COLDMAKER

COLDMAKER

DANIEL A. COHEN

HARPER
Voyager

Harper*Voyager*
an imprint of HarperCollins*Publishers* Ltd
1 London Bridge Street
London SE1 9GF

www.harpercollins.co.uk

First published by HarperCollins*Publishers* 2017
1

A catalogue record for this book is available from the British Library

HB ISBN: 978-0-00-820715-1
TPB ISBN: 978-0-00-820716-8

Set in Meridien by Palimpsest Book Production Limited,
Falkirk, Stirlingshire

Printed and bound in the UK by CPI Group (UK) Ltd, Croydon CR0 4YY

MIX
Paper from
responsible sources
FSC
www.fsc.org **FSC˚ C007454**

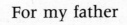

For my father

PART ONE

Chapter One

The roasted heap of rubbish was mine to rule.

Still, I was careful to check the alleyway nooks to make sure it stayed that way. I dragged my feet across the ground, grains of sand scraping beneath my heels, and listened for the rustle of sudden movements. On nights like these, blissfully dark and cool, I was never the only Jadan lurking in the dark.

I forced out a grunt, the kind taskmasters sometimes make before unfolding their whips, but no hidden mouths sucked in worried breaths. I tossed a handful of pebbles into the heavier darkness just to be sure, but the only response was silence.

As far as I knew, I was alone.

Standing above the pile, its bitter stench biting my nose, I was left with a smile so large it accidentally split a blister on my upper lip. However, my mood was too fine to be disturbed by small pain.

Glinting in the starlight, the rubbish sizzled with possibilities. Mostly the heap would consist of inedible grey boilweed leaves, dirtied up from cleaning and scrubbing, but there were always treasures to be found within. And, thanks to my newest invention, the Claw Staff, my recent rummagings were no longer followed by angry slices on my arms, greasy smells, or nasty fluids staining my hands.

A thin sheet of sand still dusted the top layer, meaning I was the first to arrive. Other Jadans would sift through these mounds of boilweed in the hope of finding a nibble of candied fig, or a discarded fruit rind to chew into a hard pulp. Of course, food was always a welcome find, hunger being one of my longest relationships, but I had a deeper itch. Something that my kind shouldn't have.

Or at least didn't usually have.

Once satisfied that I was alone, I finally reached under my clothing and undid the twine keeping the Claw Staff pinned tightly against my thigh. I'd done my best to make my invention compact, but it had nonetheless chafed like a restless scorpion during the day's errands.

'What are we going to find tonight?' I whispered to the metal.

The Staff gleamed in the dim starlight. There was no time to linger. Rubbish heaps, especially those behind sweet shops, were popular destinations for Jadans out past curfew, and I wouldn't be alone for long.

I shook the Staff's poles out. The final length got stuck, so I swiped my fingers across my forehead. I was usually a bit sweaty on missions like this, so I smeared the moisture against the carved notches, allowing the pieces to slide out easily.

Swinging the Staff upside down, I brought the sounding orb to my ear and flicked the teeth on the opposite end with my fingernail. The orb was actually just a chunk from a cracked bell, but its vibrations helped let me know what the Staff's teeth found in the rubbish's belly.

My heart started to flutter thinking about all the sounds waiting for me.

I thrust the invention in deep, and the orb answered with a tense ping. This was an alert I knew well, since glass was my most common find. Yanking the camel-leather strip that ran through the middle of my invention, I closed the teeth and pulled out a long chunk of broken vase.

I greedily ran my tongue over the small glob left on the glass, ignoring the gritty sand. Sweltering heat had turned the honey sour, but it was a departure from old figs at least. I polished the spot to a shine, careful not to cut my tongue on the edges.

Churning the Staff again, the orb made a dull, earthy sound and I pulled up an old box filled with scrapings of gem candy. I dabbed a finger into the tiny crystals and let them dissolve slowly in my cheek, but I kept the rest as a present for Moussa. My friend needed the sugar's happy tingle more than I did these days.

Next came a piece of hardened sweet bread, a pinch of discoloured almonds, and half a candied fig which I chewed happily until something moved at the edge of the alleyway, catching my attention.

I figured it was another Jadan waiting their turn, so I decided to move on, considering my haul was already better than most nights.

Gathering everything up, I lined the bottom of the boilweed bag that my father had artfully stitched for these purposes. The design was perfectly unassuming. I could hide the bag anywhere I needed to during the day, even with treasures inside, appearing as just another pile of useless grey leaves.

Scrambling to the roof of the nearest shop, I crouched down immediately, the shingles below me still hot to the touch. I shifted my weight back and forth between my finger-tips, my knees quickly growing warm. Sucking down the juice from the gem candy, I watched another Jadan attack the rubbish. The boy was younger than me, his knees knobbly and frail. A long piece of boilweed had been slung around his head as a makeshift patch, and I wondered how long ago he'd lost the eye.

Now that I was gone, the boy dived hungrily into the pile, desperation clear in his movements. Thankfully for him, I'd already disposed of a big glass shard near the top.

'*Pssst.*' I cupped my hands around my lips. '*Pssst.*'

He didn't startle, but neither did he turn around. I wondered if he was half deaf too.

'Hey,' I called a little louder, still barely more than a whisper.

He didn't stop his rifling, rummaging so fast he must have not cared about sharp edges, willing to trade blood for food.

'Family,' I called.

He turned around and bared the few teeth he still had left, giving me a feral hiss. In my barracks we all looked out for each other, but I knew it wasn't like that in every barracks. This boy didn't seem used to kindness. I reached into my pocket and grabbed the piece of stale sweet bread, tossing it down as a peace offering.

Not waiting for a response, I crossed the rooftops, crawling flat. The first Khat's Pyramid stood tall on the horizon, its peak cutting deep into the night sky. The monuments of the Capitol Quarter were all impressive, with their precise stone-work and decorative flags, but no buildings, not even the other pyramids, came even close to the first Pyramid's height or splendour.

I didn't have much time to dawdle, but looking up so high made my heart ache with wonder. Cold was falling to the land beyond the Pyramid as the World Crier let loose from the sky above. Deciding the Crying was worth a pause, I rolled onto my side and gazed into the night sky. Thousands upon thousands of pieces of Cold were shooting from the sky every hour, brushing through the dark. I knew that most of the Cold falling in the Khat's massive Patches would be small Wisps, but there would be Drafts, Shivers and Chills in there too. I squinted, trying to look for any particularly large streaks, hoping that tonight might be one of those rare times I was lucky enough to see a Frost, the most sacred of all Cold.

I didn't, but Frosts only fell once every few weeks, so the chances were slim anyway.

In the morning, hundreds of Patch Jadans would scramble through those brown sands, digging up all the Cold for the Nobles whilst taskmasters would watch, their whips at the ready, making sure it was all collected.

I tried to imagine the time before the Great Drought, when Cold was Cried throughout the entire world. When we were young, we were told stories of lands flushed green and alive, where you could walk a hundred feet in any direction and pick fruit as big as your fists. Where the Cold would break on mountain rocks, cooling the air and the boiling Rivers, so that you could swim, and drink straight from the current. And every city had bountiful Cry Patches, their gardens swollen and lush.

Now Cold only fell for the Nobles here in Paphos.

Everyone else was unworthy.

I sighed, knowing it wasn't good to dwell on a past I couldn't even remember. Eight hundred years later and the world was lucky that Cold still fell at all.

I rolled back over, the hard callouses on my palms making it easy for me to shuffle quickly and quietly without tearing my skin. Shadows flitted silently on the nearby rooftops, crawling in a similar manner. Some figures chanced moving at a crouch, their knees hugging their shoulders, but task-masters knew to look up to the roofs. Keeping flat was my best chance of survival.

Most Jadans huddled around the Butcher's Quarter, hoping to gnaw on the piles of old lizard bones, but I never went pilfering over in that part of town. The ones that sought to lord over the old meat had traded in mercy long ago, and rancid scrap wasn't worth a brick lodged in the back of the head.

I made my way towards the Sculptor's Quarter, knowing these alleyways wouldn't be so crowded. A Sculptor's leavings were never very satisfying for a hungry Jadan, but I needed materials for the board game Matty and I were creating, and every once in a while I'd find a little ceramic carving. My young friend had the rules just about finished, but we needed a few more pieces to round out both sides of play.

The Sculptor buildings were works of art themselves, with statues of famous Khats of the past chiselled into their stone walls. A Jadan was supposed to drop to their knees if they looked directly at an image of the Khat, but since I was already crawling, I decided there was no need.

The pile of rubbish closest to the back door of Piona's Moulds looked most promising, so I climbed down to the alley, giving my invention a stern look. 'Find me something good,' I whispered.

It obliged.

A ping . . . a barely cracked chisel.

A harsh scraping . . . three sheets of sandpaper, still a bit rough.

A thrum . . . a small chunk of marble that I think might have once been a Khat's nose, with powerful, flaring nostrils. The chunk was a bit big as it was, but I figured I could shape it up and let Matty decide its fate in the game.

By the time I'd reached the Ancient Quarter my knees were bruised, but my bag had a satisfying heft.

Only three Ancient Shops existed, large domes of white limestone, with curved doors locked by chain upon chain. These shops were only ever frequented by the Highest of Nobles, as the domes contained relics from before the Great Drought, sold for extraordinary sums.

Legend had it that their shelves were stocked with metal machines which moved on their own, hourglasses which told time without sand, and lanterns which needed no fire to survive. The walls were without windows, and every time I passed by I wished I could invent something which could help me hear through stone.

My scuttling was halted at the sound of laughter coming from below.

'So I told my father,' a young Noble slurred, popping a Wisp into his wineskin. He downed a swig, red liquid sloshing down the front of his fine silk shirt. 'I have no idea where the Chill went! Must be one of the new Jadans. I believe you've purchased a bad batch of slaves at auction, dear man.' He held up a fat bejewelled ring for his friend to see. 'Yes. *Definitely* stolen by one of the slaves. Oops.'

Grinding my teeth, I moved on.

The walls of the Garden Quarter came into view, fifty feet high and smooth as glass. The place could house three of my barracks, and I could only imagine the paradise I'd see if I could somehow catapult myself over their walls. There would be more figs than we would be allowed in a lifetime, not to mention the grand things we never got to eat, like orange-fruit, plump grapes, baobab fruit, and Khatmelons.

Carrying on, I passed the row of Imbiberies. Most Noble festivities were held in this Quarter, constituted of lively shops only open at night, serving mead and music. I paused to listen to the melodies escaping from the windows, but I was spurred onward by the crack of a taskmaster's whip, followed by a high-pitched pleading.

A few more stubbed fingers later, I finally reached my favourite spot, landing softly on my feet. The Smith Quarter were situated on the far west side of the city, removed so the loud bangs didn't bother anyone. The back alleys were studded with anvils, as the kiln fires made the buildings too hot to work in all day. The waste ditches were always plentiful, filled with oily mounds of boilweed waiting to bestow gifts.

I manoeuvred the Staff into the heart of the biggest heap, my chest tingling with anticipation. After some heavy sifting, the sounding orb made a series of happy pings.

An old hammerhead, bent and rusty.

A chunk of bendy tin.

Half a dagger hilt.

Five links of chain, still attached.

A rusty hinge.

My bag expanded and my chest filled with the one good warmth this world can offer. I wanted to kiss my invention, but fearing what my cracked lips might taste, I said a silent prayer of thanks to the World Crier instead.

Even though the Khat's Gospels assured us his Eyes were closed to Jadankind, I was thankful all the same. The Crier above never plagued me for being out after curfew, and for this I was always grateful.

I thrust the Staff in one last time, all the way up to my knuckles, my wrist straining to pull it through the pile. The exhausted muscles in my arm groaned until at last the orb gave a shout, long and high.

I frowned, not recognizing the sound.

It took a few pulls for the teeth to clamp around the mystery object, and with careful speed, up came a miracle.

Or a disaster.

Breath caught in my throat, and my knees went weak as I picked up the Shiver with shaky hands.

It was more Cold than I was rationed in a month.

My brow prickled with sweat. I often came into contact with Shivers, but never like this. Never one that I could keep for myself. Smuggling bits and pieces home was one thing, but if anyone found a Shiver in my possession, my body would be the first to be hurled by the dead-carts into the dunes.

I brought the beautiful round of Cold closer to my face, entranced by its lovely sheen.

A part of me knew I might get away with keeping it. I could shave off pieces and share them with the rest of the Jadans in my barracks. I could tinker with it for hours.

Maybe even use it for my Idea.

My fingers trembled as I weighed my options. This was a once in a lifetime find. Once in a hundred lifetimes. My vision went light, my body swaying beneath me as my balance faltered. Taskmasters were out there, and I had to decide quickly.

My forehead beaded with more of my namesake sweat, my heart throbbing with the terrible decision.

I tossed the Shiver back on the pile, seething with frustration.

I'd heard enough warnings throughout my life about us Jadans trying to keep any Cold for ourselves. Often these stories ended in curses that melted our eyes, and angry spirits rising up from the deepest cracks of the Great Divide to carry us back into the darkness. I had never seen anything like this happen in real life, but I didn't want to chance it. The World Crier had taken Cold away from Jadankind for a reason, and who were we to go against eight hundred years of punishment?

I turned away from the Shiver to avoid any further temptation, when, for the second time that evening, my heart nearly stopped.

A figure was watching me from the rooftops. Her braided hair framed a Jadan face hardened by thought, and I could tell she had been watching me for some time, her focus directed on my Claw Staff rather than on the Shiver.

I froze, guilty about my temptation. But before I could say anything, she moved, darting off into the night.

I climbed back to the nearest ledge to get another glimpse of her. But what I saw next made my jaw drop even more than finding the Cold.

The girl was running, proud, high, and fast, her back completely straight for all the taskmasters in Paphos to see.

Jadans didn't run like that, ever. We were inferior, and we were supposed to show it at all times. Her posture was an outright scandal, and my back ached just watching her move.

By the time I caught my footing she was half a dozen rooftops away, her spine as straight and rigid as a plank of wood. Surely she'd be spotted. Surely this would be her last night racing along the rooftops. I sighed, praying that her death might be quick.

I crouched down once again and started crawling home. I'd gathered enough materials for the night anyway.

I tiptoed around Gramble's guardhouse, making sure the sound of crunching sand under my toes was minimal. My Barracksmaster turned a blind eye to my night runs, but that was all he could do. If he caught me in the act, the Khat's law required punishment for both of us.

I inched towards the loose panel in the wall of my barracks. Taking one last look up at the sky, my eyes searched for Sister Gale within the flurry of stars. She was bright and shining, blowing tonight's air cooler than most nights, and I gave Her a quick nod of thanks.

The panel into my barracks came away easily, and I slipped inside mine and my father's private room. The cracks in the ceiling let in just enough starlight for me to make my way to bed.

Abb, my father, was already lying on top of his blanket, dreaming. I hovered over him for a moment, noting the terrible new angle in his nose. The side of his face was puffy, and in the morning, I knew his eyes would be ringed in crusty purple bruises.

Most nights when I chanced sneaking into the heart of Paphos, I'd come home to find him waiting up for me, ready to eagerly appraise each new piece of treasure and ask what I planned to use it for. I couldn't wait for the morning, as I was dying to tell him about both Shiver and the girl.

I reached out and placed the almonds I'd found beside his bed. Then, I reached into my bag to sort through my treasure. My new metal links rattled as I filed them away, but Abb didn't stir. He must have had a long shift over at the Pyramid.

Having tidied my treasures into their respective holes in the ground, I settled onto my blanket and closed my eyes. My remaining few hours were spent dreaming of Cold.

Chapter Two

I awoke with a start to my father hovering over me, smiling as he crunched the almonds.

'You didn't wake me,' he said reproachfully, wincing as he chewed.

I sat up, blinking away the images of long hair and an unseemly posture. I stretched from side to side as I drank in the morning light which filtered through the slats in the roof. I could already tell the Sun wouldn't be taking it easy on us today. The air inside the room was already stifling, thick with the sky's hatred.

'You were asleep,' I said.

'Well, that happens every night,' replied Abb, swallowing the last almond. 'Not a good excuse.'

I raised an eyebrow. As I'd guessed, the bruises now marked his face. 'Looked like you needed it.'

He ignored my comment, changing the subject instead. 'So, what did you find?' he asked, poking me gently in the chest.

The memory of the Shiver shot back into my mind. 'I—'

He held up a hand. 'On second thoughts, I believe I can figure it out by myself.'

'You're not going to guess—'

He held a finger up to his lips, a playful look in his eyes. 'I said I can figure it out. You certainly didn't learn your *listening* skills from me, Little Builder.'

The name was one of my father's continuous jokes, referring both to my inventing and the fact that I still had many years to go before I was assigned to become a Builder like himself. I liked it a lot better than my other nickname.

I shrugged, blinking the sleep away from my mind. My body pleaded for more, but there was nothing I could do until later. Thinking about my new finds, I assured myself the sluggishness was a worthy price.

Abb walked over to my tinker-wall, bearing down upon the stores of materials. I'd dug different ditches for each type, and his fingers swept along the space above the piles.

'Ah, a new chisel,' he remarked, pointing to the tool pile. 'Good find.'

I nodded, my mouth dry and dusty. I tried to dredge up the sweet taste of candy dust, but crawling around all night had given thirst control over my cheeks. I was eager for the bells to ring so we could start our rations, as my head was throbbing from lack of water.

'Lusty metal,' Abb said humorously, staring down at the chains. 'One day you'll be old enough to understand that joke.'

'Links,' I corrected, rolling my eyes. 'And I understand it just fine.'

He winked, giving me a knowing smile before bending over the pile of jars, fingers snatching something off the top. 'Where'd you get this?'

He turned around, something foreign in his grip.

At first glance I didn't recognize what he was holding up. The golden-hued vial was unblemished, and I didn't remember picking up anything like it. The jars in my stash were usually empty and broken, and I turned the decent ones into medicine vials for Abb. This one, however, looked as if it belonged on the display shelves of an apothecary. The sleep was still thick in my brain and I couldn't come up with an answer.

Abb came closer, holding it out to me. 'So, what is it?'

'I don't know.' I squinted, trying to make out the greenish material inside.

Abb's face broke into a coy smile.

'Well, it looks like the colour of a birthday present.' He chuckled, smacking the vial into my palm. 'Or part of one at least.'

My mouth gaped as I held the vial out to a sunbeam, illuminating its contents. The inside gloop was viscous and slick.

'This is for me?' I asked, stunned. I shook the small vial, the jelly wiggling inside. 'Is this groan salve?'

'It is indeed,' he said, with a slight puff of his chest. 'Mixed carefully with a father's pride.'

'How'd you get it?'

'If you must know the truth.' He shrugged, going quiet for a moment. 'It fell from the sky, specifically for you.'

I shook my head, somewhat serious. 'You can get into trouble for lies like that.'

'I've lived long enough for trouble and I to have grown a mutual respect,' Abb replied simply, scratching his fingernails across the frizz on my head. 'But if you're worried, better use it up quick.'

I pushed his hand away, smiling, and took the cap off the salve. It smelled like a taskmaster's feet, but I knew it was the best remedy for an unforgiving sting. I'd only ever been lucky enough to find a nip or two before, never a full bottle.

Abb then reached into the top crate of my invention-wall, retrieving one of my crank-fans. It was still a work in progress, since Nobles never threw away good blades, but I'd managed to file down some sturdy awning as a decent substitute.

Abb held the fan in front of his face and turned the lever, spinning air across his cheeks. The little thing gave a garbled whirr, its bearings rusty, but his face lit with delight. Once he'd finished with it, he gave it an appraising nod, as if all was right in the world.

Harsh light now tunnelled through the roof, brighter and more invasive. I could feel the hungry morning heat tasting its first bites of my face. I slapped my cheek, trying to wake myself up a bit.

'The sky had something else for you, Little Builder,' Abb said after a few moments, putting the crank-fan back in its crate.

'This groan salve is already too much,' I said. Sometimes Abb's thoughtfulness overwhelmed me, his gentle heart highlighting the brutality of the previous father to whom I'd been assigned. 'And would you stop saying the *sky* had things for me?'

Abb considered the ceiling, stepping out of a strong spear of light. He reached into his pocket and retrieved some things that made me reconsider everything that had happened the night before.

With shaking hands, he offered me three small, gleaming Wisps. I didn't miss the pleased twitch in his lips as I took them.

My heart raced looking at the three pieces of Cold. I knew Abb was okay with me breaking a few barracks' rules like sneaking out in the night, and reclaiming rubbish, but never had he encouraged me to break a holy law.

'We can't have our own Cold,' I said, stunned. 'You've said so yourself.'

He nodded, bobbing his head up and down. 'Perhaps that *was* true.'

Three tiny Wisps paled in comparison to the might of a Shiver, but it was illegal for a Jadan to keep even the smallest measure of Cold.

'What do you mean?'

Abb dropped the Wisps in my lap, so I had no choice but to take them. 'In a way, truth ages, just like we do. You aren't the same as you were a year ago, nor will you be the same on your next birthday. I think you're ready for some new truth. So take the Cold. Use the Wisps, or hide them.' He put a hand on my cheek. 'Who will know?'

I froze up at his words. How could my father, the best Jadan I'd ever known, encourage such blasphemy?

'But what about the World Crier?' I replied, a lump in my throat. 'He'll know.'

Abb gave an understanding nod. 'He let the Cold travel this far.'

'So?'

Abb sucked his cheek, seemingly testing a bruise from the inside. From the look on his face it was quite painful. 'So, there are the Noble laws, and there are the Crier laws. They're not always one and the same.'

I paused, feeling myself getting flustered. This wasn't a subject we'd ever broached, and I was uncomfortable with his disorienting words. 'But the Khat . . .'

'They're not always the same, Micah.' He stretched his fingers, striped with sizzling ribbons of light. 'But this might be a conversation for another time. Let's leave it there for now.'

'Thank you,' I said in a thin voice, petrified that the Crier might punish me for having the Wisps. But then again, Abb had no signs of plague, or evidence that demons had tried to rip out his eyes, and he'd have been in possession of the Cold for at least a night.

'Ah, but you can't thank me yet.' He smiled. 'That's not the last of your gifts.'

'No more,' I said, taking shallow breaths just in case. 'I'm going to have a hard time using all of the others.'

Abb's face suddenly turned serious. He glanced at the thick boilweed curtain that served as a door, even though I'd heard nothing from the other side.

'This is not a gift to use, Micah,' he said, his voice suddenly heavy with emotion. 'But one for you to remember. Promise me.'

I nodded, a bit afraid of this serious turn in him. A small smirk or tiny laugh usually hovered somewhere about his lips, but right now his face was iron.

Abb placed his fingers on my sweat-riddled forehead. His quiet voice rose and fell in a beautiful lilt I'd never heard before, one which sucked the silence out of the room and transformed it into something more profound, beyond language. My father had a good singing voice, but this felt different from the times he'd forced out the 'Khat's Anthem' or 'Ode to the Patch'. The devastatingly beautiful sounds coming from his lips left my head reeling.

Then the words stopped almost as swiftly as they'd begun.

'Again,' he said in a stern voice, 'listen.'

I nodded, trying to ready my ears this time.

He repeated the lovely melody, and I caught every last syllable, filing them away like the most precious of my findings.

—*Shemma hares lahyim criyah Meshua ris yim slochim*—

'Did you get it?' he asked, voice soft.

I nodded, concentrating so hard that my ears rang.

'What does it mean?' I asked.

'However would I know a thing like that?' he asked, removing his fingers and backing away, a bit of the trademark humour returning to his eyes. 'I don't speak Ancient Jadan. Now get out of here and find your friends.' He attempted a broad smile, but winced, the sunlight claiming the bruises on his face. 'They're probably eager to give you their own birthday gifts.'

Matty smirked, hands gently slapping his knees in anticipation. 'What'cha get me?'

The three of us huddled together in a corner of the common chamber, away from the shabby grey flaps that divided the family sleeping areas. Sitting on the sandy floor, our legs were crossed and knees touched so we'd take up the least amount of space.

'What did I get *you*?' I asked. 'I never thought you would be so greedy.'

Moussa scowled for the group, but aimed a private wink my way. 'Grit in your figs, Matty. It's Micah's birthday. You should just be glad that he got home safe.'

Matty's face turned bashful. 'Spout always gets me something when he goes out. Always.'

'You have got to stop calling him that.' Moussa let out a pained sigh. 'Don't you know that no one calls him that any more?'

I shrugged. In truth, most Jadans in our barracks – and indeed in the streets – still called me Spout, a nickname I'd come to terms with a long time ago. It wasn't just enough that my loose forehead wasted more water than other Jadans my age, they had to *remind* me of the fact.

'I don't mind "Spout",' I said. 'As long as Matty doesn't mind me sweating on any future gifts.'

Matty lowered his head, eyes going to his lap where his hand was stroking the small feather that I'd fashioned him from metal and fabric. I don't know why Matty kept up this fascination. Clearly the creatures were extinct, no possible way they could survive in the harsh conditions after the Great Drought.

'Did'ja see any birds?' Matty asked, his tone still hopeful, even after all this time.

'Here's the thing,' Moussa said, giving Matty's ear a playful flick. 'Why would a creature live in the sky and *choose* to be close to the Sun? You should know it would crisp up after a few flaps.'

I rehearsed what would surely be Matty's next words, holding back my smirk. My small yet vibrant friend said the same thing every time: *You know, Cold lives up—*

'Y'know,' Matty said right on cue, guarding the side of his head against another flick. '*Cold* lives up in the sky too. So if there was any birds left, they'd prolly come out at night.'

'No sign of birds yet,' I said, cutting off whatever cutting remark Moussa was preparing. 'But I promise if I see one, I'll lure it back for you.'

'Y'know that they sing, don'cha, Moussa?' Matty said, swiping the feather through a small pillar of light that was sneaking through the ceiling. 'You could prolly lure one down, if you tried hard enough.'

I looked over at Moussa, hoping the talk of music might cheer him up a little, but he said nothing, his expression remaining sombre. Moussa's Patch birthday was nearing, and lately he hadn't been in the singing mood, which was too bad, as his voice was arguably the best in the barracks. On top of that, Sarra and Joon had taken to spending their free hours in one of the empty boilweed divisions, which I imagine didn't help Moussa feel any less forlorn.

Matty tucked the metal feather behind his ear, licking his dry lips. My small friend looked almost as ready for water as me. 'One day you're both gonna see I'm right. I know it.'

'Doubtful,' Moussa said under his breath.

'However, I *do* have gifts.' I leaned forward conspiratorially, trying to brighten the mood. 'And news.'

Matty stuck out his palm, his smile practically spanning the common area.

I produced the marble nose chunk. 'For our game. I figured you'd know what to do with it.'

Matty wiggled his eyebrows in delight, taking the carving and holding it up to his face. 'Howsit look?'

'A bit big,' Moussa said with a contemplative look. 'But you should know, most things are big compared to you.'

Matty stuck out his tongue. 'Just wait some years. When I'm turning fifteen like Spout I'm going to rest my elbow on your head all the time.'

Moussa craned his neck to full height. 'We'll see about that.'

I then pulled out the box of gem candy remains and laid

it on the hard sand at Moussa's feet, opening the lid. 'For you.'

'It's not *my* birthday yet – thank the Crier,' Moussa replied, shaking his head. He reached into his pocket and pulled out a handful of gears, nearly free of rust, and with most of their teeth. 'For *you*.'

My eyes went wide with shock. 'Where? How did you . . . Thank you. They're perfect.'

'They're not much.'

I put a hand on his shoulder. 'Once I need them, they'll be everything. Tinkering is only fun when you have things to tinker with.'

Matty's face dropped, guilt flooding his face, and he tried to hand the Khat nose back to me. 'For you?'

I laughed. 'Just figure out a place for it in the game. That's good enough for me. It's about time we finished that thing.'

'I should of got'cha something,' Matty groaned.

'Really, I don't need anything else.'

Keeping his head slumped, Matty reached out his arm and tilted his hand backwards, offering up his 'calm spot'. I touched my thumb to the splotchy birthmark on his wrist, which for some reason comforted my young friend whenever he felt like he'd done something wrong.

'Family,' Matty said.

'Family,' I repeated, letting go and gesturing both of them closer. 'So last night I was in the Smith Quarter and found—'

A foot dug into the sand near my knee, spraying up a light coating into our faces. Then a gravelly voice said: 'They put it *in* the ground!'

I sat back to look into the loopy face of Old Man Gum, grinning at us through a mouth full of black gaps. As he was the oldest Jadan in our barracks, with skin dark as soot, we had to show him respect, even though he never made much sense.

'Morning, Zeti Gum,' Matty said, offering the youthful term of respect.

Gum bent down and patted us all on the head, then, without another word, he wandered back to his private space, tucked aside the boilweed curtain, and slumped back to his ratty blanket. There was enough space to watch him land directly on his face and tap the ground, listening for a response.

Matty picked up the metal feather Gum had accidentally knocked from his ear, and slipped it in his pocket.

'Anyway,' I said with a smile, 'last night, when I was in the Smith Quarter, I found a *full* Shiver in the boilweed.'

Matty's eyes went wide. 'Did'ja touch it?'

I gave a slow nod, feeling a lump in my throat.

Matty angled his head to look at my palms. 'Did'ja hands burn up?'

I splayed them wide, calloused yet unharmed. 'Nothing.'

Moussa looked at me, astounded. 'Where is it now? You didn't try to keep it, did you?'

From the concern in his voice, I thought it best not to mention the Wisps that Abb had given me. My stomach churned at even the thought of betraying the Crier. It was probably best to bury the Wisps and never speak of them again.

'It's still there,' I said, keeping my voice down. I looked around the barracks to see if anyone could overhear us. 'I think so at least. I don't know for sure, because when I put it back there was a girl watching me.'

Matty's face broke into a coy smirk. 'A girrrl . . .?'

I reached across and flicked him on the arm. 'Listen. There was something different about her. She was—'

'Spout.' The desperate voice came from over my shoulder.

I turned around and found sweet Mother Bev hunched over, hands on her knees, panting slightly. 'Can I use a crank-fan, darling?'

'Of course, you never have to ask.' I went to get up, but she put a gnarled hand on my shoulder.

'I'm still able,' she said with a cracked voice, shuffling off. 'Blessings, child. May fifteen be Colder than fourteen.'

I watched her walk away. I hated it when she said things like that, as blessings were supposed to be saved for the Khat and Crier only.

When I looked back, Moussa was dabbing his finger in the gem candy dust. He gave me a sheepish look. 'Thanks, Micah.'

'Don't mention it. So this girl,' I held my palm up like a blade, trying to approximate her posture, 'she was running on the rooftops like this.'

Matty frowned. 'Smacking the wind?'

I shook my head with a chuckle. 'No, her *back*. She ran with her back completely straight. A Jadan, running like that. Crazy, right?'

Moussa paused and then gave a long shrug. A few boilweed flaps began rustling behind us, bodies in motion, so he lowered his voice. 'Here's the thing. That's weird, I suppose. But she was already out, breaking one rule. What would stop her from breaking two?'

I hadn't thought of it like that, but something about the memory still bothered me. We weren't supposed to move like that, so tall and proud, and it almost felt like a worse transgression than hiding Wisps.

I slipped the gears into the candy box and placed it against the wall. From the amount of light basting the roof, I knew the chimes would be ringing soon, and we needed to get ready.

'Spout,' a deep voice boomed.

I turned back and found Slab Hagan looming over our group, his meaty body blocking at least five beams of sunlight from reaching the floor. One of my scorpion traps dangled in his hands, the face of the box shut and sealed.

'Morning, Hagan,' I said.

'I'll eat it when you done?' Slab Hagan asked, his eyes gleaming with hunger. I never understood how he maintained such a frame on a Jadan diet, even supplemented by the occasional insect.

'Please,' he added in a gruff voice.

I made sure the springs of the trap were tight so the scorpion wouldn't escape, and put it aside for later extraction. 'Of course. It's yours.'

Slab Hagan gave something of a thankful bow, and hulked away to his place near the main doors. Jadanmaster Gramble offered double rations of figs and a thick slice of bread to whoever was first in their respective lines, and at this point the Builders just let Slab Hagan have the honour.

The morning chimes rang out and everyone scrambled from their boilweed divisions into the common area, donning dirty uniforms and breathing heavily. The air in the chamber was already thick with the Sun's heat, and was only getting hotter. The four distinct lines settled together, stretching from wall to wall of the main chamber: Patch, Builder, Street, and Domestic. I landed near the end of my line, the Street Jadans, tucked between Moussa and Matty.

The chimes were all still ringing with ease, and my head swivelled upward, admiring my handiwork of pulleys and cables. Other Barracksmasters used whips and chains, and in severe cases, sprinkles of acid to wake up their Jadans, but Gramble was kind, and he deserved a kind system for rousing us. It had only taken a few days for me to tinker my bells idea into reality – Gramble had access to all the materials he wanted – and I'd received triple rations for a week. Now, to get the system to sound, all our Barracksmaster had to do was pull a lever beneath the sill of his guardhouse window.

I pressed a finger to my hard and scabby lips, ready for water. Looking around the lines, I caught many of my family looking over to me, knowing today was the day I turned fifteen. I got a deranged wave from Old Man Gum, a round of smiles from most of the Domestic line, a playful flash of ten fingers and then five from Avram, and a dozen other little gestures of love.

Gramble's key flitted inside the lock of the main doors, the tink of metal replacing all the conversations in our rows. The doors flung open and our ruling Noble waddled in, dragging the rations cart behind him. Our tired faces cracked with excitement at the sight of the sloshing buckets. Of course, the relief would be short-lived, as the daylight behind him was already baring fangs.

Gramble unhooked the Closed Eye from the side of the rations cart, spinning the pole so the symbol would stand above us. The copper representation of the Crier's Eye had its lid sealed shut to our kind, just as the Gospels dictated. It was a reminder of the sins of past Jadans, which the Crier could never forgive.

The Patch Jadans were first for rations, since they had the longest distance to cover and the hardest days ahead. At eighteen, life became excruciating for the young Jadan men, and many of their bodies looked frail from overuse, skin tanned black as shadow. The Sun showed no mercy to those tasked to work in the deep sands, collecting all the Khat's new-fallen Cold. At the front of the Patch line, Joon kneeled before the Closed Eye, tucked in his chin, and said in a clear voice: 'Unworthy.'

Gramble nodded, offering in return a cup of water with a single Wisp, and a double ration of figs. The rest of the line of Patch Jadans followed suit, kneeling and offering their regrets to the Eye before passing through the door to face the brutal light of the day.

If a Patch Jadan survived for five years in the blistering conditions, they became a Builder, repairing streets and walls and erecting monuments to the Khat. The Builders were next for rations, Slab Hagan leading the group. He kneeled, but was still almost as tall as Gramble.

'Unworthy,' his large mouth boomed.

The cooped-up air in the main chamber began to grow stifling, Sun making its impatience known. Soon it would be warmer inside the barracks than outside, which was saying something.

Abb successfully roused both his patients still stuck in their boilweed divisions – a silent wave of relief sweeping the lines as Dabria coughed her way to her feet – and my father filed in behind the rest of the Builders, giving me a wink before kneeling for rations himself and sweeping through the main doors.

Once the Builders had all left, the Street Jadans were next.

Ours was the largest group, Street Jadans compromised of both boys and girls aged ten to eighteen, and it took a little while before I reached the rations cart. Moussa looked back and gave me a little nod just as he passed through the doors.

I kneeled, dropping hard against the sand. I felt as if I should say the word louder than usual today considering the three Wisps hidden under my blanket. 'Unworthy!'

Gramble nodded, beckoning me to stand.

'Spout,' he said, the nickname always tilting his bushy eyebrows with amusement.

'Sir.' I eyed the bucket of water longingly. A night of scavenging always left me famished.

Gramble scooped up a sizable portion of water and then passed it my way. But before I could take it in my shaking hands, he snatched it back, a glib smile on his face.

Then he reached into his pocket and held up a Wisp, dancing it across my eyes.

'Sir, I—'

He dropped the extra Wisp into the cup and pressed it

against my chest. 'Congratulations on making it to fifteen, boy.'

I stood there, shocked at my good luck. I felt the Closed Eye glaring at me from behind its lid, knowing my guilty secret.

'Come on now, Spout, drink up!' ordered Gramble. 'The Domestics are still waiting their turn!'

I trembled as I lifted the water to my lips, the cool liquid splashing across my blisters and cuts, lighting up my tongue with pure ecstasy. After a night of swimming the rooftops, the water tasted of pure and complete decadence. My stomach wasn't prepared for the splash of Cold, clenching up tightly at first until it relaxed and enjoyed the gift.

Gramble gave me a large handful of figs and ushered me through the doors, the sunlight smacking me in the face like a fist. However, as hot as the sky was, no pox struck me down, and no spirits from the Great Divide came to drag me under the sands to my death. I could only assume that since I hadn't actually *asked* for the three Wisps, the Crier might spare me the wrath.

I moved fast, needing to reach my corner before the morning bell tolled. Jadanmaster Geb was lenient on lateness, but plenty of taskmasters would be waiting in the shadows to make up for this tolerance, hoping to catch their own Jadan and have some fun at our expense.

Chapter Three

Every Jadan's life is planned from start to finish.

We're born and raised in the Birth Barracks, and when our minds start getting spongy we're sent to the Khat's Priests to learn the Crier's doctrines and rules. Once we turn ten, the girls with the lightest skin and most comely faces are assigned to be Domestics, and the rest are given a street corner, patiently awaiting orders from a taskmaster, merchant, or Noble of any kind.

A Jadan can always be purchased outright by a Noble, but this comes at a high price, and most Nobles are happy borrowing any Jadan they see fit.

I had three more years of Street duty left, and I wanted them to last as long as possible. My corner was one of the most vibrant in Paphos, and I served under one of the finest Jadanmasters.

Moussa ran ahead of me until he took a sharp turn in the direction of the Bathing Quarter. I kept onwards towards the heart of Paphos, the Market Quarter, snaking my way across my favourite rooftops and deserted alleyways. After five years on Street duty, the pads of my feet were hardened and leathery, immune to the heat of stone. As tough as my heels had become, however, my toes were still susceptible to bites, so I made sure to keep an eye out for forked tongues rising in the gaps. It was rare to run into a Sobek lizard, as they usually didn't stray far from the boiling water channels pulled off the River Singe, but it was important to stay vigilant. The lizard's poison couldn't kill, but errands were quite difficult with a splitting headache and hives.

I speeded up as I spotted two other Street Jadans from another barracks in a nearby alleyway, crouching over a pile of billowing smoke. One of them was holding a sizable shard of glass against the sunlight, focusing the ray on some smouldering boilweed. Both mouths were sucking in large breaths, wafting the fumes towards their faces with sooty fingers, stifling coughs. They'd have to smoke quickly if they were going to make it to their corners in time, but they didn't seem too concerned.

Some Jadans claim the boilweed makes errands pass like a pleasant dream, and taskmasters' whips feel like soft kisses. I'd tried the smoke once, but it just made me feel sick, and the residual cough had earned me more than one slap on my throat.

Sweat gathered on the lobes of my ears and I cursed myself for wasting water; every drop counted in this hotbed of a world. I was the only one of my friends who still had the problem. Spout was about as accurate a nickname as any.

Keeping the safe route into the Market Quarter took me longer than I would have liked, but fortunately the day was still early, and the warning bells hadn't yet rung. Most of the Nobles I would serve today were still asleep, cool under their thin sheets, the richest being fanned by their personal Domestics.

I jumped from a low roof onto the edge of a shop and bounded onto Arch Road. I scrambled over to my corner and pressed myself against the wall. Placing my hand at my sides,

I fell into my best slave stance: shoulders rounded, chin down, a slight bend at the hip.

The wall of my corner was slightly pronounced at the top, offering me a few fingers of luxurious shade. Keeping my chin tucked, I watched the other Street Jadans out of the corner of my eye, slipping out of the surrounding alleyways just as the morning bells rang out. I was happy to see the Jadans I knew still on their respective corners, none of them having fallen at the hands of a taskmaster yet.

The final ring was our cue to begin the 'Khat's Anthem'. I cleared my throat and launched into the song along with everyone else.

> *The Crier's might upon his name*
> *Worthy of the Cold*
> *Dynasty forever*
> *Service for your soul*
> *Blessed be our master*
> *Who keeps us from the sands*
> *His holiness the Khat*
> *Who saved life upon the lands*
> *Holy Eyes have long forsaken*
> *Those of Jadankind*
> *But the Khat is made of mercy*
> *For those blind to the Cry*
> *He keeps us from the darkness*
> *He gives us hope and grace*
> *Long live the Khat and all his sons*
> *Who saved the Jadan race*

Jadanmaster Geb skipped onto Arch Road just as the song finished, a big smile on his face. As always, his robes looked new; these ones a jolly shade of green, bright enough to be seen all the way from Belisk. He wore a head wrap of matching green, meticulously tied to hold back his long hair enough to show off his dangling emerald earrings.

There was a reason Geb often had enough Cold to buy such extravagant outfits. From what I understood, Jadanmasters received bonus Cold for keeping their slaves obedient and swift. Since we all appreciated his kindness, there was something of an unspoken pact among the Arch Road Jadans to work hard to make him look good. Even though Jadanmaster Geb was from a High Noble family, and didn't technically need to work, every Jadan on Arch Road welcomed his presence. Taskmasters didn't appreciate his softness, or the fact that his skin was darker than most High Nobles, but Geb was confident enough not to care.

He checked us off one by one in his ledger, and stopped in front of me, bending over and slapping me lightly on the cheek. 'Salutations, Spout.'

'Sir,' I said, happy to bask in his shade.

'I appreciate your promptness, as per usual,' he said, and I could tell that he meant it. 'I challenge that if all Jadans were as dutiful as you, the commerce of Paphos would run smoother than silk through fingers. May this birthday be filled with swift and important errands.'

Even the fact that Geb called us 'Jadans' rather than 'slaves', or 'Coldleeches', or 'The Diseased Unworthy', spoke a lot about his character.

'Thank you, sir. That means a lot, sir.'

He nodded, walking off with a skip in his step to check off his other Jadans. I had to work hard to keep the smile off my face.

After the first hour of morning passed, the street began to fill up with hordes of Noble shoppers. Out of my peripherals I caught them passing back and forth, chirping about the deals of the day. Merchants yelled from their doorways, waving silky dresses and big hats. Women held white umbrellas and wore sun-gowns made of thin fabric that flowed down their legs like water, whilst men wore crisp suits, so white that I almost had to shield my eyes. Sometimes when a Noblewoman got too close I'd catch the intoxicating scent of perfume, and I kept my nose ready for every whiff.

The moustached vendor at the nearest watercart passed out flavoured water to Nobles in exchange for small goods. Most traded food or make-up for the water, but I saw one Nobleman trade away a wooden doll. Fine pieces of wood-work were rare, but some Nobles liked to overpay traders to show off their wealth.

Another Noble habit I'd never understood.

The second bell of the day rang, and then the third, and still no one had chosen me for any errands. I was usually happy keeping to my corner, relaxing in the shade my little overhang offered, but today, idle time allowed my thoughts to wander to the Idea.

I began to sweat, straining towards safer topics.

I'd had the Idea for some time now, but I'd never had the Cold needed to make the particular invention work. Now that I had the three Wisps, my main excuse was gone, and I needed to come up with something else that might dissuade me.

The Crier might turn a blind eye to me *having* the Cold, but using it for my own benefit would surely be my downfall.

Just then something in the alley across from my corner caught my attention. Most Jadans used the alleyways to get around for errands, and I usually ignored the shadowy move-ments perforating the lively bustle of Arch Road, but this dark outline was different, as it was keeping completely still. Jadans on errands could get lashes for dawdling, so I tried ignoring the stationary figure at first, but something about the stance resonated with me louder than the morning bells.

My curiosity grew stronger than my caution and my eyes began to rise.

A gasp nearly exploded from my chest.

It was the girl. The Upright Girl.

Her posture was like the beginning of a cautionary tale about obeying the Crier's rules. If any taskmasters caught her standing that still *and* that straight they'd have the Vicaress break her back in a hundred places and string her crooked body from our road's namesake Arch.

The girl's face was perched out of my view, and I had to get a better look, so I chanced raising my head just a nudge.

Long hair flowed down her shoulder in a single braid, knotty yet still nicely sheened. Usually only Domestics wore their hair long, considering it would be torturous out in the streets, catching the heat and bundling it against your head. I couldn't make out the details of her face, but the sun shed light on her feet, highlighting fresh wounds staining her ankles.

Had she followed me all night and morning? How else could she have found me?

The shout of a passing Noble startled me, and I slammed my eyes back to the ground. When I looked again the girl was retreating, her rigid back slicing into shadow.

Chapter Four

The hand fan on the shelf was the exact shade of pink I needed.

I held up the smeared parchment the High Noblewoman had given me, just to make sure, and found the stain of lip grease to be a perfect match.

She was going to squeal with delight.

The handle of the fan was made of ornate pearl, engraved with curling song words. The blade looked to be both sturdy and wonderfully frayed. This had to be one of the nicest pieces in Paphos, and I had visions of Jadanmaster Geb earning commendations for my wonderful find.

I breathed in the air in Mama Jana's shop, warmer than I remembered.

Most shopkeepers didn't let us in if the room was chilled, claiming the crushed Cold was wasted on Jadan lungs, but Mama Jana was a good-natured woman who treated me as if I was more than a pair of dirty feet, and I brought her business whenever I could. She was a lowborn Noble – meaning she got the minimal Cold rations delivered from the Pyramid weekly, unlike the bounty bestowed on the Khat's immediate relatives – and she could use all the trade I could muster.

The shop was unassuming, its entrance deep in the alleyway off Mirza Street, but this modest façade hid a feast for the eyes and the purse, and was the first stop for many Street Jadans. Its walls were concealed by stacks of goods, overlapped in disarray, jumbling together cheap headdresses, thin sandals, fine beadwork and leather waterskins. Often I imagined combing through these mounds with my Claw Staff, its orb sounding to alert me to items pre-dating the Great Drought. In this fantasy, I'd then smuggle the treasures back to my barracks, and take them apart, examining their craftsmanship for hours.

At the front of the shop was an entire area dedicated to the Closed Eye: racks of Closed Eye necklaces, Closed Eye candles, Closed Eye paintings, Closed Eye parasols, Closed Eye robes, and even a full suit of armour with the Closed Eye branded into the chest. There was a giant Closed Eye Khatclock, but its hands were broken and it was kept in the back of the shop. Most Nobles sported the holy symbol some-where on their bodies, a reminder of the Jadan fate from which they were saved, and a symbol of their closeness to the Crier. I'd never seen Mama Jana wear one, but there was plenty of Cold to be made in religious tradition, so the shop was kept well stocked.

Mama Jana removed the pink fan from the shelf and set it on the glass counter, stretching out her aged back.

'For this beauty? One Shiver, four Drafts, four Wisps,' she said, tapping out the different Cold amounts with her brightly painted fingernails as was her habit. I noticed, however, that a few of them were chipped, and that her voice sounded more annoyed than usual. I checked under my feet to make sure I hadn't dragged in too much sand.

She clucked her tongue, noticing my dismay. 'How much did the Wisp-Pincher give you?'

'Sadly the High Noblewoman didn't give me enough,' I said, knowing that I had to keep my tone fully respectful for my masters, even in the privacy of Mama Jana's shop. I let my head sag, holding the lips of the velvet bag open for her to see.

'One Shiver, five Wisps!' Mama Jana exclaimed with a dismal shake of her head. 'And some snooty clod expected a festival piece? Is your High Noblewoman wanting that I should come out and fan her myself? Has the Sun baked her head empty? Why have you brought me this nonsense, Spout? You know better.'

'Sorry, Mama Jana,' I said, letting myself bend forward, my heart sinking. The last time I'd found an item this perfect, Jadanmaster Geb had sneaked me a stale crust of bread at midday rations.

I stuffed the greased parchment back into my pocket, figuring I'd have to try Gertrude's Windmakers instead, even if Gertrude made Jadans stand at her window, offering us half the quality and twice the attitude.

'Thanks anyway,' I said, my eyes trailing to the row of lip pipes she had displayed on the counter, making a note to myself to keep an eye out for a chipped pair as a gift for Moussa on my next nocturnal expedition.

I bowed, letting my eyes gloss over the new assortment of belts in the corner. It was always good to know your stock when the Nobles came demanding.

'Spout,' she halted me, as I prepared to walk out the door.

I stopped, my ears perking up. 'Yes, Mama?'

'What about if I had a job for you,' she said, tapping her fingernails against the glass counter, giving the fan a wave.

'Always, Mama Jana.' I bowed again, stepping forward and holding out my hand for one of her Noble tokens. 'Let me just finish this errand and I'll come back and—'

'I should get priority over some nitwit,' she said, playfully swiping my hand away with the pink fan. 'Besides, the job is here. And if you can do it, I'll give you the fan for what you have in that purse.'

I nodded, keeping my eyebrows from rising. That was quite the deal.

She gave me a long stare and then shuffled over to the door, turning the sign to closed. The beads jangled as she drew the dense gold curtains over the window, shutting out a disappointed Jadan face that had just arrived.

With the only light coming from candles, the place took on a different look. Flickering darkness gave the objects around the shop a mysterious hue that made me believe some Ancient wonders really did live beneath the piles.

She moved to a nearby table stocked with gold-rimmed eyeglasses and ruby-studded crowns. Hunching over, she picked up something cumbersome, straining to bring it over to the counter.

Even in dim light I recognized the contraption immediately. Cold Bellows.

One of my favourite inventions, and since Mama Jana was drawing attention to it, I had a feeling I knew why the air in the shop no longer tingled.

'This hunk of beauty is broken,' she said, gesturing to the space around her, her wrinkled face pinched with annoyance.

I put on a sympathetic expression, although in truth I couldn't imagine the bliss of working inside a Cold room every day. I'd have given up some of my choicest tinkering fingers to have swapped places for even a few days.

She motioned to a table that was empty except for a thick hammer and a metal screen. 'I've been having to crush Wisps by hand for days now,' she said, wiggling her fingernails, showing off the cracks in her polish. 'Dreadful stuff.'

I felt my stomach clench, looking at the door to make sure no taskmasters were trying to peer through the beads. I could get in a lot of trouble if anyone found out I had an affinity for tinkering. In the eyes of the Khatdom, the only thing worse than a disabled Jadan was a Jadan with *too* much ability.

Mama Jana patted me on the shoulder, her jagged fingernails scratching my skin. 'Quit your worrying. No one will see you.'

I gave a nervous nod, the sweat beading on my forehead.

'I've kept your secret this far, child.' Her voice was tender. She spun the crank on top of the Bellows, which offered no resistance, meaning that the machine refused to crush whatever piece of Cold she'd stuck inside. 'Can you fix it for me?'

'I don't know,' I replied in a small voice. 'I've never even held Cold Bellows before.'

She reached under the counter for her stunning wooden tinker box, which she placed before my eyes, opening its lid to reveal the fine set of iron-handled tools that gleamed in the candlelight.

'I believe it's time to change that,' she said, swatting air over her face with the pink fan. 'So, do you want to finish your errand or not?'

Back on my corner, I held my arms high and waited, my token in one hand, and the fan in the other. I kept the pink blade extended to block the harsh light of the sky, enjoying a rare moment of complete shade. If any taskmasters gave me trouble about blocking the Sun I could tell them my specific instructions. 'All Jadans look alike to me,' the High Noblewoman had told me with a haughty scoff. 'So do make sure to keep the fan open so I can spot the pink.'

I was happy to oblige.

My limbs still felt shaky after my fingers danced inside the Cold Bellows, a sensation which wouldn't be going away anytime soon. The fix had been simple enough – just a gear out of alignment – but cracking apart the shell of the machine was like having a conversation with its Inventor himself.

When it came to learning from the tinkering minds I usually only got to peek through cracks, all my understanding resulting from such furtive pursuits, and even though it was Mama Jana who now got to enjoy the Bellows, I was the one brimming with gratitude.

I kept my head down and watched the parade of fancy Noble feet pass under my eyes. I spotted shoes with fine glass clasps, shoes with polished leather, shoes decorated with petrified scarabs, and even a large pair I could have sworn had a few Wisps concealed in the heel.

Wisps.

My mind shot back to the Idea. If I could have turned around and slammed my head against the wall to banish the thought, I would have. Pursuing such a thing would be like begging for the Vicaress to pierce my innards with her fiery blade.

As the day passed, Arch Road had become filled with hordes of High Nobles, all looking for ways to rid themselves of their fortunes. Purses swung low with amounts of Cold which could keep my entire barracks alive for weeks. Jadans ran about too, keeping themselves pressed against the city's walls and alleyways, their errand tokens raised above their heads. The three taskmasters stomping along the end of Arch Road kept their heads constantly raised, looking out for any breaches of Street rules.

Bell four rang out, and right on cue my Noblewoman began approaching. I recognized her by her pudgy ankles that didn't quite fit into her rare mahogany sandals. That extent of her girth was a sign of status so high I assumed she might be on speaking terms with the Crier himself.

I wanted to puff my chest out with pride, having earned her exactly what she wanted. And not only that, but I'd acquired the fan by doing something I would normally have begged to do.

I could already hear Jadanmaster Geb's praise in my ears.

Until the strangled feet stopped under my nose, and the legs went stiff.

'I said red, you little shit! Red! Red! Red!' the Noblewoman screeched, voice shriller than nails on glass. 'Red! Are your eyes as worthless as your people?'

I seized up, nearly dropping the fan. My stomach tightened, knowing what I was in for. This was one of *those* Noblewomen.

'Taskmaster!' the woman yelled, spinning side to side, pudge on her neck jiggling. 'Taskmaster!'

I fumbled in my pocket for the parchment she'd stained with the lip grease, keeping it in my hand for proof. I knew better than to argue, but I could still hope that Jadanmaster Geb would get here before a taskmaster, and see the truth.

Her ankles disappeared further out onto the street, leaving my line of my vision. 'Taskmasters! Right now! This Jadan has wronged me! Tears to my ancestors, I've been wronged!'

I tried to swallow away my fear, but my throat was too dry. Foot traffic in the street slowed as many of the Nobles readied themselves for the entertainment. The jangle of Closed Eye necklaces reached my ears as onlookers held the shut lids in my direction. The three taskmasters began to race down the street, excited to get to play with their whips, but they were all stopped short.

'May I ask what the problem is, madam?' Jadanmaster Geb's green shoes stepped into view.

'You don't look like a taskmaster,' the High Noblewoman said after a pause, a sneer in her voice.

'Ah. This truism resonates well, as I am a *Jadanmaster*,' replied Geb calmly. 'And I am in efficiency and disciplinary charge of the slaves on Arch Road.'

'You look more suited to be in charge of pretty sun-dresses.' She tittered. 'Although with skin that dark, maybe Jadans do suit you even better.'

'I can assure you, madam, that I am High Noble. Now again, what seems to be the problem?' he asked, ignoring both slights. There was a distinct crispness to his tone. Geb was quite adept at recognizing those who threw fits just to stave off boredom.

'I told it to get me a red one!' Her words were full of self-righteous pain. It was almost as if I'd stolen her child and tried to raise it as a Jadan. 'Does that look like red to you?'

Geb's shoes turned towards me. I couldn't plead my case, so I made sure to hold the parchment stain-side out.

'On first viewing of this parchment I find that the stain is clearly pink,' Geb replied, understanding my intention. 'And exquisitely matches the colour of the fan. A magnificent find.'

'I know, but I said—'

'The stain is decidedly pink,' Geb repeated calmly. 'Is this parchment what you gave Spout as a basis for the errand?'

'I don't know where it got that!' The lie was delivered with such force that for a moment even I almost believed her. 'Now I want punishment. Get me a real taskmaster with a whip!'

The three taskmasters inched their way forward, but Jadanmaster Geb outranked them, and when he gave them a halting raise of his palm, they stopped. He pulled out a piece of parchment that I recognized as a writ of return. 'I'll have Spout exchange it at once.'

'No.' The High Noblewoman's feet waddled my way and the fan and token were snatched from my hands. The impatient Sunlight smashed into my face. 'I don't have time for that. The ball is at bell six and I need it now. This Jadan leech has wasted two of my Shivers!' – another lie – 'And if I have to suffer for its idiocy then so does it. Punishment.'

A pause and a sigh. 'What is it you wish?'

'I want him in the Procession.'

Dread flooded through me, making me go weak at the knees.

'The Procession is only for Jadans who break one of the

first three Street rules,' Jadanmaster Geb said with calm authority. 'This . . . *infraction* doesn't qualify. How about a more appropriate punishment?'

'What if I go and find the Vicaress myself?' she asked, venom in every word.

'Be my guest,' Geb said, shrugging so high his shoulders tapped the dangling green earrings. 'My guess is that she's at the Pyramid, as per usual. But I imagine she'll impart similar sentiments to mine, and I wager you'll be late for your ball.'

'Fine. Then whippings,' the High Noblewoman said, delight coating her voice. 'But beat the water out of it, then. I mean, look at its forehead! Obviously it has too much! Greedy little Jadan leech.'

A whipping was almost tender compared to what Jadans had to endure in the Procession. I was seething with frustration, but I couldn't help feeling some small relief.

'How many lashes do you request?' Geb asked.

'Until he faints,' she declared to the street.

The audience seemed satisfied with the request, and I could feel dozens of eyes on me.

'Is that all?' Geb asked, unsheathing a punishing rod that was also somehow matching green.

'Yes.'

'Fine. You might want to stand back. Look up, Spout,' Geb commanded in my direction.

I raised my head, fear stiffening the rest of my body. However, his eyes were soft, and he gave me a conspiratorial smile.

'Arms up,' he said.

I did as he commanded, hoping he would take it easy on me.

'Spin.'

I turned around and felt him tugging at my shirt, making it look as if he was fixing something. I could feel the heat of his breath as he leaned in and whispered, 'Pretend to faint after the first hit.'

He stepped back, and then I heard the rod cut through the air, to land on my shoulder. The blow was quite strong – he had to make it look real – but the pain wasn't anything I couldn't handle. I doubted the bruise would be bigger than my thumb, barely even playable in Matty's shape game. I gasped loud enough for my audience to hear, and then crumpled to the ground, not daring to move.

'Enjoy your new fan,' Geb said to the High Noblewoman. 'Praise be to the Khat.'

'That's it?' she asked, aghast. 'One hit? No—'

Geb cut her off. 'You requested until he fainted. He fainted. Praise be to the Khat. I believe we are done here.'

'But it's faking! It—'

'Your words, not mine. Now please, allow me to do my job or I will be submitting a writ of complaint to Lord Suth that a member of his family is interfering with one of the Khat's Jadanmasters, and by decree six, stanza twelve of the Khat's law, which prohibits High Nobles from—'

The woman gave a venomous huff, and I heard her heavy feet pad away.

I kept still, trying not to breathe in too much sand from the ground as the rest of the audience dispersed to a chorus of disappointed moans. Soon enough they'd be swept up in the fervour of trading precious Cold for useless goods and forget all about me.

After a few moments, hands swept under my armpits and lifted me up. 'Thank you, sir,' I said, as he set me on my corner.

He gave me a firm pat on the shoulder, glaring at the three taskmasters, who were still waiting nearby, just in case. 'Liars are not beneficial for my operations. As always, you did exemplary, Spout. Perfect shade of pink. Like I imparted, more Jadans like you, smooth as silk through fingers.'

Chapter Five

The last of the Street Jadans trickled in, and eventually the sloping right wall of the common area was completely lined. Although most of us had some sort of painful trophy to show from the day, we'd returned in one piece, another shift having survived the Sun.

At the end of the day, Jadans' mouths were usually too thirsty for small talk, but it never usually stopped Matty from keeping my ears occupied.

'Hey, Spout,' he practically shouted.

'Yeah,' I said, trying not to move my lips too much for fear of them cracking.

He dug a finger in his ear, shifting his jaw. I wondered if his Jadanmaster had boxed his ears again. 'Wanna play "whatsit"?'

I nodded. My mind was still racing from tinkering on the Cold Bellows, and in truth I would have loved to ponder quietly on that, but I had sworn to myself long ago that I'd do anything I could to keep Matty happy.

My friend lifted off his shirt and pointed to a series of fresh lashes on his shoulder. I winced, knowing how much they would still sting. As soon as the curfew bells rang and we were allowed off the walls, I would give him as much of the groan salve as he wanted.

'Whatsit?' Matty asked.

'Hmmm.' I traced the lines on Matty's back, trying to come up with something good. 'It's the three paths that Adam the Wise took through the sands to the Southern Cry Temple.' I touched the first path. 'This one is where he had the vision that the Drought was coming.' I touched the second. 'This is the one where he found the white fig tree.'

Matty gave a thoughtful nod. 'Pretty good. I figured it felt like that.'

I took my shirt off next, careful not to rotate my arm too much. I pointed to the bruise on my shoulder that Geb's rod had given me. 'Whatsit?'

Matty's small fingers traced the outline of the bruise. 'Dwarf camel.'

'A camel?' I smirked. 'That's all you see?'

Matty shook his head. 'No. Course not. It's a camel that carries the Frosts from the Patches to the Pyramid.'

I pretended to wince. 'That's one strong camel.'

Matty shook his head. 'Frosts are almost as light as air.'

I raised an eyebrow. 'How would you know? Jadans aren't allowed to touch them.'

'Because they don't fall 'smuch as the other Cold,' Matty said, as though it were obvious. 'They prolly don't weigh a lot since they float in the sky so long.'

I chuckled. 'You might be onto something.'

Matty lifted his chest off the wall so he could look across me to Moussa. 'Hey, Moussa. Whatsit. Your turn.'

Moussa looked down at his feet, keeping his eyes decidedly off the piece of front wall reserved for the Patch Jadans. 'I don't really feel like playing.'

'What? You didn't get any marks?' Matty asked.

Moussa gave a resigned shrug. 'A few. I just don't want to play.'

I gave Moussa a light nudge with my elbow. He shook his head, but I countered with a look that asked him to play along. At ten years old, Matty was still young enough to find beauty in such a world, and Moussa and I both knew that sort of innocence was something worth prolonging.

Moussa sighed, lifting off his shirt in a long pull.

Matty's face dropped. I had to hold back my grimace.

Moussa's chest was riddled with fresh bruises. It looked as if he'd been tossed down the Khat's Staircase. Puffy welts wrapped around both sides of his stomach, and from my limited training with Abb, I thought Moussa would have at least one cracked rib.

Jadans weren't allowed to get off the wall, so instead I turned to the side and placed my hand gently on the back of his neck, pulling his forehead against mine. 'Sorry, brother.'

Matty had tucked himself back against the wall, his face mortified. Moussa leaned across me so he could give Matty a weak smile, his dry lips cracking. 'Right, I thought we were playing whatsit? So whatsit?'

I looked over all the bruises, imagining the strength that must have been behind the blows. 'It's a song.'

Moussa nodded gently. 'What song?'

'We can call it the "Jadan's Anthem",' I said, hoping he'd play into it. 'It's about time we had one of our own.'

Matty's face lifted, a sly grin on his lips.

Howdin, who was standing on the other side of Moussa, shot us a fierce stare. 'Don't blashpheme like that.'

Moussa shrugged. 'Listen. I'll make sure the words won't be blasphemy. Besides' – he nodded to the main doors—'no one's going to hear.'

'The Crier will hear,' Howdin said, his face anxious, looking at the slats in the ceiling, the Sunlight finally retreating.

'Here's the thing. The Crier doesn't listen to us,' Moussa said with a huff, prodding at his bruises. 'Closed Ears, too.'

Matty leaned forward, looking over the bruises. 'Whatsit sound like, Moussa? Our song?'

Moussa finally cracked a smile, pointing to the bruise above his belly button. He sang out a long note, and my ears shuddered with delight. It'd been a long time since I had heard my friend sing, and I'd missed his voice.

'The Jadan's work upon the sands,' Moussa sang, hopping from bruise to bruise on his stomach. Then he stopped, his burned lips searching for the fitting words.

'Those who need the Cold?' I offered.

'Those who need the Cold,' Moussa sang softly. He seemed satisfied, and moved his finger back to the first bruise, hopping along the painful spots:

> 'The Jadan's work upon the sands
> Those who need the Cold
> Family forever
> Older than the old
> Blessed be . . .'

Howdin was pushing as far away from Moussa as he could, but Howdin had always been a little twitchy. The rest of the Street Jadans looked on, smiling. Considering we had to drone the 'Khat's Anthem' every morning, most nearby ears seemed eager to listen to something else – so long as Moussa kept his word about staying away from blasphemy.

'Blessed be the birds,' Matty offered with a smile, tucking the metal feather behind his ear.

Moussa laughed, which was almost better than the music.

'Listen. Why don't we sing for something real?' He thought
it over and then picked up where he had left off:

> 'Strength to the forgotten
> Who still bleed for the lands
> So maybe the World Crier
> Might release their han—'

Moussa was about to move over to the bruises on his side,
when the Patch Jadans burst in through the main doors.
They always came together, and were always last to make it
home, but Joon led them right to their wall, settling into
their stances.

Moussa darkened at the sight of their leader, quickly finding
interest in his own feet.

At last, everyone was home.

Old Man Gum began to wave his arms about, pointing to
the chimes. The bells began to ring, our curfew officially set.
We couldn't prove it, but we all knew that Gramble took pity
on the Patch Jadans and waited until they got home to ring
the bell, instead of judging by his Sundial. Anyone not home
in time didn't get rations, which, considering the little we
were given, was torturous.

Our Barracksmaster passed through the doors, dragging in
the rations cart. He came around with the Closed Eye, and
we all kneeled for our evening portion of figs and cooled
water. Then everyone stepped down from their walls, parents
and children sweeping together in hugs that often looked
painful, limbs careful not to squeeze too tightly. Matty hovered
beside Moussa and me, always looking a bit awkward when
this time came. A few years back Matty had been assigned
Levi as his father, and not all fathers were like Abb. Levi was
a man of scowls, who often expressed his disdain at having
such a 'pathetic excuse for a Jadan' forced upon his lineage.

Moussa exchanged a cursory wave with his assigned mother, Hanni, which was the extent of the affection I ever saw them show one another.

Abb began making his way over, a broad smile on his lips, calling to us while pointing at the bells that had now finished ringing. 'Hey, boys. Did you have a good *chime* today?'

I slapped my forehead.

Abb shifted around the hugging bodies. 'Good chime? Like good *time*. Get it—'And then his eyes went to Moussa's skin, his expression slipping as the bruises registered.

'Moussa, come with me, we'll get the healing box,' Abb said. 'Now.'

Moussa didn't react, having got lost in a feverish stare. Sarra and Joon were now embracing in a lingering hug, doing their best to squish out any air left between their bodies.

Abb put a gentle hand on Moussa's shoulder. 'Trust me, kiddo. When it comes to broken hearts, the one with the hammer is never the one with the mortar. Now let's get you looked at, make sure you don't have any cracked ribs.'

Moussa nodded, knowing better than to argue with the Barracks Healer when he looked that serious.

'What'cha sad for, Moussa?' Matty asked with a curious tilt of his head. 'I never even seen you talk to Sarra.'

Moussa's hands balled into shaky fists, shooting a look of pure disdain down at Matty. 'I was going to!'

Matty gave a single frightened jerk and then fell into his slave stance.

'Moussa . . .' Abb warned.

'Sorry.' Moussa sighed. 'Family.'

Matty slowly reached out his trembling arm, tilting his wrist back.

Moussa rolled his eyes and then touched Matty's 'calm spot' with his thumb.

'We've got enough Nobles yelling at us,' Abb said with a nod. 'You boys don't need to add to the noise.'

I gestured to Matty's back with a stab of my forehead.

Abb leaned over and graced Matty's injuries with a glance. 'You too, featherbrain. Let's get you *Patched* up. Get it?'

Moussa groaned, but Matty smiled.

'Use my salve,' I said. 'Save your medicines, Dad.'

Abb raised an eyebrow, but I knew he'd be proud. 'And are you going to tinker while I work, Little Builder?'

'I'm going out,' I said, lowering my voice so the swarming families on either side wouldn't hear me.

Matty looked up, worried. 'But the Procession is soon. The taskmasters are prolly going to be all over. Stay here and help me find a place for that marble nose.'

I tapped the side of my head. 'I'm working on my own thing. Don't worry, I'll be careful.'

'What are you trying to find?' Moussa asked in the subtle tone he used when he was curious about my tinkering.

I paused. I intended to find more sheets of waxy paper tonight, which would be a vital part of the Idea; I thought if I didn't say it out loud, maybe I could convince myself to give it up, but I knew it wasn't only finding materials that I craved. My mind kept returning to the image of a rigid back.

'Something different,' I said.

I sat cross-legged on the roof, hoping the Upright Girl might finally appear out of the darkness. Most of the night had already passed, and still she had yet to show her face or braided hair.

In truth, there had been no need to come back to the Blacksmith Quarter, to the alley where the girl had watched me deny the Shiver, and I should have been back in Abb's room, deep in sleep. With the Procession coming up, it wasn't safe to be outside the barracks at this time of night. The taskmasters had their own quotas, and the closer it got to the ritual, the more desperate they became to fill them.

I'd been sitting in the same spot so long that my feet had fallen asleep. The light from the stars bathed the Smith Quarter in a soft glow, and in the distance I could see the last streaks of the Crying over the Patches, now swollen with Cold. I thought about my three Wisps and how they had once fallen into those same sands. A tired Patch Jadan would have picked them up and added them to his bucket. What might that Jadan think if he knew those Wisps would end up under my blanket? What might he think if he knew my Idea?

Abb would be worried by now, but I didn't want to leave the roof yet. I had no clue what else I could do to draw the Upright Girl out. I continued to keep my back at a scandalous angle, straight and uncomfortable, hoping that it might be the key to her trust. I could have sworn I sensed her out there, in the shadows of Paphos, watching me.

A part of me thought I might just be imagining her presence, so desperate to think she was there that I was creating faces in the shadows and conjuring dark figures at the corners of my eyes. Even the Jadans plundering the rubbish heaps had gone home now, taking advantage of the last hours of darkness to get some sleep. At this point, I thought, even the taskmasters must be in their beds.

My Claw Staff waited impatiently by my side, sitting on top of the pile of waxy fabric it had dredged up, urging me to go home. I'd got what I wanted. After working on Mama Jana's Cold Bellows, I was now riding a dangerous current of inspiration. The boilweed heaps behind the flower shops had offered me the rest of what I'd need for my next invention. Since the waxy fabric was used to protect the flowers from the Sun as they were delivered, I figured it must also be good at keeping Cold in. Now, I had the Wisps and the materials to make the Idea happen.

I needed to firm up a few new excuses on my crawl home.

In the distance, the Crying finally stopped, and even the stars began to dwindle. The night wind continued to bring in cool air. I yawned deep, enjoying a few moments of Gale's breath, and then finally let my back settle into the crook it was used to.

I sighed. It was time to go.

I packed up my things and strapped the Claw Staff back to my thigh. Taking one final glance into the alley just in case, I began crawling the long expanse of rooftops back to my barracks. If I was lucky I'd get a few hours of sleep, enough to take the edge off.

I'd just crossed into the Garden District when I saw her.

She was lying flat on her stomach, just like I was, her body huddled on a nearby roof. I wanted to call out, but I wasn't sure if she was lying motionless because there was a task-master lurking in the alley below. My heart began to pound in my chest, nervous for what I might say to her.

I crept over to her, slowly, so the waxy paper wouldn't rustle in my boilweed bag. Shuffling up from behind, chest hammering, I noticed she looked smaller than I remembered, and her uniform was dirtier. She remained still. I picked up a few pebbles and tossed them forward so they'd land just beside her legs.

No reaction.

I couldn't tell if she was just dismissing the stones, or if she was unconscious with heatstroke. I took a chance and lifted myself to my knees, jolting my head from side to side, but the street seemed clear as far as I could tell, so I gritted my teeth and stood up, rushing over to her body.

Then I stopped short. The body wasn't hers.

And it was dead.

Kneeling down, I extended my Claw Staff and rolled the corpse over. The boy's head had a long piece of boilweed slung over one eye. I recognized him as the feral prowler from last night. I had to put a hand over my mouth to stifle my choking, wondering how the few beetles crawling over his face had been able to devour so much of his remaining eye.

The boy's limbs were stiff, the blood having pooled in the lower half of his body, and I knew there was a chance he'd been lying there for most of the night. I spun around looking for a loose brick or big chunk of stone. Finding a piece on the next rooftop, I tapped beside the body, trying to scare away anything that might sting or snap from the folds of skin.

'Family,' I whispered, making sure the boilweed sling was still tight around his head. Manoeuvring the eyepatch revealed something shiny and smooth tucked away in the empty socket, and I realized that's where the boy must have hidden the items precious to him. He was an Inventor in his own right. He'd had a need and had created a solution. It was crude, and simple, and beautiful; and although I yearned to know what sort of plunder he'd been keeping in there, I thought it best to let the boy carry his secrets into the darkness.

Making sure the nearest alley was deserted, I rolled the body to the edge of the roof, stepping clear of the little brown insects. One big heave and he was in the air, a hard thud following below shortly after.

In the morning, the dead-cart Jadans would patrol the alleys, but not the rooftops. The boy deserved to rest in the sands with our other fallen kin.

There were dozens of different reasons why he might have died, all unfair, and all perfectly believable. He was born Jadan, which meant he was born in debt. A Noble had probably demanded his eye for some unintended slight, and thus doomed the boy to a very short, very desperate life of scavenging half-blind in the darkness. Anger seethed in my chest. My hands balled into fists, stopping tears that begged to be released. This boy wasn't alive eight hundred years ago. He had nothing to do with the sins behind the Great Drought, and he didn't deserve to reap the punishment. None of us did. But still, the Crier continued to forsake us.

Scuttling away, I touched the waxy fabric in my bag, deciding I should use the opaque material for something else. Something less offensive to the Crier. But it was hard, knowing how much needle and gut Abb had in the healing box, how easily I could stitch the body of the Idea together. How perfect it would be.

Jadans could die anywhere, and for anything. There didn't need to be a reason. Really, I should just take the leap, considering most other paths had us ending up like the eyepatch boy anyway. The Crier hadn't cared about my other inventions. The crank-fans went against tradition, too, alleviating some of our suffering; and I had about a dozen of those.

My fingers trembled, thinking about putting the crushing chamber of the Idea together. If the Crier didn't like what I was planning, then He wouldn't have let me get this far.

Perhaps His Eye genuinely was closed to the Jadan people.

Either way, my feet itched to step into the unknown.

Chapter Six

Five days later I stood on my corner, back hunched against the sizzling sky, thinking again about the three Wisps.

The Gospels told us to focus on one thing only during Procession day: the mercy of the Khat, and how he'd saved the Jadan people from extinction. Though I was supposed to reflect on the fact that I wouldn't have any Cold without his benevolence, I couldn't stop thinking about what I'd done.

I hadn't been able to help myself.

While bringing the Idea to life, I'd fallen into something of a trance, my fingers moving by themselves, my mind simply following them. The tinkering had started slowly, hesitantly, but as the night went on, starlight diving through the slats to encourage my work, things began to feel right. More right than anything else I'd created.

Which was clearly wrong.

I'd finished the Cold Wrap in the early hours of the morning, everything coming together better than I could ever have hoped. The design was simple enough: I'd fashioned two layers of waxy paper into a garment that wrapped around my chest. Thanks to Abb I knew how to stitch a wound properly, and so I was able to sew the layers airtight, leaving a bit of space in between the sheets. With a small metal grate, some springs, gears, and skill, I'd tinkered together a small chamber to crush the Wisps, which I put on the side of the Wrap.

The Idea was similar to Mama Jana's Cold Bellows, where the Wisps could be crushed throughout the day, slowly spilling the Cold; but in this case, instead of the Cold going into the air, it would filter inside the Wrap itself, meaning I could wear it under my uniform and secretly keep myself cool throughout the day.

That was the theory, at least.

I still hadn't been able to get myself to try it out, my hands trembling each time I touched the crushing lever, but I didn't know how much longer I might be able to refrain.

Once I used the Wrap, there was no going back. This was a blatant disregard for a Divine decree. This was blasphemy and rebellion, all rolled into one garment. The Crier had forbidden Jadans from having Cold any more for a reason. He wanted us to feel the burn of His Brother Sun for eternity. Yet, there was still no sign of his discontent.

A sheen of sweat covered my forehead just from the thought. I wanted to wipe it away, but I didn't dare move in the presence of so many taskmasters, Priests, and Nobles.

The Procession was the most popular event in Paphos, and there were eyes everywhere. Every initial Khatday of the month, the Street Jadans were reminded of what happened to those who broke one of the first three rules.

Caught out at night: chained in the Procession.

Found with stolen property: chained in the Procession.

Off the corner without a Noble token: chained in the Procession.

Arch Road was now filling with spectators, all waiting to watch the Vicaress do her work. Some Nobles even made a full day out of it, following the Procession throughout each Quarter, stretching out the entertainment.

Finely dressed Noblewomen stood in little groups, holding their colourful display of parasols and chatting about all the pain the dirty slaves deserved. They drank flavoured water and ate orangefruit, scattering the precious peels on the road. I could smell the baking citrus, and my mouth grew even more parched. High Noblemen in gleaming white sun-shirts proudly conversed about the brutal techniques they used to keep their personal Jadans in line. A few painters sat on stools, parchments stretched over easels, ready to be inked. Brushes and quills were poised in hands, eager to capture the twisted expressions of pain.

I knew from the Domestics that High Houses paid good Cold for those images to hang on their walls. The Closed Eye was everywhere. Most Nobles displayed the symbol on a necklace, but I also saw stout-brimmed hats with the Eye woven in. Ceramic versions swung on long golden chains. Boilweed sculptures of the Eye, painstakingly glued to precision. A few waterskins, with the Eye painted on their bellies, each drink a reminder of Jadan thirst. Small children holding small cotton pillows in the shape of the Closed Eye, hugging them close, stroking their soft fabric.

'Micah.'

I gave a start. I hadn't heard Jadanmaster Geb sneak up on my right.

'Look up,' he commanded gently.

As Geb usually did on Procession day, he was adorned entirely in red: crimson robes, a fiery headscarf, and ruby sandals. Those who didn't know Geb might think the colour scheme was a cruel insult, but in fact, it was a testament to his kindness. After the Procession, Geb often helped the punished Jadans back to their corners, and since he was dressed all in red, nobody had to feel guilty for smearing his clothing with blood.

'How is the state of your shoulder?' Geb asked. His face was sombre. I think in a way he hated the Processions almost as much as we did; each one of his Jadans caught was a direct failure for him, meaning a deduction from his pay and seeing one of us hurt.

'Very good, sir. Thank you for your mercy.' I made sure to sound properly gratified. 'And thanks to the Khat for his mercy.'

'Well said.' He gave me a satisfied nod, his garnet earrings rocking back and forth. 'You give your people a good name, Spout.'

'I try to, sir.'

He gave a sad gulp and then walked off to find a spot near the Temple. I checked my slave stance as the Nobles continued to spill onto the street. Finally, the bells rang out, the crowd quieting.

The Procession started.

I couldn't see their faces, but I could hear the chains swinging between their legs as they were marched down the street. A part of me was always glad I couldn't lift my head at this stage, as I was never eager to witness such a dreadful display.

A few taskmaster feet marched alongside the row of the damned, their dirty toes peeking from their sandals, plagued with fungus. Jadans only got one bucket of steaming water a month to bathe with, and it was a mystery to me how we managed to stay cleaner than the taskmasters did. 'Hate poxes the skin faster than Sun,' Abb had once said to me.

The chains rattled heavily, chiming with the sound of excitable Nobles ready to catch the demonstration. The Jadans were led to the front of the Temple, my brothers and sisters gathered up onto the lowest step. I could feel their fear coursing through the streets, making my heart clench.

We all knew what was coming next.

I heard the crackle of the blade before I saw the fire.

The Vicaress of Paphos.

'Heads high!' Jadanmaster Geb yelled down the street. In one motion, we all lifted our heads.

The holy figure slid down Arch Road, all poise and grace.

The Vicaress – like all the women in the Khat's family – was beautiful. She had a light complexion, and eyes of a startling blue that was never found in Jadankind. She wore a dress fashioned from dark, fine silk, which clung tightly to her body's every curve. Her long black hair was styled above her head, decorated with a gold pin adorned with a Closed Eye. In her hand, she held a fiery blade straight above her head, the metal collecting angry light from the Sun and casting it around the street. A ring of flames blazed along the circular hilt, dripping tongues of fire into the sky. Although they sometimes licked at her hands, she never flinched. Rumour had it a Vicaress held a truce with pain itself, agreeing to give it out with merciless expertise, and in return, she'd never feel any herself.

Flanking her sides were two young Noble girls from the Khat's close family. They wore sun-dresses of the purest white and faces stretched with glee. Each girl carried a basket overflowing with Rose of Gilead petals, ready to be laid at the Vicaress's feet. They laughed as they plucked handfuls of the red petals and scattered them about carelessly, littering the street with velvety colour.

Abb had told me there was a huge garden laid out behind the Pyramid which only grew the Roses of Gilead. He said he'd often look out from under the giant slabs of stone on his back and admire the flowers, flourishing under the constant trickle of Cold water.

The Vicaress twisted her blade, the shine from the flames smacking my face. I managed to keep calm, head forward, not twitching; although I thought I felt her eyes go to my forehead.

She passed beside me as the song started.

Always the same song.

The words were a mystery to Jadans and Nobles alike, but the song haunted our dreams. They formed the song that Sun would sing if it ever succeeded in burning the world to sand. Yet it was a lovely melody. Intricate, with long dips and gentle shakes, flowing from the Vicaress's lips as naturally as pain flowed off the end of a taskmaster's whip.

Some of the Nobles along the street tried to join in, muttering along. But the melody was too complex for humming. A particularly jolly couple near me were swaying their fingers in the air, trying to predict where the notes might go, although it proved too difficult for them. They smiled brightly with each misplacement, popping Khatberries into their cheeks, red juice dripping down their chins.

Even from my corner, the fear coursing through the veins of the chained was palpable. I thought about my Cold Wrap, and how quickly I'd be added to the Procession if any taskmaster discovered me wearing it. I'd never felt the Vicaress's blade, but each victim said the same thing: it was pain you could never prepare for, and once you felt the burning slice, you forever trembled every time you stepped off your corner.

From stories around the barracks, I knew Abb had been tortured in the Procession twice, both times before I was assigned to him, but he'd always refused to tell me anything more about it.

Down near the end of Arch Road a Noble voice yelled, 'Burn them all!' He was half-heartedly hushed by a few voices in the crowd, but the cry was mostly overlaid with titters and huffs of agreement.

The Sun shone directly overhead, pouring onto the fiery knife. The Vicaress continued to flow down the road, blade high and reverent.

Eventually she made her way to the front of the Arch Road Temple, the Noble girls emptying the rest of their baskets with a shake before skittering off to the side. At last the Vicaress stood still before the chained.

She lowered the tip of her scorched blade, drawing it back and forth between the prisoners' faces. A few tensed up, but

I think most were in shock. The taskmasters stood behind the small bodies, making the chained look ever feebler.

The Vicaress's blade drifted to the leftmost Jadan, and we all cringed in the knowledge of what was to come. Only the sacred word would keep them alive, but the space where the declaration ended was also the place where the torture began.

The first Jadan was a little younger than me. His legs trembled, while the edges of his face seemed to melt from fear. His shirt showed signs of tearing where a taskmaster must have already taken out his own punishment.

The blade waited to cleanse him of sin.

'Unworthy!' the boy pressed out, his voice nearly breaking with effort. It was said that the louder you made your status known, the less time the fiery metal sizzled in your body.

Every Noble on the street cheered at the word, waving their Eyes. A child near me tossed his plush Eye into the air, catching it with a huge smile.

The Vicaress nodded to the boy's taskmaster. Meaty paws held his shoulders as the Vicaress chose her point of entry.

The top portion of the blade slid into the boy's side, right under his ribs, and the scream that followed curdled the air. I flinched, praying no one saw me move. The fiery metal was then removed with careful precision and the boy wobbled on his feet, screaming in pain, his eyes rushing back in their sockets.

The Vicaress then stepped in front of a girl of fifteen or sixteen, who fainted at the sight of the blade before her. The taskmaster behind her was ready, easily catching the slight body and keeping it upright. The Vicaress reached into her pocket and pulled out a cube of Glassland salt. She gently waved it in front of the girl's nose until it released its smell. The girl jolted awake, her eyes popping wide in surprise and fear.

Then the tip of blade was rested over the girl's heart, waiting to see if she would make the declaration.

'Unworthy,' the girl squeaked loudly.

The crowd erupted with glee as the metal was pressed into her shoulder, hissing with fury.

The girl's scream was so huge that at first it came out silently, lips straining to expel the sound. Then it erupted in a wave that washed up and down Arch Road, leaving Noble applause in its wake.

The Vicaress went straight to her next prisoner, another girl, this one younger than the last. She barely looked old enough to be doing errands. The Jadan boy next to her tried lending a calming hand on the girl's shoulder, but the Vicaress shook her head. She lifted the hand from the shoulder and sliced away his little finger with practised ease. The flesh tumbled to the ground, leaving the boy staring at his hand, his mouth gaping for a scream.

The Vicaress pressed a hand to the boy's lips for silence.

A few Nobles whooped. My hands pulsed with anger, aching to wrap around their necks and strangle them to silence. Then I quickly remembered my place and unclenched my fists, tilting my head against the watchful sky.

The Vicaress turned her attention back to the young girl, who seized up, forgetting what she was supposed to do. She would know the word as well as her name – we all did – but fear often did strange things. I willed the word to her lips, my mind screaming it across the street.

The dagger was drawn over the girl's heart, flames hungry.

Then came a moment which would change everything.

'Worthy!' a voice screamed from the rooftops. 'Worthy! They're all worthy, you filthy Sunwhore!'

A few bright parasols dropped in surprise. The nearest artist's quill swung across his easel in shock, his painting ruined. All the taskmasters' heads swivelled behind them, looking up to the Temple roof. Some gasped, but many remained still with shock, struggling to understand.

Up on the roof, a small figure shielded her face with a mask of boilweed. To everyone on the street, her identity was a mystery.

Everyone except me.

Her posture was astoundingly rigid, and even though her hair was now unbraided, it tumbled to just the right spot below her chin.

And she was holding a Shiver.

My Shiver. It had to be.

It gleamed bright and brown in her hands. She must have doubled back that night and kept it for herself.

In one movement, the Upright Girl raised the Shiver above her head, and with a strong swing of her arms, hurled it down like the World Crier Himself.

The Shiver struck the steps beside the chained Jadans and exploded in a crack of Cold, the air rushing down the entire street, sending the Rose of Gilead petals swirling. The crowd shook as their robes were blown back, the Cold air swarming every inch of their bodies. When the Cold washed over my face I couldn't hold back the gasp. I'd never felt anything so devastatingly wonderful, and I knew I might never experience anything like it again.

'Worthy!' the Upright Girl's voice boomed over the crowd before she turned to flee.

It was the first time I'd ever seen the Vicaress lose her composure, an unsettled look creeping into the corners of her eyes. A look like fear.

All the taskmasters moved after the girl immediately, scrambling to find a way onto the Temple roof; but even if they managed to get up there, they would have no luck catching her.

I knew how fast the girl could move.

The Vicaress pointed the blade at the empty roof, murder in her eyes, as the Rose of Gilead petals drifted back towards the street.

Chapter Seven

Tradition demanded that while waiting on the barracks wall we keep our eyes closed and mouths shut until we are given our evening rations. It wasn't like Gramble could hear us from his guardhouse, especially if we kept our voices hushed, but most Jadans kept quiet out of respect and fear.

Tonight was different.

For the first time since I could remember, tradition was ignored by absolutely everyone. The main chamber of our barracks was thick with conversation. Whispers reached my ears from every direction.

'I heard she's the Sun's daughter. And that her face is one giant flame, that's why she has to hide it.'

'If her face was a flame, it would have burned the boilweed mask.'

'The boilweed was from sky's crib. It's magic.'

'She has to hide her face, because one look and your eyes melt to sand.'

'You ever seen anything like this?'

'Not since the Twin Frosts fell a few generations back.'

'But never so blatant.'

'Never.'

'Rebellion?'

'Hush! To what point? Can't rebel against the Crier.'

'I heard the Vicaress caught the girl and is roasting her on a spit on top of the Pyramid right now.'

'She going to eat her?'

'The Sun is. We'll be picking up her bones in the morning. They'll want us to mix them with the straw and clay.'

'Well, we know what this means. Bigger quota. I'd bet a finger on it.'

'Damn it, how can they possibly make the quotas bigger.'

'She screwed us all. They're going to want triple Shivers tomorrow to make up for it. We won't get our breaks.'

A scoff. 'Breaks!'

'I heard she's from Langria.'

'Langria's not real.'

'Why'd she smash it in the Market Quarter?'

'Didn't like the prices.'

A playful slap. 'Be serious.'

'Spout was there. He might know.'

Eyes turning towards me.

'Think of how long she could have lived on that Shiver for.'

'We all could have.'

I looked across the barracks at the expanse of boilweed divisions, doubting many of us would sleep tonight. Nothing this dramatic had happened in Paphos since that young monk from the Southern Cry Temple ran through the streets naked, prophesying the end of the Great Drought. Of course, that monk had been a Noble, so his punishment was simply confinement in a dungeon until his sanity returned.

None of us could have ever had the bravery to do this. And if the Upright Girl got caught, being roasted on a spit would be getting off lightly.

I turned to Moussa who stood beside me. A hand went

into his pocket, and he pulled out a pinch of the gem candy dust I'd given him the other night. Shrugging, he offered it to me first.

I shook my head. 'Have you not eaten it yet?' I asked, knowing full well how hard it must have been not to devour all the sugar the second it was in his possession.

'I saved it for a special occasion.' Moussa gestured around the room. 'Seems appropriate now. Bad times are ahead.'

'You think?'

Moussa's face soured. He smelled of a long shift, and his breathing was still a bit wheezy and shallow. Abb had said his rib would heal within a few weeks. 'They always are.'

From my other side, Matty said: 'I want to meet the Shiver Girl. She's invincible.'

'Invincible, huh?'

'*And* did'ja know she can fly?'

I paused, holding back my smile. 'How do you know?'

Matty gave me a look questioning if I was being serious. 'Because the Vicaress didn't catch her.'

'But what if the Vicaress *did* catch her, but the Boilweed Girl is just invincible,' I replied.

Matty thought about it, his face scrunching with the effort. 'That's prolly it. I'm jealous you got to see her.'

Moussa's eyes went dark. 'Here's the thing, Matty. You're too young to understand how bad this is. She's a plague.'

'Ten's not that little.' Matty smiled, bright and big. He reached into his pocket and pulled out the metal and yarn feather, waving it in front of my eyes. I wasn't sure how the thing hadn't been confiscated yet, since he always kept it on him during his errands. 'Especially if you don't know long you're going to live.'

I was stunned, my stomach flipping into a horrified knot. I looked over at Moussa for help, but he looked just as taken aback.

'Matty,' I said. My chest squeezed, but he had a point. I couldn't help but think of the one-eyed boy I'd delivered to the alley; he'd looked even younger than Matty.

Matty kept waving the feather, possibly oblivious to how sad his statement came across. His smile didn't falter as he watched the yarn dance.

Moussa tried to step in. 'You can't look at it like—'

'I don't mean it in a bad way,' Matty said. 'It's like, some things prolly don't last as long as they should.' The feather caught the first of the starlight through the roof. 'It makes 'em special,' he continued. 'And then you can hope they come back.'

I felt my throat swell shut, struggling to keep the tears out of my eyes.

'For now, let's just assume we're all going to work the Patches together,' I said. 'And then the Pyramid, and we'll all die as old men with grey hair.' I tried on a smile, but it didn't fit. 'Maybe we'll even finish your board game.'

'Grey hair like Zeti Gum?' Matty thrust the feather across the room like a sword.

Old Man Gum was standing with the Builders, but he was facing the wrong way, and seemed to be attempting to carve something into the barracks wall with his fingernail.

'Greyer,' Moussa said, the humour returning to his voice. 'I guarantee the hair on our toes is going to be grey.'

'Whatsit feel like, Spout?' Matty asked, talking above the rising whispers of our kin. 'Getting touched by Big Cold.'

I sank against the wall, thinking. 'I can't really explain it.'

Matty gave me a pleading look. 'Can you try?'

I swivelled my head to Moussa, who gave a curious shrug.

I closed my eyes and sighed. I'd never forget the feeling, but it was difficult putting it into words. 'It was like the Crier himself was lifting me into the night sky. And Great Gale putting her lips right on me.'

Moussa arched an eyebrow. 'Like you know what a kiss feels like.'

I gave Moussa a playful nudge, making sure not to hit his ribs.

'I'm going to kiss the Boilweed Girl,' Matty said.

'You mean the Upright Girl . . .?' I asked, letting the words sink in.

'Upright how?' Moussa asked.

I held up my palm and made it straight like a knife, the same way as before.

Moussa paused, his face sinking with a frown. 'Wait, you don't think . . .'

I nodded. 'I definitely think. She stood the same way. And where do you think she got that Shiver from?'

Matty's eyes widened, his voice rising. 'But'chu touched it? Does that mean the Vicaress is going to come after you too? You're smart and everything, Spout, but you're prolly not invincible like her.'

'No.' I shook my head. 'But the Upright Girl came to my corner the other day and watched me from the alley. I think she has something to tell me. That may have even been why she chose the Market Quarter.'

Moussa's face went so dark it practically melted into shadow. 'That's a really terrible idea. The Vicaress has got the same holy blood as the Khat. And she's going to find your *Upright Girl* soon, and when she does, you won't want to be anywhere near her.'

'This girl is different,' I said, feeling foolish for defending someone I knew nothing about. 'I can feel it.'

'Micah, she's the enemy,' Moussa said with a snarl. The bars went back up behind his eyes. 'She's going to bring bad times for all of us, all for some stupid *waste* of Cold.'

Before I could speak, Old Man Gum pounded a fist against the wall, right before the chimes went off above our heads.

All the conversation ceased immediately, every Jadan falling into perfectly subservient poses: shoulders in, chin down, slight bends at the hip.

Gramble came into the barracks with his rations cart, a look of deep disturbance on his face. I hoped it was just from our talking and nothing more.

'Barracks forty-five,' Gramble called out, in a tone of voice that was very much unlike him. 'There has been a certain disturbance today during the Procession. I am aware that a few of you disobey the rules and sneak out of here at night.' I tried not to look too guilty. Gramble then waved about a piece of parchment that had a freshly cracked wax seal. 'This ends tonight. Writ from the Khat himself has it that any Jadan caught out at night will be executed on the spot, and their Barracksmaster will go without pay for a month.' His eyes were boring into mine now. 'This sneaking about ends tonight. All of you.'

Gramble went around with his Closed Eye and gave out the evening rations. When it was my turn to declare myself 'Unworthy' I did so in a shaky voice, unable to look my Barracksmaster in the face.

'I told you,' Moussa said as we broke free from the wall, a grim veil over his eyes. 'Bad times are ahead.'

Chapter Eight

Metal footsteps clanked in rhythm to the 'Khat's Anthem'.

Holy Eyes have long forsaken
Those of Jadankind
But the Khat is made of mercy
For those blind to the Cry

The heavy steps sounded from the distance, their clunking so sharp I knew the shoes must have steel soles. I steadied my voice, doing my best not to draw attention to myself. Unless Jadanmaster Geb had decided to go with an armour theme for his outfit today, then this was someone else stomping down Arch Road.

He keeps us from the darkness
He gives us hope and grace
Long live the Khat and all his sons
Who saved the Jadan race

The anthem finished and Arch Road went silent, but the footsteps carried on in slow progression. I kept my chin tucked in, listening to the scratch of a quill on parchment before each thundering shuffle.

The Sun was scrutinizing everything closely, its rays focused and strong. My corner's tiny lip of stone was no match for the sky's flare, and I could feel the moisture beading out of my forehead. I knew every Jadan on their corner would be wondering the same thing: who did these footfalls belong to, and where had our Jadanmaster gone?

The sky seemed eager to lap up our tension.

'Spout,' a smooth voice announced.

I nodded, keeping my head tucked in. 'Yes, sir.'

There was another rustle of parchment, and a fine pair of leather shoes came into my vision, their bottoms cupped with iron. 'Peculiar. That's what the scroll says. But Spout is not a name.'

My chest squeezed with worry. I noted the ease with which this new Nobleman was speaking, as if he already belonged here. 'My Barracksmaster calls me Spout, sir. So do most of the taskmasters and Nobles who know me.'

'Look up.'

I hadn't realized how sweaty I was until I jerked my head up, flinging a big, globby droplet from my forehead, which, thank the World Crier, fell *just* shy of his fancy shoes.

The Nobleman above gave me a disgusted look from a flat and broad face. Light grey stained the hair at his temples, and a deep scar crossed his face from forehead to ear. He had the look of an assassin from one of the High Houses. His stance was commanding, accentuated by a knotted red rope around his shoulders; and his hand was cupped gracefully around a crisp roll of parchment.

The man scribbled something onto his sheet. 'Gramble is your Barracksmaster?'

I nodded, the sweat stinging my eyes.

His lips thinned, the scar settling deeper into his face.

Stepping back, he announced to the whole street in a booming voice: 'Ears! I am Jadanmaster Thoth. I am now in charge of the slaves in this Quarter, as Jadanmaster Geb proved to be ineffective. For the next two years, you will be under my supervision. You will receive water and figs at bell three and bell seven. If you miss water because of an errand, then you will receive an extra portion on the following bell. Praise be to the Khat.'

He relaxed his chest, lowering his voice so that only I could hear it. 'I know that Gramble takes certain lenience with his slaves, but I assure you that I am not as soft-hearted as he.'

'Yes, sir,' I said.

'What is your given name?'

'Micah, sir.'

Thoth kept his expression firm. 'Rules six, seven, and eight for a Street Jadan, Micah.'

I didn't hesitate. Taskmasters had been asking me to recite the rules since I was a scrawny thing, all knees and elbows. 'Rule number six: a Jadan will do whatever errand their superiors ask, unless it involves the direct harm of another superior. Number seven: a Jadan will be as unobtrusive as possible. Number eight: all forgotten Noble tokens will be handed over to the Jadanmaster at the end of the shift.'

A long pause hung between us, my eyes begging to go back to the street. Staring into Thoth's severe expression was nearly as unpleasant as getting pinched by a scorpion while trying to extract its venom.

'*Spout*. I understand now. Humorous.' Thoth reached out a finger and swiped it across my forehead, rubbing the sweat in between his fingers. 'Does this seem unobtrusive to you?'

'No, sir.' I pleaded with my forehead to stop this nonsense. 'I'm sorry, sir.'

Thoth leaned over, blocking the Sun. I'd have thought this would have been a pleasant distraction from the heat, but

Thoth's eyes were nearly as fiery as the sky itself. 'Irrelevant. You shouldn't be sorry. Because it shouldn't be an issue.' He scratched something onto his parchment without breaking his gaze. 'Your water rations will be cut in half for the time being. If you have water to waste in sweat, then obviously you have too much water inside you.'

His pronouncement was worse than a dozen lashings, and I felt light-headed at the thought. I made sure not to show my dismay. 'Thank you, sir.'

Running his tongue across his lips, he carried on down the street without another word.

I was still shaken by the news that Jadanmaster Geb was gone. I couldn't help but feel responsible. He must have been fired because the Upright Girl had picked our road to waste that Shiver. And although I couldn't prove it, I couldn't shake the feeling that she was trying to reach out to me.

Moussa's words echoed in my mind, and I could feel my fingers aching to wrench into fists. No full water rations, no sneaking out after curfew, and no more Jadanmaster Geb.

Bad times were ahead indeed.

The High Nobleman wrapped his wife in a passionate kiss, stroking his fingers through her yellow hair. When he backed away, a look of forlorn longing had settled on his face. 'I'll miss you, darling.'

She slapped him on the chest playfully, right above the Erridian House symbol, her wrist adorned with bracelets of every precious metal known to the World Cried. 'You can always come in with me, my sweet pomegranate.'

Brushing the back of his well-manicured hand against her cheek, he said: 'Music is only music when there are spaces between the notes. Take some time to enjoy your own company. I can attest to its wondrous properties.'

She blushed, her light complexion showing off the rosy

colour in her cheeks. Two Wisps dangled on gold chains from
her ears, each one delicately painted with a silver Closed Eye.
These looked like the kind of earrings that Edom's Adornments
sold. I knew from experience that jewellery from Edom's cost
about a hundred times more Cold than the Wisps themselves.

She flicked her hair back and lowered her voice, bringing
her lips sensually close to his ear. From my corner, I couldn't
make out what she was saying, but after she nibbled on his
earlobe, a blossom of devious excitement ran through his
face.

Bell six had just rung out, and I was trying to survive on
half rations of water. I felt so thirsty I had half a mind to
find one of the boiling waterways, drop to my knees, and
guzzle the water straight. I'd been made to drink water in its
natural state before, bubbling over with heat, and although
I knew the burning would rub my throat raw, it would still
be better than the thirst.

'What would I do without you?' the bejewelled woman
asked as she drifted away, her fingertips lingering on his.

'You'll never have to answer that question,' he said, with
a beatific smile. 'Now go and find something lovely to wear.
But don't judge the garment for its jealousy, for it will never
be able to compete with the one whom it gilds.'

My lips felt as if they might crack in half from the slightest
movement. The Sun seemed to be funnelling itself straight
onto my head, and even with half its normal water in my
veins, my forehead was beginning to bead with sweat. I
prayed Jadanmaster Thoth wouldn't come over, or he might
take my water rations away completely. Then the only way
off my corner would be in a dead-cart.

The Noblewife waved her partner goodbye, gliding down
the street and dashing through the oak door to Solomon
Weavers, a broad smile etched onto her entire face.

The Nobleman saw her off with a constant wave, and once

she was inside he immediately marched over to my corner. I made sure to drop the focus of my peripherals so he didn't think I was spying.

'You,' he commanded in a harsh voice. If I hadn't seen him walk over to me, I'd have thought it was a completely different person speaking to me now. 'Slave boy.'

I didn't hesitate. 'Yes, sir.'

'You look ill.' His tone was rife with disgust. 'Are you usable?'

'Quite usable, sir,' I said, eager to get out of the direct line of the Sun. I felt as if the sky had been nibbling my edges all day, and there wasn't much time left before I fainted.

'Fine.' He snapped his fingers under my nose, directing me to look up.

I found a pampered face, desperate not to show its real age underneath its layers of caked make-up. He looked over his shoulder, making sure the High Noblewoman was still inside, and then adjusted his parasol so it completely blocked the Sun from the side of his face. Reaching into a discreet pocket in the pleats of his sun-shirt, he pulled out a piece of folded parchment. 'I need you to pick up something heart-shaped and deliver it to this Noblewoman at this address. Knock four times, fast. She'll know who it's from, but make sure you tell her to meet in the *alley* behind Sistrum in the Bathing Quarter just after bell fourteen.'

I nodded. 'What sort of heart-shaped item, sir?'

He backhanded me before I was ready, sending what little spit I had out of my mouth and cleaning my forehead of sweat.

'*Any* heart-shaped item, you dolt.' The High Nobleman's powdered face contorted with rage, spittle ruining the perfectly applied gloss on his lips. 'Any.'

Immediately, metal footsteps clanked my way, their heavy sound throbbing in my ears. Their pace was steady, each footstep thick with authority. 'Is this slave giving you a problem, sir?' Jadanmaster Thoth's voice was controlled and smooth, the perfect match for his gait.

The High Nobleman adjusted his parasol, expression teetering on the brink of outburst. 'Do you make it a habit of choosing idiotic slaves with which to populate your corners? Are you a sympathizer?'

'Apologies.' Thoth gave a slight bow. 'From what I understand, this slave's previous Jadanmaster was practically Jadan himself.'

The Nobleman waved a hand emphatically towards the tip of the Pyramid in the distance. 'No wonder the Procession was such a disaster and the scum hasn't been caught, if the Khat has incompetent Jadan-lovers running his Quarters.'

At these words, Thoth's eyes lit with fire, as though the Nobleman was accusing him personally. He composed himself, his words dripping with guile. 'Not as of today.'

The High Nobleman paused, painting Thoth with a curious look. 'Very good. Because I need to be able to count on the *discretion* of these creatures.'

Dipping into something of a bow, the red knots rolled on Thoth's shoulders. 'Assurances. Allow me to demonstrate.' He turned towards me, bending over so he could get a closer look. I could tell his eyes were searching for sweat, but luckily the Nobleman's blow had dried me up. 'Micah, tell me the errand which this distinguished High Nobleman has just entrusted you with.'

I gave a small swallow. 'Yes, sir. The Nobleman wishes for me to—'

I couldn't finish my sentence, as everything went black.

When I came to, I realized I was sprawled out, one side of my face pounding, pressed against hot stone. The sole of Thoth's shoe was searing my other cheek, his weight crushing my skull downwards. The steel plate under his heel had absorbed the heat from the Arch Road, and I could feel the Sun living in the metal. I couldn't help but try to squirm away as the searing spread over my skin, burrowing deep. Thoth pressed harder, bending my nose, and I struggled to breathe. Face on fire, I sucked in a mouthful of street dust and sputtered, trying not to choke on the grains and pebbles.

I was suddenly released, strong arms bringing me back to my feet and setting me in place. Instinct told me to bring a hand to my cheek to nurse the fresh sting, but from the look in Thoth's eyes, I could tell that this instinct would have had me killed.

Thoth placed his rod under my chin and tilted it up. 'Jadanmaster Geb may have allowed you to discuss your errands, but Jadanmaster Thoth expects complete and utter secrecy. Do you understand?'

I nodded, the burn blossoming across my cheek into a deep swell. 'Yes, sir.'

Thoth nodded, a sanguine grin spreading across his face. 'Micah, tell me about the errand this High Nobleman has entrusted you with.'

My stomach clenched. 'I'm sorry, sir, I can't.'

Thoth gave another satisfied nod, and then jammed the butt of his rod into my stomach, jerking the air clean from my lungs. I could feel eyes on surrounding corners being drawn to my *oomph*.

'Tell me,' Thoth said. 'Or you get another one.'

I caught my breath, knowing this was all for show. Thoth had been waiting for an opportunity to make an example of someone on Arch Road, to prove his rule, and I just had to ride it out. 'I'm sorry, sir, but I—'

The rod came harder this time, and I gasped for air.

'Micah,' Thoth said calmly. 'Tell me what errand you have been—'

The High Nobleman stepped in, holding out a hand. 'I get it. Lovely display. Normally I'm one to relish these little larks' – he gave a nervous look over his shoulder – 'but I'm afraid I must have this errand in motion. My appreciation, Jadanmaster, for proving your worth. You are no sympathizer, and I allow you to take your leave with honour.'

Thoth bowed, making sure to cast his gaze over the watching Jadans on the corners. 'My pleasure.' He then gave me a final look, his eyes ablaze, before marching away, his footsteps echoing from the fronts of the nearby shops.

The High Nobleman's eyes again went to the door of Solomon Weavers, and he was quick to produce a bag of Cold and a Noble token, which he hurried to hand over.

'Fast and quick, you little piece of dung,' the High Nobleman said, shooing me off my corner just as his wife appeared in the background.

Half out of the door, her hand waved frantically. 'Come quick, Ulyssipher, my love. You simply *must* see this sun-dress. On sale for a Shiver and three Drafts!'

In the time it took for the words to reach our ears, the High Nobleman's face had softened immensely. He looked as passive and innocent as a child, his expression full of wonder as he hoisted his large Cold-purse back over his shoulder, hustling down the street. 'Coming right now, my sweet mulberry!'

I darted to the nearest alleyway to scrape the sand from my tongue. After a few gritty passes with my fingernails, I realized something else had sneaked into my mouth during my desperate breath; something soft, now pressing against my upper gums. Trying not to think of the agonizing pain in my cheek, I fished up and found a tiny flower petal, one from the Roses of Gilead.

The Domestics must have missed it after the Procession.

The petal would have sat near my corner, bright red, yet

undetected. Small and fragile, certainly the runt of the basket, it had been flung towards me by a burst of Cold that never should have happened.

I knew the Crier didn't get involved with my kind, so the petal couldn't have been any kind of sign, but looking at it sent my mind to the Upright Girl's crazy posture, and then to my Cold Wrap, gears turning in my head. If the girl hadn't been caught after wasting that much Cold, why was I so scared of my three little Wisps?

By the time I'd reached Mama Jana's, the burn on my cheek had taken shape.

I ran my fingers over the tender spot, feeling the raised skin, but it wasn't until I sneaked a look at my reflection in her shop window that I realized I'd been branded. The Closed Eye had been inscribed in the metal on the bottom of Thoth's shoe, and it was now imprinted on my cheek.

The burn was superficial, and I knew it would clear with some rest and salve, but I felt violated. I ran a hand over the spot and felt tears welling in my eyes, desperately missing Jadanmaster Geb.

What had become of him? Kindness towards Jadans seemed less and less welcome in the World Cried, and I worried that Mama Jana might be next to fall. A part of me was scared to grab the handle to the shop door because I might find it locked, its owner having been dragged off to the dark pit the Vicaress reserved for her enemies.

I was just about to open it when something caught my eye on one of the alley's walls.

I looked around, checking there weren't any taskmasters nearby, and then ducked into the shadows. I had to blink a few times to adjust my eyes, but even after things became clearer, I still couldn't understand what I was seeing.

Someone had crafted a symbol on the wall in green paint.

I stepped close enough to smell the brick, and traced the air above it with my fingertips, careful not to smudge the design.

An 'Opened Eye'.

It looked like the raised skin on my cheek, but in the centre, instead of a shut lid, the eye was wide open.

I stepped forward and examined the smears of green, my heart in my throat. The discovery filled me with a dark terror, and not just because graffiti was illegal in Paphos. Without knowing exactly what an Opened Eye meant, I had a feeling it was probably worse than waving two knuckles to the sky.

I decided it was best not to linger.

I skittered back to the front of the shop and pulled open the door, to be greeted by a puff of air so Cold it made the pain in my cheek disappear.

Mama Jana waved me in, as she finished stowing her new Cold. I sometimes wished the levers and teeth of her lockbox would break so she might ask me to fix it, but as it was, she spun the dials, and the latches pulled together with a satisfied click.

Mama Jana breathed the air deeply with a bright smile. 'Thanks to you, dear boy,' she said, tapping her fingernails on the glass, 'my home is once again breathable.'

'Don't mention it,' I said, trying to match her smile.

Mama Jana pointed to the Cold Bellows, displayed proudly on a nearby table. 'I swear that thing is now giving me twice the Cold at half the twists. Whatever changes you made, I wish you could do it to the world itself.'

'Mama Jana,' I said, as politely as I could, even though the question was burning a hole through my pocket, 'may I ask you something?'

She gave a roll of her wizened eyes. 'Some Noblewoman short you again? What do you need and how much you got in that purse? I swear, my kin are getting more miserly by the week.'

'I need something shaped like a heart,' I said. 'And I was given six Drafts. But that's not what I meant.'

Mama Jana was out from behind her counter almost before I could finish my sentence, sweeping past her impressive display of parasols. 'Heart-shaped, eh? What kind of item?'

I remembered the Nobleman's backhand against my face as I said, 'Any item, please.'

She moved towards her stack of jewellery boxes, but looked at me with a double-take. 'What's that on your cheek, Spout?'

I covered the burn with my hand. 'Nothing. Nothing but the Sun. I'm fine.'

'I know I'm not outside much, but I didn't think the Sun had that much bite.'

I quickly pulled together a lie. 'Well, sometimes—'

'I won't press,' she said with a shrug, cutting me off. 'What is it you wanted to ask, child?'

I cleared my throat. 'Did you see what was painted in the alley next to your shop?'

Mama Jana made a face I couldn't read. 'Unfortunately, yes. First the Procession, and now those symbols shooting up around the streets. It's like there's something in the air!'

'If you don't mind my asking . . .' I tried to keep my voice calm. 'What does it mean?'

'I have no clue,' she replied. A tic was beating in her cheek. 'But I've already sent word for cleaners. It should be scrubbed off by the next bell.' She then turned to drag her hands along the stacks of boxes, and lifted one out that was perfectly heart-shaped, studded with fine crystals.

She smiled, her eyes searching my face for something. 'Just in luck. Six Drafts on the nose.'

I gave a grateful bow after making the exchange. 'You never cease to amaze with your goods, Mama Jana – or your kindness.'

She bit her bottom lip, almost as if debating something but

she let it go with a sigh. She looked older than ever today. 'Come back soon, Spout.' Her gaze didn't waver. 'I'm sure a piece of my home is likely to break any day now.'

'I will,' I said, bowing again and shuffling backwards.

As I was leaving, I turned to wave at her, but she didn't see me, as she rooted for something underneath the counter: a jar. I could have sworn its lid was the same colour green as the Opened Eye, and she stuffed it deep under a pile of sun-dresses.

Chapter Nine

The puffiness over my father's eye was slowing the game down considerably. I'd offered him some of my salve but he'd refused to take any. For a Healer, he was remarkably stubborn about not numbing his own pain.

Abb picked a card from the pile. 'You're normally better than this, Little Builder.'

I fanned out the backs of my cards, proving how many I'd collected. 'I'm winning, *Old* Builder.'

'Not at Conquer,' Abb said with a smirk. 'You're normally better at hiding things.'

My eyes flicked to the spot where I'd buried the Wisps, but the patch of ground seemed undisturbed. I drew a new card, painted with the plump face of Khat Horem VI, who was known for bleaching his skin bone white. 'I don't know how anyone besides you or me would find them,' I said.

Abb selected a card, bobbed his head from side to side, and then flung it at my face. The card flew sideways, coming fast at me, and I ducked out of the way enough to only catch a glance on the ear.

'That bad a hand, huh?' I asked with a chuckle after

recovering. 'We could always play Match. No skill required there. You might even stand a chance.'

Abb pointed to my cards, now splayed in front of him where he could see most of them. My face dropped and I flipped them back over, but it was too late.

'See,' Abb said, his face smug. 'Not so good at hiding things.'

'Not when you play dirty.'

Abb shifted so he could show me the bottoms of his blackened feet, stained with oil and mud. 'Us Jadans don't have much choice.'

I sighed, changing the order of the cards in my hand. I picked out the River Singe card and flicked it down between us, placing it under his Khat Luddit III. 'Here. Wash yourself.'

Abb raised his eyebrow. 'You actually playing that? Or is it just a joke?'

I shrugged, a smile on my lips. 'You tell me.'

Abb gave a flourish with his hand. 'I've taught you too well. Now what are you hiding?'

I paused, pretending to shift my cards. 'Nothing.'

'That's one heavy piece of nothing.'

I gave a one-armed shrug, rubbing my belly. 'I think maybe Gramble gave my bad figs this morning. That's all. Now are we going to play?'

Abb raised the eyebrow over his good eye. 'Come on, Spout, give your old man *something*.'

I flipped a card from my hand. 'Need a Cry Temple? I've got North and East.'

Abb chuckled. 'You little scoundrel.'

'If I am, it's your fault.' I shrugged and turned the card back. 'Raising a kid takes practice. Maybe you'll get the hang of it one day.'

'I didn't have you from the start, so it doesn't count.' Abb gently folded his cards into a pile, his gaze following the beams of starlight back up to the ceiling. 'Now talk to me. See, I won't even look.'

I let a long pause sit between us. 'You'll think I'm crazy.'

My father's voice was gentle. 'I already do. In a good way. Now spill.'

I sighed, trying to figure out why I was having such a hard time talking. 'It was *my* Shiver. The one the Jadan girl destroyed.'

Abb nodded, a contemplative look on his face. 'I see. Where'd you find it?' he asked.

I paused, trying to shake the words loose. 'The Blacksmith Quarter. In the boilweed piles. I pulled it out with my Claw Staff, and held it for a few moments, deciding whether I should keep it or not.'

'And so you didn't.'

'I didn't. I put it back on the pile, but when I turned around, she was there watching. She ran away, but she must have come back later.'

'Let me do some fatherly deduction here.' He tapped his bottom lip. 'You think you're the reason she tossed the Shiver. And in doing so, you think you've angered the World Crier and got your Jadanmaster fired, and brought down this new Jadanmaster who gives you half the water and twice the beatings. And – again this is just a guess – you're assuming it was a punishment for your temptation, and that you should probably stop tinkering just to be safe.'

I nodded, a lump in my throat. As always, he was spot on. 'Yes. That's exactly what I think.'

Abb didn't even look up from his hand. 'Well, you're wrong.'

I set mine on the pile. 'What do you mean, "wrong"? How can you just dismiss it? Just look at your eye. All the task-masters in Paphos are now making a point, trying to get us in line. What if it's my fault?'

Abb levelled his eyes to mine. His face was impossibly calm. 'It's not.'

I felt a fire burning in my chest. 'You don't have any proof of that.'

Abb flipped over my cards and started helping himself to all of the hourglasses. 'You think you're the first Jadan to think like that? That the Crier singled you out? That you're responsible for all the pain around you?'

I suddenly felt very young and naïve. 'No.'

Abb whistled, holding up one of my cards in triumph. 'Ah, so you've been hoarding the Glassland Glazier this whole time. No wonder you were winning.'

'Can you be serious for a second, I—'

'The Nobles hold up a Closed Eye for a reason.' Abb gestured to the bottom of my tinker-wall. 'Speaking of . . . I see you know about its opposite.'

I went stiff.

'The Opened Eye,' Abb clarified. 'The one you carved into that piece of wood.'

Once again I was silenced at his words. How did he know about the secret carving I'd done the night before? Even though I knew it was an incredibly needless risk, I hadn't been able to help myself. I'd taken my chisel and done all the work outside, smuggling it back in under my shirt when he was asleep. And I'd made sure to hide it at the back of the bottom shelf. I lowered my voice, all too aware of the curiosity in my tone.

'Your turn to spill then,' I said quietly. 'Does the symbol mean what I think it means?'

'What do you think it means?'

I paused, speaking almost in a whisper. 'Worthy.'

Abb rifled through his cards, eventually picking out the single Crier card in the deck. It was forbidden to draw any image of the Creator, so I'd settled for doodling a Frost to represent him.

'What do you know about Langria?' Abb asked.

'Same as everyone else,' I said with a shrug. It was a children's tale, passed down through the generations amongst Jadans despite being frowned upon in the Khatdom. 'The land as North as North goes, where everything is green and alive, as it was before the Drought, and Jadans are free.' I tried to steal my cards back from his hand, but Abb gave a masterful dodge. 'It isn't real though, is it?'

Abb licked his dry lips. 'If it's not real, then why is it kept quiet?'

I paused, not having thought about it like that before.

'Get your carving,' Abb said with a gesture to my tinker-wall.

I dug the wooden piece from beneath my useless Dream Webs, blowing out the sand before handing the carving over.

'Okay.' Abb settled it at his side, wiggling the Crier-Frost card instead. 'In the beginning, the Crier was feeling lonely, and with his first tear he created the World. The second, the Jadan people.'

'Yes.' I gave a teasing smile. 'That's what happened.'

'And the lands were green and healthy,' Abb said, ignoring my tone. 'And animals roamed, fruit grew and music played.'

'Yes,' I said, although Abb sounded so sentimental I decided not to tease him.

He fished around for a card, finding the one painted the colour of fire and sat it next to the Crier. 'And from deep in the black, Sun saw what his Brother had done, and he got jealous. Sun tried to do the same, to create something beautiful, but every time he tried Crying something into existence, it dried up. So, after failing over and over, Sun decided to ruin the World. Every day he showed up and burned away what he could. The Crier, not able to banish his older Brother back to the eternal black, decided to create Cold instead. And Cold fell from the sky every night and broke over the mountains, and cooled the boiling seas, and turned sand into soil, and the land itself survived.'

I couldn't help it. 'Yes, Dad. I know the story.'

'Indulge me,' Abb said. 'Or do you already know everything about everything, oh wise Inventor?'

My cheeks flushing, I let him go on.

'And cities grew, and wonderful things were discovered, the unknown was tamed. And for a long while, the Jadan people were happy. They fell in love and made music, and they lived in peace with nature, and—'

'And then eventually came the Great Drought,' I said, moving him along.

Abb shook his head with a sigh. 'Brilliant mind, no patience. Anyway, yes, the Great Drought. The Jadans angered the Crier with their sins, and Cold stopped falling everywhere except the Patches of the first Khat. Most of the land died, we became slaves, and the Khat and those closest to him became Nobles. Brief enough for you?'

I pointed to the carving. Abb picked it up and ran his fingers gently over the pupil. 'That's what this symbol is about. Not everyone thinks that Jadans deserve to be slaves after all this time. And that's what the Opened Eye is about. It's the hope that maybe one day the Crier will end our punishment and Cold will fall again for Jadans. Some say it happened up North already, in Langria, and that the Nobles are keeping it a secret. Others say it's still a long time away.'

'Why would the Crier change his mind and end the Drought though, after all this time?'

Abb gave me an odd smile before turning his eyes back to the ceiling, enjoying the starlight.

I scoffed. 'None of that answers my question. How do you know I'm not being punished for being tempted by that Shiver?'

Abb started shuffling the cards, putting the deck back together. 'Because I've been tempted by bigger Cold than that.'

I gave him a sceptical look.

'Back towards the end of my Patch days,' Abb said matter-of-factly, 'I touched a Frost. Took off my digging gloves and picked it up with my bare hands.'

My eyes nearly bulged out of my head. 'Wait, what?'

Abb gave me a nonchalant look. 'I was working one day and I found a Frost. The Patches are huge and no one was around. Instead of immediately finding a taskmaster like I was supposed to, I undressed my hands and ran my fingers all over it. Big old thing. The size of my head. And unlike other Cold, it was cool to the touch. I'll never forget the feeling.'

I didn't understand if he was being serious or not. The Khat's Gospels decreed that any Jadan who touched a Frost directly would bring upon himself his immediate death. Everyone knew it was one of the most forbidden things a Jadan could do. 'How can you still be alive?' I gasped.

Abb finished putting the deck back together, and got up and stretched his back out, letting loose a few severe cracks. 'Ah, perhaps I am getting old.'

'Don't *getting old* me,' I said, standing up too. I wasn't as tall as my father, but I could still look him in the eye. 'Answer my question.'

'How would the Nobles know?' Abb twisted back and forth, trying to loosen his spine. 'And as for the Crier, he didn't kill me, but he did do something rather drastic.'

I gave him a searching look. 'What did he do?'

Abb went over to my tinker-wall and picked up the Cold Wrap off the middle shelf, placing it gently against my chest. 'He gave me you as a son.'

I moved my feet up and pushed them down again, kneading the top of the dune.

My Rope Shoes were once again allowing me to walk the surface of the sand, proving to be one of the most effective of my creations. I rarely came out to the dunes, so the shoes never got much use, but when in action they always kept me from having to struggle along with my legs buried up to my knees. By spreading my weight over their thick metal frames, which I'd threaded with taut rope, I was able to glide across the crest of the dunes like the wind itself.

But just because I had the right equipment didn't mean I had the nerve.

I looked over my shoulder, trying to keep calm. My barracks were only a few dunes away, yet I couldn't have felt further from home.

Why did I feel the need to push my luck with the Crier? I peeked under my shirt. Such a simple thing, yet something so dangerous.

Abb had thought it was funny that I'd refused to try the Wrap inside. But I didn't want to put him or the rest of our family in danger by drawing the Crier's attention to the barracks. If I did this, I'd told him, I would do it alone, with no one else around. He had opened up the loose panel in response.

Now I was here, thin clouds of sand washing over my skin, preparing to fall out of the Crier's grace. Taking a deep breath, I pulled my eyes towards the stars, searching for any comfort Sister Gale could offer.

I shouldn't have rushed Abb through the Creation story, because he'd left out my favourite part. Sister Gale always deserved a mention. It only took me a few moments to pinpoint Her, as she was in full form, striking a bright pose in the sky.

There were a few versions of the Sister Gale story. Everyone accepted the feud between the Crier and Sun; but how Sister Gale fitted in was always up for debate. Mother Bev had told me the version I liked best, where Gale was the Peacemaker of the eternal family, coming each night to the empty battlefield left behind by Her Brothers, kissing away the wounds of Nobles and Jadans alike.

I closed my eyes and felt Sister Gale's comforting breath washing away the heat from the sands.

It was time. The Crier had let me get this far, so I might as well go a bit further.

My fingers went to the crushing chamber, touching the tiny Wisp. I told myself over and over that Abb had survived touching a Frost. And the Upright Girl had destroyed a Shiver. If they were alive, then crushing something as small as a Wisp shouldn't earn the Crier's wrath.

I hoped.

My heart began to pound. I reached under my shirt and plucked hesitantly at the waxy fabric.

I knew I was just stalling.

I looked up to Sister Gale, Her stars winking impatiently at me. She knew I was just stalling, too.

Taking a deep breath, I closed my eyes tightly, said my apologies to the Crier, and then twisted the Wisp until I heard a small crack. The Cold gave way, and the crushing chamber went cold against my chest.

A pleasant tingle slipped around my chest, clouding my skin with delight. The cool air filtered in from the chamber exactly as I'd hoped, and the feeling was unbelievable. Even better than I could have hoped for. I forgot the pain of my burned cheek, and the thirst in my soul, everything replaced with pure Cold. My lips begged to turn up at the edges, but I didn't dare show any joy.

I paused, waiting for claws to pop out of the sands to drag me under. Or for a giant piece of Cold to soar down, straight at my head, knocking the life out of my skull.

But nothing happened, except an ecstatic deepening of the Cold.

I couldn't believe it, but the Wrap was a success. My smile

broke free, and in that moment, it was almost as if the sands were parting at my feet and revealing my future.

I was an Inventor.

I gave another hard twist, and the rest of the Wisp cracked. The Cold was now rapturous, flooding my body with deep tingles. I drank Wisps in water every day, but this felt different; this felt unhinged, and ancient. And a part of me never wanted it to end.

And then my skin realized it wasn't used to the temperature, and began arguing against the change. I tried to calm myself with deep breaths so I might continue to enjoy the moment, but the stitches on the fabric were straining tight. The cool air was filling up faster than I'd expected, too concentrated, burning my skin with a new sort of fire. My lungs strained as the waxy layers continued to tighten, the prison of Cold constricting my breath.

I managed to wriggle free from my shirt, but as much as I clawed and prised, the Wrap wouldn't come off. I tried to breathe, but the pressure was becoming too much, my body unable to break from its hold.

I knew this couldn't possibly all be coming from a single Wisp, and dread filled my entire body.

The Crier was angry, and he was going to kill me with my own invention.

Only then did I understand that I should have built some sort of proper release. Abb had taught me to sew too well. I flipped open the cap to the chamber, trying to let the Cold have an escape that way, but I'd installed a one-way flap inside to protect against just that.

My fingernails only slid helplessly across the waxy fabric as I struggled to breathe.

I was about to drop to my knees and beg the Crier for forgiveness, when I heard a sound from behind me, a soft padding through the sands.

The Crier had finally sent His spirits to whisk me away.

I spun around, but I was met by a Jadan face.

I would have cried out, had I had any air left to give.

The Upright Girl struggled towards me over the dunes, using her hands to keep her balance. Her back was still rod straight, but she looked more like the rest of us as she scrambled to reach me, her ankles struggling against the sand.

When she finally came over to me, she dug a hand into her braided hair and pulled out a thin metal blade, half of it wrapped in boilweed for a makeshift handle.

I squeezed in another thin breath as she stabbed.

At the last moment, her hand shot sideways, the tip of the blade slicing across the belly of the Wrap. The material made a popping sound, and Cold air spilled through the slit as fast as it could. The girl's ruffled braid blew back, revealing an impressed look on her face.

I gasped heavily. The Cold had bitten my skin, and I knew I'd have something of a rash – but the Crier had let me live.

The girl sheathed the knife back in her locks and stepped close, so much so that I flinched, not expecting the proximity. Without a word, she reached for the fabric at my chest, but I couldn't feel her touch, as my skin had gone numb.

She tested her fingers gently on her cheek. 'Wisp?'

I nodded, still trying to catch my breath.

'Where'd you steal it?' she asked, as if two Jadans meeting on top of a sand dune in the middle of the night – one of them wearing Cold – was completely normal.

'Give me a second,' I said, expelling what was left of the chilled air in my lungs, my heart settling to a reasonable pace. My body was tingling from the experience, not used to something so opposite from the Sun.

The Upright Girl watched me recuperate, keeping quiet.

She was half a head shorter than me, but only because I had the advantage of the Rope Shoes. The starlight trickling onto her face showed hazel eyes, bright and defiant.

Something was very different about her. And it wasn't just her rigid posture. She didn't have the sallow complexion so many of us had, nor the hunger-sunken, ashen cheeks. Her skin was dark like mine, but its texture was smooth, almost glowing. She looked . . . alive.

She crossed her arms over her chest, her intense gaze boring into mine. 'You had a Wisp in there. So why didn't you take that Shiver?' she asked. 'From the rubbish pile.'

My chest heaved up and down. 'That's your first question?'

'It's what I want to know. Unless there are other things you want to talk about . . .' And then she smiled.

It wasn't the same beautiful way a Noble girl might smile, all dolled up with red gloss and teeth clean of food.

It was the smile of someone who knew more than I did.

I was enamoured, and couldn't think of what to say.

From the way my father talked of past loves, or even the way Joon bragged over evening rations, I'd have thought being entranced by a girl would be pleasant, but my brain was completely frazzled by Cold, and my body was too distracted with awkward squirming to appreciate the moment. In fact, I don't remember ever feeling so uncomfortable.

'First time you've been alone with a girl?' she asked with a straight face.

I blushed. 'No, I— I mean. It's just—'

She shrugged. 'What is that thing?' Around your chest.'

'It's called a Cold Wrap,' I said, wishing suddenly that I could be anywhere else. 'And thanks for cutting me loose.'

I was glad her eyes stayed up at my face as she asked: 'What are *you* called?'

I hesitated for a moment's pause, deciding on which name to give. 'Micah.'

Instead of introducing herself, she pointed to my torn invention. 'Is it because a Shiver's too big?'

'Sorry?'

'You left that Shiver in the boilweed.' She spiralled a finger towards the Cold chamber. 'Because it's too big to fit in the chamber thing?'

'Wait, one second. What are you even doing out here?'

She shrugged. 'I live out here. You're not very good at answering my questions.'

I first thought I'd misheard her. 'You live in the sands?'

A flash of amusement passed through her eyes. 'No one lives in the sands. They would die. What was that pole you were using the other night? I've never seen one before.'

'Claw Staff,' I replied, trying to keep my voice down.

'Claw Staff?' she echoed. 'You named it Claw Staff? Couldn't you think of anything better? You *must* have had other options.'

My face went sour. 'What's wrong with Claw Staff?'

She smirked. 'Nothing.'

I thought my blush might burn the skin off my cheeks.

She gestured to my barracks. 'You sneak out more than most Jadans, don't you. I've seen you. What do you do with all that rubbish you steal?'

'It's not rubbish,' I said, indignation flooding my chest.

She gave a wry smile, clearly enjoying seeing me rise to the bait. Then she pointed to my feet. 'Where'd you steal those?'

'I didn't steal them. I made them.' I looked down at the Rope Shoes, finally feeling steady enough to speak. 'From my "rubbish".'

'Ah. So you make things,' she said, as if it was something she'd been mulling over for some time. 'I like that. Stand on the sand. Use something besides your hands to dig through the rubbish. Crush the Cold and keep it close, like a Bellows for your body. You have good ideas.'

'Wait. My turn to ask,' I said, trying to be as firm as she was; although I couldn't believe she'd distilled all my inventions so succinctly, considering those were exactly my thought processes in their creation. 'Why did you throw that Shiver on the street? That could have got you killed.'

She tapped a finger against her lip. 'You mean like how we can get killed for stepping into the wrong alley. Or for walking the wrong way. Or for buying a Noblewoman a pink fan instead of a red one?'

I raised my eyebrows. 'Do you make a habit of following people?'

'You're easy to follow,' she said matter-of-factly, walking her fingers through the air. 'Some people are very slow.'

She struck a nerve. 'No I'm not. And why are you following *me*?'

'No particular reason.' She shrugged, but I noticed that she wasn't looking at my face. 'I get bored sometimes.'

'What's your name?' I asked.

'Shilah.'

I extended a hand. 'Micah.'

She sniggered. 'I know. You told me.'

I ignored her. 'All of Paphos is looking for you. Everyone's angry at what you did.'

She rolled her eyes. 'I know that, too.'

'You got my Jadanmaster fired,' I said.

A dark look found her eyes. '*All* Jadanmasters should be fired.'

'So why did you do it?' I asked, not understanding how such a system would work. 'You must have known if the taskmasters couldn't find you they'd just take it out on other Jadans.'

She didn't hesitate, her words taking on a harsh edge. 'Because Shivers are supposed to fall for Jadans too. So I made it happen. And it was beautiful. You felt how beautiful it was.'

This was the strangest conversation I'd ever had. 'But what about the Great Drought?' I asked.

'What about it?' she replied, her voice resolute, hands going back over her chest. 'You drink Cold every day. You just used a Wisp that you weren't supposed to have. Are you dead? Did the Crier send a Draft from the sky to rip a hole through your chest?'

My cheeks grew hotter. 'It was my first time using a stolen Wisp! And anyway, for a second I thought the Crier had sent you to kill me.'

Shilah gave a serious nod and then reached into her pocket, pulling out something and tossing it over to me.

I caught the small Khatmelon, with wide eyes. It was one of the most expensive fruits in the city, so expensive that even some Nobles couldn't afford them. And this one was not yet ripe, as if it had just been plucked from a garden.

'Eat it,' she said. 'Then tell me if the Crier wants you dead.'

I looked at her straight in the eyes. 'Where'd you steal this?'

'What makes you think I stole it?' As she crossed her arms over her chest, I noticed a dark stain peeking out from her sleeve.

She noticed me looking and yanked up the fabric, proudly showing me a tattoo that made my jaw drop even further. I had to squint against the dim light to make sure, but there, in black ink, the Opened Eye was stained into her skin.

'I did it myself,' she said proudly. 'Don't look so surprised,' she added, catching the look on my face. She tapped the back of her neck at her barracks markings. 'You have one too. Mine just happens to be a tattoo I wanted.'

I gave her an annoyed look. I had the suspicion she'd get along well with Abb. I pointed my finger at the design. 'Fine. But that one goes against everything the Crier has commanded.'

She offered another knowing smile and then pulled at

the uniform on her chest. I tried not to let my eyes linger on her, holding in a breath and conjuring thoughts of tinkering instead.

She raised her eyebrows, but thankfully she dismissed it, pointing instead at my feet. 'Can I have those?'

I blinked, tilting my head with curiosity like Matty often did.

'Please,' she added.

I unstrapped my feet. I could always make another pair, I wasn't likely to get my hands on another Khatmelon.

Shilah examined the shoes for a moment and then bound her feet inside, kneading the sand like I'd done. 'Thanks, these will help.'

Then, with a smile, she turned and began sauntering back down the dune, her back straighter than ever. 'And I think you meant it goes against what the *Nobles* have commanded, not the Crier,' she shouted over her shoulder.

'But they're His chosen people,' I called.

'Come back out here in a few nights and I'll find you,' she said, walking down the slope. 'Take some time to think things over. Your first Jadan Cold only happens once.'

My legs had already sunk up to my ankles as I watched her walk south, in the direction of the River Kiln. I couldn't understand why she'd head that way, as there was nothing there except more dunes, and boiling water that couldn't be crossed. 'Do you want to come back to my barracks?' I called after her, fearing she was walking off to an uncertain death. 'My father would take you in. We have a private room!'

'I don't think so.' She turned back, her long braid whipping around. 'Please do try not to get yourself killed. I could use someone like you, Micah.'

'What do you mean, like me?'

Even from a distance, her smile was like another wash of Cold against my chest.

'Someone who makes things,' she replied. 'An Inventor.'

Chapter Ten

Two nights later, the Khatmelon had become perfectly ripe.

High Nobles expected their Jadans to know how to tell good fruit from bad, even the rarest kinds. The Khatmelon now had a hollow sound when I struck my knuckles on the rind, and its colour was a startling green.

I could have eaten the fruit at any point and been immensely pleased – even the toughest, starchiest melon would still have been a divine change from our ration of figs – but I wanted the surprise to be that much more perfect when revealed.

My lips curled into a smile without breaking any blisters. Gramble had been taking pity on me since Thoth had begun his crusade to dry me out, filling up my water rations extra high whenever he could. My head was still constantly light, but living was now at least bearable. I made sure to clean my forehead of any sweat before reaching my corner, so Thoth had no reason to take away my rations altogether.

But that wasn't the only reason behind my smile.

Shilah still hadn't been caught.

Thoth and the rest of the taskmasters stalked Arch Road like sand-vipers, snapping and thrashing at the smallest mistakes; but that only made things clearer.

For the first time, I was witnessing the Nobles struggle to retain their control over us. A Jadan had done something despicable, something so unholy that the Crier should have snuffed her out on the spot, yet she had gone unpunished.

The sound of snapping fingers came from the other side of Abb's boilweed door, and I hopped up from my blanket, stowing the Khatmelon in my pocket.

'You don't have to announce yourselves,' I said to my friends as I let them in. 'I think we're past that.'

Moussa ran his hands over Matty's scruffy hair. 'Shorty insisted.'

Matty huffed. 'I'm not that short.'

I waved them in and ushered them over to my blanket. 'Sit, sit.'

'Abb said you had something to show us,' Matty said, eagerness apparent in his eyes. He had a fresh bruise on his arm. All of Paphos had been on edge since the incident at the Procession, including the Jadans.

My heart started beating with anticipation. 'I do.'

Matty's eyes shot to my tinker-wall, scanning the shelves and piles. After a moment, his face dropped. 'Did'ja lose the Rope Shoes?'

'Sometimes I think you know my stuff better than I do. Forget about the Shoes.' I took the Opened Eye carving from the top of the wood pile, and then found a thick beam of starlight to use for illumination. 'This is more important.'

'Oh, I seen that,' Matty said, eyes lighting up. 'Prolly. Once in the Garden Quarter.'

Moussa nodded. 'Me too. In the Bathing Quarter. Do you know what it is, Micah?'

I sat with them on the blanket, a smile breaking free across my whole face. 'It's called the Opened Eye. But I also have something else, something even better.' I licked my bottom lip, savouring the moment. Putting the carving down by my side, I pulled out the Khatmelon, bouncing it up and down in my hands.

'You found that in the boilweed?' Matty asked, astonished. His hands went out, but he snatched them back, a guilty look in his eyes.

I shook my head, knocking the rind so they might hear the hollow sound. 'I found it in the hands of a girl.'

Matty's head tilted so far I thought it might topple off his neck.

My smile grew. 'The most wanted girl in Paphos, I might say.'

'The Upright Boilweed Girl?' Matty's jaw dropped. 'Did'ja talk to her?'

Moussa's face darkened. 'Micah, you know better . . .'

'Can she make herself avisible?' Matty asked.

'You mean invincible?'

'No.' Matty slapped his hands over his eyes. '*Avisible.*'

'Oh, *in*visible.' I chuckled, handing over the melon. 'I don't think so.'

'Matty, when have you ever seen a Jadan make themselves invisible?' Moussa asked with an amused shake of his head.

Matty shrugged. 'She got away from the Vicaress. Maybe she can.'

'Plus,' I said with a shrug, winking at Matty, 'you can't actually *see* someone who's invisible.'

Moussa shook his head again, but a grin lifted his cheeks. 'You shouldn't encourage him.'

I got up again and grabbed my sharpest blade. 'Anyway,' I sliced into the fruit and let the scent carry through my whole head. 'She had the Opened Eye tattooed on her arm, and she set off into the dunes after we spoke. I have a feeling she knows some secret the rest of us don't.'

Moussa's disappointment thickened his voice, and when he spoke, it was almost a growl. 'That's impossible. Nothing exists beyond those dunes.' He held his piece of melon away from his body as if it might turn around and bite him. 'I'm serious, Micah, this is dangerous. The taskmasters are working double shifts to try to find her. You shouldn't get caught up in her lies—'

I didn't want to listen to him. My heart swelled at the scent of the melon, hope pushing away all the hunger and thirst and pain. I took a bite of my own piece, and it tasted like freedom.

'Moussa, please, let's just enjoy this.' I began singing between bites. *The Jadan's work upon the sands.* Come on, Moussa,' I said, now standing on top of my sleeping blanket. 'The "Jadan's Anthem". You wrote this. Sing with me!'

'The thing is, I don't want to make the Crier angry,' Moussa said, in an almost pained voice.

'The Upright Girl is still alive,' I said, licking my palm. 'I'm still alive. Abb touched a *Frost* and he's still alive. You've sung it before, and *you're* still alive. If the Crier didn't want us to share this melon, he wouldn't have let it get this far.'

Moussa observed us, our chins dribbling red juice. A fearful look passed through his eyes.

'The Gospels don't say we can't eat melon,' I said.

Moussa sighed and took a small bite of the rind. He swallowed, and couldn't hide the joy the taste brought to his lips. He began to mumble: *'So maybe the World Crier . . .'*

I held a hand against my ear. 'I can't hear you.'

Matty's grin was full of melon. 'Yeah, Moussa. We can't hear you!'

Moussa took another bite, sucking up all the juice, and sang louder. *'So maybe the World Crier, might release their han—'*

The chimes rang out.

Our faces turned towards the door as one. It was past rations time, and there was no reason for Gramble to be calling everyone together to the main chamber.

Moussa spat out the pulp, scratching at his tongue. Matty quickly wiped down his chin with a handful of the boilweed door.

'Relax, both of you,' I said, putting my melon down on the blanket. 'It must be Old Man Gum messing with the wires again.'

The chimes kept ringing, however, strong and heavy, and together we stumbled into the hallway heading towards the main chamber. Worried murmurs swept towards us, whispers brushing along the walls, and the closer we got to the chamber, the bigger the sense of dread filling my stomach became.

When we reached the room, dozens were milling about, outside of their divisions. No one seemed to know what was going on, and we stared at the chimes, worried conversation hissing in the air.

Old Man Gum stood very still in the centre of the room, waving two knuckles at the chimes. I thought I could hear him saying 'In the ground,' over and over.

Abb clapped his hands and called out: 'Lines! Everyone, lines.'

No one stopped to question him as we stepped into our normal spots, trying to keep order in the near dark. Matty kept close behind me as we swept into position, holding a hand on my back as if to make sure I was still there.

By the time the chimes stopped ringing, we were mostly organized, and Gramble's key sounded in the door. Each scrape of the metal sent a wave of dread into my stomach.

The doors swung open and every body went stiff.

It wasn't news that our Barracksmaster was bringing.

Inside swept a figure wrapped in tight black silk, a fiery blade in her hand. The circle of flames lit up blue and merciless eyes. In the half-light I could make out petrified faces, and our shadows trembled on the walls.

I felt Matty's fingers tremble, pressing harder against my skin.

Gramble did a long count, his voice breaking as he spoke. 'Twenty-one Patch, forty-eight Street, thirty-nine Builder, and thirty-six Domestic. They're all here, Highness.' Times were rare, if ever, when I'd seen Gramble afraid, but from the look on his face, he might have been thrust in one of the Jadan lines himself.

A sourness began rising in my throat, replacing the sweet taste of melon. The Vicaress prowling the street was one thing, but to find her here in the barracks was unheard of.

'Barracks forty-five,' she said, her voice a storm and whisper at the same time, 'one of your own has betrayed you, and the Crier is displeased. He is looking for her, through me.'

Gramble kept his eyes averted from the flames. I thought for a moment he was staring at me, but I couldn't tell from my position in the Street line.

'With the help of dark forces, this girl has eluded the Crier's vision,' the Vicaress intoned, her voice calm and collected. 'I am to be His ears.'

Gramble's voice rose. 'Everyone remain calm. The Vicaress is here to look for the betrayer. Follow her orders and everyone will be fine.'

The Vicaress turned slowly towards our Barracksmaster, her lips thin. 'The Crier does not require you to talk.'

He nodded, bowing his head down low.

'You are all aware of the blasphemy that happened during the Procession, so I shall make this simple,' the Vicaress said. 'Our Lord and Creator had been blinded in this, so He needs to hear the demon's voice. Women in this barracks. When I point the holy blade at you, you will say "*worthy*" and nothing else. You shall say it loud and clear, and I will consider any faltering a sign that you have something to hide. This needs to be nothing other than simple. Most of you obey the Gospels, and have no reason to draw upon His wrath.'

Matty tugged at my shirt, and I reached back, steadying my fingers over the birthmark on his wrist. Moussa's back heaved up and down in front of me. I wanted to tell them both that we would be fine, that the Vicaress wasn't here because of the melon, that she was only looking for Shilah. This was just a coincidence. All we had to do was obey, and the Vicaress would move on to barracks forty-six without incident.

The Vicaress finally broke her stance, moving smoothly past the line of Patch Jadans, but she stopped towards the end, a curious look on her face when she came alongside Liran. She bent down and prodded his thigh with the handle of the blade, twitching her lips as if she was dissatisfied. Liran managed to stay still under her scrutiny, which was more than I could have done.

Standing up straight, the Vicaress intoned over to Gramble: 'I've just got word. The Crier wishes this Jadan to have two extra figs per ration. Your Patch Jadans should be thick enough to withstand the demanding work.'

Gramble gave a relieved nod. 'Absolutely, Highness.'

Her shiny lips thinned. 'I thought I told you, you need not speak. One more outburst and I'll consider it a sign that *you're* trying to hide something.'

Gramble's face turned to stone.

The Vicaress moved over to the Builders. Only four women were physically adequate to remain in that line – those women who couldn't cut it as Builders after ageing out of the Street Jadans got sent to the Glasslands – and the Vicaress stopped at Zipporah. Zip had arms that could keep up with any of the men, but she was easily flustered. As soon as the flames came within spitting distance, one side of her face began twitching.

The Vicaress pointed her blade down at Zip's chest.

Zip hiccuped and then shouted: 'Unworthy!'

The blade sizzled as it slipped into Zip's shoulder, nearly causing her to topple over in pain.

'Worthy,' the Vicaress said calmly, shaking the blade an inch deeper. 'The Crier needs you to say "worthy". Let's try again.'

Tears welled in Zip's eyes.

The Vicaress licked her lips, smearing the black gloss. 'The Crier doesn't approve of Jadan tears. They are waste. Hold them back and speak.'

'Worthy,' Zip shouted, her voice shattering at the end.

The Vicaress closed her eyes and nodded. 'That wasn't so hard.' She moved on to the other women Builders, everyone else thankfully getting the word right. Since none of them had Shilah's voice, they were safe.

The Vicaress headed for the Domestics. She moved with a confident gait, her eyes blazing with purpose. The fiery dagger was kept high, the flame's light licking the line of women.

Suddenly, Old Man Gum hopped out of his line and jumped in front of the Vicaress, pointing a gnarled finger at her. 'The Khat tried to send Him away! They put it in the ground!'

The Vicaress fumbled her grip, the flames around her blade dancing wildly. Her eyes opened wider, which was the most I'd ever seen her lose her composure, even more so than at the Procession. Without warning, she kicked out with her heel and cracked Gum's leg sideways. Gum crashed to the ground, his head slamming against the hard-packed dirt, and didn't let out so much as a yelp. Once on his side, she pressed the flat of her blade against the protruding bone of his knee, sealing all the loose flesh.

Yet he didn't cry out.

'Women only,' the Vicaress said, stepping over Gum. She readied the knife to thrust into the old man's heart, but her expression grew calculated and she refrained, standing up straight instead. 'The Crier has judged.'

Moussa was breathing so hard I thought he might faint.

The Vicaress moved on as if nothing out of the ordinary had happened, stopping beside the first girl in the line of Domestics. Dani's face managed to stay strong against the heat of the blade.

'Worthy,' Dani said, her voice overly firm, almost to the point of insolence.

Deciding the tone was fair, the Vicaress lowered the blade, taking a single step to the right and aiming the point instead at Jardin's heart.

'Worthy!' Jardin shouted, her hands shaking.

The Vicaress closed her eyes, picking the sound apart for clues. She continued down the line, coaxing out the shouts from each Domestic. The blade remained in the air, each body it left unharmed brought me the smallest relief.

The Vicaress would finish her hunt and leave. Everything would be okay. I'd give Zip the rest of my salve, and by tomorrow, she'd barely even feel the sting. And I'd take some metal rods and bearings and I would build a support that Gum could wear around his knee.

Everything would be okay.

Slowly, as the Vicaress made her way through the lines of women, my pulse began to relax. 'Worthy' had been shouted dozens of times now.

I wiped my sleeve quickly across my forehead while she wasn't looking, removing any sweat.

At last the Vicaress had heard every Domestic voice in the barracks and she slowly sauntered back to the front of the Street line. When she turned to look over our line, the blue in her eyes glittered like gemstones in the light of her dagger. I hated myself for finding her beautiful.

Our line, the Street Jadans, had most of the youngest girls, and I prayed that this would all be over quickly. The Vicaress pointed her blade at the girls' hearts one by one, skipping over the boys.

'Worthy,' Rachiel called.

'Worthy,' Jakie shouted.

'Worthy,' Hanna managed to get out.

As the Vicaress passed Moussa, I held my breath, and tipped my eyes down. Matty's fingers wiggled out of my grip, and I could tell he was doing the same.

An old tale said that the Vicaress could read Jadan minds. A simple meeting of eyes, and she would know the secrets of your heart. I'd dismissed the idea then, but it came back to me now. I smelled the flames as they swept next to me. My heart thundered loudly. Heat grasped at my face, and the blade hovered beside my ear for a moment. My knees threatened to drop me, knowing she could sense my secrets – but she moved on, satisfied that I had nothing to give.

And then, all of a sudden, the black silk stopped rustling.

'Who's this?' the Vicaress said, amusement in her voice. She snapped her fingers calmly. 'Barracksmaster.'

I heard Gramble waddle down the row, and my heart tried to stop.

'Who is this?' the Vicaress repeated sweetly.

'That's Matthew,' Gramble said carefully. 'We call him Matty.'

My legs started to wobble at the realization. Matty. Matty didn't know Shilah. It was me who'd used the Wisp. I was just about to speak up, when—

'Barracksmaster,' the Vicaress said, almost like a song, 'how old is this boy?'

Gramble thought about it for a moment. 'Ten. He's pretty fresh from the Priests.'

The silence was thick in the room.

'But he's a good Street Jadan,' Gramble said, his voice not so confident. 'He—'

The shadows shifted, the blade having shifted too. 'That's enough, Barracksmaster. I didn't ask. Good or not, this boy is too small for ten. Sun must have tampered with his development and I'm afraid that the Crier can't trust the results.'

I felt the sand at the back of my feet slowly grow wet. Nobody spoke.

'I'll have a proper replacement sent in the morning.' The Vicaress's voice turned caressing. 'The Crier wants you back, boy. He'll fix you, He'll get you ready for service in the afterlife.'

Matty spun slowly, holding out his 'calm spot' to me. His hand trembled with fear as he bent his wrist back as far as it could go.

'Don't touch him,' the Vicaress scolded. 'He's been tampered with.'

And I froze.

Time slowed down. Then the sound of metal sliding through flesh came. A single whimper, and a small body slumping against the ground followed.

The Vicaress finished questioning the last few girls in our line, and then left the barracks, not once looking back at the lifeless corpse resting against my legs.

Once the main doors shut, I dropped to my knees and wrapped my whole hand around Matty's birthmark.

'Family,' I choked out, gripping tight. The only thing my mind could process was how thin my friend's wrists truly were. 'Invincible.'

But there was no response. He was gone.

PART TWO

Chapter Eleven

I only coughed a few times, the Droughtweed smoke mostly agreeing to stay down. After two weeks of coming to the makeshift hut, I was getting used to the burn.

The Roof Warden sat cross-legged beside his billowing cloud, running his fingers up and down his knees. The Jadan Peddler was his own shade of darkness, his skin even darker than Moussa's, which left me wondering if the Sun had any effect on him. I'd known of his business for years, but I'd never had reason to seek him out before.

'Don't give up on me now, *Spout*,' the Warden said, lost in the smoke. 'You paid for six huffs.'

I choked in another breath, leaning over the fuming pile. The embers winked in the belly of the smoke, black plumes tickling their way around my face and neck.

The Roof Warden imported his Droughtweed supply from Belisk. The plant was a special strain that grew along the banks of the Hotland Delta, and inhaling it did things that regular boilweed couldn't. I held the laced air in my chest, pinching my nose in the hope that I could keep the stuff down. The longer the hold, the longer the numb.

The image of Matty's lifeless face would soon melt from my mind, and I could go about my errands in peace.

I let out the breath slowly, but I couldn't quite make it steady. As I coughed, I had to close my eyes, the smoke burning and forcing out tears. But the tingles had already started at my feet, and I knew they would spread quickly.

'Growing up so fast,' the Warden said, his eyes like endless pits. I squinted, trying to take another look at his pupils, which reminded me of quicksand. 'Two more times. That's all, *Spout*. And keep it clean. Don't want to break the magic for the next customers.'

Finding my composure, I turned my head and looked through the crack in the tent flap, watching the row of bodies sitting on the roof, all waiting impatiently to get their daily fix. Some scratched, some rolled their necks, and some looked as if they would throw me off the roof if I didn't hurry up.

The Roof Warden's supply box sat by his side, stocked with stolen waterskins, half-eaten figs, and even a few Wisps. It was incredible what a bit of flint, a foreign supply, and loyal customers could earn someone. I desperately wanted to ask him how he never got caught by the taskmasters – a small tent could only do so much to keep a low profile – but I knew he took remarks like that as threats. Rumour had it that the last Jadan who tried to extort free huffs from him never even made it to the dead-carts.

My mind hadn't yet floated as far as I had hoped, so I took the next dose of smoke through the nose. The oily black burned again like fingers scratching at my brain, but it seemed to do the trick, as my ears had begun to pulse with calm nothingness. After a moment I could barely think at all.

I probably didn't need the last breath, but I took it anyway. I had to get my trade's worth. My eyes went to my crank-fan stuffed on the side of his supply box, and I heard a voice in the shadows of my mind.

'Yeah, Moussa!' Matty's voice echoed. 'We can't hear you!'

The shock made me lose control of the smoke, spitting out my relief.

I quickly went to sneak a replacement, but the Roof Warden leaped up and wrapped his hand over my mouth and nose, pushing me out of the tent.

His body was larger than mine, and his grip was like a slab of Building stone over my face. Woozy from the smoke, my feet scrambled across the roof tiles as he pushed me. Then his fist jammed into my gut, heaving the stolen smoke out. I dropped into a fit of coughing.

'I don't play that, young tears,' the Warden warned, gritting his teeth, which right now looked too numerous to count. I blinked, and his teeth looked normal again. 'You better bring me something smart if you want to play tomorrow.'

My eyes narrowed, hate filling the now empty cavern in my chest. 'I can find my own boilweed to smoke. In case you hadn't noticed, it's in every rubbish heap.'

'Good luck! You'll be coughing up shit and snot for no high.' The Warden's eyes were laughing, but his lips were firm.

'I don't—' My fingers clawed at the colours in front of my face. 'I'm still alive. Abb is still alive.'

'Loser kid,' one of the Jadans in the line behind me said. 'Junkie loser.'

I spun on my knees, waving two knuckles at whoever had spoken, ready to strike and claw. The emptiness was consuming, and I felt too dry even to cry.

'Who's Abb, young tears?' the Warden asked, a spry grin dancing across his lips.

'I—'

Matty's voice cut me off, sharp and distorted: 'We can't hear you, Moussa! Whatsit!'

I put my hands over my ears, trying to shake him loose.

It wasn't my fault. It was Shilah's fault. She was the one that started this whole mess. She'd tossed the Shiver off the roof; she'd given me that cursed Khatmelon.

It wasn't my fault.

'I'm sure I'll be seeing you tomorrow, Spout,' the Warden said, slithering back towards his tent and waving the next Jadan forward.

One of the other Jadans waiting his turn was scratching at his face. Beetles skittered out from the giant hole he was making in his cheek, but after a moment the hallucination dissolved.

Waves of heat splashed from the sky, trying to knock me on my back, but there was a shield being built now, brick by brick. And silence.

The Sun had no power over me. The smoke was making me invincible.

It wasn't my fault.

Six months ago, on the final Khatday of the year, Gramble had walked through our barracks doors and ushered in a group of new barracks members.

I remember the group being mostly girls, but there at the end, cowering into himself, was a boy who had arms like sticks and a face that knew joy but had forgotten how to smile. I'd wondered if the Priests had decided to teach him hunger over everything else. Gramble assigned parents, doled out old sleeping blankets, and the girls were gathered into hugs by their new mothers. Hair was stroked and worries were eased, the new Jadans giggling as their mothers preened.

Then it came time for the boy, standing there digging a tiny toe into the dirt. Gramble checked over his list, grumbled a few things as he scratched his stomach, and did the dreadful thing we all knew was coming. Levi was slouching against the back wall when his name was called. His arms tightened across his chest, but other than that he didn't acknowledge his new child.

I gave a silent groan, knowing how much Levi was dreading the day he would be burdened with a son; but the boy looked up at his new father with a disheartening amount of hope.

His eyes only met empty air.

Gramble left, locking us in, and everyone went about greeting the new Jadans. The boy was ignored by the Patchies, but got hearty handshakes from the Builders, and a few kisses on the cheek from the Domestics – I remember Jardin giving him two. But after the friendly faces came and went he was left alone, blanket under his skinny arm, gaze lowered.

I walked over towards him. 'Hey,' I said, waving my hand under his face to draw his attention back up. 'I'm Micah.'

The boy looked up. His eyes were damp, but they lit up at my voice.

'What's your name?' I asked.

'Matty,' the boy said, the first tear finding the middle of his cheek. 'Matthew.'

'A nickname, huh?' I said, drawing my smile out. 'I have a nickname too.' I prodded myself on the chest. 'Spout.'

Matty's head tilted sideways. 'Spout?'

I laughed and pointed another finger at my forehead. 'Because I sweat. See, we both leak. We're going to be great friends.'

Matty leaned in. 'He doesn't want me.' We both looked over to Levi grumbling to Slab Hagan in the corner.

'That doesn't matter,' I said, giving him a clap on the shoulder. I made sure not to hit him too hard, because I didn't want to shatter any skinny bones. 'The rest of us do.'

Then I noticed he had his fingers clutched tightly around something.

'What have you got there?' I asked.

Matty held out his shaking hand, opening his palm. A small carving of a bird rested in the centre, one wing missing and the beak cracked. I recognized it as a piece from a game the Khat's Priests made us play in the slave schools called Drought. The purpose was to guide the Jadan tokens to spots under the Khat's sigil in the centre of the board. Some of the game pieces represented the great things our people had ruined by angering the Crier.

'You like Drought?' I asked.

Matty sniffed, his eyes flicking back and forth. 'I hate Drought. I like birds though. I'm going to see one one day.'

I nodded, picking up the piece, hoping he didn't really believe that. 'Will you tell me when you do?'

Matty gave a hesitant nod.

'So look at this. *You* like birds, *I* like to make things.' I held the dilapidated bird carving between my thumb and forefinger. 'How about we make a new game together. And this will be the first piece?'

'Can I help with the rules?' he asked in earnest, eyes filling with life.

I smiled. 'You can make them all if you want.'

He thought about it for a second. 'It'll prolly take me some time. I want to get it right.'

I laughed, gesturing to the barracks. 'We have all the time in the World Cried.'

The Droughtweed high started to fade as I choked out the last few lines in the 'Khat's Anthem'. Usually the floating sensations lasted until the second bell, but the Roof Warden's fist had speeded up the process immensely.

The Sun was taking advantage of my weakness, striking from every angle imaginable; my lip of stone on the wall was all but useless today.

Metal footsteps replaced the melody, coming towards me,

and I begged my forehead to keep the sweat inside. I made sure to tuck in my chin more tightly, and the Sun used the opportunity to bite my neck, its fangs piercing deeper than normal.

Thoth's shoes came into view, and his voice was a growl. 'Micah.'

'Sir!' I said, too loudly.

Thoth took out his rod from the sleeve on his ankle and my heart started to beat. Heavily. The thumping grew loud in my ears, and for a moment I thought it might be a drumbeat. He tilted my head back, the light stinging my eyes.

'Why was your hand twitching when you were singing?' he asked.

I gulped, trying to come up with something believable. Truthfully I hadn't even realized I'd been moving. 'I'm sorry, sir. I felt a scorpion on me. I was trying to brush it off, as a sting would keep me from perfection at my errands today.'

Thoth licked his lips, the scar tugging across his face. 'Considerate, but not allowed. During the "Khat's Anthem" you show respect. If the scorpion bites you, then it bites you.'

'I'm sorry, sir.' I swallowed hard, my head going fuzzy with fear. 'He wasn't my fault.'

'*He* wasn't your fault?' Thoth repeated, his eyebrow arching towards the sky. 'What do you mean, "He wasn't your fault"?'

My tongue faltered, begging to be bitten. I hadn't meant to say *he*, it had just slipped out.

'The scorpion,' I choked, not knowing what else to say.

Thoth tucked his scarf back in place and commanded: 'Street rule sixteen.'

Easy. I took a breath, relaxing in the knowledge that I'd had all the rules memorized since childhood. Rule sixteen was the one that had to do with—

'Lemme help,' Matty whispered from far away, my vision swimming.

My jaw seized up and my mind went blank. 'Rule sixteen. Rule sixteen is . . .'

'Promptly,' Thoth commanded.

I cleared my throat, my tongue so dry it felt as if it wasn't even there. I had no idea what rule sixteen was, and I had to spit out something that sounded reasonable. 'A Street Jadan will make sure that whenever the Khat's name is said, it is with complete reverence.'

Thoth bent closer to me, enough so that I could smell some foreign spice on his breath. 'What is happening with your eyes?' he asked. 'Why are they red?'

'I was stung,' I said, my insides starting to tremble. 'On my way here. That's why I thought the scorpion might still be on me.'

Thoth sounded amused. 'And where were you stung?'

'My back, sir.'

'Proof,' he said.

With a heavy heart I lifted off my shirt and spun around, hoping some old scar might pass as a potential sting. I closed my eyes tightly while I waited, whilst a spectrum of dark colours coalesced across the back of my eyelids, swirling into the Opened Eye. I wanted to scratch it away, but I couldn't move.

'Dress yourself,' Thoth commanded. 'And spin back around.'

I did as I was told, tense as I waited for his judgement.

The Jadanmaster reached into his pocket and pulled out his bottle of ink and feather quill.

'I'm sorry, sir,' I said, my voice gravelly and distant. The words pulsed in the air in front of me. 'I deserved the scorpion bite. I'm unworthy.'

Thoth inked up the quill, the black liquid dripping off it. Lifting the nib to my forehead, he began drawing, each stroke of the brush like the touch of a razor. When he'd finished the symbol, and gone over it twice, he stowed the quill with slow movements.

I knew what would be waiting on my forehead.

A triangle with a vertical line dissecting it in half.

Unusable.

Whenever Jadanmaster Gramble had made a slave unus-able, it had been out of kindness, letting them rest for a few bells if they were feeling sick or had had a particularly taxing last errand. I had a feeling Jadanmaster Thoth's motives might be different.

In the distance, I saw a black streak floating through the sky and I almost gasped, thinking it might be a bird.

Then I realized it was just ink dripping into my eye.

The sweat finally broke free on my forehead and the last of the Droughtweed left my system. Sobriety slammed my mind like a fist. The Sun exploded over Thoth's shoulder as he brought the rod high, my insides buckling in shame and regret.

It was all my fault.

Chapter Twelve

Abb wiped on another layer of the groan salve, his calloused fingertips scraping against the wounds. 'Is Moussa still avoiding you?'

I winced as he spread the gel across a painful spot on my shoulder, and my answer came out as something of a snarl. 'What do you think?'

'Easy there,' Abb said. 'I can talk to him for you if you want.'

'Abb,' I said with a warning.

'Yes, yes. You're old enough to fight your own battles. You've even finally grown your first hairs on your chest. I get it.'

I didn't fall for his baiting. This was no place for jokes. My body was more bruise than anything else, and my mind wasn't faring much better. Thoth had decided the beating wasn't sufficient enough to validate the unusable symbol, so to ensure that I was left a useless wretch, he'd taken away my day's entire rations as well. When I'd stumbled into the barracks earlier, I had barely made it to the Street wall, gasping with each step, to then stand shoulder-to-shoulder, in a line with my family, yet completely alone.

'Almost done.' Abb gave the wound a final pat. 'There.

Nice and sticky. Just think, when you're out collecting materials, now you don't need pockets. You can just roll around in the boilweed and bring stuff back on your skin!'

'That's not funny,' I said, stomach churning with frustration.

'I think it would look very funny. You crawling back through the panel, all dressed up in—'

'Just drop it,' I said, eyes going to my dying tinker-wall. I'd smashed most of my creations in the sands behind the barracks. Now the shelves were practically bare, save for the few things that the barracks relied on me for, and Matty's board game near the bottom. If I ever saw Shilah again, I'd vowed to wrestle back my Rope Shoes and destroy them too. And then I'd march her straight to the Pyramid. 'I'm done with that.'

Already the salve was working, a cool tingle replacing the stings, but I felt guilty for the relief. If not for Abb's insistence, I would have left the salve for those Jadans more deserving.

'You can't give up on who you are,' Abb said, his voice turning serious. 'I understand you need to take time to mourn Matty, but—'

I spun around, my face heating up. 'And who am I? A damned slave who spat in the face of the Crier and got my friend killed. That's who I can't give up on?'

Abb sighed. His eyes were soft, even though I was being difficult.

'Seven,' he said after a long silence.

My teeth were clenched so hard I wondered if they might crack. 'Seven what?'

He paused, gathering another layer of the salve and going after the rash on my forearm. I tried to pull away, but he was much stronger than me. He slowly drew my arm towards him and began applying the medicine.

I wanted to strike him, to ball up my other fist and hit him, but I knew that wouldn't make me feel any better.

In circular motions, Abb spread the tingling salve. 'In the last week, that's how many Builders have been killed at the Pyramid, two of them I knew by name. I suspect we might have even been friends if we were allowed to have conversations.'

I swallowed, trying to steady my resolve. I knew what he was trying to do, but it was useless. The Crier had made it very clear that I'd crossed the line.

'And do you know the reason they were killed, Micah? Not from Sunstroke. Or thirst.' Abb met my eyes, his gaze blazing even in the dim light.

I felt my face grow even warmer under his gaze. 'Because it was their time.'

'It was because the taskmasters in the Monument Quarter got bored. It's high up, it's hot, and it's monotonous work keeping the Jadans in line. We're an obedient bunch, and there is not much for them to do.' Abb shrugged, speaking as calmly as if he were discussing the procedure to mix clay. 'So, every once in a while, they decide they deserve to have a little fun; but they've been whipping us and berating us their whole lives. The usual tricks don't get their juices flowing any more.' He gathered some moisture in his mouth and spat on the ground. 'Glory be to the Khat.'

My eyes widened with shock, but he kept going.

'So the taskmasters have a game.' Abb's gaze dropped. He went to work putting the finishing touches on the salve, smoothing it out with his fingers barely touching the skin. 'They call it *Obey*.' He was still calm, but he practically spat the word. 'Every couple of days, they'll find a Jadan who maybe coughed after inhaling some powdered mortar, or someone who accidently fell to a knee while carrying his load.' His eyes flicked to my forehead with a pointed look. 'Or maybe someone who was sweating too much. For justi-fication.' Abb voice was matter-of-fact, but his words were smouldering at their core. 'And that Jadan will be taken to an empty chamber in the Pyramid with nothing inside it except a Closed Eye nailed to the wall. And then the task-masters will test the boundaries of their power. They'll command something, anything, just to see what we might obey. How far we might be prepared to go. And we're unworthy Jadans, so what choice do we have, right? It's the Crier's will. And if we refuse, we get tossed off the Pyramid.'

He cleared his throat, emotion in his voice. 'That's the seven.'

I paused, letting the idea wash over me. I'd never heard the Builders discuss such a thing before, and as despicable as it sounded, I knew there was no point arguing. The Nobles were chosen, and we were not.

'Maybe the Jadans that get picked for Obey did something to upset the Crier. And it's a justified punishment.'

'Justified.' Abb's face dropped, pain in his voice. 'You think the Crier has kept us alive all these years just to decide our fate in this way? By seeing if we are willing to drink spoiled ale until we vomit? Or to see how high we'll fill up a water-skin with blood? Or what we might do to our bodies, with glass and with rods, and fire, while the chosen sit back and laugh?'

I felt my face stiffen with shame. I wished he would now let me suffer in peace. 'The Nobles are our betters. We have to listen for a reason.'

Abb nodded slowly, rubbing his slimy fingers around the rim of the bottle to try to save the excess salve. Then he went to my tinker-wall and blew the sand off the top shelf. 'You're a special kid, but you're still a kid, Micah. You have to trust me when I tell you Matty was killed because the Nobles are scared. Power is a fragile thing, and what happened at the Procession was a crack in their chains.' Abb placed a hand on my cheek. 'You can't give up on what you want, son. The Vicaress didn't kill your friend because of the Cold Wrap. Or because of a little Khatmelon.'

'You don't know that,' I fired back, the memory burning my tongue. 'You can't know that.'

'I can't, can't I?' Abb's eyes narrowed. 'So tell me, if you're such a disappointment to the Crier, then why is the girl who destroyed a Shiver still out there? You think the Crier can single you out for using a Wisp, but can't find a girl who did that?'

He had something of a point, but I couldn't stop thinking that Matty's blood was on my hands. Hands that would never again tinker. Hands that should only serve the Nobles, and pick Cold from the Patches, and carry stone.

'The Vicaress said dark forces are hiding Shilah,' I countered. 'And if I could, I'd turn her over just to make sure no other innocent Jadans die.'

'Dark forces,' Abb scoffed, reaching for the handle of one of the few crank-fans I'd saved, giving it a whirr. Then he turned back, his voice like iron. 'Why are you alive, Little Builder?'

'I'm alive . . .' I let my head sag, my chest a dark pit. 'Because . . .'

Abb slammed a fist on top of the tinker-wall, the shelf buckling. 'Why are you alive?'

I stiffened, not expecting such a reaction. I replied with a voice so severe I wondered if it might shake the entire barracks. The emptiness inside me was all-consuming, chained around my neck and pulling me down. 'So I can suffer! So I can feel all of this darkness! So I'll obey too!'

Abb nodded, as if he had been expecting that. He grabbed the nearest bucket, dumping out the last of my metal scraps. Then he swept across the room and jarred open the loose panel. His eyes were so full of love that I wanted to scream again.

'I'm going to show you a secret, son,' he said, taking a deep breath. 'It's out there, deep in the sands behind our barracks. And it's been around since even before the Great Drought. You want to know why the Nobles hold up a Closed Eye when they call us unworthy? Here's your chance.'

I was stunned. The southern sands were just dead land, and there was nothing out there except dunes and eventually the rocky banks of the River Kiln. 'What are you talking about?'

Abb tapped his foot impatiently. 'I'll show you. I'm going to take you there. It's hard to see, but I think you're finally old enough to know the truth.'

'We can't go outside at night,' I said, although he'd struck my curiosity. 'Gramble—'

'We can, and we will.' His eyes finally hardened. 'Don't you want to learn the truth?'

'I—'

Abb grabbed me hard by the wrist and pushed me through the panel. I tried to wriggle out of his grip, but it was like a breath trying to resist the wind. He pulled me to my feet and brushed the sand off the sticky patches of salve on my arm. Outside, I tried not to look at the rubble that had once been my beloved inventions. Metal edges from my smashed Teleglass glinted in the starlight, and tiny gears from what was once my Sand Sifter peeked out of the shallow hills of sand. Dozens of my designs, crudely disassembled, each shred of debris reminding me of what I'd lost.

Abb smiled and put a consoling hand on my arm. 'Have I not been a good father?'

I couldn't lie. 'You have been.'

'And so you trust me?'

I paused, thinking about his bare hands touching the Frost. 'For the most part.'

'I'll take that.' He shoved the bucket against my chest. 'Now fill this with sand.'

I lifted an eyebrow, but Abb just stabbed his hand at the nearest dune.

'If you want to see the truth, you need to fill this with sand,' he said.

I sighed, dropping to my knees and scooping a handful. My fingers struck something solid and I tried not to think of what invention it might have come from. I continued, and soon the bucket was full. My limbs were still shaky from being so exposed.

'All the way,' Abb ordered, his voice suddenly hard as iron.

I stuffed the bucket, patting the top smooth. My father had never spoken so harshly to me before.

'Okay.' Abb started walking South, the thin patch of dirt behind our home quickly swallowed up by the dunes. 'Follow me. And don't drop the bucket. It's very important that you don't drop the bucket.'

'Why? What are you taking me to see? There's nothing out here.'

'I told you. The truth,' Abb said simply, continuing to stride out into the sands. 'Don't drop the bucket.'

I got to my feet, the bucket already heavy in my arms, and followed him. My legs buried themselves deep with each step, the burden weighing me down. I had no idea why I'd need to carry a supply of sand, when there was an infinity of buckets'-worth in every direction; but I listened.

We trudged into the dunes, neither of us speaking. I felt my forehead grow wet with effort, my aching muscles shaking. Thankfully the salve was helping to keep the sharpest pain bearable, but still my legs shook. My eyes scanned the surface of the dunes for any prints from my Rope Shoes, but of course there was nothing. Shilah couldn't secretly survive out here, it would be impossible.

Abb reached the top of the next dune and looked back.

His face was hard and his eyes narrow, but he didn't say anything as he carried on.

My breathing speeded up as I struggled down the slope, and I was unable to fill my lungs fully. I shifted the bucket, trying to find the best way to carry it, but nothing relieved the burning in my arms.

'Keep up!' Abb kept walking, cresting another dune, and if anything, picking up the pace. 'We have a long way to go yet!'

I snarled, feeling my throat beg for relief. My heel struck something solid on the rise of the next hill, and I wondered if it was a stone, or the skull of the last Jadan stupid enough to wander these dunes. The bucket quickly became more than cumbersome, and I had to double my effort. The gentle wind was no longer enough to keep the sweat from my face, the beads dripping into my eyes.

I made it to the top of the next dune, high enough for me to see the rolling whitecaps of the boiling River Kiln in the distance. Abb was waiting for me there, eyes fixed on the stars, something off about his face. It took me a moment to pinpoint what bothered me, but I realized it was because for the first time in my life, I was seeing him cry. 'What do Jadans need?' he asked in a soft voice, fingers at the corners of his eyes. He gathered the water and then held it up to the sky, almost as if proving the tears were real.

I shifted the bucket, trying to rest it on top of my knees.

Abb's eyes shot down, his voice nearly cracking with emotion. 'Don't drop that.'

'I won't,' I said.

'What do Jadans need?' he asked again through clenched teeth.

I tried to catch my breath, but Abb turned and stormed down the dune, marching as if the taskmasters were at his back with their whips flying. I gave a deep sigh and then hurried after him, my chest heaving.

We met on top of the next dune. My forehead was now dripping, and my lungs felt weak from all the Droughtweed I'd been forcing down my lungs.

'Where' – I sucked in a heavy breath, almost a wheeze – 'are we going?'

'What do Jadans need?'

'Why are you asking' – my words faltered, lacking the air to push them out – 'me that?' My mind was as blank as when Thoth had asked me about rule sixteen. I had no idea what he could possibly want from me, and the bucket was getting heavier by the second.

Abb's expression hardened again, and he turned, heading for the final dunes by the banks of the Kiln.

'Wait!' I called, but he didn't slow.

I caught up with him on the last dune before the riverbank, and I felt as if my chest might explode. I looked out over the River Kiln, bubbling with anger, and at least felt satisfied in the knowledge that all that was out here were the un-crossable waters. Abb was mistaken; there was no ancient truth to be found.

'The scorpion traps. The crank-fans. Star-slides. Rope Shoes. Fire-snuffers. All the things you made.' His hands were fists. 'You must know the answer. What do Jadans need?'

I couldn't quite form words yet. The bucket slipped through my sweaty fingers. I was close to fainting, my head swim-ming in a haze of thirst. 'I don't know!' I shouted, desperate to let go. Or to stop. Or to fall to my knees and give up completely. My bruises felt as if they had never been treated with the salve in the first place, each contusion hammering me with pain. 'I don't know what Jadans need!'

Instead of heading towards the waters, Abb turned left and started sweeping along the banks. I wanted to scream and hiss and spit. It was as if he wanted me to die out here. My body had been broken and depleted to begin with, and now every step was torture. I knew I probably didn't have enough moisture in me to make it back.

'Stop!' I yelled.

He marched along the rocks, keeping up the pace.

'Please! Abb!' My body was hotter than a blacksmith's fire. 'I can't do it any more!'

'What do Jadans need!' was the only reply.

'I don't Sun-damn know!' The edges of my vision were creeping towards black as I stumbled onto the banks. Hot flecks from the Kiln were carried by the wind and pricked my cheeks with heat. 'I don't know!'

Abb suddenly stopped, turning around and marching back. For a moment I felt relieved, but then I saw the intensity in his eyes and I wondered if he was going to hit me.

'Of course you know,' Abb yelled. 'You've always known. It's why you tinker, it's why you create!'

I could only concentrate on breathing, trying to keep my body from giving up altogether. The bucket was practically bucking in my arms, trying to get me to drop it to the ground. 'What the hell is this about? There's no secret out here! You're going to kill me!'

'You're going to kill yourself,' Abb snarled. 'Why didn't you drop the bucket?'

'Because you told me not to!'

He stepped up and reached a hand into the bucket, grabbing a fistful of sand and tossing it over the banks to the sputtering waters. 'The Khat's Gospels.'

I struggled to suck down even a single breath.

He grabbed another handful of sand, his eyes wet with sorrow as he tossed it into the wind. 'The lies of the *Great Drought*.'

Another handful. 'The street rules.'

Another. 'Quotas in the Patches.'

Abb snatched handful after handful of sand out of the bucket, calling out after each toss, his voice rising in volume.

'The Closed Eye.

'Droughtweed.

'Lessons from the Priests.'

He was practically roaring now.

'Curfew!

'Taskmasters!

'Jadanmasters!

'High Nobility!

'Errands!'

Now he was using two hands, the sand flying.

'The Procession!

'Barracks!

'Rations!

'Lashings!

'Obey!

'The Sun!'

At last he scraped the bottom of the bucket, pulling up the last of the sand. My arms cried out with joy.

Abb waved the final fistful of sand in front of my face and then let it sprinkle through his fingers slowly. 'The Vicaress killed twenty-two Jadans the same night Matty died. Each one in their own barracks, for the same reasons such as being too small, or being too frail. You think the Vicaress never saw Matty on the streets before? Or Jadans his size? Why did she wait to kill him until that night? Because she needed to make a point! She needed to take back the power!'

The bucket was empty, and, although my chest felt as though I'd been poisoned, I wheezed deeply in relief, close to crying.

'I don't understand,' I said.

Abb snatched the bucket away from me, setting it on the ground. 'It's how power works, Micah. It's the reason behind everything. Do you know how much Cold falls in the Patches every day, how much has been harvested since the Great Drought? How many Frosts?'

I shook my head.

'None of this life is necessary. The Khat has enough Cold in the Pyramid to rebuild fallen cities. Enough Frosts to make at least some of the world as it was. Yet it is not the Cold that he treasures. It's the control.' Abb kicked the bucket. 'You trusted me, and I gave you a burden. That's them, Micah. That's how the Nobles win. They keep us docile and under their heels. They give us burden after burden so we won't think. They lie to us and tell us it's the Crier's will, so we forget about ourselves and obey.'

I hunched over, acid from my stomach dribbling up to my lips. My back felt as if I was being beaten all over again, and I had a suspicion that even with Sister Gale's help, I might be too overheated to make it home to the barracks.

Abb came over and put a hand on my back.

'I'm close to the edge,' I said, drained of all energy. 'You'll have to carry me.'

'Absolutely not,' Abb said. 'You need to drop the bucket.'

I pointed to the bucket resting on the ground and turned, my whole face on fire.

'Not this bucket,' Abb said, snatching the pail and then going to the banks of the Kiln, careful not to slip on the rocks. He kneeled down and scooped up some of the steaming water. As he walked back, the bucket swung at his side, spray sloshing over the rim, but he ignored the scalds.

He set the bucket down, and put a hand on my shoulder. 'You're different from the rest of us, Micah. You know that. I know that. And Nobles are going to try to break you for it. They are going to steal what's precious to you, to distract you and to dissuade you. They can't abide Jadans who think about what our people need. It was the reason your first father did what he did to you. The Crier didn't give me you as a son. I took you as a son. I took you from a man who feared the change you represent. Drop the damned bucket, Micah. Think for yourself. I know what greatness you are capable of, and my hope is that one day soon you will know it as well. The Opened Eye is about proving our people are worthy of freedom. Maybe you'll make a weapon. Maybe you'll make an army. Maybe you'll make something so beautiful that even the Khat will have to take notice and bow.'

'I don't understand what you're getting at. I'm just a Jadan who can tinker a bit,' I said, my breathing fast and thin. 'I'm just a slave like everyone else. Trying to be different will just make the Crier angry.'

'If that's true, then stay. Don't drop the bucket. Die out here. Jadans have no need for another broken soul.' Abb's mercy left his eyes as he plucked out a Draft from his pocket and held it up to the night sky. The Cold went into the bucket of steaming water, the bubbles immediately stopping as the water grew cool before my eyes.

'I stole that Draft from a High Noble,' Abb said as he began walking away, trudging back into the dunes. 'If you think the Crier punished you for a Wisp, then He certainly wouldn't want you to drink a stolen Draft. If you think Jadans are only supposed to suffer, then sit here and suffer. Let it all end.'

I gave the water a desperate look, my forehead still leaking into my eyes.

Abb reached the top of the nearest dune, turning with a hard look. 'You can let the Kiln boil your bones for eternity. Or you can drink all that Cold, make it home, and live to change our world. Either way, there's no turning back.'

Chapter Thirteen

'Um . . . Boy?' a quiet voice asked, followed by the clearing of a throat. 'Are you crying?'

I swallowed hard, trying to summon the tears back inside my eyes. A pair of gold slippers popped into my vision, their fancy glass buckles purple and perfectly stained. I imagined one shoe alone probably cost more than all the materials I'd need to remake my tinker-wall.

This was most probably a High Noble.

I wiped my face with the back of my hand. 'No, sir. Just a bit of sweat. My apologies.'

'Are you alright?' the Noble asked.

I narrowed my eyes with suspicion. No one asked us if we were alright. In fact, it was usually a habit of theirs to make sure we weren't. I readied myself for another pink fan incident, feeling comforted at the idea of the salve I had left in the vial under my blanket.

A mug rested in the Nobleboy's hands, steam rising off the top – an odd choice considering the heat. I smelled honey. Whoever this was, they must have a lot of Cold in their purse.

'I'm perfectly usable, sir,' I said.

The mug was lifted to his mouth and he took a sip, smacking his lips. 'Would you mind looking up?'

I raised my neck to find a boy only a few years older than myself. His blond hair was neat and long, his complexion was milky, and he wore the thinnest, most decadent sun-shirt that I'd ever seen. Gold-rimmed eyeglasses rested on the bridge of his nose, and a jewelled waterskin was slung across his chest.

This was definitely a High Noble.

'You wouldn't happen to be Spout, would you?' he asked, sipping again.

My stomach dropped. Most Nobles never cared to know our names, and it felt safer that way. 'Yes, sir. But my given name is Micah.'

The boy gave a satisfied nod, eyes shifting back and forth to check if we were alone. 'Good, because Mama Jana didn't really give me much of a description.'

An awkward pause sat between us. I cringed on the inside, wondering what might spur Mama Jana to put my name on a High Noble's lips.

'Can I call you Spout?' he asked, sounding almost hopeful. 'I like Spout. I had it in my head on the way over.'

'Yes, sir.'

He didn't seem to be in a rush for an errand, and I was hoping he would hurry up and reveal whatever horrible game he was intending to play. I still had Abb's story about 'Obey' in my mind, and since the dunes, I felt far less patience towards Nobles than before.

'I'm Camlish by the way. You can call me Cam if you want, though,' he said. He thrust out an immaculately groomed hand and I grimaced, expecting a strike against my chest. The horrified look in his eyes made me realize this wasn't his intention. He snatched his hand back, pushing his glasses back up his nose. 'Are we not supposed to shake hands?'

I'd seen Nobles shaking hands to seal a deal or something like that, but never with a slave. I wasn't sure if shaking hands violated a Street rule, but I had to assume it was punishable. The Khat wouldn't want unnecessary contact between a slave and a Noble.

'I don't think so, sir,' I said.

'Please, no sir. Just Cam is fine.'

I could see him struggling to come up with something to say as he jiggled the mug in his hands. 'My cousin warned me about drinking Oolong tea. He said the more I'd drink the more I'd need to get out of bed in the morning. Have you ever tried Oolong tea?'

'No, si— Cam.'

He yawned and then pressed the mug my way. 'It's nice. Would you like a sip?'

My eyes nearly fell out of my head at the offer. To my knowledge, no High Noble in the history of Paphos had ever tried to share drinks with a Jadan, so I knew I had to be ready for whatever maliciousness this boy was planning. I would have guessed the drink was poisoned with something to make me vomit had he not been swallowing it himself.

'That's not allowed, sir,' I said. 'Praise be to the Khat.'

Cam snorted. 'Praise be to the Khat indeed.' He looked at me from head to toe. 'So how do you know Mama Jana?' he asked, conversationally, as though he actually cared.

This was becoming a very unsettling conversation, one I was keen to end quickly.

'Is there an errand you need help with, Cam?' As soon as the words left my lips, I realized I could be beaten for the insolent tone. Before the Draft and Abb's bucket I'd have never dreamed of talking that way to a High Noble, but the words had slipped out on their own. Yet Cam only gave a satisfied smile, as if he'd been hoping for a reaction.

'Sure,' he said, casually, pushing the glasses back up his nose. 'I guess that would be the proper way to do this.'

'What's the errand?' I asked carefully.

Cam clacked his teeth as he collected his thoughts. 'Nothing in particular. I planned to go to the Apothecary. Would you like to come with me?'

Heat flushed my face at the question. 'Jadankind is here to serve Noblekind. I am required by the Khat's law to help you with any errand.'

Cam looked a bit disappointed. 'Well, let's do that then.'

I held out my hand for a token, but he met my palm with a look of curiosity until he unslung his waterskin and held it out to me. 'Would you like some water? There's a few Wisps already in it. You can drink it all if you want.'

I swallowed hard. 'Please,' I said, confused at whether this High Noble was acting dumb, or simply had the same mental affliction as Old Man Gum. 'Your House crest.'

'Ah, of course.' Cam took the waterskin back, and reached into his pocket to reveal a coin that made this whole situation all the more bizarre.

House Tavor.

The Tavors were the closest family to royalty outside the Pyramid. They weren't as wealthy as the Erridians, or as well connected as the Drylads, but Lord Tavor was said to be the Khat's choice for successor should he die without a proper heir.

Cam wasn't just High Noble.

He was the *highest* of High Nobles.

Looking at the coin in my palm, I let my body slump further, wondering what Mama Jana had got me involved in. This had the appearance of some cruel test Thoth might arrange, yet Cam seemed strangely . . . *genuine*.

Cam smiled warmly. 'Shall we?'

*   *   *

The door triggered a deep gong that was followed by a series of reedy buzzes that descended in pitch, filling the air with a long seductive ringing, like a wet finger circling glass. I stepped inside the Apothecary.

I followed Cam across the threshold, and my eyes found the small contraption near the door responsible for the sounds. A nearly invisible chain connected the door to the squat box, which was branded with Ancient symbols and forged from a dark wood that looked too thick and healthy to have grown in this world. I ached to see its inner workings.

The shop was painted dark, and the nearest shelves to the door were filled with vials of liquids and jars of powders, arranged by colour. Each ingredient had line after line of indecipherable descriptions. Golden statues were scattered about the place; gilded creatures, extinct since the Great Drought, like cats and gazelles. A stout metal jackal sat sentry in front of a crate of scrolls, each impressively sealed with the Khat's wax sigil. I saw Dream Webs and Gale-Catchers hanging up near the ceiling, waiting to filter the air.

A pair of double doors swung open from the back, a thin mist rising from the darkness behind. A few more gongs rang from among the shelves before the shopkeeper swept out of the doors, his silver-gloved hands hiding his face. His whole body was draped in patterned silk, robes flowing down past his knees and sweeping along the floor. Capping off the outfit was a headscarf, emboldened with a Closed Eye so vividly stitched it seemed to jump off the black material.

'Welcome, travellers, to the Mind's Bazaar.' The shop-keeper's voice dripped like honey. He reached into his pockets and tossed out powders that glittered through the air, shining against the mist in a dazzling cloud. 'The only place in Paphos where the Sun can be banished, where you might taste the ether, and miracles rain like Cold in the Patches, and—'

The shopkeeper stopped mid-flourish, confusion painting

itself over his moustached face. 'Young master Tavor,' he said. His tone had turned nasal and slightly annoyed. 'Are you aware that there is a slave behind you?'

Cam nodded, and even from behind I could tell he was rolling his eyes. 'A Jadan.'

'You never bring slaves,' the shopkeeper said. 'I didn't think you practised the Decree of Unworthiness.'

The Decree of Unworthiness stated that it wasn't just enough to *call* Jadans unworthy, but rather it was every Noble's duty to reinforce our degradation. The doctrine justified all kinds of cruelty, and was the reason why so many Nobles wore Closed Eyes out in public. It was also why games like 'Obey' would always plague our kind.

Cam's shoulders stiffened. 'Of course I do. I'm not going against the Khat's wishes, I just like to run my own errands if I'm honest.'

I tried not to cough from the powder drifting into my lungs.

The shopkeeper looked truly puzzled. 'So why the slave—'

'The Jadan has a name,' Cam said, annoyed. 'Micah. You don't need to keep calling him a slave.'

The shopkeeper bowed, but his gaze remained sceptical beneath his bushy eyebrows. 'Very well. What are you and, ah, *Micah* looking for today?'

The air inside was cooler than in most shops, and I hoped Cam would draw out the transaction for as long as possible. As they were talking, I had surveyed the room, taking in all the wondrous things it contained: the sarcophagus that was being used to grow blue moss, the boulder that had been split in half to reveal a belly full of crystal, and the little red eyes glaring out from small cages near the back of the shop.

'I didn't feel any different after the glow cream,' Cam said, giving me a quick glance and lowering his voice. 'Six times a day and it's made no difference.'

The shopkeeper gave an understanding nod, calm and collected. 'Alchemy isn't an immediate magic, young master Tavor. It's subtle and mysterious, and can take many months, nay *years*, for it to show any sign of it—'

Cam took the purse from his hip and shook it, encouraging the distinct sound of large Cold knocking together. 'Do you have anything quicker than subtle and mysterious?'

The shopkeeper eyed the purse, his eyes hungry. 'Ah, well, there are some things. Some *quicker* potions that might have the desired effects. If instead of common scarab we use the powdered bradford beetle from deep in the Glasslands, and add just a dash of—'

Cam held up his hand. 'That sounds good to me, Lasah. You know I'll take it.'

Lasah sized up the purse. 'It's quite expensive. There is also, and this is most unfortunate, a Jadan-cleaning fee, since I'll have to scrub the floor where he is standing. I never thought to bring it up before—'

Cam's sigh cut him short. 'Have I ever turned you down before?'

Lasah bowed again, the long silk sleeves of his robe brushing the polished ground. 'Please just keep your sl— *Micah* – close to the door. Jadan essence can be toxic for my ingredients.'

I sneaked a look at my feet, grimacing at the sand I'd dragged in, but Cam winked at me, putting his hand on my shoulder. 'We won't move.'

The shopkeeper hopped around the room, picking vials off shelves and uncorking them, testing their freshness. Or perhaps testing for the opposite. I couldn't imagine the skills that the job required. The rubbish heaps I plundered were never successful in teaching me what was safe and what might turn me into a raving lunatic with one sniff.

Cam yawned again, finishing up the last of his drink. 'And

more Oolong tea as well, please, Lasah. No rush, just when you get a chance.'

Lasah was dumping a white crystalline power into a mixing bowl. 'Of course. For you, tea is on the house.'

Cam tapped his foot as he turned to me. 'So, Spout,' he said, 'do you like music?'

I tried not to let my face go slack. Jadans weren't encouraged to like anything. Either this High Nobleboy was so sheltered that he didn't understand a Jadan's place, or he was toying with me.

I gave a polite nod, keeping my eyes pinned to Lasah's work.

Cam's ears perked up. 'Great! What kind of music?'

'The "Khat's Anthem",' I said without pause.

'Yeah, the "Khat's Anthem" is fine.' I could hear a groan in Cam's words. 'What else though?'

I kept my eyes down, not knowing what to say. Matty, Moussa and I made up music together all the time – or rather, we used to – and I listened to what escaped from the Imbiberies when I went out at night, but most Noble music was foreign to me.

'What about Mirrlah City songs?' Cam asked, hopeful. 'Or the most recent Belisk court jesters' stuff? Or the hymns from the northern nomads – the ones who travelled back from the Great Divide? Have you heard them yet?'

I shook my head. 'I don't know that music.'

Cam sucked his cheek. 'Well, I suppose that makes sense.'

We both fell silent, the only sound being Lasah grinding his mortar and pestle.

'So, Mama Jana told me you're very smart.' he said.

'Smart, sir?'

'Cam, not sir,' he corrected and stuck the empty mug in his pocket. 'And yes, she told me you were . . . *unusually* smart.'

'We're not allowed to be smart,' I said, wishing desperately that he would just wait quietly and leave me alone. 'We're only supposed to serve the Khat and his chosen.'

Cam sighed, lowering his voice. 'Well, that's not what she told me.'

Lasah peeked over his mixing bowl, looking just as confused as I did.

'Do you have a girlfriend?' Cam asked.

My face flushed so deeply I knew it would be visible even against my dark skin. 'No. We're not really allowed that either. The Birth Barracks—'

Cam gave me a playful punch. 'Don't worry. I'm not judging. I don't either. That's why I'm here. But Lasah said the glow cream is supposed to get rid of all imperfections.' Cam pointed to a few red spots on his face, the kind that only showed up on light Noble complexions. 'I know it's shallow, but I feel them all the time.'

I was too stunned to speak. Cam was talking to me like an equal, like a friend even. Surely a group of taskmasters must be waiting behind the cabinets, whips in their hands, ready to punish me any minute now for believing in the kindness of a High Noble?

I nodded, keeping my eyes lowered.

Lasah tipped the cream into a jar, screwing on a lid and tying it up with a thin strip of boilweed. The shopkeeper swept back across the room, past a board pinned with dead insects – some as large as my fist – and around a table stocked with the skulls of small animals. He stopped at the statue of the jackal and lifted the head back, revealing a secret store of green leaves in its neck. Taking a scoop, he portioned out a bit into a small bag and tied it with a red ribbon.

'Here you are, young master Tavor. Oolong tea. Enchanting Glow Cream,' Lasah eyed Cam's Cold purse again as he pressed the jar and bag into Cam's hands, 'which is very potent, much more so than the last. One application a day should do it.'

Cam emptied the purse onto the nearest table, spilling a Shiver, two Drafts, and a handful of Wisps. The shopkeeper looked dismayed at the fortune.

'Master Camlish, this isn't quite enough,' Lasah said by way of gentle chiding. 'For the Enchanting I used a pinch of grainlick, and essence of tear-berry, an—'

'Ah, I see. How much do I owe you? Can I bring you the rest of the Cold tomorrow?' Cam asked. 'You know my family is good for it.'

He wasn't lying. From what I knew, the Tavors had enough Cold to buy a hundred of these apothecaries.

Lasah gave a respectful bow, and as he dipped, he shifted the Closed Eye on his forehead to point it in my direction. 'Four more Drafts should do it. And that will also cover the cleaning fee.'

Cam swept aside some of the mist that had risen to eye level, and beckoned to me to leave.

'Oh,' Lasah called from behind us, 'and if you send a slave to bring the Cold, make sure it knows to stay at the entrance and not to come in! The Mind's Bazaar is a delicate oasis in the—'

Cam shut the door behind us, trapping all the Cold air back inside. He pocketed the jar and the bag of tea, and then looked back and forth, as if pondering something important. Then, looking at me with a sincere shrug, he took a left and started walking.

I lagged behind him by four or five paces, trying to decipher what might be going on in his High Noble head. My body growled from the quick swap of blessed air to harsh Sunlight.

Cam peeked over his shoulder with a smile before he began jogging. Hesitantly, I did the same, but his longer legs allowed

him to go much faster than I could. I was also worried I
might crash into another Noble. Cam then waited for me,
putting a hand around my shoulder to stop me.

'You're not a camel,' he said. 'Walk beside me?'

I was suddenly aware of how wonderful Cam smelled.
There would most likely be a beating when the Nobleboy
realized I'd tainted him with my Jadan stink.

I awkwardly fell in with his stride as we went forward,
knowing this proximity would draw unwanted attention from
passers-by. I made sure to hold up his Tavor coin as high as
I could to show that I was just doing as I was commanded.

'So,' Cam let me go and clapped his hands together, 'you
must know these streets better than I do, Spout. Where would
you buy chocolate? It's my favourite thing, but I don't know
where the best places to get it are.'

'I know a good shop on Canar Street,' I said after a pause.
'Sometimes they have dates that they dip in the chocolate.'

Cam pulled out a secret bag of Cold and weighed it in his
hand, giving me a mischievous smile. 'We should have just
enough.'

Chapter Fourteen

'I know you're still angry with me.' I set the board down in front of Moussa, stirring up a bit of sand off the common chamber floor. 'But this isn't about me, this is about Matty. We're going to sit here and play the game, and wherever he is, maybe he'll get a smile out of it. You don't even have to talk. Just endure my presence.'

Some of our family members looked over to us, smiling. The rift between Moussa and me was still a mystery to them – Moussa still hadn't told anyone about his theories behind Matty's death – and most of barracks forty-five was ready to see us be friends again.

Conditions were worse than ever, a hundred backs desperately trying to heal before the next lash. The taskmasters had shown no signs of reining in their malice, making up new rules on the spot that might allow them to dish out discipline. They weren't even looking for information any more. Shilah still hadn't been caught, but the Nobles had stopped mentioning that fact. Instead, we were constantly told that any rebellion would be punished.

Moussa looked cornered, but he didn't dart off to the nearest boilweed division, like the last few times I'd tried to talk to him. He lowered his voice so it might be overlaid by the chatter in the room. 'Listen, Micah. It's not that I'm—'

I folded into my legs, sitting across from him. 'Of course it is. But Matty loved both of us, and I think he would want us to be friends.'

Moussa's teeth clenched at my words. 'Matty would want to be alive,' he spat at me.

I swallowed hard, opening the lid to the little box of pieces. I'd carved notches into the board and the pieces themselves, so they wouldn't shift around too much. I began to arrange the small chunks of marble, and little bits of tin, and jade dice around the swirls of colour that Matty had painted on himself. When I got to the small bird carving Matty had smuggled in, my fingers trembled too much, so I left it in the box.

'I know,' I said. 'So let's at least keep this part of him alive.'

Moussa kept his eyes lowered, letting the silence stew. He was covered in fresh bruises, and one of his eyes was almost swollen shut. His hands were clenched as he stared at the empty boilweed division, which didn't seem so empty at the moment, as the curtain was rustling. 'Fine. But let's play in the corner. And I'm not going to talk.'

We moved away from everyone, Moussa not meeting my eyes as we sat back down. I explained the rules Matty and I had concocted so far, and Moussa just about cracked a smile when I mentioned that the small staff piece could only move backwards, unless you sang when you rolled the dice, then you could move forward.

'That rule was for you,' I said quickly. 'He really cared for you.'

Moussa didn't say anything, but he stayed put, examining the staff piece he held in his hands until he gave a small laugh. 'He prolly did.'

I finally pulled out the metal feather that had spent so

much time nestled behind Matt's ear. 'We need a rule for this, too.'

Moussa visibly jolted at the sight. 'You kept it?'

'I took it off his body,' I said. The memory made my eyes burn.

Moussa finally broke, with the intensity of someone who has held back for too long. I wanted to go over and embrace him, but I feared that might send him fleeing.

'We loved him,' I said, a lump in my throat as I tried to remember the way Matty had so simply put it. 'Not everything lasts as long as it should.'

We stayed quiet for a moment, but it felt good to be in Moussa's company again. I picked up the dice and cast them, still unsure of what the numbers would mean exactly. 'On another note,' I said, finally breaking the silence, 'something really weird happened to me today.' I decided my main game-piece would be the twisty bit of blue rubber Matty had deemed the River Jadan. 'There was this High Nobleboy, right. A Tavor. And he had me help him with errands all day, but he didn't make me actually do anything. He didn't even want me to carry his bags.'

Moussa gave a small shrug, brushing the last of his tears away. He picked a piece for himself and I could tell he was intrigued, so I pressed on. I rolled the dice again and moved my River onto the garden space. 'He kept asking me things about myself. Almost as if he *cared*. Whether or not I like to paint things, or if I'd ever tried frollock cheese, or—'

'You can't talk to the girl any more,' Moussa cut me off.

I lifted my head up to him in curiosity, but I couldn't meet his eyes. 'Huh?'

'The Boilweed Girl,' he said. 'The Upright Girl. Whatever. If you really want us to go back to how things were, you can't talk to her any more.'

I hadn't wanted to bring her up, but the mention of Shilah

had sparked something inside me. Since venturing out onto the dunes with Abb, I'd thought about trying to find her, but hadn't worked up the nerve to walk back out into the sands and wander around for hours on end. Especially without any Rope Shoes. 'Shilah?'

Moussa's face went dark. 'You know her name?'

A couple of people looked over to us, but I smiled back reassuringly. 'Yeah,' I said. 'But I haven't talked to her since.'

'You can't.' Moussa sniffed, a bit of dry blood trying to peek out of his nostril. 'Here's the thing. Maybe Matty's death was just because he was small, and because the Vicaress was angry, but regardless of that, she tempted you against the Crier.' He was clenching his fists again, his knuckles almost white with effort. 'Now Zeti Gum's dead too. And Paphos is like one big ache. She did that. She made everything worse for us.'

I wanted to slam my fist down and argue that Paphos needed changing, that I didn't *want* us to go back to how things were, but instead I took a big breath. Sending Moussa storming off wouldn't help anything.

I picked up the die and tossed it into his lap. 'Okay. I understand. No more Shilah. But for now, can we just remember our friend?'

Moussa's chest heaved with a deep breath as he held up the dice. The smile took a long time to reach his eyes, but it came nonetheless. 'Like the time he hopped on your back and called himself a Jadan shield?'

I licked my lips, and smiled too. 'Or the time he found those eggs and smuggled them back so he—'

Moussa mimed a shake of his head, pretending to empty something from his ear into his palm. 'Lizard brain! I gotsa a lizard brain, you guys!'

I grinned, happy to have at least one of my friends back. I felt ready to move on now, to be myself again. The urge to tinker had even returned, a new Idea forming in the back of my mind. It was an impossible feat, completely unattainable, but an interesting thought nonetheless. I knew it might be possible to hone the Idea into something achievable, but to do so I would need to spend time mentally working through things, before my fingers went plundering. Immediate death was the new punishment if Jadans were found outside after curfew, but for some reason I was no longer scared to step into the unknown. The Crier had left me alive, after all.

Moussa rolled the dice and looked over the board and all its pieces. 'So how do you win?'

I picked up the makeshift metal feather, brushing it through a beam of starlight spilling through the roof. 'I don't know. But I'm going to figure it out.'

Chapter Fifteen

I found Cam beside my corner before the Sun was even fully
ablaze. He was the only Noble around, and was once again
taking little sips out of a steaming mug, absorbed in a thin
book, and squinting against the glare from its white pages.

This was now my third day in a row of meeting with Cam,
and I was starting to get worried. At this point, we'd gone
on so many errands that I was running out of ways to avoid
his scrutiny. I'd kept my answers clipped and vague, but
Cam insisted on knowing everything about my past, apparently fascinated by the life of a Street Jadan. He showed no
signs of stopping, either. I was wondering if his aspirations
were to become a Jadanmaster, and I was his choicest method
of study.

'Morning, Spout,' Cam said, perking up as I slipped out
of the alleyway opposite. He pocketed the volume as I
approached, so quickly that I didn't have a chance to make
out the design on the front. 'How's Abb?'

'He's usable,' I said, hating the fact that I'd let slip any
information about my father. Someone I cared for could
always be used against me if Cam grew tired of being kind
to me. 'Thanks for asking.'

Cam gave me a mischievous grin, tapping the side of his head. 'And Moussa?'

'Usable,' I said. 'Thank you.'

Cam gave me a playful nudge as I hopped onto my corner, almost throwing me off balance. 'Don't be so glum. Are you ready for today? There's plenty to be excited about.'

I nodded, falling into my slave stance. The naïve side of me wondered if I might use my new obsessive High Noble to explore my Idea, subtly picking his brain about materials that were only available to the rich and powerful, but I knew I shouldn't allow myself to trust his kind.

The other Jadans on Arch Road eyed me with less curiosity than on the last couple of days, but none of us understood why this Nobleboy kept singling me out. Cam had mentioned Mama Jana a few times on our errands, but he had yet to mention how they knew each other. The only thing that gave me any sort of comfort was the fact that she didn't seem to have told Cam about my tinkering, as he'd yet to steer the topic anywhere in that direction.

Cam pulled out a Tavor token, gleaming silver, waving it about in his fingers. 'Let's go.'

'I can't,' I said, eyeing the street from side to side, hoping Thoth was still far away. 'I have to be checked in.'

'That's right.' Cam sighed, downing the rest of his tea. Then he tipped the mug upside down, letting the honey drip down to the rim so he might lick it off. Looking around, he absently lapped up the dripping sweetness. 'I'm hungry. I'm going to find us some breakfast somewhere. What do you like?'

Another question I'd never thought would have been asked. At this point, any food at *all* was what I liked. Thoth had continued to halve my rations of late.

'Figs,' I said quickly.

'Figs?' Cam echoed. 'No, that's boring,' he smirked. 'I'll be right back. Don't go anywhere without me.'

I watched him stride away, wondering what in the World Cried Mama Jana had got me involved in.

The first bell chimed, coaxing the 'Khat's Anthem' out of our collective throats. Lately every Jadan on Arch Road seemed to be having trouble getting the melody out, as most of us had been starved or beaten to the point where even singing was a struggle.

Whispers of blame still fell on the 'Boilweed Girl', but I'd begun to wonder if the taskmasters caught Shilah they would even tell us. It looked as if they were having too much fun being this much crueller to us.

Metal footsteps thundered my way, and I was glad my forehead was dry.

Thoth greeted me with a big gob of spit to my face.

'Fine morning, Spout!' Thoth said with delight as he wiped the corner of his mouth. The spit tingled on my cheek, still fresh with Cold. 'That will be your water ration for the day.'

I nodded, trying not to let my hands clench.

'Response, slave?' Thoth asked in a calm voice.

'Thank you, sir.'

'Thank you?' Thoth's eyes darkened. 'Ungrateful. I think I deserve more than that. I just gave you water from my *own* mouth. And all you have to say is thank you?'

I froze, not sure of what else I could say.

I tried to focus my mind, thinking about my impossible invention. I conjured up the image of Matty's bird carving in my mind.

'Eyes,' Thoth commanded, his voice reminding me of the flies that circled the dead-carts.

I lifted my face with swift obedience.

Thoth spat again, this time rubbing the spit into my eyes. I knew struggling would only make it worse, so I did my best to keep still.

'Now I've given you two rations of water.' Thoth backed off a bit. 'Very generous on my part. What do you say?'

'Thank you very much, Jadanmaster Thoth.'

He regarded me for a moment, the scar on his face deepening as his eyes narrowed. 'Better, I guess. Still not nearly good enough.'

He slowly took the rod out of its sheath and slid his hand along the length of the metal. One heavy strike later and I was on the ground, curled up, the side of my knee smarting as if I'd been bitten by a colossal Sobek lizard.

'So close,' Thoth said.

'Unworthy,' I tried between quick breaths, the pain in my knee blossoming. Considering I was still conscious I knew he hadn't shattered the bone, but it brought flashes of light to my vision all the same. 'Bless you, sir. Praise be to the Khat.'

'You're on the ground, where you belong. That's a nice start. But how dare you not address me from your knees? Have you forgotten *everything* about being a Street Slave?'

I squirmed into the proper slave kneeling stance. My knee gave out in a wave of agony, but I pressed against the pain.

Thoth bent lower, his mouth right next to my ear. 'Unworthy indeed. Don't forget who keeps you alive.'

He grabbed me by the back of my shirt and lifted me up. I could barely put any weight on my leg without my knee screaming in protest, but he left me alone, moving down the line to check on the rest of my kin.

Cam returned, moments later, swinging through the arriving shoppers. A huge smile rested on his face, and I noticed a few round bumps in his side pocket. He came up to me, patting the pocket. 'You ready now?'

I nodded, holding back a wince. I limped off the corner, trying to walk as normally as possible.

Cam followed the pain from my face to my knee. 'What happened? I was only gone a few minutes.'

'It's nothing.' I tried to remain calm, the Sun licking my forehead and enjoying my hurt. 'What can I help you with today?'

Cam frowned. 'But shouldn't you—'

I fixed my eyes on him, and my tone came out unexpectedly harsh. 'What can I help you with?'

I held my breath. Any other High Noble would have demanded blood for such a tone. Yet Cam seemed to enjoy my fire, his face opening with delight.

'The Ancient Quarter,' Cam said. 'Think you can make it that far?'

Walking helped.

By the time we were out of the Market Quarter, I felt able to carry something other than myself again. I just hoped that whatever Cam wanted in the Ancient Quarter was small and light.

Cam led us into a sheltered alley behind the Kay Street Cry Temple and stopped me.

'I'm sorry they treat you like this,' Cam said, pointing to my knee. 'That *we* treat you like this.'

'Cam, you've been nothing but—'

He held up a palm. 'If they can blame all the Jadans for the actions of one, then I can blame all the Nobles for the action of one.' He swirled his hand, the gold bracelet on his wrist jangling. I tried to spot a Closed Eye pendant, but there was none. In fact, I didn't remember seeing any Closed Eye on him at all, which was peculiar. No Eye necklace, no Eye parasol, not even an Eye handkerchief.

'Maybe this will help,' Cam said, his hand going to one of the bulges in his pocket and pulling out something wonderful.

An orangefruit.

A piece of food so expensive, it made Khatmelons seem like common currency.

Cam pushed it into my palm. 'Better than figs, right? Had to get him to go through his reserves, but a smart shopper knows the merchants tend to keep the good stuff for themselves.'

I paused, too shocked to know what to do. Last time I'd eaten something forbidden to my kind I had lost one of my closest friends. My heart clenched, and my hands tensed.

Cam looked at me, waiting for me to take a bite.

I knew I needed to get over all this fear. I had to drop the bucket.

I bit into the fruit, my eyes wild as I ripped and gnashed it with my teeth. Cam said something about not eating the rind, but I couldn't stop myself. The flesh was plump and juicy and I furiously licked the juice off my forearms when I was done.

Cam had been kind enough to look away during my savage display, leaving me with some dignity. Neither of us mentioned the orangefruit again that day.

Cam led me through busy avenues and across prominent squares, brushing at the outskirts of the Auction Bazaar, home of happy shouting and furious bargaining. Thirty or forty vendors were belting out promises above each other: better goods for smaller Cold, spring-loaded quills, foreign chocolate, musical instruments, jewellery, and even sculptures – the kind made from the red clay which unlucky Jadans were made to agonizingly scrape from the banks of the Singe.

Street Jadans made an effort to stay away from the Auction, unless their Noble specifically requested they go there. The goods were always more expensive than at traditional shops and getting to a vendor without bumping into a Noble was near impossible.

'So, speaking of the actions of one,' Cam said, as if it was no big deal, using the noise for cover. 'What do you think of the Boilweed Girl?'

I stiffened, my knee threatening to buckle. 'Sorry?'

Cam put his hands over his head and then mimed tossing something to the ground. 'Shivers and Frosts, Spout! The Boilweed Girl. The talk of Paphos. Surely you must have heard, considering you have ears, and you live in Paphos.'

'She's obviously a menace,' I said carefully.

Cam ran his tongue over his teeth, something crossing his eyes. He lowered his voice, making sure no one was around. 'I don't think that's obvious at all.'

'I—'

'No pressure,' Cam said, throwing up his hands in mock defeat. 'Say no more. The Ancient Quarter awaits.'

Soon the three domes came into view. My heart beat faster at the idea of going inside.

The Great Drought had not only destroyed beauty, it had also destroyed beautiful ideas. In the face of starvation, what good were tinkerings and inventions? Considering the World Cried was still struggling to survive eight hundred years later, the indulgences of the past had been lost.

My heart thundered in my chest as we approached the nearest dome. Above the entrance was a system of old glyphs I couldn't read, and I assumed Cam couldn't either. It was a language from the time when there were many other tongues.

'Heart of the Past,' Cam read, pointing at each letter. 'Preservation. Duty. Tradition.'

I raised an eyebrow.

Cam shrugged, patting the thin book in his pocket. 'I have a lot of free time to study.'

I nodded, but I still didn't believe that was all it was. Most High Nobles couldn't tell the difference between a Cry Temple and a Cold Thermae.

Cam went to knock on the door, but before his knuckles could reach it, a clay window slipped open, revealing a pair of dark eyes within.

'No Jadans,' the voice commanded.

Cam let his arm slump, faking an injury and pointing at his shoulder. 'But I need him. I can't carry—'

'No Jadans.'

The clay window slammed shut and Cam sighed, giving me an apologetic look.

I had already expected as much, not having hoped enough even to feel disappointment, so I pointed to the nearest alleyway. 'I'll wait in there.'

Cam sucked his teeth. 'Fine. But only because I really need to get something in there. Don't leave without me.'

I nodded and headed to the shadows, glad that I might get to wait out of the Sun. I took up my position, and watched Cam negotiate with the hidden eyes, having to pass his huge Cold purse through the slot to prove he could afford to shop there.

Slumping against the wall, I sighed, spending the next few minutes with my eyes closed, enjoying the taste of orangefruit still on my tongue.

'What are you doing, little slave?' a sweet voice asked.

My heart sank and I resumed my slave stance as a burly-armed taskmaster glared at me.

I tried to keep my voice calm, holding out the Tavor token. 'Pardon, miss, but I'm on an errand. I was not allowed in the Ancient Shop with my *High* Noble' – I made sure to emphasize the distinction – 'so he commanded I stay here.'

'Yes?' Her mouth pulled into a wicked grin, revealing a set of yellowed teeth.

I quickly pointed in Cam's direction. 'If you'd like to go and check with him, he's in the—'

Without another word, she grabbed me by the wrist and

dragged me deeper into the alley, away from the domes. My shoulder felt as if it was being ripped from its socket, and I prayed she wouldn't be able to smell the orangefruit remains on me.

'Lying Jadans are no good. Lying Jadans are a burden on the Khat.' She spoke sweetly, yet I couldn't miss the venom that dripped from her words.

'I'm not lying, miss. Please. I really am on an errand. If you'd just—'

She gave my arm a sharp pull, and my words caught in my throat.

'More lies.' She kicked aside a few small piles of boilweed to make a path.

'I swear, miss. If you'll just let me—'

She ripped my shirt over my head and spun me against the wall, pressing my naked chest into the brick.

'What's this?' She jabbed a finger against my back and I winced against the pain. 'Has no one punished you for your lying today, little slave?'

'No, miss.' My chest was thumping. 'But my Jadanmaster withheld my rations so—'

'Good!' she spat, hissing in my ear. 'Your kind doesn't deserve rations.'

She scraped a sharp fingernail in a long line down my back. Pain flared.

'Skin so soft.' She talked in the same bored tones. 'You'll learn truth in pain. Pain will cleanse you. Praise be to the Vicaress.'

I closed my eyes and tried to prepare myself as I heard the gentle swish of the taskmaster's whip being unravelled. I thought I heard more than one tail swinging through the air, waiting to carve into me. My breath stopped in my chest.

'You will leave here with a valuable lesson for all your people, little Jadan,' she droned.

'Wait!' Cam's voice called, and I nearly collapsed with relief. My eyes shot open, but I didn't take my forehead off the wall.

'He's with me.' Cam's voice was calm, but authoritative, like someone used to being obeyed.

Yet she didn't move. 'Stand back, please,' she said calmly. 'This Jadan needs to be taught a lesson. It's the Crier's way.'

Cam begun waving his hands, growing animated. 'No, he doesn't. He doesn't. It was my fault. Look, here's my crest. I'm from House Tavor.'

'Move aside, please.' Her voice was frustratingly composed. 'This is not your business. Out of the alley would be best.'

'Didn't you hear me?' Cam's voice took on an authoritative edge that I hadn't heard before. 'Look. *Tavor.*'

'I don't care what House you're from. This is the Crier's work. And He has the highest House of all.' I heard her lick her lips. 'I'll ask you one more time, please.'

This was the point at which I knew things in Paphos had become really bad. A High Noble would normally only have to clear his throat and the taskmasters would stand at attention. But Shilah's stunt had poisoned the natural order, and discipline had begun to overrule status.

'Spout didn't do anything wrong,' Cam said. He sounded almost frantic now, and I could tell he was worried. 'Here, I just spent most of my Cold, but I have a little left. Take this for your troubles.'

She didn't reach out her hand, but simply looked at him impassibly. 'You shouldn't try to bribe a taskmaster, little Noble. It's quite frowned upon.'

'Look, if that's not enough, I'll bring you more—'

'Bribing is not the Crier's way,' she said calmly.

My heart leaped to my throat. Cam wasn't going to be able to save me with words or Cold. I was going to get all the tails and more. Probably the Procession.

'If you stay there,' the taskmaster said, 'your pretty shirt might get stained.'

'Eyes above! Why won't you listen to me?' He was shouting now. 'He's on an errand with me, you daft, stupid—'

I heard the crack before I felt it. Fire erupted across my back and my whole body went stiff. I clenched my teeth as tightly as I could, as pain blossomed through me. I nearly tumbled to the ground.

'WHAT ARE YOU DOING? STOP!' Cam screamed, followed by a crash that sounded like wood, with a chink of metal spilling after.

'The Crier's will,' the taskmaster commanded. 'Let him take his punishment.'

'LEAVE HIM ALONE!'

I felt blood ooze down my back. I squirmed beneath the throbbing. Another crack, and the pain was something out of a nightmare.

'PLEASE! STOP!' Cam's voice broke.

'The Crier's will.'

Tears came to my eyes and I stared at the brick through a watery veil. The second lash had been worse than the first, and I didn't think she planned on stopping.

The whip swished through the air behind me, and I braced myself. But then something soft pressed against my body before the next crack. A howl of pain swelled through the alleyway, but surprisingly, it hadn't come from me.

'Oh. Oh no,' I heard her say, followed by the sound of her feet racing away.

The soft something was still pressed against my back, and I distinctly heard whimpering behind my ear before the pressure lifted.

Wiping the tears from my eyes, I turned to find Cam on his knees, eyes scrunched in pain. I stepped around him and saw the deep trail of red against his sun-shirt. And next to him was a decorated wooden box with one of its sides split, gears and guts spilling out.

Suddenly the pain in my back didn't feel so intense. A *High Noble* had just taken a lashing. For a Jadan. For *me*.

'Cam,' I said, kneeling down. 'Are you okay?'

Cam sucked in deep breaths, tears welling at the corners of his eyes.

'I—'

Cam brought a hand around to his back, his face aghast. 'You live through this *every day*?'

I gulped, giving a nod. 'Yes – but are you okay?'

'This isn't right.' Cam's face grew hard, and for the first time, I saw the boy beneath. Cam was different from the rest. He cared, he truly did. 'This shouldn't be. This shouldn't happen to you.'

I looked around, gathering my bearings. It was only half a bell's walk back to my barracks and I had just enough salve left to soothe a virgin whipping.

'She'll get what's coming to her,' Cam said, his breathing still fast and full of pain. 'I promise.'

I lowered my hand, helping him to his feet. I couldn't imagine what it would cost him to get his fancy sun-shirt cleaned of all that blood. And I didn't want to think about the artefact he'd dropped to save me.

'Come on,' I said. 'I'll take you to my barracks.'

'What's there?' he asked, his face twisted with pain.

'You get a Jadan beating,' I said, 'you get a Jadan healing.'

The loose panel came away smoothly, and I slipped into Abb's room. Cam waited outside, clutching the remains of his mystery box, the crank on the side bent out of place. I wanted to examine what he'd bought at the dome, but I didn't have time.

'Shirt,' I said, uncapping the salve when I came back outside.

'Can we go in?' Cam asked, eagerly appraising the panel. 'I've never actually been inside a Jadan barracks.'

I shook my head, scooping out a generous portion of the gel. 'No. We— It's not a good idea. My Barracksmaster sometimes walks through during the day, to make sure none of us are hiding from our duties.'

It was a lie, but it was the best I could come up with at the moment. Gramble either spent the day sleeping in his guardhouse or blowing his hefty salary at the Imbiberies. In truth, I wasn't quite ready for Cam to see my tinker-wall, to reveal such a secret.

'If he catches us, I'll just tell him it was my idea,' Cam said with a shrug.

'This will only take a second.' I gave a weak smile. 'Shirt.'

Cam peeled up his shirt and I flinched at how pale his skin was. I wondered if the Sun had ever even tasted his flesh. The red was vibrant against his back, but I didn't think he would need stitches. It looked worse because I wasn't used to light skin, which showed everything more vividly.

I pushed aside his long blond hair and spread the salve across his back, and after a few moments, Cam's body seemed to relax.

'I'm really sorry,' I said.

Cam shook his head. 'No. This is good. All Nobles should know how this feels.'

This boy was irrational. I hoped no other Tavors heard him talking like that, or they might take away his crest.

I gestured at the box. 'What is it?'

'A music box,' Cam said, turning the crank, which didn't do anything. 'It's my cousin's birthday. I was hoping this would be a good gift for her. She loves music.'

'When is her birthday?' I asked, knowing I should just shut up.

'Tomorrow,' Cam said with a sigh, wincing as I rubbed on some more of the salve.

I paused, taking a dangerous leap. 'Leave it here.'

Cam spun, giving me a confused look.

'There's someone' – I kept my eyes down – 'one of my family. He might be able to fix it.'

'Fix it?' Cam raised a puzzled eyebrow, although I could have sworn an amused smile flashed across his face. 'How would a Jadan know how to fix something from before the Great Drought?'

'I don't know,' I said, already regretting my decision. 'But he can try.'

Cam shrugged, and then winced. Then he spun the useless crank again. 'Can't hurt, I guess. Want me to put some of that salve on your back? Your lashes were worse than mine.'

'I'm fine,' I lied, wiping my fingers onto the inside of my shirt, greasing the cloth with a mixture of groan salve and High Noble blood. 'I'm used to it.'

Cam gave a frustrated huff through his nose. 'And that's a damn shame.'

'Let's get back.' I looked up at the Sun, its heat pulsing down strongly. I didn't think it liked the idea of me getting my hands on something so precious as a music box.

But the Crier had kept me alive, letting me drink that Draft.

And Moussa was my friend again.

And a High Noble had even taken a whipping for me.

Things were different now. Changing.

I stowed the ancient treasure behind the panel and waved two knuckles at the sky, welcoming its blazing hate.

Chapter Sixteen

For the first time since we'd met, Cam was wearing dark colours.

His sun-robe was a deep shade of red, and the sight of it made my throat tense up. The colour reminded me of how Jadanmaster Geb dressed on Procession day.

Cam had two mugs of Oolong tea this time, steam billowing from the tops. I remembered how hard it was to sleep after my first bad whipping, and I wondered if he had been able to rest at all. My back was fiery to touch, but my slave skin was no longer surprised by the sting.

Still, I hadn't slept much. Not because I was hurting, but because the night was one I hadn't wanted to end.

Cam's eyes had dark circles underneath them this morning, but still, he smiled brightly and greeted me with a little bow that every other Jadan around must have seen as a sign of insanity. I hoped Thoth didn't catch sight of the movement.

'Morning, Spout,' Cam said, leaning against the wall beside me. 'Sorry I'm late.'

I almost smiled at the thought of Cam being late. Like he owed me the debt of showing up at all. 'Morning, Cam.'

Cam leaned in, eyebrow going up. 'So how did the thing go?'

I cleared my throat, flicking my eyes in Thoth's direction, who was glaring at us from the end of Arch Road, near the Temple. 'Perhaps you can give me a token and I can show you,' I said, 'somewhere else.'

Cam moved both mugs to one hand and fished around in his pocket, his face lighting up with intrigue.

'Cam,' I whispered. 'Don't look so happy. Jadanmaster Thoth doesn't like happiness.'

Cam frowned for a second, his eyes following mine down to Thoth. My Jadanmaster's feet now looked poised to stomp our way and make trouble.

'Don't look,' I said, a bit panicked.

'Oh, him?' Cam broke into a huge smile, giving a polite wave, keeping his voice hushed. 'That's the one who beat you with that rod for nothing?'

I paused, the Sun heavy on my forehead. 'Yes.'

Cam nodded, continuing to wave as if he was the happiest boy in Paphos, giving Thoth a sincere thumbs-up.

'Scumbag,' Cam said under his breath, his face all smiles. He held up the token with a flourish and waved it about so Thoth could see.

'Piece of Sunshit Jadanmaster,' Cam murmured in Thoth's direction, through a broad smile. 'You're a disgrace to Noblekind. You're probably House Erridian, aren't you?' Cam gave another thumbs-up. 'Hope that stupid knot-scarf chokes you.'

I froze, not expecting such a tongue on a boy of refined birth; but Thoth only huffed at Cam's display, not able to hear the actual words, and turned his attention to the Jadan on the nearest corner, touching his neck and wrenching the boy into a deeper hunch.

'He probably just doesn't know how to *deal* with happiness,' Cam said, turning back to me. 'There's a difference. All the Cold in the World, and still most Nobles are miserable pricks. I feel like it's proof enough that things here aren't right.'

I took the token and hopped off the corner, leading Cam deep into the secluded alley where I'd hidden the music box.

'Hold on,' Cam said, skirting around me.

I stopped, aching to get to the hiding place.

Cam put his mugs down on a stone ledge and then added a few Wisps to his waterskin. He took a sip, gave a satisfied nod, and then pressed the drink my way.

'You look bad,' Cam said. 'Drink.'

'I—'

'I know,' Cam said with a roll of his eyes. 'You can't. You insist. Blah blah. Just shut up and drink. All of it.'

I sighed, knowing it was better not to argue. He hadn't turned me in for the orangefruit, so I knew I was safe. Besides, Thoth had spilled my water rations at my feet that morning and made me sip it up from the stone. I still had sand in my teeth, and it would be a relief to swill it out.

I drank the whole waterskin in one continuous gulp, trying to capture every moment. I was suddenly reminded of Abb's bucket, and wondered what the Khat would think of this Nobleboy giving extra water to his slave.

'How's your back?' I asked, wiping the back of my mouth.

Cam slung the container back over his shoulder and grabbed his tea, sipping both mugs, one after the other to keep their levels even. 'Don't worry about me. What about you? You've got yours on bare skin.'

I shrugged, leading him down through a narrow opening, into the dim light between buildings. My boilweed bag hadn't shifted since I'd set it there that morning, and I took out his treasure. 'Just more scars for the collection.'

Cam's eyes darkened, but then widened with joy when I revealed the music box, fixed and polished.

My heart tingled as I remembered all the fun the invention

and I had had the night before. The piece had started as a complete stranger, but it had whispered its secrets slowly, and my hands had listened. The system of bumps and gears its Inventor had used were ingenious, striking different-sized pipes and flicking metal stems as the crank turned. There were a few interchangeable rollers for different songs which had kept Moussa entranced for hours. The work had filled me with purpose, the invention and I eventually connecting, becoming each other's keeper. I felt sad letting it go.

I spun the crank, drawing out the soft tinks and chimes, making sure both ends of the alleyway were clear of spectators.

Cam's face looked as if he'd just been splashed with his own bucket of Cold. 'Shivers and Frosts! It's fantastic.'

I shrugged, trying not to seem too proud. It was my mysterious *family member* who'd fixed the machine, after all.

Cam waited a long pause, his face flushed with intrigue. 'You want to know a secret?'

My heartbeat picked up. 'What?'

'It didn't work,' Cam said, lips puckered with a laugh.

'I know. I— My friend fixed it.'

'No,' Cam said, like this whole thing had been a big joke. 'When I bought it at the Ancient Shop. It didn't work. Got it at a great deal, too. I was going to have Leroi fix it for me last night, but it looks like there's more than one genius Tinkerer in Paphos.' Cam winked. 'And he's in your family, nonetheless.'

I felt my head tilt. 'What? Who's Leroi?'

Cam smirked, polishing off the tea and putting the mugs in his pockets. 'You'll find out soon enough.' He carefully took the music box, giving it a big kiss. 'Well, thank you very much, Spout.'

I gave a small bow, sad that I didn't have more time to spend with the treasure.

'I have a few things I have to do at the Manor,' Cam said. 'I guess I still don't know the exact rules.' He was careful with his next words. 'Is there any way to, um, reserve you? Not that you're property or anything like that. I just . . . you know, want to make sure—'

I held up my hands. 'It's okay. I understand. Unfortunately not, but I promise that if anyone else sends me on errands, I'll do them quickly.'

'Okay, good, because tomorrow I want—' Cam nearly dropped the music box, his eyes widening. 'Wait!'

'What's wrong?'

Cam didn't answer, skirting around me so fast I thought his robes might catch on the stone wall. My stomach knotted, wondering what might have set him off.

Then I saw it.

Cam had stopped in front of an Opened Eye, painted on the stone in gold. His hand snapped out to point at it, finger stiff.

I couldn't believe I'd missed seeing the symbol earlier, considering it was so close to where I'd left the music box; although the gold colour blended almost flawlessly against the beige brick. The Eye was only more apparent now that the Sun was higher and spilling more light into the alley.

'Did you paint this?' Cam asked, his pointed finger circling the pupil. But his question was full of hope, not accusation.

'No,' I said quickly.

Cam's eyes narrowed, searching me for the truth.

'I swear,' I said. 'It wasn't me. I don't even know what it is.'

'You don't?'

I shook my head, oddly cross with myself for lying to him.

Cam looked at me, then, holding one finger to his lips, he reached under his shirt and drew out a necklace. The chain jangled down over his shirt, holding up the symbol's twin. He looked down at the Opened Eye and then straight back at me. 'Yeah. I don't either. I have *no idea* what this symbol could mean.'

Then he reached into his chest pocket and pulled up the thin book he'd been reading, to reveal the Opened Eye inked on the cover.

'No clue whatsoever,' he said, drawing out the words, letting the book slide back in.

My throat went dry.

The second bell rang out overhead and Cam sighed, putting the necklace away. 'Damn. I need to go, I'm going to be late. Sorry, Spout.'

I tried not to look at the golden Opened Eye on the wall, but it seemed to be calling me, even more so than the last time I'd seen it.

'Listen, I know your people have every reason not to trust mine,' Cam said, adjusting the box. 'But you can trust me. We'll talk more tomorrow.'

I gave the smallest of nods, my stomach still dancing from all the Cold I'd drunk earlier.

Cam walked a couple of steps, but he stopped, and turned back to face me. 'I think I understand now. I mean I did already, but now I'm pretty sure she was right.'

'Hmm?'

'Mama Jana. When I went to her, she told me— You know what, forget I said anything.' Cam waved with his elbow as he darted down the alley, music box carefully held out and red robes billowing. 'See you later, Spout! Don't have too much fun without me!'

Black smoke spilled from the roof of the Arch Road Cry Temple.

The oily cloud stood in a long plume, menacing against the already harsh sky. Every Jadan still left on their corner seized up, wondering if they'd be sent to snuff the flames out. I looked down at my uniform and deliberated how much sand I might be able to carry if I folded the bottom into a pocket.

The shops in the Market Quarter rarely caught fire – the poor Jadans stationed in the Blacksmith Quarter couldn't say the same – and last time flames broke out there, many Jadans had left the buildings with melted bodies.

But the black smoke wasn't just coming from the Cry Temple: all above Paphos, black trails marked the sky. Each Quarter had its own plume, which meant it wasn't an accident. This couldn't mean anything good.

Then came the Priests.

Usually the white-robed holy Nobles remained sequestered in the holy houses, manipulating the minds of young Jadans, but now they filed down the road in two neat rows, each of their hands wrapped around a silver pole, hoisting a Closed Eye overhead. They spun the poles in slow turns, rubbing their palms, the Eyes rotating and casting their judgement on us all.

As the Priests hummed a low chant, taskmasters began to emerge from every corner, swarming onto Arch Road. Their whips were out and cracking, shouting for the Jadans to return to their corners. The whips didn't seem to care how quickly the Jadans were obeying. I was already on my corner, but I felt as if I could feel the sting of every lash, my hurried family members crying out. I longed to do something, but I was stuck.

The two lines of Priests flanked the middle of the street, pausing all at once as someone gave a shrill whistle. The taskmasters stopped their torment long enough to politely ask the Noble shoppers to stand to one side of the road, so they may commence whatever monstrosity this was going to be.

Then Jadanmaster Thoth's voice boomed out. 'Holy day!'

I could only see him in my peripherals, but his bearing

was intense as he prepared his ink and pen. 'Corners, slaves! Holy day.'

Whips cracked some more. Legs scrambled.

This was all happening so fast I had no idea what to make of it. The Sun was directly overhead, and everything was so clear. The white of the Priests' robes was nearly impossible to look at straight on without wincing, and it felt as if the Sun was using the fabric to flood the street.

'There shall be a day of Cleansing,' Thoth bellowed. 'In order to draw the poison out. Praise be to the Khat. Paphos shall once again be purified.'

I hadn't heard of a Cleansing before, and from the looks of my kin, neither had they. The Gospels commanded a Procession each month, but that was the only big event in Paphos I could recall in my lifetime.

The Noble shoppers all seemed elated at this little bit of fun. They gathered together in happy clumps, pulling out their Closed Eye necklaces, chattering excitedly.

Then came the sounds of the chains.

The line of Jadans was marched down the road. The Priests dipped their poles inwards in order to make a looming steeple under which the chained would have to walk. Some of the Jadans were whimpering, shackles chafing their ankles. Every one of their faces looked confused, as if they hadn't expected to end up in this crowd. And there seemed too many of them. Even in the Procession the numbers never got this high. Dozens upon dozens of prisoners were marched into place on the steps of the Temple.

Black smoke continued to pour out of the chimney. The scent in the air changed. It became stale and murky, and the street smelled of rot.

Thoth marched down Arch Road and gave all the cornered Jadans an unusable symbol. When he got to me, not only did I get the ink on my forehead, but he made me stick out my tongue so he could draw one there, digging the tip of his quill as deeply as he could.

For the next half-bell, we waited in silence, my mouth tasting of blood and ink. I was too shocked to make any sense of this. Looking over at the Cry Temple, I could almost see the toxic air rising from the shackled Jadans.

Then came the light of the dagger.

The Vicaress flowed down Arch Road like blood over glass, moving slowly and deliberately. The flames of her blade gave off the same black smoke as the Temples. The smell of death intensified.

'The Blasphemy continues,' the Vicaress said, forgoing her usual song as she swept over to the Cry Temple. She walked alone, no young girls dressed in white or Rose of Gilead petals within sight.

One of the Priests dressed in an elaborate white gown, peaked at the head like the Pyramid, stood behind the Vicaress's left shoulder and shouted out what she said in a voice loud enough for all of us to hear. 'The Blasphemy continues!'

'First the girl affronted the Khat by dropping the Shiver. Now the mark of Evil has been seen on the walls of Paphos. Trying to convince you of something that is *simply untrue.*'

So it was the Opened Eye that had caused this. Had one of the taskmasters seen me with Cam? Was the Vicaress going to snatch me off my corner and put me in front of the rest of the chained?

'Five of the markings have been spotted in this Quarter alone,' the Vicaress continued. 'The Sun is trying to corrupt your minds, unworthy children. But fear not. I will cleanse this city, so you may once again survive in the merciful arms of the Khat.'

She lifted her palms towards the sky.

'You may have seen the Opened Eye, the Trickster's Mark, the Firemaker's Brand.' The Vicaress raised her dagger high.

'But I shall remove the Sun's words from your ears. I will drive the lies from your heart!'

And that's when I knew that the Vicaress had to be a fraud. She had no direct access to the Crier, she couldn't possibly. If she was cleansing those who'd seen the Opened Eye, then I would be among the chained. I'd looked at it more than once – I'd even carved one – and here I was, still on my corner, watching innocents get punished. That was the shattering of the last link in the chain of doubt. Maybe I couldn't invent the outlandish things I dreamed of, but I would make things. I would make dozens of things. Hundreds. I'd tinker until my fingers bled. As long as I lived, I'd squeeze my mind for Ideas until it went black.

The Vicaress advanced on the first Jadan on the Temple steps. She lowered her fiery blade, her blue eyes hardening as she muttered incantations in a language that seemed made up.

The head Priest couldn't replicate the sounds she was making, so instead he started another low hum that the rest of the Priests copied.

Then came the screaming.

Chapter Seventeen

Mother Bev tried her best to stand tall, but so many years of a proper slave stance had left her back one giant crook.

'This is not the Crier's will,' Bev said, straining to address us all. 'The Gospels are one thing, but this has gone too far.' She coughed, obviously not used to speaking so loudly. 'They are making up their own rules now.'

Voices rose in the chamber, some in agreement, some in fear. The Cleansing hadn't only happened on the streets. The Vicaress had made sure her wrath had spread to the Builders, Domestics and Patch Jadans as well. Priests had run rampant around Paphos, with weapons of their own and carrying out vicious acts of her Cleansing. But considering the white-robed holy men weren't as precise with a blade as the Vicaress, the Jadan death toll was far higher today. Many of the survivors had even been chained to their own dead-carts and made to carry their fallen kin out to the sands.

Our barracks alone was missing two members. We still weren't sure if Miggy and Cariah were on dead-cart duty or stacked in the dead-carts themselves.

'Today was an act of savagery,' Mother Bev said. 'And it forces us to respond with savagery of our own.'

Slab Hagan's massive body loomed beside her, waiting patiently to provide his counter-argument. 'We must obey the Crier. We must be grateful for life.'

Mother Bev looked as if she was about to breathe fire. 'Grateful? For what should we be grateful? For the starvation? For the torture? For the—'

'The Vicaress had to cleanse us!' Slab Hagan said. 'The Boilweed Girl defiled our name. We were tainted. Now we are clean.'

Mother Bev spat on the ground, waving two knuckles at the roof. I'd never seen her this angry before, and I hoped she wouldn't break anything. 'This was *not* the Crier's work. And the Boilweed Girl is probably dead already. The Nobles might have even drawn those marks theyselves, just to make a reason to prove their might.'

'And what do you want us to do, Bev?' Dabria called out, her voice shaking. 'Rise against the chosen?'

'This was not the Crier!' Mother Bev shouted, trying to hobble into a menacing stance, but only raising her head enough to reach Hagan's elbow. 'This was an affront to the natural order! This was innocents being slaughtered. The Crier will be on our side if we fight back.'

'If He was on our side He would Cry again for us,' Steeven said. 'Even if this wasn't His direct order, nothing has changed. The Khat gets all the Cold. We have to obey or we all die.'

'So? We die,' Bev huffed.

'Easy for you to say!' someone shouted. 'You've already got a foot in the dead-carts. What about us who don't want to be punished and sent to the eternal black!'

Slab Hagan nodded in agreement, crossing his meaty arms over his chest.

I shot a questioning look at Moussa, querying whether I should speak up. He shook his head, whispering: 'Let the elders go first.'

'Abb!' Mother Bev called. 'Get up here and talk some sense into these cowards!'

'Not cowards,' Slab Hagan grunted. 'Loyal.'

Abb sighed, dropping his healing box. Everyone went quiet as he walked towards the main doors. He put his hands behind his back, collecting his thoughts, and finally turned to face us, keeping his lips sealed.

Small conversations rumbled around the chamber, but were quickly hushed by Mother Bev.

'I have been under the heel of the Nobles for thirty-seven years,' Abb said. 'Some of you have served longer, some of you are just getting started. During that time, I have learned a lot about the World Cried. Even in shackles, I have known love. Even against the whip, I have seen beauty. But mostly I have seen our struggle. We serve so we may survive, but today was different,' Abb said quietly. 'Today was wrong.'

A round of disagreeing huffs pocked the air, but Bev held her hands out for silence.

Abb continued: 'If you truly believe this Cleansing was a normal part of Jadan life, then I suggest you look away now. For all you others . . .' Abb slowly reached into his back pocket and held up my carving of the Opened Eye, finding a beam of starlight to illuminate the details. I gasped, as I thought I'd chucked the thing out into the dunes with the rest of the purge.

It took a moment for the onlookers to register what it was, and some shrieked, holding up the blankets to shield themselves. A few gasped like I had, sucking in quick breaths. Hagan winced away from the carving, as if he'd just been whipped, but Bev looked at the symbol as if it was a Frost.

'This was their so-called blasphemy, but it is just a symbol. It is just a symbol until we decide it's more. In thirty-seven years I have learned that the Nobles can punish us for disobedience,' Abb said, his voice filling with steel. 'They can punish us for lying. They can punish us for not meeting our quotas. They can punish us even out of boredom. As they alone hold life in their Patches.' Abb took a deep breath, the carving beginning to shake in his hand. 'But they cannot punish us for having hope. When we are not allowed to hope, then this life is already the eternal black. Whether it's real or not, the Opened Eye is as much a part of our people as our chains. We must be like my son, and look at the things that can be changed. We cannot abandon—'

A metallic clinking sounded at the main doors, and Abb went silent, pushing the carving back in his pocket. Everyone turned towards the doors.

Gramble burst in, his eyes rimmed red as if he'd been crying. 'Shut up! All of you! I try to let you have your peace, but I can't pretend I don't hear this commotion! Wasn't today hard enough? Do you really want more lashes to fall on your shoulders?' He slammed his hand against the door and a deep boom thrummed in the air. Then he waved about a piece of parchment with what looked like the Khat's seal branded into the paper. 'They sent these to all the barracks! If you knew what I'm supposed to— What she wants me to—' He slammed his fist again, the door vibrating deeply. 'Just go to bed!'

Then he crashed the doors shut as violently as he could, and locked us in.

Abb waited a few beats and then pointed to the hallway leading to his room. 'All who want to discuss further about what we can do,' he said, voice soft yet firm, 'my quarters.'

Most Jadans turned away. I heard a few of them curse Abb under their breath for the carving. The Patchies all fled silently to their own private quarters, too obedient a bunch to make a fuss. But a small batch of the Builders and a few Domestics ignored their boilweed divisions and made their way towards Abb's room, fear and determination fighting on their faces.

I joined them, surprised that all I felt was an overwhelming desire to go outside. Steeven was right when he said nothing had changed in terms of Cold still only falling for the Khat. But my new Idea – however impossible it might be – had to do with just that problem. The Cold only fell in the Patches, but it was still up there. It still existed above, in the heavens or the blackness. I touched Matty's bird carving in my pocket, wondering yet again about the nature of flying. About the nature of how Cold fell to the land.

In that moment, I didn't need discussion. I needed to look up at the stars.

I needed to figure out how to touch the sky.

Chapter Eighteen

The heavy door swung closed behind Cam and me, sealing out the Sun. I'd never been inside the Paphos Library before, and the sensation was overwhelming. Not only was the room delightfully Cold, but there was a certain sense of awe in the air. As if the building itself knew more than Cam or I ever would, even if we lived a hundred lifetimes.

The Bookkeeper took his droopy eyes from the pages long enough to cast us a sceptical glance, the dim candlelight and bald head making him seem even older than he was. He hunched over further, moving his gnarled finger along lines of text as if desperate not to lose his place.

'Camlish Tavor,' the Nobleman said in a gravelly voice.

'Hello, Humphrey,' Cam said. 'I know.'

Humphrey frowned, eyes still on the paper. 'You never bring Jadans in with—'

'Thank you, Humphrey.' Cam took a Shiver out of his Cold purse and plopped it on the desk. 'Like I said. I know. But I figured, why fight it? Got to grow up sometime.'

Humphrey looked over at the Cold, one barren eyebrow trying to rise, but stuck in a mere quiver. 'A Shiver is a bit much for a borrow fee. Unless you're trying to take out some early archives.'

'No, thank you, sir. But I would like to reserve room six, please.'

'The Empty room, I see?' Humphrey snorted and then hawked something slimy into a little basin on the desk. I tried not to think about the poor Jadan who had to clean that bowl. 'Two Drafts per bell. Two for a candle in your lantern. You're here often enough to know the rates.' His eyes narrowed as they swept over me. 'What are you two planning on doing in the Empty room for three hours?'

'One hour is fine,' Cam said, leaning forward and lowering his voice. 'But the extra is for your discretion.'

'Discretion for what?' Humphrey asked with a frown, his face one big question mark.

Cam made a point of looking from side to side, patting his pocket as if he was carrying something important. 'Let's just say I'll also be needing the *Vicaress Compendium on Jadan Torture for Truth Extraction.*'

Humphrey's wrinkled face drew into a delighted smile, as he lit a candle in the base of a lantern. 'I see you're growing up indeed. So you want to learn about Jadan pain, do you?' He gave me a toothy grin. 'Probably good to know how to control your slaves if you're going to take over the Crest someday.'

Cam gave a gentle bow. 'My sentiments exactly, my dear man.'

Humphrey sat back in his chair, hands going behind his head. I sneaked a peek at what the old man was reading and recognized it as the Khat's Gospels. All the books in Paphos to choose from, and he was reading the one he most probably knew off by heart already.

'Don't want to practise at home.' Humphrey tapped a finger against his lips. 'Is this a surprise for your father? To show him you're not a boy any more?'

Cam gave another bow, his blond hair tumbling over his

shoulders. 'You may as well be a Tavor yourself with how well you know the family.'

'Kindly said.' Humphrey looked delighted and then reached under his desk to retrieve four boilweed sacks. 'These go on the slave's hands and feet, to protect the books. Jadan skin is riddled with Sun – *Khat Baroques the Benevolt*, verse twenty-two – and just so you know, if he touches a book, you buy it.'

Cam threw the little sacks at me, his face turning harsh. 'What are you waiting for, then? Put them on.'

I nodded, making sure to look properly scared, as Cam had asked before we entered. I covered my hands and feet, feeling rather foolish.

Humphrey gave a modest little clap. 'You'll be a Lord yet, young Camlish Tavor.'

Cam bowed. 'The Cleansing yesterday has got me thinking. These Jadans don't know discipline any more.'

'Rightly said.' Humphrey creaked forward, his bones as excited as his face. 'I've been worried about that myself. What you planning on first. Pressure points? Strangling? Teach it commands?'

Cam patted his pocket again. 'Blunt objects. I want to see what spots make them squeal the most. And I believe room six has the thickest walls.'

'That it does.' Humphrey looked so proud at the declaration. '"They shall know pain, for the aches and disease, kept under holy cudgel so the Chosen might step on their backs and rise off the sands."'

'*Khat Illuminus II*,' Cam said without pause. 'Verse sixteen.'

Humphrey looked as if his mouth might get stuck in a smile as he took a key off a little rack and tossed it to Cam. 'Nothing quite like wisdom of the past. Praise be to the Khat.'

'Praise be to the Khat,' Cam echoed.

Humphrey pointed to my forehead. 'And look at the thing

sweating. You've already got your Jadan scared. Well *done,*
Camlish!'

Cam nodded. 'I'm sorry to cut our conversation short, but
I'm quite eager to get started.'

Humphrey hawked up another something terrible and
added it to the slimy basin. 'Not at all, Camlish Tavor. By all
means.'

Cam nodded and slapped me lightly on the back of the head.
'Follow.'

'Bless you, sonny,' Humphrey said as we wandered into the
stacks. 'The World Cried needs more young Nobles like you.'

'*High* Nobles!' Cam corrected with a bratty smile.

'Rightly said. High Noble indeed!'

I slumped over, wandering in Cam's path, trying not to slip,
as the boilweed sacks made me glide across the smooth stone
floor.

'Sorry,' Cam whispered as he led me down the streets
of scrolls and books, past many ceramic busts that seemed
to be tossing me dirty looks. 'I need to keep a low profile.
Humphrey is nice to me, but all he reads is the damn Gospels
and it has suffocated his mind. All these books don't seem
to inspire him to branch out.'

'I understand,' I whispered back.

Cam slapped himself on the back of the head. 'At least
now we're even.'

I smiled.

'Seriously though,' Cam said. I could sense the regret in
his tone. 'I feel really terrible. I didn't mean to bring up the
Cleansing so casually, I'm so sorry—'

Just then another lantern bobbed around the corner, held
by a stern-looking Noble holding a single book under his arm.

Cam cleared his throat and dropped into a harsh tone.
'How dare you lag behind so far, slave. I should have you
whipped for your incompetence.'

I moved closer, making a point of cowering. 'Sorry, sir.'

Cam gave a frustrated huff and turned to the Nobleman. 'Jadans. What are we to do?'

The Nobleman nodded but didn't say anything, before moving down the row, picking up his pace.

'I swear, your kind is about as stupid as—' Cam stopped, making sure the man was out of earshot. 'Anyway. I'm really sorry. I'm glad you're alright though. I swear that this time, the Vicaress—'

A light bobbed out of the shadows, revealing a Noblewoman this time, her rosy lips pinched so tightly that I thought they might be in danger of fusing into one.

Cam brought himself to his full height. 'The Vicaress is an inspiration for us all. Now don't make me hurt you more, slave scum.'

'Good for you, young sir,' the Noblewoman said with a haughty grin. 'Show them their place.'

'I don't even know why we keep these things around any more.' Cam grabbed a handful of my uniform and dragged me down the rows. Once we were alone again, he let go, smoothing out the wrinkles he'd caused. 'Sorry again.' He bowed his head bashfully. 'I hate how well I can play the part of the spoiled Noble brat.'

'It's like you're a natural,' I replied teasingly. My face immediately stiffened. The words had just slipped out, reminding me of something that Abb would have said, and I couldn't believe my tongue had let go of something so foolish. This was a High Noble, not Moussa, and I couldn't say things like that.

Cam's eyes widened. 'Did you . . . did you just make a joke?'

'I'm so sorry,' I lowered my head. 'Please don't—'

'Thank the Crier,' Cam said, pulling me into a one-armed hug, careful not to hit me with the lantern. 'I was worried. You're always so serious with me.'

Squeezed against him, I was reminded of how wonderful he smelled, and I pulled away carefully so as not to contaminate his clothes.

'Cam. Why are we here?' I asked quietly once he let me go. The events of the previous day still had me on edge.

'Well, room six really does have thick walls,' Cam whispered. 'And I don't want people to overhear what I have to say. Plus, there's something in the library that I want you to see.' He smiled, giving me a light punch on the shoulder. 'I'm so happy you actually joked with me. *Like I'm a natural.* Hilarious.'

I nodded, wondering how this Noble boy had ended up being so different from the rest of his kin. He held the lantern out, ushering me down a new aisle, this one filled floor to ceiling with scrolls so old one breath from Sister Gale might rip them to shreds. At the end of the corridor hung a large painting, menacing even from this distance.

As we closed in on the painting, Cam's good mood seemed to deflate. The painting depicted sprawling land, green and lush, slowly being consumed by fire. The dark-skinned figures in the foreground scrambled up a mountain towards a glowing piece of Cold, which, from its size, I assumed was a Frost. The Jadans were trampling on each other, pressing one another down into the flames. They all had bloody horns, fangs dripping with flesh, and wore wreaths of intestines across their chests like whips. And while they were busy bludgeoning each other with Cold, brandishing glass blades, and ripping off each other's skin, the fire underneath crept closer to their feet.

It was the most horrific scene I'd ever witnessed.

Cam folded his arms across his chest. '"The Cause", by Armus Josiah. Painted sixty-two years after the Great Drought.'

I'd heard of 'The Cause' before. Sometimes on the streets young Nobles would stop at my corner and look at my forehead, asking where my horns were. But even with all the descriptions, I hadn't expected it to look so brutal.

I nodded, feeling that it might make me sick if I looked at it too long.

'This painting,' Cam said, 'is one of the most notable works in existence. I wanted you to come here because I need you to understand something.'

I held back a retch. 'What?'

'That Nobles like Humphrey, most Nobles,' Cam's expression was harsh, 'they believe this nonsense. They believe the Jadans brought their fate upon themselves all those years ago, and that as a Noble they are special and chosen.'

I nodded. 'I know that.'

Cam took a deep breath. 'But even if I'm a Noble, I want you to trust me. I understand why you would have every reason not to. But I need you to know that I don't want to do you any harm.'

'I trust you,' I said. 'You did jump in front of a whip to save me.'

'Not enough. Here's to Humphrey.' Cam checked back down the row to make sure we were alone. Then he gathered a big gob of saliva and spat right on the painting. Wiping his mouth with the back of his hand, he said: 'This painting is all lies. Just like the Cleansing. I don't believe in any of this for a second.' He tapped the spot under his shirt where the necklace was. 'And even though people are scared to admit it, I'm not the only one.'

I stared wide-eyed at what he'd just done, the wet lump dripping down the canvas. Even though he was a High Noble, Cam could be punished severely for defacing something so precious to the Khatdom.

'It's a copy,' Cam said, seeing the panic in my eyes. 'But if I could get to the real thing down in the locked archives, I'd spit on that too.'

I swallowed hard. His expression told me this was true.

'Come on,' Cam said, nodding back down the row.

He led me through the library to the section of private rooms, neither of us saying a word. Quickly Cam unlocked a door, the lantern in his hand illuminating a room which was completely empty, save for a single table with two chairs behind the door.

Closing the door behind him, Cam gestured for me to sit as he put an ear against the door. Eventually he seemed satisfied with the silence, taking the opposite seat and putting the lantern on the table.

'So,' Cam said, idly playing with his silk sleeve.

I nodded, not used to the feel of a chair under me. I'd only really ever sat on rocks or ledges, and wasn't used to such comfort. 'So.'

He pointed to the boilweed sacks over my hands. 'You can take those off, by the way.'

'Thanks.'

Cam tapped his fingers on the table, lips twitching back and forth. I could tell he'd been thinking about this moment for some time, and was worried about what might happen next.

After a long stretch, I realized I'd have to be the one to break the silence. 'Is there something you—'

'You fixed the music box,' Cam declared.

'No. It was my family—'

Cam shook his head. 'If this friendship is going to work, we need to be honest with one another. I need you to trust me.'

I let out a long breath at the word 'friendship'. 'Yes. I fixed the music box.'

An enthusiastic smile cut broadly across his face. 'Brilliant. How did you know what to do? From what I understand, Jadans aren't allowed to own things, let alone tinker with them.'

I shrugged, struggling to find my words. 'I steal things from rubbish heaps at night. Usually I don't think too much about what I'm making, the pieces just tell me what to do. That's what happened with your music box.'

'Which she loved by the way,' Cam added. 'Thank you for that.'

'I'm glad.'

Cam gave a smug smile and then got serious again. 'What do you make?'

'Small things. Things that might be useful.'

He paused. 'So what you're telling me, since you've had no teacher and have to do everything in secret,' he clucked his tongue, 'is that you're a *natural*.'

I kept a straight face, and then my smile broke.

Cam leaned forward, the lantern light casting his shadow long across the brick wall at his back. 'What do you know about the Great Drought?'

'Same as everyone else I guess.'

Cam nodded. 'So very, very little.'

I shrugged.

'What if I told you,' Cam said, 'that there is nothing that proves the Crier wants you to be slaves?'

I felt my face flush. 'What about the fact that He stopped giving us Cold?'

'Did He?' Cam asked, tilting his head. 'Or did someone else just take it away?'

'I don't understand.'

Cam leaned in, speaking quietly. 'Some people say the first Khat had a hand in the Great Drought. That he made a deal with the Sun for power.'

'I—'

Cam held up his hand. 'It's just one of many stories. But I'll let Leroi explain the real theories to you. He's better at it.'

There was that name again. 'Who's Leroi?'

'There's only one member of my family that I truly respect. My cousin Leroi,' Cam blushed, his mood changing, 'and he is dying.'

I paused. 'Dying of what?'

Cam's expression hardened. 'Of himself.'

I tilted my head.

Cam's eyes flashed to the door. Then he screamed loudly at the top of his lungs, his voice breaking in the middle from the effort. My hands flew to my ears.

'STOP!' Cam screamed. 'PLEASE! STOP! UNWORTHY!'

Then he stopped abruptly and shrugged, giving me an apologetic look. 'Just in case Humphrey's out there listening. Anyway, Leroi runs our tinkershop at the Tavor Manor. He's kind, and generous, and a genius, and right now he's determined to drink himself to death. And not from Oolong tea, mind you.'

'Why?' I asked, my ears still ringing.

'Because his assistant died,' Cam said bluntly, rubbing the front of his throat. 'An assistant that he cared for very much, and who happened to be Jadan.'

I had a feeling I knew what was coming next.

'So I went to see a friend named Mama Jana' – Cam tapped again at the Opened Eye necklace under his shirt – 'the one who gave me this. Like I said, I'm not the only Noble who believes we should all be equals. Mama Jana keeps good relationships with Jadans she thinks are different, who might prove our beliefs to the rest of the world. So I asked her if she knew any Jadans that might be good in a tinkershop.'

'And she gave you my name.'

Cam smiled. 'She did. But honestly, if I had met you on my own I'd have known there was something unusual. Special.' He pointed at his eyes. 'Even the way you looked at that music box. It's all in here.'

'So, what can I do to help?' I asked, although I felt that I already knew what Cam was about to suggest.

'I know I'm asking a lot, especially since, after this Cleansing, you probably want to be with your family.' Cam took a deep breath. 'But if you're willing, you can let me buy you. You can let me set you up in our tinkershop, where you don't have to steal, where there's no Sun, where you don't have to make only basic things in the dark.'

I felt my heart hammering in my chest, hard enough to crack stone.

'Give me three days to get the right papers,' Cam said.

I paused for a few beats, and then gave a single nod.

Cam reached across the table, and we shook hands, like equals. Then he got up, cupping his hands around his mouth and aiming his screams at the door. 'MAKE IT STOP! PLEASE! MAKE IT STOP!'

Chapter Nineteen

Abb was sprawled out on his blanket, threading a needle back and forth through a piece of boilweed. He'd been at it for some time now, deathly quiet as he practised his stitching. He didn't need the practice – Abb was so good he could probably stitch together the Twin Rivers if the Crier gave him a big enough needle – but in the past this method had been a proven system to get me to talk. He knew if he strung along the silence, doing something repetitive, I'd get annoyed and eventually spill whatever secret I was guarding.

He knew me all too well.

But I held back. I wanted to tell him about Cam, about the library, about the life-altering offer that every Jadan dreamed of, but I wasn't quite ready for the idea to become real.

Going with Cam would mean I'd have to leave Abb behind. To leave my family in this time when things were only going to get worse. When they needed me more than some drunken Inventor did.

I didn't crack, so after a while, Abb got up and made his way over to my side of the room. He bent down, gave me a very serious look, and then swiped the boilweed across my forehead, dragging a thin layer of sweat away with it.

I tried not to react, but a laugh escaped me. 'What are you doing?'

Abb scrutinized the sheen in the dim light, giving a nod. 'Bleeding skin is never dry when you stitch it. No point in practising unless it's realistic.' He gave me a respectful nod, almost as if addressing a Noble. 'Do carry on.'

He returned to his blanket, diving back into silence, poking the boilweed over and over. It irked me that Abb was always so certain he'd outlast me.

'That Tavor Noble offered to buy me today,' I said, wanting to slap myself for giving up so soon. 'To set me up in the tinkershop in his Manor.'

Abb went still, leaving the needle poked halfway through.

I didn't move from the blanket or turn in Abb's direction, instead I looked over at my tinker-wall. I'd worked hard every night since returning from our journey with the bucket to try to recreate some of what I'd destroyed, gathering up my scraps from the sands. Most of my creations were dented, looking a bit on the sickly side, but they existed once again.

I hadn't got too far, but there was at least one of each. I'd finished a crank-fan, a gear flyer, and a colourscope. I'd rescued a few carvings, a scorpion trap – both spring-loaded and bait designs – and an hourglass. My Claw Staff. Sound stretcher. Syringe. And half a dozen other little things I'd be leaving behind.

And if what Cam said was true, I'd never have to worry about scavenging for materials again. I'd get to assist a real Inventor, and maybe in time to become a real Inventor myself.

I just wished Abb would say something.

I finally looked his way, trying to process the devastating idea that I might never see him again. Abb was still, staring up at the starlight through the slats.

I must have broken his heart.

'I'll sneak out at night,' I said quickly. 'It's not like I won't see you again. I'll even steal from their gardens and bring you and Moussa food.'

Abb still said nothing.

'I'll bring everyone food,' I said. 'I'll bring figs. And dates. Orangefruit, if they have them to spare.'

Nothing.

The sweat had returned to my forehead. 'I know you want me to stay here and figure out how to fight back with you and the rest, and I know I said I would, but I think I could do some good at the Manor. A little while back I had this idea—'

Abb finally shifted, sitting up straight and staring directly into my eyes. 'Did you say, in their *tinkershop*?'

I nodded, ready for him to shout at me that I was a fool. That Nobles didn't just buy you and give you your dream. That Cam was just toying with me, playing some elaborate new game the Nobles had created since traditional torture had got so old.

'*That* sort of tinkering?' Abb pointed to my wall. 'Like what you did with his music box?'

I nodded with a gulp.

Then Abb got up and his body started tensing up. I thought at first maybe he was going to hit something, or that he was having some sort of spasm, his body rejecting the idea of us parting ways, but then I realized the truth of what was happening.

'Are you kidding me?' I asked, smile breaking. 'That's your reaction?'

Abb clapped his hands and started swaying awkwardly in the worst display of dancing I'd ever seen. 'Don't be mad that your old man moves like the wind!'

I slapped my forehead, the smack wet and loud. 'You're the most embarrassing father in the entire World Cried.'

'Lucky you, Little Builder!' Abb threw his hands up

and hopped over his blanket, nearly tripping over his healing box.

'Stop!' I said. 'By the Crier's name, I take it back. I won't go. Just make it stop!'

Then it got worse.

Abb started singing, clapping his hands to a jagged rhythm.

> 'The Jadan's work upon the sands
> Those who need the Cold
> Family forever
> Older than the old'

'How do you even know the "Jadan's Anthem"?' I asked, trying to slow him down.

Abb stopped his horrifying movements long enough to shake a finger at me. 'You forget; I was there when it was written! Now where was I . . .?'

His voice got louder and I was desperately glad no one was around to witness my shame.

> —'Blessed be the forgotten
> Who still bleed for the lands
> So maybe the World Crier
> Might release their hands.
> They never fall to Sun
> Dooby dee and dooby dun'

Catching the look on my face after the last verse, Abb clenched me in a hug and ruffled my hair. 'Maybe I forgot a few words,' he shrugged, pulling back and giving my cheek a light smack. 'Micah, this is it. This is the greatest day in both of our lives! This is the Crier proving everything we hoped. Apparently we should all be touching Frosts in the Patches.'

'Don't even joke about that.'

'Who's joking? I break a holy rule, and now years later you're getting the best fate a Jadan can receive. House Jadans have all the shade they want, and you'll only have one family to worry about instead of serving every nasty Noble on the Street. And, oh wait, that's right, you're going to be working in a *tinkershop*!' Abb's smile was so bright it seemed to be sucking up the starlight around us. 'I'll tell you what, if I were as strong as Slab Hagan, I'd burst into the Pyramid and rub my dirty Jadan hands over every single Frost if it meant you'd get to stay in that Manor.'

I shook my head. 'Please don't.'

Abb flexed, kissing the muscle on his arm. 'Good thinking. All the women in here would be so disappointed if my body looked like Hagan's.'

'It's not fair though,' I said, ignoring a strong desire to roll my eyes. It was a tad upsetting that the finest mood I'd ever seen my father in was because I was leaving. 'You all need me here.'

'Micah,' Abb put a hand on my shoulder. 'What in the Crier's name made you think that anything about this world is fair? You don't like the way things are, then use your new life to change them. Drop that bucket.'

'There you are with that nonsense again,' I said, a bit of heat rising from my chest to my face. 'I don't know what you expect of me. It's not like I can Sun-damn tinker us to freedom.'

'Maybe not.' Abb looked up at the holes in the roof, kissed his finger, and then held it to the sky. 'But I've seen it.'

'Seen what?'

Abb gave me a devious look. 'There's something back there. An idea. You haven't been able to stop staring at the stars all week; it's written all over your face.'

It never failed to unnerve me, how well he could read me.

Telling him about the Manor was one thing, but telling him about my new Idea would make me feel truly foolish. 'I don't know what you mean.'

He started the song and dance again, and I got up to head for the boilweed door.

'Tell me, and I'll stop!' Abb laughed between verses. 'It's the only way!'

I grunted. 'Fine! But it's so insane that you'll want to break out your healing box and try to spread some salve on my brain.'

Abb bowed, dipping back down to his blanket, a huge smile across his face. 'Good thing Gramble just gave me a new vial. Now spill, kiddo.'

I took a deep breath. 'Okay, it's more of a concept than an actual idea. I was thinking—'

Just then, a soft rattle came from the side of the room, the loose panel shaking against the casing. We stopped talking for a moment. 'Must be the wind,' I said. Abb nodded at me to continue.

'I was thinking—'

The panel rattled harder, angry almost, ready to burst inwards.

Something was out there.

I bent down, snatching up my reassembled Stinger from its hiding place on the bottom shelf, tucked behind Matty's game. The weapon wasn't full, but I'd gathered enough scorpion venom for its capsule that I knew it could take down the Vicaress herself. No one besides Abb or myself used the loose panel – anyone else sneaking in or out of our barracks would go through the fake wall in the uniform closet – unless it was a last resort.

Then there was another violent shake of the metal, this one including a thump that sounded like a foot. The panel had to be slid, not forced. Someone unwelcome was trying to get in.

My knuckles went white around the Stinger. I'd promised

myself I wouldn't use such a weapon unless it was a last
resort, but with how things were headed in Paphos, I was
glad it was in my hand.

The panel finally slid across and fell to the ground, revealing
a shock of dark, braided hair and pointed cheekbones I knew
all too well.

My tongue tasted dust and my heart raced. 'Shilah.'

'Hey, Micah.' She began to slip through the space. 'I heard
singing,' she said in a toneless voice. 'Figured it was a good
time to come in.'

'That would be my father,' I mumbled, blushing furiously.

Abb relaxed, raising his eyebrows at me. I decided not to
respond; my face was already flushed.

Shilah stood up, as though she sneaked into random
barracks all the time. From the corner of my eye, I could see
Abb noting the way she stood, so rigid it was almost like she
was bending backwards.

My fingers ached to reach out and touch her. As if I could
try to guide her posture back to normal.

Abb's smile broke open and he gave a small wave, so
embarrassing that I felt like diving outside and hiding in the
sands. 'Hi! I'm Abb. I'm Micah's father. Are you his girlfriend?
He didn't tell me about you.'

Shilah didn't seem to find this amusing. Then, after a
moment of reflection, a hint of a smile slipped onto her lips.
'Your son would have to be quicker on his feet. I need
someone that could keep up.'

Abb looked over to me with a wink. 'She's great. You'd
be lucky indeed!'

I thought my cheeks might explode from embarrassment.
'Abb!'

He threw his hands up in defence and then started towards
the boilweed door. 'Don't mind me. I'll give you both some
space.'

I gave him a pleading look. 'But—'

Abb waved again. 'You can tell me about your idea later. I'll leave you two alone.' He paused, giving me a wry look. 'You should definitely ask her to be your girlfriend.'

If my father hadn't been so much bigger than me I would have tried to clamp his mouth shut. The door flapped shut behind him, but not before he'd given me another exaggerated wink. 'Don't worry. I'll snap before I come back in.'

I picked up a wad of boilweed and chucked it at the closed door, careful not to trigger the Stinger.

When I looked back, I found Shilah's eyes flitting across my tinker-wall, her face still expressionless. I'd hoped she might look impressed.

'Seems like there should be more,' she said.

'I've had a strange week,' I said.

'I know,' Shilah said, the corners of her mouth upturned. 'I watched you destroy all of your stuff.'

I raised an eyebrow, my heart still thumping fast. 'You watched me do that? You couldn't have come to say hello, and maybe stop me?'

'That was your business.' She shrugged, shoulders tossed back. 'And then you had your father ask me to be your girlfriend. Bit of a desperate move.'

I felt my stomach clench, my mortification growing. 'I didn't tell him to do that. I didn't even tell him about you.'

She sauntered past me, giving off hints of sweat and dirt, yet for some odd reason I felt my nose following her, finding it impossible not to inhale. She smelled like the deep sands.

'Sure,' she said, bending down to the bottom shelf and touching my Dream Web. 'What do you call this, a *Sand Sifter*?'

She used the same sarcastic tone as before, and it made me think about the night I tried the Cold Wrap, and how so much had changed in such a short time.

'Why'd you draw all those symbols on the walls?' I
ventured, having a strong feeling that my guess was right.
'They got some Jadans killed.'

She stood up, her face so close to mine that I had to step
back.

'What makes you think it was me?' she asked.

I looked at her incredulously. 'You're telling me it wasn't?'

'I drew some, yes,' she said, gesturing at the wall. 'But do
you think I'm the only one in Paphos who believes in the
Opened Eye?'

'I—'

'Is that a weapon?' she asked, stone-faced, pointing to my
Stinger.

I almost forgot I'd been carrying it, and I went to tuck it
back on the shelf before I hurt someone. I hadn't had enough
time to gather the amount of scorpion poison that I'd lost
the night it had been destroyed, but the dose in the chamber
now was still hefty enough to keep someone out for days.

'Wait,' she said, putting a hand on my arm. I felt a jolt
travel through me at the unexpectedly soft touch. 'Can I
trade you for that? I could use a weapon.'

'It's kind of dangerous.'

She gave me a harsh look. 'That's the point of a weapon,
isn't it?'

Our faces were so close together that I could smell her
breath, with a hint of Khatmelon. It brought back a flood of
memories and I had to retract. 'Trade for what?'

She stood up and grabbed the new pair of Rope Shoes that
I'd fashioned. 'Put these on. I left mine outside.'

'Why?'

She smiled, and for a moment, her sarcasm faltered. 'I
make things too. Different things, but I think you'll want to
trade. Come on. And try to keep up.'

*   *   *

'Welcome to my home.'

'So,' I said, heart sinking as I realized Shilah was truly insane. We'd come to the last of the rocks, the only thing waiting at our feet being a large drop from the cliff to deadly water below. 'You live in a boiling river.'

'Yes,' Shilah said, hand gently wrapped around the Stinger. 'All my life. Born in the Hotland Delta, and I swam all the way here. Did I mention I can breathe underwater? I find it best to sleep on the hot clay at the bottom of the river, and sometimes I make friends with the bubbles.' She pointed off into the distance. 'That's Shem. And that one is Michael.'

I started to back away from the edge of the cliff, now slightly nervous about the fact that Shilah was armed and I was not. Luckily enough my Rope Shoes were a lighter pair than hers – this time made with thinner metals – so I could probably outrun her back across the dunes if need be.

She looked at me with a grin and then turned back to survey the Kiln, the current steaming and fast and hungry. 'Also, if you're going to be my partner, you can't be such a gullible idiot.'

'Who says I'm going to be your partner?' I asked, glad that she was just playing around, and that the Sun hadn't baked her head full of false visions. 'I don't even know you.'

Shilah smirked, keeping her focus on the water. 'That's the part that bothers you, huh? Not the idiot thing.'

'Seriously,' I said, annoyed that I'd agreed to come. I should have been spending these last few nights with Abb and Moussa, not traipsing around the sands with a troublemaker like her. 'Why are we out here?'

Her smile faded, and her cheeks became as rigid as her back. If there were still wars in the Khatdom, she'd suit being a warrior. Her face was stoic and poised, and I wanted to reach out and touch the angles of her cheeks, just to feel what such a thoughtful face was like to touch.

'You shouldn't trust him,' Shilah said. 'That Noble who keeps pulling you in.'

'Cam?' I asked after a moment, shaking off the trance.

She gave me an impressed look. 'No title or even a full name? Maybe there's hope for you yet.'

I shrugged. 'It's what he asked for.'

She stared across the River Kiln at the empty sands beyond. 'Why did he take you to the library?'

I smirked in turn. 'You've got to stop following me, you know. It's very creepy.'

'Not following,' Shilah said, annoyed, slipping out of her Rope Shoes and flexing her toes against the rocks. 'Judging. You think I would just bring anyone here?'

I gestured to the raging waters. 'Okay. To your home, right? I imagine it's a lovely place to spend—'

She jumped off the cliff.

My stomach clenched and I darted to the edge, looking over in horror. The Kiln would cook her alive in a matter of minutes, and I felt my head go light thinking about how loud her screams were going to be.

But she looked up at me from a long ledge jutting from the rock face below, shaking her head. Then she slipped inside some sort of cave underneath where I stood, the angle making it impossible to see inside. I placed a hand against my chest, feeling the thumps reverberating across my palm.

And then I smelled something impossible.

My nose wrinkled, knowing it couldn't be true. The only time I had smelled anything like it was when I had crawled near the Garden Quarter. But this time it was much heavier, more potent, tickling my nose with its earthy bitterness.

I peeked over the cliff further and saw the edges of dark greens and even darker browns.

Impossible. It couldn't be what I thought it was.

Shilah popped her head back out, pointing to a series of rungs she'd hung down the cliff's edge. 'Try and keep up. You can use them if you're scared.'

'I'm not scared,' I said, heart beating. 'I'm shocked. Is that—'

'Soil,' she said, rubbing her finger along an exposed leaf, which was attached to some sort of creeping vine. 'Welcome to Little Langria.'

I could scarcely breathe, winded worse than when Thoth had driven his rod over and over into my stomach. 'Did you say Little *Langria*?'

'Keep up!'

I had to grip the ladder tightly as I climbed down, worried the strength in my hands might give at any moment. The smell of the soil was almost too much for me to bear, and I tried not to look directly at the plants spilling out of the cave mouth until my feet were firmly set on the ledge.

The cave was bursting with life. Green plants flooded the insides, all different shapes and sizes, stretching up the walls and deep into the shadows. Berries of half a dozen colours winked out from the vines, juicy and plump. I recognized many of the fruits from the Market, but it was miraculous to see them still attached to the source. Huge figs melting off the branches. Vibrant apricots clustered tightly. A small Ahmanson tree sat near the cave mouth, offering yellow pods that dangled off each branch. And a Sever Ficus loomed above the mess, dazzling with its scarlet fruit. And there were persimmons, and limes, and even pomegranates, which looked as if they were nursing so many seeds in their bellies that the bulbs were about to drop.

'What, in the Crier's Eyes, *is* this place?' I asked, almost too overwhelmed to press the words out of my mouth. 'Do the Nobles who own this know you're here?'

'No Nobles allowed in Little Langria.' Shilah gave a winsome smile, peering through a thicket of vines and leaves as she stowed the Stinger somewhere. 'I told you, I make things.'

'This is mad,' I said, my head swimming with all the delicious odours.

'No,' Shilah said, practically bursting out from the bushes and jabbing a finger at my face. 'This is the opposite of mad. This is what happens when you know what's real.'

I was starting to feel faint, and I knew I should probably move away from the edge of the ledge, lest I fall backwards and exchange this paradise for the hungry waters below.

'I—' I took one step in, my tongue failing me as what she said registered. 'I don't— you made— no Nobles?'

Shilah put a hand on my lower back, and helped lead me to safety in the cave. The healthy brown soil gave slightly under my feet, squishing in between my toes, and it was cool, unlike the infinite sands I was used to. It felt like the Sun had never tasted this cave, and I couldn't help but wonder if Shilah had used the Stinger on me while my back was turned, and this was death.

'I don't understand,' I said, feeling the tears come to my eyes. If Shilah had built this, then the place was a miracle. Not a miracle like drinking the Draft, or finding the Shiver in the rubbish, but a true phenomenon that went against every law of nature that I understood.

Shilah grabbed a pail from the side of the cave. It was attached to a long rope, the end tied snugly on a cone of rock. She tossed the bucket over the edge of the cliff, letting it fall to the waters below, the rope instantly going taut. Giving a heave, the sleek muscles in her arms tensing, she brought the haul back up, boiling water sloshing over the rim.

Then she dived back into the cave, a few moments later coming out with a handful of Wisps. Dropping two of the Wisps into the pail, she then removed a small cup from a nook in the wall and began doling out little rations for each of the plants, the soil growing darker at her offerings.

'It took me two years to make,' Shilah said, giving an extra long drizzle over a plant with blue berries that I did not recognize. 'But I did it. A fully Jadan Garden.'

'You made this place?' I asked, the truth sinking in as I slumped against the nearest wall, knees crumbling against my chest. What was an Inventor in the face of this miracle? What were trinkets held against a secret fountain of life? What did I know about anything, if this place could exist, right under the nose of Noblekind?

She nodded.

I swallowed hard, pushing away a single tear that threatened to run down my cheek. It was all so beautiful, and I wished Abb was here to see what I was seeing.

She came over to me and offered me a scoop of Cold water, which I drank down in one gulp. Then she slumped against the wall, our sides touching. Pulling up her sleeve, she once again showed me the Opened Eye mark she'd inked into her skin.

'If all this is real, and you made it without Noble help,' I said, gesturing to her lush garden. 'Then that means . . .'

'Correct,' she said, a finger running around the Opened Eye. 'We don't have to be their slaves. The Crier looks down every night, and still He lets me keep this place. They use His name to make their lies seem real. But He loves us, Micah. The Drought was not His doing. I truly believe that. And I think He's been trying to end our suffering ever since, but He can't.'

I pulled my knees closer to my chest, trying to contain my tears. 'So it's all lies.'

Her hand went under her shirt and removed a piece of old parchment, folded many times.

I was still trying to process everything I was seeing. The

Crier hadn't punished Abb for the Frost. He hadn't punished me for the bucket. He hadn't punished Shilah for a whole Garden.

'Is the Crier even real, do you think?' I asked, throat choked up. 'Or is everything about everything a lie? Did the Nobles just make the Crier up?'

'I don't know what's real.' Shilah unfolded the parchment, revealing it to be a map of the Khatdom; but it extended further than any map I'd ever seen. Up North, above the River Singe, above the Glasslands, above the City of David's Fall, even past the Great Divide, was a small area marked with the Opened Eye.

'But I plan on finding out,' Shilah said, tapping the spot. 'I'm going to go where Cold falls everywhere. And crops grow huge and juicy, way bigger than mine. And there are lakes filled with Cold water where you can swim without getting burned. And there are birds singing, and all kinds of animals that are supposed to be extinct. And when you walk, you walk on grass instead of sand and mud. Jadans aren't slaves in Langria. You'll see.'

The map began shaking in my hands.

She put a hand over mine, keeping it steady. 'But I don't want to go alone. I can survive out here alone, but there's so much I can't do on my own. So I've been waiting for someone else who believes.'

I felt sweat prickle on my forehead, and I moved the map aside so I wouldn't stain the ink if any drops fell. 'How do I even know what to believe any more?'

'The map was my mother's,' Shilah explained gently, getting up and picking a selection of fruit. 'The best Jadan I've ever met. She told me all about Langria. And that she'd heard some runaway Jadans from Paphos would march—'

'Are there secret Cry Patches?' I blurted out, trying to think clearly in spite of the fact that my whole world seemed to be tumbling around me. 'Patches that the Khat doesn't know about? Is that where you get your Cold? Is that how Langria could be real?'

Shilah laughed, plucking an apricot and adding it to her collection. She came over and dropped all the fruit in my lap. The rush of the current below was soft at the mouth of the cave, and it almost sounded like the River was tittering along with her.

'With questions like that,' she said with a grin, 'I think I picked the right partner after all.'

Chapter Twenty

White smoke broke through the sky this time.

Every Jadan on their corner stiffened, watching the thin clouds billow above the Cry Temple. Thoth's earlier walk down Arch Road had warned us that something like this might happen, as he drew an unusable symbol on each of our foreheads and commanded us to kneel until told otherwise. He'd scratched his quill across our skin wearing an expression of firm purpose, although he hadn't said a word about what we should expect.

The Priests in white showed up again, but this time, they lined the corners beside us, kneeling down and laying their Closed Eye poles at their sides. Their chants were different now, the tone more reverent and quieter. The taskmasters were back in droves, but their whips remained curled at their hips, and they too dropped to their knees at the sight of the white smoke rising.

Even Thoth had set himself gently down to the ground, taking care not to wrinkle his uniform, as he knelt with the rest of us.

Not a single word was spoken for a full bell. Noble

shoppers appeared at the edges of the street, but it was clear something was happening, so they remained to one side, silent.

I felt the ink drip into my eyes, the sweat practically pouring from me now. Shilah had made sure she returned me to my barracks with a full stomach of both miracle food and Cold the night before. I'd never felt so full of life, the juices of so many fruits still on the back of my tongue. My dreams too had been like nothing I'd experienced before, and when I woke up, it was with clarity, and ideas involving the sky and stars filling my brain.

If Shilah could make a Jadan Garden, then maybe I could make something impossible too.

My body felt whole, and my mind felt as if it was flying rather than trudging through the dunes. I'd hoped to have a normal day of errands during which I might half-heartedly consider Shilah's offer of running away together and searching for Langria.

But I could think of nothing other than the distinct sound of the ram's horn, and the thickening of the white smoke that was now rising all over Paphos.

Rams had gone extinct with the Drought, and their horns were very rare, only used on holy occasions. I'd heard the instrument sounded only twice in my life: once when the Khat had his firstborn son, and once in honour of the Vicaress of Belisk when she was called up to the Crier. If I could even believe that such things happened any more.

The horn sounded out closer, blaring in a series of extended blasts. I could tell its player was nearing Arch Road. The Priest and taskmasters hadn't moved from their knees, although some of their expressions had soured from being in contact with the hot stone.

And then the Khat's chariot appeared.

I'd only ever seen the structure in paintings or in stories, but I recognized it instantly.

The chariot was being carried by four of the largest Jadans I'd ever seen, so fierce that they made Slab Hagan look like a well-fed infant. Four golden poles extended onto each of the Jadans' muscular shoulders, and they marched down Arch Road in perfect unison so their cherished bounty would remain stable. Armoured soldiers of the Khat flanked the sides of the chariot. They too marched in unison, weapons lowered, moving as one unit, the sound of their boots booming a thousand times louder than Thoth's metal soles. The golden curtains on the chariot were drawn, lined underneath with the same kind of waxy paper as my Cold Wrap, and I almost broke into a smile of recognition. If my own experience was anything to go by, the air in the chariot would be so cool that the Khat would need a dozen layers of windcloth just to feel comfortable.

The idea that the Khat wasn't any more divine than I was still tugged at the edges of my sanity. The man behind those golden curtains had power, huge and reaching, but it wasn't the kind he claimed. It couldn't be. For a Jadan Garden existed. One which had nothing to do with him, yet thundered with beauty.

The chariot, along with its pageantry, was gone almost as quickly as it had appeared, turning the corner and disappearing onto Maan Road, the ram's horn blaring loud and leading it into the next Quarter. I noticed that some of the Priests beside me had bent all the way over so they might kiss the road that the Khat had crossed.

'Rise, slaves!' Thoth called out, as if he'd been waiting for his cue.

All the Jadans snapped up, while the Nobility followed at their own leisure. Some of my kin were shaking, their knees

wobbly from having witnessed the 'divine' in the flesh.
I wished I could show them what I had seen, and tell them
what I had been told over the past few days. Would their
knees tremble then?

A black-clad figure now stood in the spot where the chariot
had appeared, and for the first time, the Vicaress was not
holding her fiery blade.

Instead, her hands clutched a large black bag, velvety and
bulging at the seams.

Behind her was an extraordinarily large rations cart being
pushed by two lackeys in white, a tub of boiling water sitting
between baskets upon baskets of figs.

The Vicaress spoke, and the lackeys repeated what she said
loudly enough for the whole street to hear.

'The Crier assured me He is pleased!' the Vicaress said,
her voice echoing around her. 'You, Jadan people, have taken
your Cleansing without incident. And the Sun has been
banished from your hearts. The Crier wishes to reward you
for your service. First with a sighting of your divine ruler,
and second with a gift of rations. Do not be afraid! Bask in
the fact that you made it through, here to serve the Creator
once again. You shall feast on figs and choose a Wisp from
the holy bag to drink in your water. Together, we shall
celebrate the Crier's delight.'

The Jadans around me first stood still in disbelief, but
as the lackeys began to hand out fistfuls of figs, their faces
slowly filled with excitement. The Vicaress herself held the
bag open, giving each of the Jadans a seductive smile as
she encouraged them to reach inside and select a piece of
Cold for their water.

I watched what she was doing with a detached sense of
awe. The Vicaress knew she'd overstepped her bounds, going
against the Gospels, so she got the Khat involved and imple-
mented this scheme. Abb's secret meeting about fighting back

was probably not the only one in Paphos, and the Nobles knew they'd have to do something. This bribery was nothing but an attempt to quell any future resistance, and the worst part was, it would probably work. More than anything, more than all the figs or Cold in the Khatdom, the Jadan people wanted to feel that the Crier hadn't forgotten about them. An eternity serving Noblekind in the afterlife was far better than spending an eternity in the black.

The Vicaress slid in front of me, and I held my breath, trying not to inhale her intoxicating perfume.

She opened the bag, offering me a smile that could make the Pyramid crumble down to its foundation. 'Pick one, boy.'

My hands were shaking, but I'd been a slave long enough to know what my facial expression should be. For now, I reached in and pulled out a perfectly nice Wisp, round and shiny. A Priest handed me the communal water goblet, so I dropped the Cold in and drank it all down in one delicious gulp. Figs were shoved into my hands, and the Vicaress moved to the next corner.

I almost wished the smoke above the Cry Temple was black again.

Not because I wanted any more pain for my people, but because I knew after this little peace offering, the Opened Eye would no longer show up on any walls for quite some time. Abb was right, the Nobles would do what it took to keep their power, and this little token of appreciation was a better motivator than any lashing. It was what the Jadan people had always been desperate for.

The Nobles were lying to our faces, and we'd been taking it for hundreds of years, and I knew right then that I couldn't possibly leave to try to find Langria while all my family was stuck here, suffering and—

The Vicaress gasped, which triggered a rustling from the nearby taskmasters.

'This Jadan has chosen a black Wisp from the bag!' the Vicaress said, hand over her chest. 'He has not been Cleansed! The Sun is still in his heart! He must have drawn one of the Firemaker's Brands!'

All eyes were drawn to the scene, and we watched the cornered Jadan tremble in front of her, a black Wisp in his hands. The piece of Cold looked as if it had been dipped in paint, and left to dry, covering it in an unnatural sheen. The Jadan looked at the thing with a face full of confusion, his hands shaking.

'Taskmaster!' the Vicaress snapped, pointing at the nearest one. 'Take this Jadan into the Central Cry Temple. He still has secrets.'

The taskmaster sprang to his feet and grabbed the Jadan by his arm, wrenching him down Arch Road. The black Wisp toppled to the ground, and was picked up by the Vicaress, who brandished it so all might see, before stowing it in her pocket.

'Fear not!' the Vicaress said, spreading her arms to us. 'If the Sun is not in you, you have nothing to worry about!'

The rest of the Jadans on Arch Road reached into the bag much more slowly when it was their turn, but when their hands came out of the bag holding a regular Wisp, their smiles were only bigger.

I knew what they'd be feeling. That the Crier truly cared for them, keeping their hand away from any black Wisps, and giving them cool water and figs. The eating and drinking would usher in one of the happiest feelings imaginable.

For just a moment, they were once again worthy.

Apparently anger also made me sweat.

I was discovering this new fact about myself, heart stewing with rage, as I stood on my corner and thought about the vile things the Nobles made us suffer. They were ruthless and calculating but most of all, they were liars. We weren't punished for our misdoings, and never would be. We'd been fed lies, all in the name of hoarding Cold.

Every other Jadan seemed delighted at their fortunes, bodies full of food and Cold, and getting some time to rest on their corners. Thoth had announced we'd all remain unusable until the white smoke disappeared above the Temples, and that we should spend our time thanking the Crier for His gifts and mercy.

But I'd spent long enough thinking about the Crier. My mind turned instead to the decision ahead of me.

It was simple: either I ran away in search of freedom, or took Cam's offer and spent my days tinkering.

Either way, I was on my way to a better life.

At least that's what I thought, until the Vicaress returned with my name on her lips, two taskmasters at her back.

I couldn't hear her voice, as she was at the far end of Arch Road, but I could see her mouth forming the word *Spout*, and Thoth's finger swooping towards my corner.

She sauntered my way, with a black wool cap dangling in her hand. I met her eyes, and they were full of mockery, the blue colour startling in its brightness. The taskmasters marched behind, one of them holding a pole with a loop on the end, the other holding a giant hammer.

I tried to cool myself, but my chest was full of fire.

'Observe,' the Vicaress said, as they arrived in front of me, 'he already knows why I'm here. Look at all that sweat.'

Thoth snorted. 'Unfortunately, Highness, that's normal for him.'

The Vicaress smiled at me, her gloved fingers gliding across my cheek. 'The Crier knows, child.'

I swallowed hard, and she backhanded my face, hard and swift.

'That's the opposite of what we need from you.' She rubbed

the wool in her fingers. 'We need everything to come *out*. All your dirty little secrets.'

I made sure not to move.

'Do you have anything to say for yourself?' the Vicaress asked calmly. 'Anything you've been hiding, *Spout*?'

'His given name is Micah, Highness,' Thoth said, adjusting his scarf.

She leaned in and licked my sweat off the tip of her gloves. 'I taste what you've been hiding, Spout.'

My body flooded with dread, but I begged myself not to let it show. I kept reminding myself that this enemy was a false prophet, and that she had no power over me.

But what had brought her back, and straight to my corner?

The Vicaress licked her lips, lush and red and plump, and then she stretched the wool out and slipped the cap over my ears. In an instant I felt the heat, the Sun diving into the black wool as if it was a long-lost lover. There was enough of a gap under my eyes that I could see her black sandals, but other than that the hat obscured my vision completely.

Her voice was close to my ear, so soft that only I could hear. 'Your friend Moussa gave you up. He chose the black Wisp, and it took quite a bit of Cleansing to get him to scream, but eventually he did. Everyone does when the Crier's wrath is involved.'

I heard the crackle of fire, and I smelled her blade come to life. The suffering had begun, my head was sweltering, and I knew things were only about to get worse. I couldn't think about the Vicaress torturing Moussa. That would only make me break, and I wouldn't break.

Someone clapped, drawing the sound of padding feet. I took a steadying breath, trying not to let the fear make me stupid. I couldn't fall apart before knowing what the Vicaress wanted to know. I could still try to lie my way to freedom.

One of the taskmasters grabbed my arm, my body jerking in surprise. He responded with a hefty smack to my face. Then my other arm was grabbed, and my hands were chained together. There was the sound of metal hammering into stone above my head, and I tried not to let the tremors shake my heart.

Already the wool was soaked with my sweat, and the manacles were cutting off my circulation. The chain hanging from my arms was then locked to a pole the taskmasters had driven into the wall above my head, and I knew there was little chance I'd be leaving my corner alive.

But I wouldn't break.

Whatever they wanted to know about my tinkering ideas, or the Shiver, or about Abb's meeting, I wouldn't let them have it.

A Jadan Garden existed.

The Crier was not on the Vicaress's side, and chained or not, I would not die her slave.

She waved her blade under my nose so I might smell its acrid flames.

'Spout,' her voice was sweet and tender, 'there's no point denying it. Moussa has told me everything. So we're going to sit here and play a few games, with all of your dirty Jadan friends watching, until you tell me everything you know.'

Her blade brushed against the skin of my arm and sent pain jumping into my skull.

Then the Vicaress peeled up the hat just enough for her tongue to hiss in my ear. 'Where is Shilah hiding?'

Chapter Twenty-one

The sand beneath my feet opened up and swallowed me whole.

And I fell towards black water.

And fell fast. There was no wind at my sides, just a wash of heat running away from the waters below, shooting back up towards the crack of light through which I'd fallen. I wanted to cry out, but my voice didn't listen, as it was already riding the heat up and away. I grasped, desperate fingers swimming through stifling air, but the harder I pushed, the harder my hands struggled against thick silence.

I suddenly hit the surface below, waves parting gently. Saltiness splashed into my mouth, and I knew this river. I let my hands glide over the surface, recognizing the waters; they'd poured out of my eyes and a hundred thousand others, and I could feel the current of tears beneath me churning. Instead of drowning, though, I was dragged forward, riding the cool black bubbles of memory into unending shadow. It was a strange realization when I discovered that there was no pain any more. I'd left pain far away, back in the world.

The river was wide, but its flow was gentle, and I let my head tilt slowly back as I watched the light being sucked into the distant split in the sky above. I was thirsty so I cupped a bit of the water into my mouth, and I tasted things of the past. Like the time I'd tinkered that little catapult for Matty to shoot pebbles against the barracks' wall. And when Abb showed me the loose panel in his quarters.

Suddenly I realized that these tears had Cold in them. Not like the Draft in the bucket of Cold, but enough to make me curious. Were the glimmering beads raining into the river behind me, or into the dark cavern which I was being swept towards? Was the cool feeling blooming or fading, or eternal?

I knew I was coming to the place where the river ended. I was aware the current would plunge to somewhere different, somewhere I wasn't quite prepared to go. I drank more of the waters, hoping that I might be able to carry some of the memories with me, and my head flooded with gentle visions of Mother Bev trying to free tangles in her daughter's hair with the combs I kept having to make her, and the most evocative answers of 'whatsit' that Moussa concocted, and the time Jardin kissed me on the cheek when I first lent her a crank-fan.

Shilah and Cam were there, but most of all I felt my memories of Abb trickle into my heart, and spread out with a deep sense of comfort. I could feel his powerful hands at my back as he sewed together a deep gash, and the time he'd accidentally triggered my Colour Wheel, laughing together until our throats burned as we tried to scrub the dyes off his face.

The current speeded up, and some instinct in me knew I was closing in on the edge.

The end.

I didn't feel the need to panic. I'd left that above too. The river felt as natural as breathing. The tears were calm and cool, and mostly I just wondered what Matty had been thinking as he rode these waters not so long ago. I hoped he'd thought of me kindly as the precipice came closer.

The current increased to impossible speeds, rocking up and down, and I felt my body surge into open air. Tumbling through emptiness. I didn't feel dizzy, or upset, or even properly sad. Life undressed itself from my shoulders, and my dreams of things left un-invented gently strained through the tiny holes in my mind, and my essence dissolved into the beautiful black nothing.

And then peace.

. . .

. . .

. . .

. . .

. . .

. . .

. . .

. . .

. . .

. . .

. . .

'Where are you?'

The words came from everywhere at once.

It had been an eternity since I'd had to communicate, so I closed my soul again and rested.

. . .

. . .

. . .

. . .

. . .

. . .

'Where are you?'

A pinpoint of golden light burst into the dark. The spot was tiny, but against the black it was everything.

It came closer, not in a straight line, but as if blindly searching for me. I tried to curl back into the darkness, like a pinch of sand tucking itself back into the bottom of a dune, but the light continued its annoying search, hurting what were once my eyes.

'Where are you?' the light asked. 'I can't see you. They put it in the ground.'

I remembered someone who used to say something along those lines, but I didn't care enough to throw off the blanket, and I pulled death more tightly around my body, tucking in the edges.

. . .

. . .

. . .

. . .

. . .

. . .

'Please,' the voice said after another hundred lifetimes. 'It's not supposed to be this way. I'm sorry. I've been ready for so long.'

I sighed, peeking out and trying not to wince against the harsh light.

'How?' I asked. 'How can I help you, so you might leave me alone?'

'The whole thing is a lie,' it said.

'Well, who was the one who told it?' I asked, annoyed, pushing myself back under.

Silence.

. . .

. . .

. . .

. . .

'You're a Jadan,' the light said. 'I need a Jadan.'

'Yes. I was a Jadan.' My voice sounded odd, muffled through eternity.

'I've been waiting so long. I suffer too, you know. Where are you? They put something in the ground.'

'What did they put in the ground?' I asked with a sigh.

'I don't know,' it said. 'The end?'

I shook what was once my head.

. . .

. . .

. . .

. . .

. . .

'Where are you?'

It was interesting to smile again after so long, but the movement didn't come back easily. 'You're not going to let me rest, are you?' I asked.

'Only a Jadan can help me.'

I grumbled, but then realized the light was pure and wonderful, and for a moment I didn't know why I'd been pushing it away. It was so grand that darkness itself quaked underneath.

'You can invent it,' it said.

'Invent what?' I asked.

'Where are you?'

I waved my arms, but then I realized that that movement could only happen in the past, so I stopped. 'Invent what?'

'Langria.'

'Langria? What's that?'

'Freedom. Life. Everything. Put it back to how it was. How I made it the first time.'

I tasted the tears again, like a rash from chains. 'I thought Langria was already real.'

'You have to make it real.'

'Then I can rest?' I asked.

Silence.

'How do I make Langria?' I asked.

'Aren't you an Inventor?'

'Not yet,' I said. 'Was I?'

The light pulsed, golden hues knocking at my door. I shrugged what were once my shoulders and it came in.

Then the most spectacular thing.

Ice.

Ice only existed in legends; the old, alive version of me never understanding what it could possibly feel like. But at a single touch I understood. This was what the Crier was made of, what He'd been trying to give our people for so long. Ice, that lived in the deep darkness; Ice was forever. I remembered certain things: an idea. Two ideas. About Cold in the sky and the stars.

'You think I can reach them?' I gasped.

'You're an Inventor.'

'Come with me,' I said, my edges still crackling with Cold. 'Come back and help me.'

'You'll have help. But I can't.'

That was when I finally felt how trapped the voice was. The gold couldn't be lifted from the darkness unless from the other side. I heard the river in the distance, splashing in my direction. I let out my eternal sigh, breathing away the last of my non-existence.

'Build it,' the light said as the waters found me. 'My Jadan Inventor.'

'I'll try,' I said.
'Promise.'
'I promise.'
'Where are you?

The wool was peeled from my head and I gasped as the street came back into view, the fading Sunlight nearly breaking my eyes. The intense smell of salts ambushed my mind, keeping me afloat.

'Where are you?' the Vicaress asked, waving the vial under my nose.

Life was too vivid and I wanted to scream, but a piece of boilweed had been shoved into my mouth to keep me from doing just that. All the thirst and aches and pain from fresh wounds returned at once, all the things she'd done to get me to talk, and I closed my eyes, desperate to return to that blackness. My shoulders were on fire, arms still locked above my head, chains taut and keeping me from the ground.

I once again felt the sears on my ribcage where the fiery blade had pierced me. And the missing bits of flesh on my knuckles. And the stiffness of the dried blood on my calves, and the bruises driven deep into the bones of my forearms.

But I hadn't broken. Shilah was still safe. The Jadan Garden was still safe.

'Welcome back, Spout. Don't think you're done yet,' the Vicaress said, tossing a cup of water at my side and throwing in a Wisp.

'Maybe he doesn't know her,' Thoth said gently. 'Perhaps this Moussa was mistaken?'

The Vicaress looked at him, a curious tilt of her head. 'Does the Crier speak to you too? Are you a holy now, Jadanmaster?'

It was curious to see Thoth standing up for me, and it made me wonder how pitiful my body must have looked.

I'd never felt so thirsty in my life, even after Abb had walked me to the banks of the Kiln.

'Apologies, Highness.' Thoth bowed, low and deep. 'I just meant your time is most valuable. I can take over for you if you like? I've memorized the *Compendium* myself, and—'

The Vicaress held up her gloved hand for silence. 'This is my work.'

Thoth bowed once more, stepping back and letting her return to my torture.

I was tempted to dismiss everything that had happened as a hallucination, just a bunch of visions firing in my mind as it was ripped apart, but something told me the voice couldn't be ignored. I could still hear the words in my ears, could still feel the touch of golden Ice at my core.

I'd spoken with the Crier.

A presence that needed me to live.

I just had to get through the next bouts of torture until they got bored. I'd scream and scream, give the Vicaress every agonizing sound she wanted, stretch my threshold to the limits.

But secretly my mind would be elsewhere.

The wool had drained me of water, but now there was something different running through my veins.

If the Vicaress killed me, fine.

If not, I had my own work to do. And Shilah and Cam were going to help me.

The Vicaress yanked the piece of boilweed from my mouth and I spat out a mouthful of blood to the stones at my feet. She gave me a delighted look, picking up another cup of water and forcing it down my throat.

Then she pulled the wool back over my eyes, the heat returning.

'Gather your screams,' her voice said, close to my ear. 'We'll try again in a few hours.'

Chapter Twenty-two

I was still blinded by wool, but I knew that distinct creak of metal, blades lifting apart. The safety latch had been opened, and the fast little clicks were calling out, notches that had been dug into the pole to give warning that the mouth was about to bite.

I would have recognized those sounds anywhere.

Mostly because I'd built the damn thing.

'Hmmm?' the taskmaster said in front of me, followed by a rustle of cloth. 'What the—'

I'd never heard the Stinger actually pierce flesh before, and the sound was uncomfortably satisfying. I felt a bit guilty for how sharp the blades must have been as they sliced through the guard's skin, but then again, I'd designed it that way; to be faster, and with less mess.

Then came the whoosh of the springs, the pop of the trigger capsule, and I knew the guard was done for, poisoned with enough scorpion venom to take down two Slab Hagans. The guard made a few half-hearted grumbles, but they didn't last long before his body hit stone.

The wool was peeled from my eyes, and the boilweed plucked from my mouth, and I came face to face with my rescuer, outlined by starlight. She had red Khatberry juice smeared over her face to lessen the shine of her lovely skin, and she blended well with the dark.

The guard was lying on his stomach, the Stinger lodged in his back, all three blades of the mouth buried in deep.

'You should have given me two vials,' Shilah said, a dark smile on her face. 'What if there was another guard? How would I have saved you then?'

I spat out the globs of leftover blood and boilweed, and licked my dry lips. There was just enough moisture to make a few desperate sounds. I drew attention to the chains with a rattle of my numb arms. 'Not saved yet.'

Shilah unslung a waterskin from her chest and tipped it up to my mouth, the cool relief splashing down my throat. I started to choke, and she slowed the flow, her fingers careful and tender. I looked over Shilah's shoulder at Arch Road. It was empty save for the limp body, but I knew the Vicaress would be coming back soon.

'How'd you find me?' I asked.

She chuckled, walking her fingers through the air. 'Like I said, you're very slow. Turns out you're even slower when you're chained to a wall.'

I smiled, irritating a few blisters on my lips. 'I didn't tell her.'

'About what?'

'What do you think?' I leaned in, the chains rattling. 'I know what I have to do. What we have to do together. I think it's why you're here.'

'I'm here because the Vicaress is an evil, lying, Sun-baked piece of shit. And she was hurting my partner.' Shilah reached into her pocket and pulled out a few long threads of metal. 'I assume you'll be able to use these?'

I tried to flex my fingers. Nothing at first, but as the cool water began to splash across my insides, they freed up. I nodded to her palm. 'That one. Third from the right.'

Shilah came close, her body folding against mine. Her dark hair brushed my chin and I inhaled her familiar smell.

'You smell terrible,' Shilah said with a smile, sniffing my neck. 'You shouldn't do this any more.'

I angled the metal into the shackles and began to feel for the give in the lock. Her eyes were narrowed as she scrutinized it herself. Catching the look on my face at her proximity, she winked at me, but kept her gaze focused. 'Just pretend I'm your Cold Wrap.'

I moved the metal in and out more quickly, trying to find the release. The Khatberry juice on Shilah's skin made her smell like the Garden. But I couldn't afford this kind of distraction. We needed a plan.

'We have to go to the Manor,' I said.

'What Manor?'

'Cam's Manor. The High Nobleboy from the library,' I said, almost tripping the pin. 'He'll take you in too. Partner.'

I could feel her body tense up at the declaration. 'A High Noble Manor?'

'I spoke to . . .' I knew how foolish it was going to sound, but the promise I'd made still rang in my ears. 'I think I spoke to the Crier.'

'What are you babbling about? I can get you more water.'

I paused. 'I think I died. And talked to Him.'

She finally pulled away from me, dropping her gaze from the shackles. 'You sound pretty confident for a dead person.'

'Maybe not died then,' I said, wishing she could feel what was in my heart. The Ice. The voice. 'But I went somewhere beyond. And He told me I had to invent it.'

'Invent what?'

'Langria.'

Shilah's voice took on an edge as she tapped under her shirt where I knew the map would be. 'How about we just *find* it? I think that might be easier than building it from scratch.'

I shook my head, resolute. 'It's not real yet. We have to make it.'

Shilah burst out laughing. 'I knew showing Little Langria would give you ideas, but I didn't think you'd take it this far.'

'What?' I asked. 'I'm being serious. The Crier told me Langria's not real. But I have an Idea that—'

Shilah's playfulness was gone. 'You're not joking?'

I shook my head, tripping the lock in one of the shackles, and moving to the other. 'I'm going to fly.'

Shilah folded her arms across her chest, looking at me as if I was crazy.

'Think about it,' I said, working fast, as I thought I heard voices in the distance. 'Cold only falls in the Khat's Patches since the Drought, right? But it used to fall everywhere. And what if it's still up there in the sky all around us. What if we could get to it?' It felt strange talking to someone about the Idea I'd been mulling over for so long, but it felt right hearing the words out loud. 'I'm going to invent something so that we can go up and get the Cold ourselves.'

Shilah's face was blank, expressionless through all the Khatberry juice smears.

My cheeks grew hot. I was hoping she'd at least be excited about the Idea. '*That's* freedom,' I said. 'The Khat can keep his Patches. We'll have our own way to get Cold. That's how we'll make Langria.'

'Micah.' She raised an eyebrow. 'This is impossible.'

Voices rang in the distance, only a few streets away, and I moved the metal thread in and out of the lock faster.

'We can't just go running into the sands with no Cold or friends or a plan. It's suicide,' I said, finally freeing myself from the shackles, rubbing my wrists as I stepped off my corner. My legs felt wobbly, and my ribs burned, but I knew I'd find strength on my path. The Idea clamoured to get off my tongue and move to my fingers. 'We'll go to the Manor's tinkershop. Cam will keep us safe. We can learn secrets, and I can try and build us our miracle. The Crier said—'

Shilah heard the voices too, her face darting to the side. 'If you'd really spoken with the Crier, then He would have told you you're an idiot. It's *impossible*.'

I gestured for her to follow me down Arch Road. We didn't have much time, as the noises were getting nearer. 'I thought a Jadan Garden was impossible.'

Shilah stood her ground. 'I'm not setting foot in a High Noble Manor. You have no idea what happens in places like that. I'm going to Langria.'

I felt myself grow angry, which I knew was incredibly inappropriate, as Shilah had just most likely saved my life. 'And what happens if I'm wrong and you actually find Langria? What about all the Jadans still here in Paphos? And Belisk? And the ones chained up in the Glasslands? Our people will still be slaves, so it changes nothing. We need to figure out how to make us free, not how to run away.'

Shilah took a quick, sharp breath, her face so fierce I felt like taking a step back. Then a deep sadness crossed her eyes, and without another word she darted into the alley and began running.

'Shilah!' I called, instantly realizing I'd shouted. The nearby voices suddenly stopped.

Shilah didn't turn back, disappearing into the darkness. I gritted my teeth, thinking about how foolish she was being, and then I began limping as fast as I could in the opposite direction, away from the nearing voices.

I was two streets away and one rooftop over when I heard men's voices shouting for the Vicaress. The taskmasters had discovered my corner vacant, the chains empty, but that didn't concern me any longer. It would be a long, hard trek, but I'd make it through the city and to the Tavor Manor.

I kept crawling, my whole body screaming in protest, but

I silenced my aches with a glance at the Pyramid. The Crying had just started in the distance, and I watched the thousands of streaks of life falling onto the sands beyond.

I thought about Matty's birds, and about flying, and about all the Cold up in the night sky waiting to be collected. I thought about buckets, and straight backs, and Abb's secret meeting at the barracks, and I pushed through the pain.

I was going to break the Khat's hold on the world.

PART THREE

Chapter Twenty-three

Licking my palms, I moistened the dried blood on my chest and drew the red smears across my face. The more pitiful I looked, the better the chance the guards might believe my lie.

Looming in front of the eastern gate were two massive Jadans, the biggest I'd ever seen. They stood rigid, holding spears so thick the metal shafts might as well have been extensions of their meaty forearms. Great slabs of armour didn't dent their stances in the slightest, and their skin was so dark even Moussa looked Noble in comparison.

In the dim starlight I could only just make out the Tavor sigil branded into each of their foreheads, and I hoped I wouldn't have to undergo such scarring to be welcomed in the Manor. Beneath the symbol, the guards' faces were focused and fierce. Rumours had it any Jadan selected to be a guard received special treatment to guarantee complete and utter obedience. Rumour also had it that the woman leading those long treatments wore black robes and had a knife that danced with fire.

I couldn't rely on the guards seeing me as family, but I had to try to provoke enough pity by making myself look truly helpless, since it was long after curfew and the guards had every right to cut my neck on the spot.

Taking a deep breath, I limped from behind the dune, dragging my left foot along the sands, only having to exaggerate my pain slightly after my encounter with the Vicaress this afternoon.

They spotted me instantly.

'That's far enough,' one of them barked, his voice gliding across the sands.

I limped closer, making my way out of the sands and onto the stone street leading up to the gates. The cuts on my chest burned like Sun had touched my skin directly, and I had half a mind to take off my shirt so they could see all the damage.

'Enough!' the other guard said.

I kept my eyes down and my arm nursed over my chest, as if it were too painful to let it hang freely. Dragging myself down the road, I made sure my whimpering was audible.

The taller guard thrust his spear out as I closed in, the point shining with menace. He waved it through the air to gather my attention.

I kept looking down.

'Think he's deaf?' the guard with the crooked nose asked under his breath.

The shorter one shrugged and stuck out his spear as well, waving it about. 'Stop there, kid!'

I pretended I was afraid, putting one hand up to defend my face, hoping I'd just look like another dirty Jadan. The Vicaress might have already put out a name and a description that could have beaten me here, and I had to be careful until I was inside with Cam.

'I'm sorry, sir,' I called, making my lips quiver. 'I can't hear very well! He pierced my eardrum. Said he'd pierce the other if I didn't finish the errand tonight.'

'Who?' the short guard asked, with no sympathy punctuating the question. 'Why? Talk louder.'

I let out a single sob.

'Speak, boy!' Crooked Nose barked.

I knew almost nothing of High Noble politics, but I did know from Cam that the Tavors had a strong rivalry with the Erridians, and so I decided that my best bet was to play on that. 'I was g-given an er-rrand,' I stammered out, careful to keep angled so the starlight wouldn't reveal my face. 'I have to deliver a message. To the High Nobleboy Camlish. Tonight.'

'Where's your token?'

'What, sir?'

'Your TOKEN,' he said, exaggerating the movements of his mouth.

I let my fingers shake, pressing my hand against my ear. 'He didn't give me one in case I got caught. Didn't want anyone to know who sent me.'

Short Guard pulled his spear back and pointed to a small table beside them. 'Leave the message there. Then go.'

I let out another sob, sad that I had to play such a wretched creature. 'I can't, sir. I can't. I wasn't allowed to write it down. The High Nobleman from House Erridian—' I stopped myself, eyes widening as I threw my hand over my mouth. 'The message has to go to Camlish Tavor, personally. No parchment. I was beaten for every word I didn't memorize.' I lowered my gaze, letting my arm flop down. 'I finally got it right, though.'

The guards gave each other a silent look, conversation jumping between their eyes. I could tell I wasn't impressing them.

'Please, SIR!' I cried out, coughing at the end. It was a real cough, and in fact, I was starting to feel woozy from all the talking. 'If he finds out I didn't tell Nobleboy Camlish personally, he'll kill me. Please, sir. I don't want to die. I want to serve the Khat. Please. He told me—'

Crooked Nose let out a grunt of annoyance. 'Fine, just stop whining. I swear, your generation is thin as soggy boilweed. A little blood and you go all soft. Wait here.' He spun the numbers on the lock and the gates clicked open. 'I'll get Master Camlish.'

Short Guard kept a suspicious watch over me as his partner went inside.

What felt like forever passed, my heart hammering, but eventually Cam arrived at the gates in his silk nightclothes. I was glad he hadn't taken a moment longer, because my head was spinning so badly I almost didn't recognize him at first.

Cam's eyes shot awake at the sight of me, and he rushed forward. 'Spout! Are you okay?'

Crooked Nose gently put his spear between us. 'Careful, sir. These Street Jadans are nasty. And he's got many open wounds.'

The guard's tone struck me as odd, as if his blood wasn't as Jadan as mine. I angled my face, giving Cam the smallest shake of my head. 'I don't know what Spout is, sir. But I have a message for you. From my master.'

Cam paused, confusion thick upon his face. 'But—'

I rubbed my ear. 'It's a secret message, sir.'

Cam thankfully seemed to pick up on the ploy. Scrunching his face in the most disdainful way possible, he exclaimed, 'Shivers and Frosts! What is this nonsense?' His spoiled tone was a match for my injured one. 'You dare wake me in the middle of the night for a message, little slave?'

'I'm sorry, sir,' I called out, putting my head down. 'I was told I had to tell you a message personally or else they'd kill my family and then they'd kill me.' I knew I was laying it on thick, but now that Cam was here, I felt free to do so. 'I'm sorry. No one else is allowed to hear it.'

I limped forward, keeping my head tilted to the side and in shadow.

'Close enough,' Short Guard announced when I was only a few paces away.

'Very well, *slave*,' Cam said with a sneer. He pushed the spear aside, making room to come through. 'If my message is to be private, let it be private.'

'Be careful, Master Tavor,' Crooked Nose said. 'He might have weapons on him.'

Cam waved a dismissive hand, walking forward. 'Bah! These little Jadans are harmless. No spines at all. I'm in no danger.'

He came over to me and leaned in, both the guards stiffening instantly.

'What happened?' Cam whispered. 'You look terrible. Why aren't I supposed to know you? What's going on?'

'I'm in trouble,' I said softly. 'The Vicaress is looking for me.'

'Why? Oh, Spout. You look like death.' Cam swallowed hard. 'What happened? Do you need water? Medicine?'

'Can you get me inside?' I asked, my vision narrowing at the sides.

Cam backed away and nodded seriously to the guards. 'Very well. I guess that is an important message.' He grabbed my collar and pulled me through the gates. 'Come with me.'

Short Guard started to protest. 'Sir, what are you doing?'

'I'm going to write him an answer to take back, obviously.'

Crooked Nose nervously cleared his throat. 'Young Master Tavor, sir. Your father said—'

Cam got right up in the guard's face – even though he only reached his chest. 'I'm the Tavor here. I'll do whatever I please. What right do you have to stop me?'

The guard nodded. 'Very well. My apologies, Master Camlish.'

'Don't worry about this little slave,' Cam scoffed. 'I'll send him out of the west gates later. And no word of this to my father, or I'll have you both sent to the Quarry.'

Cam dragged me along the path of stones leading from the iron gates. A dozen paces away stood a long clay wall, too tall to see over. He shouldered open a door in the centre, hurling us through.

My jaw dropped as we landed in a different world.

A river of grass flowed outwards, the deep green colour pure in the starlight. Not a drop of sand dusted the blades, underneath was only dark brown soil. Long spikes of grass stretched towards the sky like tiny pikes. I looked in both directions, and found that the garden seemed to surround the entire Manor. The whole place bustled with life, making Little Langria look like a single potted plant. To my left, vines crept across trellises, bearing bright berries. Thick trunks were feathered with leaves, fruit tucked in every crevice. And there were wiry bushes dripping with yellow pods. Tubs of Cold waited nearby, more than I'd ever seen in one place, with little ducts at their bases that could wind water through the dark soil.

A dozen Domestic Jadans tended the garden. They wore uniforms unique to the Tavor Manor, tools in hand to work the soil. They were wonderfully pretty, their hair long and combed, but their expressions were sunken and hollow. I knew with faces like that, they probably had to suffer far worse errands than purchasing hand fans and delivering parchment. For Nobles, beauty was a gift, but for Jadan girls, it was just another kind of chain.

'Sorry about the way I talked to the guards,' Cam said. 'I hope I didn't offend you with any of that.'

I didn't respond, my throat tightening.

The girls were spreading Cold water along the grass, their faces haunted and expressions blank. A few had trouble walking, even though their legs had no visible wounds, and they looked over at us with silent desperation.

Cam followed my eyes, his face going pale at my expression. 'I don't touch them, I swear. I would never hurt them. Ever.'

'It's okay,' I managed to cough out, my head too light for comfort. I could feel the Vicaress's blade digging around in my chest once again, and I didn't realize it until now, but I was in quite bad shape. 'Inside, please. Hide.'

Cam nodded, putting a hand on my shoulder to keep me steady. 'Come on. I have the perfect place. Just for now.'

He ushered me out of the garden and towards a set of small doors off to the side. We entered the Manor into what must have been just a hallway, but looked to me like a Palace. The air was devastatingly Cold, and the floor was tiled in beautiful black and white marble. Iron candelabras lit the place with musky-smelling candles, and ornate tapestries draped down the walls; lining the walls were cabinets full of shiny trinkets on display. The Tavor crest showed up every-where, from diamond-encrusted plaques to embroidered tapestries, to wooden instruments hung up with the crest branded along their bodies.

But what really sent me over the edge were the pedestals.

Through the hallway, prominently displayed on wooden podiums, were Chills nearly as big as my head. I rarely saw Cold that size, as it was too valuable, and never entrusted to Street Jadans. And each Chill had a coloured Closed Eye painted on it.

This Cold, each one capable of cooling a huge pool of water for days at a time, was out on display. Not used to keep the Tavors alive, or to buy things they might need, or even to grow bigger gardens.

It was an outrage.

When Cam spoke again, all I could hear was the blood rushing in my ears.

'Spout,' he said. 'Come on. We need to get you off your feet.'

I tried to answer, but the pain and emotion were too much for me, and I toppled over, everything going black.

*　　*　　*

'Spout.'

I jerked awake, trying to remember where I was. I sucked in a desperate breath, but the air was too cool for the barracks, and the walls too close to my sides. Pain registered in every one of my bones and joints. A blind panic rose in me but Cam's face appeared in front of mine, and he snapped his fingers to keep me focused.

'Spout,' Cam said. 'It's okay. Here. Drink.'

Something was pushed onto my chest, and my fingers scrambled up the pouch, my throat so dry that I couldn't speak. I tilted the water into my mouth, but found it was thick and syrupy. Even drinking was an effort.

'What happened to him?' another voice asked.

'I think he was tortured,' Cam said, adjusting his golden glasses.

'Course he was.' The words were slightly slurred. 'Khat-damn course he was.'

Silence.

'Spout,' Cam said, his attention returning to me. 'Drink all of it.'

I tried harder, but the water still tasted brackish and thick, and every gulp was painful. As I regained full consciousness, I realized I was in a storage room, and that I'd been nestled on top of a pile of soft sheets.

A candle came closer to my face, making me cringe away. I still couldn't make out the face behind it, and the light hurt my eyes.

'Will it fix him?' Cam asked, hopeful. 'Can you fix him?'

A feeble laugh. 'He'll be up and getting tortured again in no time.'

'He can help you, Leroi,' Cam said. 'He can do what you do.'

'I hope that's not true.' The voice paused and I heard gulping sounds. 'Because that'd make him just as useless.'

'Drink, Spout.'

I choked down the last sip of my water, which burned my throat. My body began tingling, numbness rising through my feet, and things began to go dark again, the candle dimming right in front of my eyes. I smacked my lips and realized it wasn't water I'd been drinking, and that everything about me was starting to sag. My lips felt the need to babble. 'I have the Idea. The Crier said. The gold light. I know what I have to—'

'Don't try to talk, Spout,' Cam said soothingly. 'It's one of Leroi's tonics, to help you sleep. And to heal. We brought a wheelbarrow and a blanket to get you to the tinkershop so no one sees. Leroi is going to—'

'Who says I'm going to do anything?' the voice protested. 'You said the Vicaress was after him.'

'He's smart, Leroi. You should have seen the music box, he—'

But I was gone.

Chapter Twenty-four

'Do you hate me?'

I don't know how the man knew I was awake before I did, but I opened my eyes, and slowly sat up from the cot. I expected pain from my wounds, but all I felt was an intense hunger stretching down to my core.

My hand went to my stomach, the gurgling loud.

A small number of wax candles burned in the room. Considering one of the last things I remembered Cam mentioning was the tinkershop, I hadn't expected to wake up in a dark, plain room with nothing but two padded chairs, a single table, and a small bed sitting flush against the back wall.

A man was hovering over the table, his silvered hair peeking out in all directions and a goatee surrounding his mouth. His lips were thin and thoughtful, and he had what was undoubtedly the palest complexion of any Noble I'd ever seen. The clothes hung loose on his frame, and it looked as though he hadn't eaten in weeks.

Without a word, he unfolded his arms and pointed at the side of the cot. My eyes followed his fingers and I found half a dozen orangefruits sitting nearby. I dug in without further invitation, the hunger all-consuming, and bit straight into the rinds.

'Camlish said you like those,' the man said. 'He brought them yesterday. The tonic works, but it burns up all your reserves.'

'Yesterday?' I asked between furious bites.

The man nodded, sitting down in his chair and pouring himself a drink from a decanter and then fitting the cork back on top. I could smell the tang of alcohol all the way from across the room.

'You didn't answer my question,' the man asked, swirling the drink, the candlelight revealing a disturbed look that could have rivalled the Domestics' in the garden. 'Do you hate me?'

Needless to say, I was taken aback. Not only had I only just met the man, but if this was who I thought it was, he was in a position to teach me everything I wanted to know.

'Are you Leroi?' I asked, chewing the last bit of pulp from the first orangefruit.

He sucked his teeth. 'Would it change your answer if I were?'

I nodded, diving into the next fruit. 'I couldn't hate a real Inventor.'

Leroi slammed his fist on the table. 'I'm a High Noble. I'm your enemy. I'll never be in line for the throne, but I'm a High blasted Noble.' He spilled some of his drink to the floor, but didn't seem to notice. 'Descended from the first Khat's bloodline. Whoop-a-dee-doo. Praise be to the bastard.'

I kept quiet, wondering whether this was all some sort of test.

The rest of his drink was gone in one gulp. His eyes fell upon the candle on the table and he went quiet for some time, staring into the flame.

'Sir,' I said carefully. 'I—'

'Jadan bodies tell stories.' Leroi picked up the decanter, not letting his glass stay empty for long. 'You've been whipped more times than I could count; cut; burned; tortured. Your arm's been broken twice. You have no fat on you, so I know you've been starved most of your life. And even now, in my very Cold study, you're sweating. Most slaves don't do that. I'm guessing that's where "Spout" comes from. Am I wrong?'

A finger went to my forehead. I was only nervous because I didn't want to say something that might have all of this taken away. I was so close. If this was his study, then real inventions waited on the other side of the door.

'He was just as Jadan as everyone else,' Leroi said quietly. 'The first Khat. Us High Nobles don't like to talk about that too much, but he was.'

My body jerked at the declaration, especially coming from someone like him. I touched my face and then pointed to Leroi's milky skin, bringing attention to the stark difference. 'He had to be different in *some* way.'

Leroi waved a flippant hand. 'Bah. That's just eight hundred years of your people slaving under a scorching Sun. And breeding control. But in a way you *are* right.' Leroi snorted, rolling the cork around in his palm. 'The first Khat was *less* than Jadan.'

I sucked in a breath. I'd never heard any Nobles talk like this before. Let alone High Nobles. The Priests and Gospels told us that the first Khat was pure, immune to sin, and that's why he was chosen.

'They why'd the Crier choose him?' I asked, feeling him out, my chest rattling on top of a frantic heartbeat. 'There had to be some reason.'

'Why, indeed?' Leroi said, stroking his goatee. 'Why do High Nobles have shorter natural lifespans? Why do High Nobles get diseases that Jadans are immune to? Like firepox. Sunspots. Achemede's shakes. Fang-rash. Hmm?'

My whole body went tense, the dizziness in my head not just from the tonic. These were questions I'd often thought about asking, but never found the right time or person. Abb only knew about Jadan diseases, which were few and often mild.

'I don't know, sir,' I said, swallowing hard, the citrus from the orangefruit burning the cuts on my lips.

'Are these not important questions?'

'They are! I just—'

'He enslaved his own people,' Leroi said, flushed with anger, squeezing the cork till it sqeaked. 'How does that make my kind "Noble"?'

I paused, finally starting to understand what he wanted to hear. Perhaps it was the haze, but I felt bolder than normal. 'I guess we're going to have to even things out.'

Leroi's eyes narrowed, and then he snorted, as if what I'd said was quite funny. 'Is that right? And what are you proposing?'

'We create something new.'

Leroi sat back in his chair, licking his lips. 'Create, huh?'

'Cam told me you're an Inventor,' I said, fingers itching to get out into the main chamber and just touch everything there. 'You make things that didn't exist before. You make the World Cried better.'

'You already know me so well.' Leroi gave a series of quick nods, eyebrows raised in a sarcastic manner. 'You're referring to the anklets of course.'

I went quiet.

'Camlish told you about my special anklets, right?' Leroi asked, the corners of his lips turned up in a wry smile. 'What I've been commanded to do? How I'm making the World Cried better.'

I shook my head.

Leroi sucked down another drink, his eyes lighting up with glazed delight. '*Lord* Tavor didn't tell me the plan exactly. But it's obvious.'

'What are the anklets, sir?' I asked. His words were

beginning to slur, and I didn't know how much longer we had until the last of his sobriety was washed away.

Leroi bit his lip, holding back a laugh. 'If you stay here long enough, you'll get one too. Crier knows how long I'll be able to keep you secret.' His eyes filled with humour. 'With the Vicaress after you, I can't get you proper papers. You'll have to hide under the floor like a beetle if anyone comes.'

'Does that mean you'll take me in?' I asked, heart thumping. I couldn't believe my body felt so healed already. The man's tonic had worked wonders, and it was obvious he knew the kind of secrets that might help me realize my Idea. I felt invincible. 'Because I know what I need to build.'

'What *you* need to build? You're the Head Tinkerer here already?' Leroi chuckled. 'That was fast.'

'No, sir.' I shook my head, life flooding my chest. 'But Cam told me you've stopped Inventing. I figure at least one of us should put this place to use.'

Leroi scratched his goatee, and then burst out laughing. 'Who are you?'

'My name is Micah Behn-Abb.' I sat up straight, trying to make my back like Shilah's. 'I've tinkered all my life with materials I found in the refuse heaps. I've had to work in secret, and in the dark, while friends around me have died. But I've created things that make my barracks better. And I've spoken to the World Crier. I believe that He led me here so that together we can Invent something to end the Great Drought.'

A heavy silence buzzed about the study.

Then Leroi let out a roar of hilarity. 'So the Vicaress actually tortured you into madness. I don't blame you for breaking. I've heard stories of what she does to Jadans.'

I got up, my legs no longer wobbly. 'What can I do to prove to you that I'm supposed to be here?'

Leroi stared at me for a long moment. It was rare that I

saw such intelligence in a set of eyes, even through the veil of alcohol. Eventually he reached for the decanter, taking a deep swig right from the bottle.

'I had an assistant before,' Leroi said, his eyes glowing with relief as he downed the liquid. 'It didn't end well.'

'And you'll have one again,' I said, keeping my voice like stone, 'and this time it will.'

'You think you have the mind for it?' Leroi took another swig, longer this time, and I worried for his safety. 'The discipline?'

I kept my back straight, trying to look as defiant as my partner. My back ached from the posture. 'Yes, sir. I do.'

He picked up the decanter again and chugged the rest of the drink. Closing his eyes and making a satisfied face, he settled back into his chair. 'Then go Invent. And wake me when you're done.'

I waited for further instruction, but none seemed to be coming.

'What shall I make?' I asked.

Leroi spoke with his eyes closed. 'I don't care. You're the one who's been tinkering all your life, *Micah Behn-Abb, Behn-Crier*. Go ahead, no one will bother you, I chained the main door.' He made a shooing motion. 'The tinkershop is right down there.'

I leaned against the door for support, my eyes flitting around the large room in wild abandon.

It was my own personal promised land.

Now I understood why Leroi would need a bare room to hand, because after one glance I was already overwhelmed.

First and foremost were the lights.

I had no idea what I was looking at. Blazing across the room were little glass domes, but instead of holding normal candles they glowed fuzzy white, so brightly that if Leroi had told me he'd trapped little pieces of Sun inside, I might have believed him.

The domes illuminated a giant room, bigger than my barracks, and every wall contained a nook, an alcove or a side passage. Every available space housed a machine or an invention. Most of them I didn't recognize. There were things that made sense, like the huge crank-fans, and the shelves of Cold Bellows, but there were also things I'd never seen in all the streets of Paphos: hourglasses filled with metal beads that fell upwards. A pool in the centre of the room, filled with gears instead of water, all interlocked and spinning. And small pyramids made of glass, Wisps floating in their liquid centres and somehow not dissolving.

Most tables were weighed down by large clay pots from which metallic wires snaked out and led to buckets underneath. An army of barrels brimmed with white sand that, knowing the exuberant wealth of the Tavor family, could be salt. A whole section of the room was dedicated to glass vials, filled with everything from slimy green paste, to milky smoke, to what looked like powdered bone.

An anvil waited patiently in front of a desolate fireplace, saddled with water buckets and sets of heavy gloves. On the shelves along the walls I saw a hundred different types of metal parts jumbled with instruments with too many angles and strings to be usable, and buckets of Wisp and Drafts, as if the Cold were as common as sand. There were meticulous piles of rare woods, and stacks of coloured glass. Lining the left wall were bookshelves overflowing with scrolls, flanked by cabinets bursting with mysterious trinkets.

Shutting my eyes, I listened to the few light hums and whirrs spinning through the air, trying to pinpoint which machines were still awake. Leroi might have stopped tinkering, but there was magic here.

I concentrated on breathing as I wandered around the

room. Each step brought a hundred new things to touch and spin and ogle, but I kept my hands at my sides, not sure what inventions might unexpectedly bite back and take off a finger, like the boxy metal frame filled with rotating spikes that looked as if it would chomp twice given the chance.

As I wandered through the mechanical wonders and the rivers of material shelves, I felt nervous beads of sweat on my forehead, trying to conjure an Idea that could prove my worth. Shilah was wrong. This was where I needed to be, and I pitied her. I wished she'd made the right decision to come here with me instead of wandering through the empty sands alone.

I stepped over a tub filled with pulped boilweed and found my answer stacked in neat sheets.

How fitting to start this new journey where the last big one had begun, especially considering the implications of the invention itself.

Piled high and precisely cut, the waxy paper called out to me with a smile.

I returned the expression.

I'd created the original with rusty tools and bent metal in darkness. Recreating it in a real tinkershop would be easy. My hands already knew what to do, and in no time the needles and gears and other pieces needed had leapt into my fingers. I grabbed a few sheets of fabric from the top and found a clean table on which to work.

It was time to make another Cold Wrap.

Three loud knocks echoed through the shop and my eyes jumped to the door.

The chain rattled, a nose peeking through the gap. 'Spout? Can you let me in?'

My stomach uncurled at Cam's voice. I stuffed my quill back in the bottle of ink, only a few strokes away from the final touches.

I hopped around the machine that dripped waste into a

grate in the floor, and the wheelless cart loaded with huge fan blades. I raced up the staircase leading to the main door of the tinkershop, undid the chain, and let Cam in.

The door swung open. Cam was holding a tray laden with meat, cheese, fruit, and doughy bread. I'd only ever eaten stale crusts, baked with leftover, thrown-out grease, and this loaf looked wonderfully pillowy and soft.

'Spout! You look like a new Jadan.' Cam thrust the tray at me. 'Leroi said the tonic would make you hungry.'

I was indeed famished, and I plucked off the first piece of fruit I could find, a little red thing with seeds on the sides, and popped it in my mouth. It was sweet, and juicy, and tasted so good I thought I might never eat anything better.

'Thank you for the orangefruits,' I said, licking the roof of my mouth, trying to taste everything about the fruit that I could. 'And this.'

'Orangefruit is the plural. And with strawberries you don't eat the leaf on top,' Cam said with a grin, pointing to my mouth.

I tilted my head, swallowing everything whole. 'Why not? It's green.'

'You sh—' Cam shook his head, peeking back over his shoulder. 'Never mind. I'm glad you're awake. But let me in, because as far as the rest of the Manor is concerned, Leroi doesn't have any assistants.'

I moved aside so he could lock us back in. He lowered the tray to me, and I snatched the rest of the strawberries with a sheepish grin.

'Has anyone ever told you that you snore really loudly?'

'I do?'

Cam nodded, tucking into the cheese, which looked to me like it might have gone bad. I wanted to point out the specks of blue on it, but he ate it so quickly that I didn't have time.

'It's like,' Cam tapped his lip, lost in thought, 'if a camel was rolling down a hill, but having fun.'

I smirked, wondering why Abb had never brought this to my attention.

And then fear and realization slammed together in my mind like two slabs of heavy stone, crushing the dreamy mood in which I'd been idiotically awash.

Abb.

I'd been so enamoured with the tinkershop that I hadn't even thought about the danger my father would be in. Leroi's tonic had left me sluggish and unconcerned, and like a fool I'd been flitting about the tinkershop puffed up with a false sense of pride and security, buzzing with purpose. I couldn't believe that worry over my father was only hitting me now, and I'd never felt so selfish in my life. The first place the Vicaress would check for me was my barracks, and she would do everything she could to get my family to talk.

And Moussa. Poor Moussa. Was he even still alive after her interrogation?

I coughed, spitting out some of the seeds.

Cam dodged the projectiles with a chuckle, somehow managing not to drop the food tray. 'You can eat those.'

'My father!' I said, nearly falling to my knees. 'She's going to go after him!'

'Abb?' Cam gave me a sceptical look, his glasses now sitting at the end of his nose. 'Shivers and Frosts, Spout! What kind of friend do you think I am? First thing I did was send out word to Mama Jana. She's been keeping her ear to the ground about your barracks and we've been sending notes back and forth every few hours.' He patted his shirt pocket, which was bulging at the moment. 'You're worth quite a bit of information.'

I couldn't breathe. 'You did? You have?'

Cam nodded sincerely. 'You and that Shiver girl are the talk of Paphos right now. Both vanishing into thin air. But from what I can tell, the Vicaress wants to keep her failures quiet, so she hasn't even shown up at your barracks yet. Everything is calm for now, and Abb is perfectly fine. I wanted to tell you, and checked on you a few times, but you were sound asleep.' His face suddenly went hard. 'Leroi was supposed to let you know. Where is he, anyway?'

I took a deep breath, trying to let Cam's words sink in and find my calm. 'Sleeping.'

'Sleeping?' Cam raised an eyebrow. 'Or *sleeping*?'

'You're right,' I said. I could barely talk over the sound of my thundering heart. 'He's a bit broken at the moment.'

Cam nudged me with an elbow. 'Good thing he works in a tinkershop. Broken. Right?'

I would have laughed, but I was nowhere close.

'Sorry,' Cam said, wrinkling his nose, as if finally smelling the obviously rotten cheese on the tray. 'Just trying to lighten the mood.'

I shrugged. 'No, it was funny. And I have a friend, Moussa, at the barracks. Can you find out about him as well?'

'Consider it done.'

A pause sat heavy between us.

'I'm glad you came to me,' Cam said softly. 'And that you're safe.'

I swallowed hard, not worthy of his kindness. 'Thank you.'

'So what have you been doing?' Cam asked, his returning chipperness grating against my layers of guilt. 'Polishing the equipment?'

I surveyed the magical land, a bit of enthusiasm finally peeking back through. 'Better.'

'Sorting the metals?'

I let the silence build for dramatic effect. 'He wants me to tinker something.'

Cam's eyebrows went up. 'Already?'

I nodded.

Cam plucked a slice of meat and chewed with his mouth

wide open, an evil grin in his eyes. 'Do I know how to pick them, or what? Spout. You've done me proud.'

I felt my cheeks flush. 'Do you want to see it?'

'See what?'

I gave him a blank look. 'What I made?'

Cam stopped chewing. A stray bit of meat flecked his chin. 'Already?'

'Already.'

'I thought he meant, like, to plan something for you to do before next Crierday. You *made* something? How?'

I gave a little bow. 'A natural, I guess.'

Leading him down the stairs and through the maze of shelves, we came to my work surface, cleared of everything except my invention, a cup of Wisps, and some inking supplies.

Cam set his tray down slowly, his hand absently going to his chest where the necklace sat. 'Is that trying to be the Opened Eye? I hate to break it to you, but it's a bit askew.'

'No.' I shook my head, picking up the quill and adding the few final distorted lines around the pupil.

'Not that I'm not all for what this almost-symbol represents,' Cam said with a smile, 'but I don't think badly decorating a shirt counts as *making* something.'

I sized Cam up for a moment. The Wrap would be a bit tight, but this time I'd remembered to build a release valve. 'Put it on.'

Cam pushed his glasses up his nose. 'Won't the ink run?'

I shook my head. 'I pressed hard. Now put it on.'

'Why's it got a box hanging off it?'

I paused, giving him a wry look. 'For someone who spat on a *very* holy painting, and who jumped in front of a whip for me, you seem *awfully* scared of a simple piece of clothing.'

Cam burst out laughing, his eyes twinkling. 'A natural.' He threaded the Wrap over his body, letting his arms hang at his sides as he looked it over. 'Hmm. Fashionable.'

'Okay, hold still.' I put a Wisp into the crushing chamber, and gave it a hard twist. Now that I'd been able to make this version of the Wrap with all the finest materials in the Khatdom, the device worked flawlessly, puffing out and holding the Cold air inside firm and tight. Cam's face lit up, not expecting the sensation, and he looked at me with a face full of awe.

The Opened Eye bloated outwards as the Wrap expanded, the symbol stretching into the right dimensions. It wasn't perfect, but it was close.

'*Now* it's the Opened Eye,' I said, running my foot across the smooth floor. 'Kind of neat, huh?'

Cam seemed at a loss for words, looking down over his chest.

'I call it a Cold Wrap,' I said. 'It holds the Cold in so you can walk around and battle Sun all day.'

'Tears above! It's so Cold!' Cam's teeth began to chatter, but his face was fixed in an expression of reverence. 'Spout. This is amazing. Everyone should have one. Why isn't this a real thing?'

A voice came from behind us: 'It is. It's called a Saffir.'

I spun around and found Leroi's gaunt body hiding in the shadow of a large shelf. I hadn't heard him come out of the study, and wondered how long he'd been watching.

'Thank the Crier, I thought you might be the Vicaress,' Cam said, hand over his chest. 'Why are you sneaking around in your own tinkershop, Leroi?'

'I've been watching,' Leroi replied, his voice quiet. I imagined he must have tinkered a recipe for a sobriety tonic as well, considering he should have been asleep from the amount of spirits he'd imbibed. 'I didn't want to interrupt Spout's work. Where did you see such a rare thing, Spout? Nobles never admit to wearing them publically. Did a Domestic describe one to you?' he asked gently.

'I just thought it would be a good idea, sir. I made one once before.'

Leroi's eyes narrowed. 'With your stolen scraps?'

'Yes.'

Leroi walked over to Cam to appraise my work. He looked closely at the crushing chamber, and even smiled at the design on the chest. 'This is good work, Spout,' he said. Then he turned back to look me in the eye. 'Tell me, I'd like to know. What did the Crier tell you? When you had your little chat.'

I was surprised at the question. 'Sir?'

Cam nearly choked, the flesh on his arms prickled from the Cold. 'Wait. You talked to the Crier?'

'Course he did,' Leroi said matter-of-factly, picking up a Wisp from the table and rolling it between his spindly fingers. There was a dark sort of amusement in his face. 'What did He say?'

'He told me that it's not supposed to be this way,' I said, trying not to be discouraged. 'He told me that they put it in the ground.'

Leroi's face jerked, settling into a frown. 'What did you just say?'

I lowered my eyes, feeling foolish. It had just been a hallucination from the pain, and the voice was just repeating what Old Man Gum used to babble. 'That's what I can remember. *They put it in the ground*, He kept saying. But I used to have a family member that said the same—'

Without another look at me, Leroi walked out of the room. After a long silence, I could hear the door to his study open. Before it slammed shut Leroi called back: 'You can stay.'

I turned to Cam, his face already busy with a hundred questions.

'What?' I asked.

Cam's body was quivering as he plucked at the Wrap around his chest. 'How do I get this thing off?'

Chapter Twenty-five

I'd been tinkering for a few hours when Cam's knocks sounded at the main door. Three raps – two fast, a pause, and then another – which was his way of letting me know it was safe, and that he was alone.

I laid down my tools to run up the steps and undo the heavy chain.

Cam checked the hallway behind him and then swept past me. He looked dishevelled, strands of his golden hair flying around him, and with dark circles under his eyes.

I locked behind us. 'Good to see you.'

'Good to see you too.' Cam smiled at me, although it was more like a wince. 'You look happy.'

My face was still flushed with excitement from setting the Glassland Blue in place on my latest invention. I still couldn't believe all the things I had to tinker with in the main chamber alone. 'Well, you're to thank. You're the only reason I'm here.'

Cam leaned back against the bannister on the stairs. He sighed. 'I just wish I could do the same for all the others in here. I try so hard, Spout, a compliment here, or a smile. I sneak them food and medicine, but most of them won't take it. No one wants to trust me.'

I nodded, unsure if I had anything to add.

'It's just— I'm so sick of how things are,' Cam said, clenching his teeth. 'The more I look, the worse it gets, and I'm completely powerless to help.'

I was almost afraid to ask, as a part of me had been waiting for the hammer to drop. 'Is it really getting worse out there?'

Cam swallowed, looking at the wall of instruments Leroi had displayed. I hadn't touched most of them: I'd blown over a few of the pipe sets but the sound had plucked my heart with thoughts of Moussa and I'd had to stop.

I tried to meet Cam's gaze, but he looked at the floor instead. 'It's okay. You can tell me,' I said.

Cam paused. 'There was another Cleansing yesterday.'

I tensed up. I'd gone a few hours without worrying about Abb, but now I was flooded with anxiety. 'Any word on . . .'

Cam nodded, still not meeting my eyes. 'Mama Jana says he's alive.'

My ears popped with relief, but my heart was still heavy.

'Was the Cleansing because of me?' I asked, trying to keep my voice steady.

Cam suddenly gripped my shoulders, facing me with a fierceness I hadn't seen in him before. 'This is all because of the Khat. Never forget that. Ever.'

I nodded, wishing that were possible.

Cam clucked his tongue. 'Is Leroi still in his study?'

I nodded, my stomach still trying to unknot. 'For going on two days straight now. He moved in all these machines and materials so he could make those anklets.'

Cam nodded, brushing down his hair. 'How do I look?' he asked archly.

I lifted an eyebrow. I hadn't failed to notice how silent both cousins became when I brought up the anklets. 'Don't change the subject.'

'Sorry, Spout.' Cam sighed, his hand going to the necklace

under his shirt. He started pacing. 'I'd rather not talk about it now though.'

I shrugged, unsure of what to say.

Cam started pacing awkwardly around the room. 'How are you getting on then?'

'Well, *I'm* making some progress on something at least.'

Cam stopped pacing long enough to give me a quizzical look, pushing his glasses back up his nose. 'Flying?'

I shook my head. 'No, that might take me a while. Especially if I'm working on my own while Leroi's working on those mysterious *anklets* . . .'

Cam's lips pinched into a thin line.

I held my hands up. 'Sorry, sorry. I'll drop it. Want to see what I'm working on?'

'Is it something new?'

I gestured for him to follow. 'Always. You're not the only one sick of the way things are.'

'I'm intrigued. Lead the way, young Tinkerer!'

I smirked, hopping towards the large platform with the giant fan mounted on the back, and the cabinet with the silver medallion-like trinkets.

'So I was thinking,' I told Cam, shifting around the table I'd claimed as my workspace. 'There's got to be other helpful things that I could make while I'm trying to figure out the big stuff.'

Cam sank into a chair on the other side, picking up the rubber strip I was going to use for tension. 'I'm all for that. What can I do to help?'

'Listen and watch.'

Cam sighed, leaning over so he could look at all the gears and springs I'd laid out, still toying with the rubber. 'Fine. But when you discover how to scoop Cold out of the sky and the whole World Cried knows your name, you be sure to tell them mine too.'

I put a hand over my heart. 'Fair trade.'

I tapped on the sheets of parchment I'd drawn the design on, glad that I finally had paper to work with. Being able to extract the ideas from my mind and plan them properly had uncovered a whole new layer of my creativity.

'This is the Decoy Box,' I said, gesturing to the various materials laid out on the table, gleaming and ready to be assembled. 'I was thinking about all of us Jadans who sneak out at night. Whether it's trying to find food, or escape something in our barracks, or even things that I don't know about—' I thought of Abb and me wandering out onto the dunes, and turned back to the table, my throat dry. 'A lot of us are out there crawling on the rooftops at night, and it's not safe.'

Cam nodded solemnly. 'I can only imagine.'

I plucked off the thick piece of Glassland Blue and the brass rod from their places and began rubbing them together slowly, easing out the horrific sound. I'd discovered this phenomenon by happy accident, a few nights back when once again I couldn't sleep and had wandered the raw materials stacks of the tinkershop instead, testing things.

Cam's face scrunched up with disgust. 'Lizards under stones, shut that off!'

I nodded, smiling through the sound, which was like someone howling after a whipping. I rubbed the pieces a bit faster, and the volume increased, sounding even more like a high-pitched moan.

Cam's hands went to his ears, and he gave me a pleading look. 'Mercy. Mercy.'

I put the rod and rare glass back on the table, the vibrations cooling. 'So I figured I'd make a system with a series of gears on notches which would be timed to rotate in—'

Cam held up a hand. 'I don't speak Inventor.'

I paused, raising an eyebrow. 'Want me to translate it to . . . "Camlish"?'

Cam laughed and bowed over the table. 'Fluent.'

'Basically, you put the box in some alley, crank this piece as a timer and then go about your business. When it goes off, the taskmasters will be drawn to it, and you can slip behind their backs unnoticed. And I'm going to paint the Decoy Boxes deep black so when the sound stops, they'll be lost in the shadows. Useful for the simple Jadan scavenger, or someone devious.'

Cam took his eyes off the table to meet mine. 'And this is something you came up with? Without Leroi?'

I nodded. I knew this was nothing which would bring down the Khat, but I felt that it was a solid invention that might be able to help someone.

Cam wobbled the rubber rope some more. 'I'm in.'

I opened my mouth, but he knew what I was going to say.

'To watch,' Cam said, catching the look on my face. 'For company. Don't worry, I won't mess with anything.'

I grinned at him. 'I might take a while. Some of this is going to be tricky.'

Cam tapped his shirt pocket, pressed into the shape of a book. 'I brought supplies. For when I get bored.'

I reached across the table and snatched the rubber strip from his hand. 'Good, because this will be quite complicated. See, the crank is going to be—'

Cam put his feet up with a wink, and then pulled out his book with the Opened Eye on the cover. 'Phew. Don't think I could have taken much more of that.'

The dribble finally reached Cam's chin.

Which meant that I had lost the bet against myself.

I sighed. I'd been using the slow trickle of spit from Cam's sleeping mouth as a challenge, racing to see if I could get the timing gears aligned before the drip hit his chin. Now I'd lost, and I owed myself three more hours of not worrying about Abb.

Or I could at least try.

I'd thought about waking Cam, as a lot of this tinkering would have been easier with an extra hand to press glue here and keep the rubber from snapping there, but he looked so peaceful that I couldn't bring myself to do it.

I was shaving down a piece of the Glassland Blue with some sandpaper when the study door slammed open.

Cam woke with a start, nearly falling to the floor, his book toppling from his chest.

Leroi's crumpled body slumped against the doorframe. His eyes were bloodshot, his cheeks were sunken, and his silver hair was outrageously unkempt. He looked like he'd aged a few years in a few days, and, if anything, his complexion was even paler than before, so pale that I wondered if the magic lights might just shine right through him.

Leroi croaked something, his voice gravelly and soft, but his eyes weren't focusing on us.

Cam and I exchanged a look.

Then the Tinkerer seemed to realize that no one was on the other side of the door, his eyes blinking furiously, and he ducked back into the shadows.

Cam yawned, wiping the dribble from his chin. 'Do you think—'

Leroi shot out of the study, his wiry arms wrapped around a large crate. The bars were too thin to see through properly, but I saw glimpses of steel, curved and sleek. Inside were dozens of different little items that I had to assume were the anklets. From here they looked like normal shackles, and I couldn't tell what all the fuss was about.

I stood up, so Leroi might see where we were, but at the sight of my face he took off, smashing and bumping his way to the main stairs. The crate was unwieldy and obviously heavy, controlling him more than the other way around. Leroi knocked against a table leg, stumbled, and sent a small shelf of starscopes cascading to the ground, lenses smashing.

'Cousin!' Cam shouted, but Leroi didn't stop. He almost didn't make it up the stairs, the weight of the crate making his feet falter – but he reached the top, and didn't look back. The veins in his neck strained with effort, purpled and bulging, but he managed to knock the chain loose with his elbow and burst through the door.

I ran behind, straight through the stench of strong alcohol, but when I got up the stairs and to the door I heard voices in the hallway. I knew I couldn't risk going out, so I stopped short. Closing the door with a sigh, I returned to my table. Cam's head was deep in his book although his cheeks were flushed. Even though the desire was now burning, I knew this would be the wrong time to ask again about the anklets, so I kept quiet and went about my tinkering.

Leroi didn't return for three days.

When he showed up he didn't come through the main door, instead appearing from somewhere in the back of the workshop. I'd already assumed there were secret passages in and out of this place, but now there was proof.

I was working on my Decoy Box when Leroi cleared his throat softly behind me.

I spun around and found a different man than the one who'd left.

His cheeks had filled out again, and his arms didn't seem so frail. His clothes were free of oil stains, his goatee was groomed, and his eyes were alive. He had sunburns all over his face and neck, his light skin baked crisp and red, although it was nothing next to the pain.

'I'm sorry,' he said.

I got up from my chair and went to the vial cabinet, picking out one of the few that I recognized. 'You don't have to be sorry for anything.'

Leroi took the groan salve with a little nod, uncorking it and spreading a layer over his burns. 'At least it's over with.'

I watched him cover his burns, wanting to flinch as he pressed against some of the spots. Matty and I could have had a heck of a game of whatsit looking over all that red. 'Where did you go?'

Leroi kept spreading the salve.

I nodded, deciding not to pry any further.

'I see you've been working on something,' Leroi said, gesturing to my boxes and putting the stopper back on the salve.

'I think it's pretty good.'

'We'll see about that.' He smiled. 'Has the Crier told you anything else?'

'Nothing,' I replied. 'Maybe He's forgotten about me.'

Leroi sat down in a chair, looking over the designs on my parchment. I'd never seen anyone's eyes move so fast, study so intently. Finally, he gave a nod. 'Well then, let's build something to make Him remember.'

Chapter Twenty-six

'It's called a Cold Charge,' Leroi said, dumping another scoop of the salt into the water tub. 'And it's the most important discovery about Cold you can learn. If you're even going to figure out the secret to flying, then I would suggest this is the best place to start.'

My heart thundered as I watched him work. Over the past few days the man had proven himself to be every bit the genius I was hoping for when Cam had first introduced him to me. Since his return, he'd finished teaching me the basics, and we'd moved on to the more complicated stuff: the beauty of Golem Gears, how to decode a Belisk Puzzle-Box, Esaw's Descent technique when soldering metals, and how to tell the difference between Hacock's Sleeping Powder from Hacock's Purging Powder; but this Cold display was what I'd been yearning to see most.

'If *we* are going to figure it out,' I corrected. I was having trouble sitting still, the excitement hard to contain. I'd made it a habit of pointing out that we were a team as much as I could, hoping that if I could make him see me as his assistant, he'd want to keep me around for as long as possible. At this stage, I had no intention of ever leaving.

Leroi dipped a finger into the water and tasted it, shaking his head. 'This needs more salt.'

'How do you know?'

'Because it doesn't hurt yet,' he said simply, scooping in more salt. Eventually he seemed satisfied, taking another taste and grimacing.

'Okay,' he said, picking up one of the Drafts he had placed on the nearby table. 'Let's talk about Cold. What do you know about it?'

I shifted in my seat, impatient for him to toss in the Draft and make something exciting happen. 'Falls from the sky. It's the enemy of the Sun. There are five different kinds. It's sort of important.'

Leroi chuckled. 'Think about your invention,' he prodded. 'The Saffir. What did you call it again?'

'Cold Wrap,' I replied with a sheepish grin.

'Promise me one thing?'

'Sure.'

'If you figure out a machine that lets you scoop Cold out of the sky, you'll try to be a little less literal in the name.'

Since he had returned from delivering the anklets, he had slowly begun to open up, and I'd met a whole different man.

'Noted. It will not be called the Sky Scoop.' I wiggled my fingers under the table, itching to know more. 'And to answer your first question, Cold also seems to be more potent in air than in water.'

Leroi rolled the Draft around in his palm, admiring the sheen. 'That's because water has a lot more of Sun in it. Sun's light passes through air with ease, so air can get cooler quickly and easily, but Sun gets *caught* in water' – his fingers clenched around the Draft – 'sucked in and hoarded.'

'That makes sense I guess.'

'And *salt* has the most Sun in it,' Leroi said, rapping his knuckles against the wooden barrel, 'since salt is what happens when the growlands get left at Sun's mercy for too long. Salt doesn't take to Cold at all.'

I looked deep into the Draft's surface. I hadn't thought much about the properties of Cold so far. I wondered if that made me a bad Inventor, but then I remembered this was the first time I'd ever been in the position to experiment with something as precious as Cold.

Leroi manoeuvred the Draft over the tub and let it fall in. I knew what to expect, but I still couldn't help my mouth from dropping open in awe.

Instead of dissolving or dropping to the bottom as nature usually demanded, the Draft hung on the surface of the water, submerged halfway in, bobbing gently.

'In a tub this size' – Leroi dragged his finger through the air, counting – 'the Draft should be gone in two weeks and six days.'

'Gone?' I asked, leaning forward in my chair.

Leroi stuck a finger on top of the Draft and pressed it down, but it refused to go quietly, rebounding against his touch. 'The tub is not all salt. There's still some water that will take the Cold. But—' Leroi walked over to one of his trinket cabinets '—Here's the interesting part.' Thrusting a hand into the back of the top shelf, he returned with a pair of black gloves and a long metal pole. The pole had a small glass dome on the end, and inside was a bit of wirework that I couldn't see properly. 'The solution doesn't change temperatures. The salt gets angry that it has to share water with its enemy, and so they fight. And the solution takes advantage of the battle.'

Leroi snapped on the gloves and dipped the end of the pole into the water. I expected something explosive – probably all the rampant energy running through my body – but the water remained still.

'Give it time,' Leroi said, reading my face. 'It's only just begun.'

I got up from my seat, inching closer to the tub. After a few quiet moments, the small dome began to light up. The shine was dim, but it was there.

'What is it?' I asked.

Leroi shrugged. 'Energy. Motion. Light. It's a lot of different things.' He pointed to the pond of moving gears, and the domes of light – which I'd learned were called 'Sinai' – and even the giant fans that needed no crank to spin on their own. 'I'm still figuring it out myself. It's a relatively new discovery.'

I pointed to the dim light on the pole, and then to the nearest Sinai, my eyebrows raised.

'Those had Shivers dissolved in their solution, not Drafts,' Leroi said, anticipating my next question. 'The bigger the Cold, the bigger the fight, and the more charge collected. The Sinai last months before they need more Cold.'

Then my finger went to the clay pots.

'Sharp mind. You can dissolve more than one piece of Cold in the solution. It compounds, getting even stronger than it should. Those are concentrated charges for bigger experiments.' Leroi gave a bashful chuckle. 'I once had grand ideas as well.'

A question popped into my mind among the flurry of new information. 'Does that mean Cold is alive?'

Leroi tapped his lip, which was still sunburned so he stopped straight away. 'That's a good question, but I wouldn't say it's alive. It's more representative. Salt is a product of death, and Cold is a product of life. Without each other they are nothing, but together they have power.'

'Why isn't this common knowledge?' I asked, my heart still fluttering. 'This discovery alone could change the way the world works.'

Leroi took the pole out, letting the tiny light subside. 'Because it's illegal.'

I looked up at him astonished. 'Illegal?'

Leroi sucked his teeth. 'The Khat's orders.'

'But think of all the things it could do,' I protested. 'If we can harness this charge from Cold, we could ch . . .'

Seeing the obvious look in his eyes, I let my words trail off.

'Sun damn,' I said. 'Change.'

'Change is a big no-no for the Khat. Hope too. Lord Tavor, my illustrious cousin, knows I experiment with this charge, but he turns a blind eye to my activities, if in return I make him,' Leroi's lips pinched briefly, 'certain things he requests.'

'But what about—'

Four rapid knocks at the main door and I shut my mouth. It was the signal that Cam was there, but that he wasn't alone.

Leroi snapped his fingers and pointed at the grate in the floor. I dashed over, pulling up the oily metal as quietly as I could, and slipping into the crawl-space underneath. We'd lined the dark area with plenty of boilweed so the nook was relatively dry for me, but its musk was still potent, and the floor was soggy from all the saltwater drainage. Leroi had felt guilty when I suggested it as my designated hiding spot, but my nose and body had experienced much worse on the streets. Leroi gently rolled the closest table over the top of the grate so as to cover me completely, yet I still had enough line of sight to make out feet.

I heard Leroi pad up the stairs, and I held my breath, praying. I'd not strayed from the tinkershop, and other than Cam and Leroi, no one knew I was here.

Breathing in deeply to try to keep calm, I made myself focus on all the things the Cold Charge could mean for my future. If the Charge could make things move, and fill them with light, then maybe it could even make them fly. Leroi was right, this could be the key to my quest.

Sweat beaded on my forehead as I waited. The sound of a closing chain reached the bars. My stomach clenched so hard I could have turned sand to glass. The sounds moved down to the main floor of the shop and closer to my table.

'It's okay, Spout,' Cam said from above, knocking the grate with his velvet sandal. 'You can come out.'

Opening the lid and looking up, my breath caught in my throat as I clocked braided hair and the straightest back in Paphos.

'Shilah!'

'So you *do* know her.' Cam gave a sigh of relief, lending a hand to help me out. 'I'm glad, because she knew you were here. Thank the Crier I got to the gates before my father did. He's been extra paranoid lately. Please tell her to have some water, Spout. She's refused my offer three times now.'

'I need to talk to *Spout* in private,' Shilah said in a way that answered at least one of my questions – I'd been wondering if she'd overheard my nickname while following me around the city. Her voice was quiet but serious as she added begrudgingly, 'Sir.'

She looked as if she'd just waded through a pit of Sobek lizards. Her robes were torn and bloodstained, and her eyes were bleary. She looked even worse than I had when I'd showed up at the Manor, which explained why Cam had been so ready to give up my hiding place to a stranger.

'Of course.' Cam bowed respectfully, his face flooded with concern.

He backed away, gesturing for Leroi to do the same. The Tinkerer seemed transfixed by Shilah, fixing her with an unwavering stare, but eventually he pulled away, crossing the tinkershop and joining Cam at the top of the stairs.

I took a small step back, worried about why Shilah might be standing in my new home, rather than halfway to the Great Divide as she'd sworn to be by now.

Shilah surveyed the tinkershop. Her eyes flicked from the rotating gear-pool, to the glass pyramids, to the magnet-clocks then back to me. 'You look good,' she said, at last. Her arms twitched out awkwardly, and for a moment I thought maybe she was having some sort of spasm until I realized what she was doing.

I stepped close and drew her into a quick embrace, breathing in deeply while we hugged. I inhaled the lingering scent of fire.

'What happened?' I asked, my heart in my throat as we parted. 'Is Abb okay?'

'Yes.' Shilah straightened up. 'And I am too, thanks.'

'Sorry. It's just . . .' My hand went over my chest, my pulse desperate. 'You scared me.'

Her hand went to her pocket, revealing a handful of black ash. 'How's that for scary?'

'What is it?'

She paused, clenching her jaw tightly. 'Little Langria.'

'What?'

'They followed me that night, from Arch Road,' Shilah said, her eyes full of so much anger that there was no room for tears. 'I thought I'd lost them, but that Sun-blackened pustule called a Vicaress followed me to the outskirts. She brought dozens of taskmasters and they searched the southern sands for days, from the barracks to the Kiln. I kept ahead of them for a while, smoothing out the tracks from the Rope Shoes, but she knew I was out there. It was only a matter of time.'

I swallowed hard. 'I'm so sorry.'

'I don't have anywhere else to go now.' She let some of the ash fall from her fingers into the grate. 'It's all gone. Everything I built. All so I could save *you*.'

The accusation struck a nerve. 'I don't know what to say. I'm really sorry.'

She met my eyes with a fierce look. 'Say you'll go with me. To Langria. Today. Now.'

'But I'm happy here.'

Shilah tossed the rest of the ash into the grate. 'Happy in a place where they keep you in the floor?'

'They don't keep me down there,' I said, smoothing my clothes. 'That's just where I hide in case anyone comes.' I hesitated, but felt compelled to ask, 'Weren't you supposed to be on the way to Langria already? Why did you stay in Paphos?'

Shilah glanced sideways, her eyes going to the tub with the Draft bobbing on top. 'Why are *you* staying here?'

'Leroi's teaching me. I'm creating things. Better than the Rope Shoes.' I could barely believe what I was saying out loud. 'Cam treats me like a brother. *Better* than a brother.' I reached out to touch her arm, but she pulled away. The heat of her skin lingered on my finger. I'd almost forgotten how scorching the world was outside the tinkershop. 'It's safe. Stay with me. There's room for two assistants. There's food, and as much Cold water as we want, and clean clothes, and—'

Shilah gave a scornful huff, cutting me short. 'Listen to yourself, talking like this. You're just a slave in a different uniform.'

'I don't want to have this argument again,' I said. I actually liked the robes Leroi had given me. They were thin and clean, and the dark colour didn't show any oil. 'I'm useful here.'

Shilah's jaw tightened, its angles smooth and beautiful, and I suddenly feared this might be the last time I would ever see her. She didn't say another word, just turned her shoulder and returned to the stairs, her back like a blade as she climbed to where Leroi and Cam were standing. She moved quickly and quietly, and I couldn't understand how the Vicaress had been able to follow her into the sands. I trailed after her, trying to think of the words that would make her stay. She was the loneliest person I'd ever met. Part of me wondered if she'd burned down Little Langria herself, just to try to convince me to accompany her.

For an instant, an image of a Jadan paradise flashed through my mind, the way she'd described it before, but I knew deep down that it couldn't be possible. If we wanted freedom, we had to make it.

'Please let me out,' Shilah said, standing in front of the door, hands clenched at her sides.

Cam had his hand on the chain, eyeing her warily. 'All good?'

I nodded. 'She won't say anything. You can let her out.'

Shilah stood tall and defiant, her hands still filmed in black ash. 'Sir,' she said, her voice a sandstorm, 'may I *go* now?'

I looked up at Leroi but he didn't meet my eyes. He was studying her as he often studied me, a pensive look on his face. After a few moments, he looked her straight in the eyes, and said, 'Stay. Please.'

Cam and I both looked up, confused.

'As another assistant,' Leroi added. 'We'll keep you safe here. Shilah, is it?' he asked carefully.

Shilah tilted her head suspiciously, staring back into Leroi's face. 'What will I have to do?' She took a few steps away, her back resting on the railing.

Cam looked to me in puzzlement, but a High Noble wouldn't know true desperation like we would. It shocked me to see Shilah so vulnerable, and not completely fearless.

'This and that. Nothing difficult.' Leroi gestured to the tinker-shop, his voice softening. 'There's plenty to be done here. Cleaning. Stocking. You can help to build things if you wish.'

Shilah's eyes narrowed, searching Leroi's face. 'What were those anklets that I saw on the other Jadans here? The guards and the Domestics.'

Leroi faltered, his voice narrowing to a hiss. 'You'll never wear one. I promise. I'll keep you secret.'

'And if I want to leave?' she asked.

Leroi took a deep breath. I couldn't understand why he seemed so set on getting her to stay. 'Course you can. Any time. I swear it on my honour. I have a passage in my study that leads outside the walls. I can show you. Right now, if you want. Just stay.'

I felt a tad slighted, considering Leroi had made me prove myself to stay on as an assistant, yet here he was offering the same thing to Shilah without question. Also, Leroi had never offered to show *me* the secret passage.

Shilah brushed ash from her hands. 'I guess I'll need a uniform then.'

Chapter Twenty-seven

'Are you awake?' Shilah whispered.

I kept my eyes closed, but I was no closer to sleep than Shilah was to Langria. My mind was still spinning from our unlikely reunion, the wobbliness toppling any Ideas I'd had for possible uses of the Cold Charge. I'd been wondering if the Charge could lift the heavy slabs of stone to the top of the Pyramid, or maybe could be injected into garden soil to help fig rations, but nothing felt serious, and nothing was sticking.

'No,' I said, shifting my sheet. I still wasn't used to being in a place chilled enough to need a layer on top, but since we had our own private Bellows to crank, the room was practically frigid.

'If you're not awake, then I guess you're dreaming about me,' Shilah said.

'I'm dreaming about the Cold Charge.' I smirked, turning my head so I could face her. Her bed had been set up so it was almost touching mine. My nights had been quiet since I'd left my room with Abb, and I was secretly glad to have her close.

'You made the right choice, coming here,' I said, turning

towards her fully. She'd taken on a new vulnerability since entering the Tavor Manor. 'Why can't you sleep?'

'I'm trying to figure it out.'

'It's pretty simple. The salt and the Cold don't mix, so the energy gets collected in the water—'

'Not that,' she said, pulling out her map again and brushing her fingers over the Opened Eye. 'This.'

'Can we please go five minutes without you trying to convince me to leave?' I asked, pulling the sheet over my chest. 'Why would you want to leave here? This place has everything.'

'I know it does.' She kept stroking the old map, movements slow and poised. Her finger wandered over Paphos, across the Erridian Bridge, around the City of the Stars, through the Glasslands, and up to the Opened Eye. 'Do you know any stories?'

I couldn't hide my surprise. 'Stories?'

She brushed the strands of hair out of her face. 'Yeah, stories.'

I indulged the thought for a moment. She reminded me of Matty, asking for a game of 'Whatsit'. 'I suppose so.'

'Tell me one,' she said, her voice small. 'My mum used to tell me stories, to help me sleep.'

Realization dawned on me. Of course she couldn't have been alone all this time. She'd lost her own Abb. She knew of the pain I'd been dreading more than anything else. My sheet suddenly lost its warmth as a chill ran across my skin.

I thought hard. 'What kind?'

'Doesn't matter.'

I paused, trying to hold back my smile. 'One time there was this Tinkerer named Salvidor Suth who wanted to figure out a better way to combine metals without—'

She reached over to my cot, giving me a playful slap across the chest. 'A *story*. I've had enough lessons for the day.'

I channelled my father, offering a goofy wiggle of my eyebrows. 'The best stories *are* lessons, Little Builder.'

I felt a pang in my heart and decided not to joke around with that nickname, at least until I saw Abb again.

'Crier above,' Shilah said with a sigh. 'Send me a new world partner.'

'Okay, I have a real one.'

She rolled onto her back, looking up at the ceiling. 'Go ahead, I'm listening.'

So for the next half-hour I told her of Klaus and Rachel as told to me by Abb when I was younger. A classic tale, from before the Drought. It didn't have any religious connotations, so the story hadn't been banned, everyone from the Southern Cry Temple to the Great Divide had heard some version of it. It was a story of love lost, adventure found, brave explorers, treasures unearthed, rulers slowly turning evil from greed, family squabbles, and even extinct beasts called 'horses' which were like camels, but stronger and faster.

At the end, I let the final words sit heavily in the darkness: 'And Klaus closed his eyes, never to open them again. He was already on his way to see her.'

The silence stretched until I was convinced that she had fallen asleep. The topsheet gently rose and fell with her breath, and I felt a subtle pride at helping her ease into her dreams. I rolled over onto my back, looking at the still shadows on the ceiling, and thought of flight.

'Mum always ended it with Klaus slicing his finger *before* the poisoning,' Shilah said with her eyes closed.

I groaned. 'And here was I, thinking she'd asked for any story—'

'Oh, hush.' She reached over and gave me another playful slap, the spot tingling after she removed her hand. 'It's a good version either way.'

'Thanks,' I replied.

She gave me a soft look. 'Do you have any more?'

'Stories?'

She smirked. 'No, sand mites.'

'How about you go to sleep?'

She turned and looked at the ceiling again. 'I don't like sleep.'

'Everyone likes sleep. You should like it best. Quickest way to Langria.'

She sucked her teeth and turned my way. 'Can we go five minutes without you trying to convince me *not* to leave?'

I chuckled. 'Maybe.'

'And sleep isn't that great,' she said. 'Your ears don't work when you sleep. I don't like it.'

'We're safe in here.' I felt my heartbeat start to quicken. 'You have to trust me, Cam is—'

'Do you have any more stories or not?'

I sighed. There was no point in trying right now.

We swapped stories for a few hours, and Shilah was the perfect audience, clapping and gasping at all the appropriate moments. It felt like being back in the barracks again, surrounded by Matty and Moussa, laughing the hours away. Shilah revealed herself through the tales she told. She was well-spoken, with a sharp tongue, and some of the swear-words she threw in could blush the red off a Rose of Gilead. She chose stories with adventure, and stretched those parts for as long as she could. From her inflections, I could detect a fondness for caravans and Peddlers.

Yet when I finished the story of Boaz and the Conquerors and her turn came up again, she seemed more hesitant than before. She sat up, crossing her legs underneath her. 'Okay. I've got another story.'

I pulled myself up too, so our eyes could meet. 'Tell me.'

'It's about the first Khat.' She'd been holding on to the

map this whole time, refusing to fold it up. Now the paper rustled a bit as her hands started to shake. 'And it's not pleasant.'

I nodded solemnly.

'You sure?' she asked.

I chuckled. 'It's just a story.'

'I want you to be able to sleep tonight. And it can be hard to hear.'

I grabbed my ear and gave it a wiggle. 'Good thing I'm awake.'

Shilah nodded, and cleared her throat nervously. 'So, before we were slaves, when Cold was Cried everywhere, and every bit of land was green and prosperous, the whole World Cried looked like Langria, right?'

'Yes, like the stories about Langria. Go on.'

'And now the only Cold gets Cried to the Khat,' she said, leaning in and lowering her voice. 'Don't you wonder why?'

'The Cause,' I said, thinking of the painting from the Paphos library, my fists clenching at the lie of it all.

She opened her palms and gave me a look that said *by all means*. 'And what exactly *was* the cause?'

'The Gospels say it's because Jadans are unworthy,' I countered, just to see where she was going with this. 'Evil things we did. Killing each other. Greed over Cold. Things like that. Not that I believe any of it any more.'

Shilah nodded. 'Nobles kill Jadans every day. And no one has more greed than those who have too much. So why would they still get Cold if the World Crier punishes murder and greed? That doesn't make sense.'

'I agree,' I said. 'That's why this place is what Jadans need.'

'Hmm?'

'Nothing,' I said quickly. 'Continue.'

She took a steady breath. 'Sometimes I go to places. The

kind of places taskmasters pretend they don't know about. Neutral territory. Jadans and Nobles both go there. And they drink and gamble, and do other things.'

I'd heard rumours about the places she might be referring to, the Drifthouses, underground chambers where it didn't matter who you were but rather what you were willing to do. It was in places like the Drifthouses where the Roof Warden got his Droughtweed supply. And where a Domestic might sneak out to earn extra rations. Fighting pits, gambling tables, rooms by the hour. Obey would just be a warm-up act in a Drifthouse. I nodded for Shilah to continue, petrified to find out what she might have been doing in a place so coarse.

Her eyes darkened and I almost felt compelled to look away. 'And I overhear things. People like to talk when they can get away with it.' She rolled up her sleeve and pointed to the tattoo on her arm. 'Lots of people have these.'

Her words hung in the air for a moment.

'What did you hear?' I prodded.

She remained at a distance from herself. 'That the first Khat made a deal with Sun. And that Sun led him to something hidden in the land, that Sun had put there right under the Crier's Eyes.'

My throat had gone dry, so I had to choke out the words. 'In Paphos?'

She gave her head a slight shake. 'I don't know where it was hidden. But it was dangerous. And there was a lot of it.'

I knew it was just a story, but the idea unsettled me. 'What was it?'

'Things that looked like Cold, but were the opposite. Something Sun created in secret to get back at his brother. The man telling the story called it "Desert". And that Sun told the first Khat that if the pieces of Desert were buried in the sand they would dissolve, and then no Cold could ever be Cried within a whole river's span. So the first Khat went to the all the cities in the World Cried, in secret, burying the Desert in everyone's Patches except for his. And all the crops went brown, except for his crops. And people starved and died from the heat. The rivers only got hotter, and the people got more desperate. So then the other kings and queens of every Jadan city in the land came and bowed to the Khat, promising everything they had if he would share his Cold. And so the Khat offered slavery.'

My hands started to shake, all of this sounding far too possible, especially after my trip to the dark river.

'The first Khat *caused* the Great Drought,' Shilah continued. 'So that he could rule everything. If he was the only one with Cold, he held life and death. And every Khat since has been keeping the secret. That Desert is buried everywhere.' She leaned so close I could feel the heat of her breath. 'Except in Langria.'

She gazed into my eyes, desperate for me to believe. I put my hand over hers, which was now squeezing my knee, and left it there. 'They put it in the ground,' I whispered. The words sounded as if they were being spoken by someone else.

'What?' she whispered back.

'Nothing.' I was trembling all over from rage. 'Everything.'

She was right.

I found no sleep after that.

Chapter Twenty-eight

'Spout.'

I looked up from the little flame, the visions of dying land still in my mind: trees cracked in half, rivers drained into the bowels of the sands, and the birds all falling from the sky.

'Spout,' Leroi said again, sitting on the base of the invention and snapping the black gloves over his hands. 'Focus. It's the most important tool of an Inventor.'

'I thought it would be imagination,' I replied with a guilty grin.

Leroi gave me a pointed look. 'Imagination is a material *and* a tool. It doesn't fit in just one box. Now do you want to see this display or not? You're the one who's been begging.'

I nodded, swallowing my frustration. I still hadn't got the nerve to ask Leroi if the story about Desert could be true, but it had been constantly playing on my mind.

I flicked the button on the Flamespark, bringing the little fire back to life. The device was simple, a bit of flint and a striking post inside at the right angle, but it was quick and useful and lit the candle on the podium with ease. I moved down the line, lighting the candles on the podiums, the tables, and the cabinets pushed to the sides so we could have a clear path all the way through the main section of the workshop. Meeting Shilah at the final row, I dipped the flame to the last wick, completing the tidy row of fire.

'Okay,' Leroi said, shrinking towards the wall. 'Both of you. Come back and join me here.'

Usually he was excited when he showed us one of his inventions, but he had been more reluctant with this one. Shilah and I scampered back through the rows of candles and met at the Sand Glider – the wheelless platform with the giant, caged fan blades on the front; a creation which I'd been dying to know about. Leroi had moved one of his clay pots to the base of the invention, this pot stout, with all sorts of black tally marks notched in columns on its sides. He pointed to one block at a time. His hands were shakier than usual today.

'Seventy-two Wisps, fifty-four Drafts, thirty-six Shivers, eighteen Chills,' Leroi said, tracing the little marks with quivering fingers. 'All dissolved over the course of a year. It's the most potent Cold Charge I've been able to come up with.'

My eyes widened at such an astounding amount of Cold. I knew all too well how much Jadan pain that Cold might have eased.

Leroi lifted the lid of the pot and sighed. 'I've had pots where I'd dissolved more Cold, and ones with less, but this mixture is the most powerful. The problem is, I've finally reached the wall.'

'Did you say ones with *more* Cold?' I asked, trying to keep the incredulity from my voice. Leroi didn't seem to be the malicious type, but I wondered if he knew the extent of the suffering in the world outside his tinkershop.

Leroi nodded, flexing his gloved fingers to keep away the shakes. 'I've been doing this for a very long time,' he said with another sigh. 'But I think maybe you two are here now, for a reason.'

'What reason?' Shilah asked.

Leroi didn't answer, instead taking the lid off the pot. Initially I thought the solution had a gold tinge, but I dismissed this as a trick of the nearest Sinai. He stepped up onto the base of the Sand Glider, which was just large enough for him and maybe one other body. The huge caged blades on the front had a copper wire that fed from the gear work through the bars. Leroi picked up the end of this wire and fed it through the mouth of the clay pot.

The blades came to life in a sudden jolt. The Glider itself vibrated, trying to buck away from the vices anchoring its hull to the ground, but the bearings of the fan were smooth, and in less than an instant, the metal was turning at a miraculous speed, hurling wind all the way across the tinkershop. Machines rattled and cabinets shook, and the line of candles behind the invention were blown out row by row in a furious current of wind. Shilah and I backed away in surprise. The candles were blown out all the way across the tinkershop, except for the last three rows, which flickered gently. Leroi let the blades spin aimlessly for a few seconds, and then pulled the copper wire out of the pot, at which point the Glider slowed down and eventually came to a standstill.

Leroi stripped off his gloves, slapping them on the base of the Glider. Kneeling, he moved his hand down to the base, which was made from some shiny green material.

'I lined the bottom with an alloy I call Slither-metal,' Leroi said, swiping his finger along the green and producing a slick squeal. 'No friction whatsoever. The idea is to have the blades propel the Glider across the sands. No roads, no bridges. If it worked, you could explore the whole World Cried, maybe find things out in the deep dunes that we didn't know about. Maybe secret Patches long forgotten. I've tried the Glider outside behind the manor, but there's still not enough charge to move it properly. I'm close, but I need more if it's to ride all the way across the dunes. I figured we might experiment with different potions to mix in to try and solve it.' He stood back up. In the half-light, I saw how sunken his face had become again, almost deflated. 'Enough charge, and we might build a different version that could push into the sky.'

'What if we ruin the charge completely?' I asked, looking at the final rows of candles, their flames tauntingly still quivering. 'All that Cold will go to waste.'

'Perhaps,' Leroi said. 'But freedom is not without its cost.'

Shilah broke free from my side, touching the cage that circled around the Glider's blades. 'We should try and get a Frost. Maybe that would—'

Leroi cut her off, his knees going visibly weak. 'Never that. Please never mention that again. Anything else. I'm sorry, but no. Sorry.' He shook his head. 'Sorry.'

Shilah and I exchanged a glance. We'd spent long hours at night discussing what secrets Leroi might be keeping. But before we could even change the subject, a furious knocking came from the main door, rattling the chain.

The pounding was frantic, wild even. It was most certainly not Cam.

Leroi's eyes widened and he snapped his fingers, pointing at the grate. We'd practised this yesterday, and Shilah and I silently flew to our hiding space, lifting the metal and tucking ourselves in. The space was big enough for two, but only just. My chest began beating harder than from just fear as Shilah pressed next to me.

Leroi gently closed the grate and pushed a table over it. The knocking grew even louder, as though the door was being pounded by half a dozen hands.

I pressed my face as high as it would go against the grate so I could see, Shilah doing the same. I could smell the Khatmint Leroi had given us that morning on her breath.

Leroi's bare feet slapped up to the landing and I heard the scrape of the chain being removed. A flurry of apologetic voices cascaded around the tinkershop, too muddled to make out. Leroi's voice broke over the din. 'Where were the task-masters?' The Tinkerer sounded frantic, his voice almost unrecognizable. 'Why didn't he get it turned? Speak!'

'A thousand apologies, Master Leroi!' another said. 'Samsiah was on an errand and didn't make it back. The taskmasters commanded us to—'

'The Manor Healer couldn't—'

'—the anklet took it clean off—'

'—found him calling out from the sands.'

'Please help him, sir. He's a good slave, and he only—'

'Take him downstairs!' Leroi broke through. 'Hurry! Now. Find a clean table.'

The voices did as he commanded. Shilah and I exchanged a worried glance. As they approached, we could see feet through the cracks in the grate, and some blood dripping, leaving a thick trail on the floor.

There was a crash of glass smashing as Leroi brushed everything off the worktop. As the feet drew nearer the grate, we could see how dirty they were. They all had thick metal cuffs around their ankles, with a large bubble shape on the sides. Shilah's expression was impassive, but she grabbed my arm, digging in tight. Her other hand went to her braid, although I didn't think she kept a blade in there any more.

'How long?' Leroi asked. 'Speak, please. Don't be afraid.'

'Less than a bell,' a voice squeaked in reply. 'Please, can you help him, Master Leroi?'

'Just Leroi,' the Tinkerer said. I heard him rifling through the shelves, his voice small. 'No master.'

'The bleeding's not stopping. We tried to stitch it—'

'Pinion's acid will eat through stitches,' Leroi muttered in reply, seemingly mostly to himself. 'It won't work.'

Leroi had never mentioned Pinion's acid in our lessons. I looked at Shilah, but her eyes were stony and remained focused on the grate.

'What can we do to help, sir?' one of the voices asked.

'Get the boilweed off the foot.'

Leroi gave an audible wince. 'It's all gone. The whole foot.'

'We tried to get him here as quickly as we could, sir. I'm sorry.'

A bottle popped and I saw some clear liquid drip to the floor. There was no reaction above, however, and I imagined that the body was no longer conscious. 'Sun*damnit*!' Leroi shouted.

I heard several sharp intakes of breath in the tinkershop.

'Sorry.' Leroi made a noise that sounded like a howl. 'I'm sorry. I just— Hold him down. I have to cauterize.'

Even our cubby-hole lit up as a flame was sparked to heat up the iron. I wanted to retch at the idea of what Leroi was about to do.

'Put this in his mouth,' Leroi commanded. 'In case he bites down.'

Leroi took a breath and the iron was brought to the flesh. The sizzle made me shudder. It was followed by an astounding sickly smell, which reached us all the way under the grate. I couldn't help myself as I let out a gag.

Shilah's grip became even tighter, her face panic-stricken. One of the Jadans followed the sound of my retch towards the grate.

'Focus!' Leroi demanded. 'Look here. Hold him down.'

The hisses and sputters subsided, but the putrid smell kept attacking us. Shilah wrapped a hand around my cheek, trying to pull my face away and into her neck to hide me from the smell, but I felt compelled to watch, struggling to keep my head afloat and the gags down.

No wonder Leroi hadn't wanted to tell me about the anklets.

Leroi's feet moved around the table, I presumed to check the body's heartbeat. 'He's going to be okay. He lost a lot of blood, but he's going to live. Now, please would one of you go grab some Cold from that bucket over there, and there's a waterskin on my—'

Leroi stopped himself. All the Jadans dropped to their knees simultaneously.

A tapping rang out from the direction of the main door, as a cane slowly made its way down the stairs. When it came into view, I saw that the cane was made of stained glass, and the legs that walked beside it were adorned in fine silk. The feet moved slowly, each step ringing a deep thud in the tinkershop.

'Cousin,' Leroi said, his voice coated in regret. 'Is this what you wanted? Is this why you had me create them? You were supposed to have a turn-key with each of the taskmasters. You told me . . .'

There was no reply, just a slight rap as the cane was rested against the table.

'He's going to live,' Leroi said, unable to get the words out fast enough. 'They brought him here in time! These Jadans should get triple rations for their service.'

I could now feel a wet hot pain on my arm, where Shilah had pierced my skin with her fingernails.

'I'll build him a new foot,' Leroi said, his words coming out even faster. 'I can attach a brace to the knee and run it down to— Cousin, just hold on a minute. He'll still be able to serve you. Please, just wait. I can make him— Cousin, please. I beg you, just—'

A voice, which sounded like Cam's but older, cut across him. 'You've brought this on yourself, Leroi. You should have kept her on a tighter leash.'

'Please let go,' Leroi implored. 'Please. I can fix him. I can—'

Fast, strangled breaths came from the table, until they

eventually culminated in a final, juddering gasp. Silence then resumed. After a few moments of stillness, the feet I was now certain belonged to Lord Tavor stepped back from the table. No other word was spoken. The High Noble picked up his decorative cane and began tapping his way back to the stairs.

The door creaked open, but wasn't immediately closed. 'Oh, and, Leroi,' Lord Tavor said, 'I see you've been tinkering again.'

A tense pause followed. 'Yes.'

'Is there a reason?' he asked, voice smooth and calm.

'It was time. I've mourned.'

'Good for you. Would you like a *new* assistant? I'm sure my son would be glad to find you one.'

My face flushed deeply at his words. Lord Tavor couldn't know we were here. Could he?

'No,' Leroi choked out.

'Because you can have one, now that we have these anklets you so lovingly bestowed.'

'No,' Leroi practically sobbed.

'The kitchens tell me you've been requesting more food. Eating more than usual, have you? Where have you been packing it away?'

'I need my strength,' Leroi said, sounding like his teeth were clenched. 'Those anklets took a lot out of me.'

The door creaked open again.

'Then I'll have the kitchens send you a whole roast,' Lord Tavor said. 'Because I expect you to make another anklet to replace the one this slave lost. I'll send someone to pick it up in a few days.'

Chapter Twenty-nine

Shilah put her hands on the table without any fear or hesitation. 'Here.'

I backed away. 'I don't think so.'

She leaned forward, putting her weight on the wood. 'If we're going to talk about important things,' Shilah said, her dark skin blending with the table. 'This is where we'll do it.'

I looked at the table, now spotless. While Shilah and I were hiding under the grate, the three Jadans had cleaned the place and then taken the lifeless body out to the sands. Now, the table resembled a workspace like any other.

I kept my distance. 'I don't think I'll be able to concentrate on—'

She let herself relax away from the table, the saddest smile I'd ever seen weighing down her face. 'Where better?'

I paused. 'Literally anywhere.'

Her hands clenched into fists, and once again I saw that fierce anger breathe its life inside her. 'This is everything that's wrong with the World Cried. We need to look the problem in the face, Micah. Here.'

I gave a resigned nod, my own anger still rising in my chest. We hadn't been able to talk to Leroi about the anklets, since after Lord Tavor had left, he'd locked himself back in his study, and wouldn't come to the door when we called for him.

Shilah pulled up two chairs, setting them across from each other, and we each sat down. After a few moments of uncomfortable staring, I grew fidgety, while Shilah kept straight and still.

'I'll make you a deal, partner,' she said in a simple voice, her hands laid flat on the table.

I tilted my head. 'Okay?'

'I admire you, I hope you know that. The way your mind thinks is different. Trying to end the Drought by flying up to collect Cold from the source is a good idea.'

I felt my cheeks flush with heat. 'Thanks. And I admire you as—'

'But I also think you're being an idiot again.'

I stiffened, stung by her words. 'I don't think—'

She held up her hand. 'Let me make you my deal.'

I clenched my teeth, and nodded.

'One week. I'll stay here with you for one week, and I'll help in any way you need. If you're not any closer to your plan, we go with mine.' She gestured to the buckets of Cold sitting on the shelf nearby and then tapped the tattoo on her arm. 'We take as much Cold as we can carry, and we go north to find Langria.'

I paused, feeling moisture spout on my forehead. 'But it's going to take me more than a week.'

'You saw what happened.' She knocked on the table. 'This place isn't safe for us.'

'But the Cold Charge—'

She waved her hand dismissively. '—Blowing out candles from across the room is a neat trick, but it doesn't help anything. It's not what we need.'

The words made my heart squeeze. 'What did you say?'

'It's not what the Jadans need,' Shilah repeated, resolutely. 'It's not what I need.'

I took a deep breath, trying not to think yet again about my father. 'What *do* Jadans need?'

She closed her eyes, sliding her fingers along the surface of the table. I wondered if there was a residual warmth left by the body, but I was still too apprehensive to feel for myself. 'Freedom.'

'Flight can bring us freedom. Just give me time.'

'Leroi said it himself, the Cold Charge doesn't get any stronger, even with more Cold, so it's not as if you can push your way into the sky. I think it's a foolish plan, and I think your talents are better used elsewhere. One week. Please.'

I allowed my fingertips to touch the underside of the table. I would miss her if she left, but I still had no desire to leave the safety and comfort of the Tavor Manor.

'I wish the Crier would talk to me again,' I said.

She slammed a palm down. 'That's not how the Crier works, Micah. This is about us. You and me. The Crier hasn't been able to save us for eight hundred years, so why start now?' She gave an angry glance around the tinkershop. 'The secrets are here, are they? In this place? Hidden away from the Jadans themselves. Fine. Show me why this is better than Langria.'

'Because I can make things here. Things which will help Jadans,' I protested.

She brought over a bucket of Cold and slammed it down in front of me. 'So do it. Make us something useful.'

'I'm trying.'

'You're spending as much time *trying* as you are hiding in grates from your *friend's* father,' she spat.

'We could make more Saffirs,' I said quickly, feeling flustered.

'Jadans don't have Cold to put in them. And they're already illegal.'

'The groan salve,' I said. 'You could help me grow more groan trees here and—'

'The Nobles would only ever take it away. You know that.' She shoved the bucket over, spilling all the Cold onto the table and the floor. 'Look at all of this. This Cold that they take out of our hands. Show me why this place is better!'

I felt my chest seize in frustration, unable to answer. 'I—'

My words were cut short as a Draft suddenly rolled into my lap. I looked at it. Then, an Idea about Cold struck me like a hammer.

My eyes went straight to Shilah's chest. 'Have we been looking at the problem from the wrong angle all this time?' I wondered.

She followed my gaze and snapped her fingers. 'Hey. We're having a conversation here.'

I shook myself out of my daze. 'Take out the map.'

Shilah raised an eyebrow, but she reached under her clothes and pulled out the folded parchment.

'On the table,' I commanded.

Shilah's eyebrows arched in surprise, the angles of her face stiffening.

'The map,' I said, with an exasperated sigh. 'Please.'

Shilah unfolded it gently, clearing away some of the tinkering debris to spread out the page. I stepped around the table to be at her side. Together we looked over the Khatdom. 'Why doesn't it say Langria? It's just the symbol. The Opened Eye.'

Shilah shrugged. Our shoulders were touching, but she didn't pull away. 'So. It's kind of the same thing.'

I let my fingers caress the symbol, tracing the pupil. 'You said that the first Khat found Desert hidden in the land, right? And then used it to poison the world.'

'It's just a story,' she said quietly. 'But yes.'

I flashed her a devious grin. 'The best stories are lessons.'

She sighed and went to fold up the map, but I reached out and put a hand over hers, keeping the paper open. Her skin was soft and cool from the tinkershop's Cold air, and I had to shake my head to not lose track of what I was thinking.

'The Opened Eye represents hope, right?' I asked.

She nodded, not pulling away, letting my fingers rest over her knuckles.

My heart began to beat faster. 'What if this isn't a map?'

'It *is* a map.'

'No, I mean, what if it's not a map to Langria itself, but a map to how we can bring Langria to the World?' I tapped my finger hard on the drawing. 'What if there's something hidden up North? If Sun created Desert and hid it in the land for the first Khat to find, then what if the Crier created something secret too? Something for the *Jadans* to find.'

I could feel Shilah's shoulder tense beside me. She thought about it for a moment and then pointed to the map. 'I'm not saying I buy any of this. But even if you were onto something, it wouldn't matter. The Eye on the map is huge, the size of the other cities. If there's something hidden in the land up North, how would we even find it?'

My head spun to the Sand Glider, looking at the clay pot still sitting on its surface. Then I found the shelf of Cold Bellows, thinking about all the cool air in the tinkershop. 'It would be hard, agreed. But look at everything we have here.' I waved around at all the machines in the tinkershop. 'I think we could do it.'

Shilah folded her arms over her chest. 'What do you mean?'

'Think about the Charge,' I said. 'It's something that the Khat wants to keep quiet.'

Shilah nodded.

'We obviously don't know everything there is to know about Cold. What else can it do?' I picked up a Wisp from the table and held it up to the light of the Sinai, the surface gleaming. 'There must be more to know.'

Three swift knocks sounded at the door.

I looked to see if I could find Shilah, but she was busying herself gathering more beakers and salt and ink at the back of the tinkershop. I ran up the stairs without her, sliding off the chain.

Cam burst in, kicking the door closed behind him. His face was red and heavy breathing punctuated his words. His glasses were askew to the point of almost falling off. 'Spout. I delivered . . . Decoy Boxes to Mama Jana . . . got back . . . they said something happened in the tinkershop. What happened?'

I reached out and put a hand on his shoulder. 'Breathe, family. Everything is okay.'

Cam didn't seem convinced, leaning around me and looking down over the railing. 'Shilah, what happened? Are you okay? Did my brothers . . .?'

I turned to find Shilah at the bottom of the landing, clutching something behind her back. 'Hello, sir,' she said in the emotionless, uninterested tone she used around him, before marching away, her back tall and proud.

Cam frowned, his chest rising and falling in rapid succession. His voice strengthened with the kind of authority he usually only used in jest. 'What. Happened?'

'She's fine,' I said, squeezing his shoulder. 'Listen, we have something important to tell you. I think I finally had an idea that—'

A loud moan came from Leroi's study, and stopped me from answering. Cam's lips thinned to a line. He paused, eyes fixed on the door. 'Spout, is Leroi back in there again?'

I felt a pang in my stomach. 'Well, Shilah and I were talking this mo—'

Cam swallowed hard. 'Spout. Is Leroi back in there? I thought he was done with the anklets.'

I gave a sad nod. 'He was.'

Cam nearly collapsed against the railing. 'So . . .'

I let my chin fall slightly. 'I don't want to say.'

'Why is Leroi in there?' Cam asked in a more forceful way.

Shilah popped her head out from behind one of the clay pots. 'Because of your Sun-damned father, that's why!'

Cam went rigid, every drop of liveliness draining from his face. 'My *father*? He was here?'

By the time I had filled Cam in on everything we'd witnessed from the grate, his face had grown so pale that I could finally see the resemblance between him and Leroi. I'd escorted him down to the infamous table, where for the last hour I'd been setting up the jars and ink and salt for an experiment, but Cam couldn't seem to find any excitement over my new Idea.

'I'm so sorry,' Cam said yet again, his eyes damp at the corners.

I poured the thick ink and water into a glass, making sure to leave enough room on top. 'You don't have to keep apologizing. It's not your fault.'

Cam had his knees pulled up to his chest, and he hugged them close. 'I'd strangle *him* if I could.' There was a deep fierceness to his voice as he said the words.

'Let's focus on this instead,' I said to Cam, pointing at all the things arranged on the table. 'You believe in the Opened Eye, don't you? We think we've found the way there.'

Cam's eyes were still stony, but he gave a nod. 'Sorry I've been distracted. Tell me.'

'Cold dissolves in air, right? Like with the Saffir. I want to watch what it does.'

He sat up straighter. 'What do you mean, what it does?'

I shrugged, scooping some salt from a barrel and pouring it into each of the inky jars. I wasn't trying to make a Cold Charge with the salt, I just didn't want the Wisps dissolving in the blackness. 'To see if it spreads evenly. To see if it rises or falls or comes together in clumps. Or if there's any metals or potions that it's attracted to more than others. I figured we need to know everything we can about Cold if we're going to invent something that can find it.'

'*We*, really? You're going to include a High Noble in your plans, even after what just happened?' Cam took a deep breath. 'I sure know how to pick them.'

'You're the only reason I'm here,' I replied, giving him a small smile.

Cam reached out and touched one of the Bellows I'd hauled to the table. 'So you put the Wisps in the ink. The ink seeps in through the little holes and stains the Cold. Then you crush it, and then watch what it does? That's the plan?'

'Unless you have any better ideas,' Shilah said with a sneer, finally settling down on a nearby chair.

'Be nice,' I said. 'We're in this together.'

Cam's head sagged. 'I'm sorry, Shilah. I'm really, really sorry for everything that's been done to you.'

Shilah took a steadying breath but didn't bite back. Cam's earnest tone seemed to appease her for the moment. 'Let's just get this over with,' she said.

'Should we get Leroi?' I asked.

'No,' Shilah said, looking over to the study, the tinkering sounds having stopped long ago. 'Let him have his peace.'

'Well then, here goes,' I said. The five jars were ready, different amounts of salt poured in each. I grabbed the first Wisp, kissed it for luck, and dropped it in the first inky concoction.

All three of our faces closed in on the glass, each of us holding our breath.

The Wisp sank to the bottom and dissolved.

I tried not to think of this experimenting as wasting Cold, and selected another one from the basket. I added it to the next jar, which had double the salt. This time the Wisp held near the top, starting to fizzle at the holes, but eventually it dissolved too. My lips pinched with disappointment, but I repeated the process over and over, finding the fourth jar to have the combination I was looking for; the Wisps sinking enough to be submerged, but staying in one piece.

I stuffed half a dozen Wisps in that jar, letting them suck up the ink.

'How long?' Cam asked.

'Few minutes should be enough.' I shrugged, turning to Shilah. 'Got any stories?'

She made a face, her eyes glaring at Cam, who physically shrank under her intensity. I'd never seen a High Noble intimidated by a Jadan in this way. The tension crackled in the room as we waited in silence.

My chest beating with excitement, I finally handed Cam the pair of thin tongs I'd found near the fireplace. 'Want to do the honours?'

Cam accepted them with a bow of his head and began fishing out the Wisps, letting them dry on the sheets of boilweed we'd laid out on the table. The ink ran off the surface of the Cold, but it was still staining the insides.

I opened the mouth of the Bellows and stuffed one of the Wisps into the vice, my fingers growing sticky with ink.

'*The Jadan's work upon the sands*,' I sang softly, closing the Cold in and wishing Matty was by my side to see this. '*Those who need the Cold*.'

'What's that?' Cam asked.

'Whatsit,' I replied with a smile, and turned the top crank of the Bellows.

Using two hands to spin it hard, I was able to shatter the Wisp all at once. The jaws of the vice collapsed in relief, and immediately a trail of black smoke rose from the mouth, slithering into the air. I leaned away as the trail widened, my heart pounding, but the black kept flooding out in my direction. I stumbled back, knocking over my chair, but the dark cloud kept coming at me. The swarm split in two in the air, half of it swinging towards Shilah, who also tried backing away. I couldn't move fast enough, the inky air surrounding me, covering my skin and diving into my lungs. It blinded me, and I choked, tasting cold and salt, the air rough with the ink. Although I couldn't see her, I could hear Shilah choking too. I tried to hold my breath, but the cloud didn't want to dissipate. I held my shirt over my mouth and filtered small breaths for a few moments, until the cloud became less dense. I wiped my sleeve over my eyes, removing the ink and coughing out the last of the black air. My vision cleared after my streaming eyes had flushed out the ink, and I watched the black cloud fade into the air, spreading out and shrinking until it was too thin to be seen.

I looked over at Shilah. Every bit of her skin had been stained black, and dressed in her dark robes, she looked like a shadow, with only the whites of her eyes and teeth reacting to the light of the Sinai.

'It went right for us,' I said, astonished. 'Like a magnet.'

'Your whole face is covered. And your neck and hands. All black,' Shilah said, smiling.

I turned to look at Cam, expecting him to be covered in ink as well, but he was surprisingly clean, his complexion only slightly dusted by the cloud. He ran his hands over his robes and skin, with a puzzled look on his face. He retched out a cough, but it seemed forced. 'Did it get me?'

'No,' I said, curiosity deepening. 'It seems to have avoided you.'

Cam's expression soured. 'Maybe it was because you two were closer. Let's try again.'

'We need masks this time,' Shilah said, grabbing a piece of boilweed and putting it over her mouth. 'And eyewear too.'

I found a few pairs of Leroi's soldering goggles, and we all strapped them on. I loaded another inked Wisp into the Bellows and cranked it hard, the cloud shooting out. Like the last one, it swarmed towards Shilah and me right away, but it barely touched Cam, passing over his body in the same impassive way it did everything else in the tinkershop. We cleaned our skin and repeated the test several times, but each result was the same.

The Cold shot right to the Jadan skin, but didn't seem to care about Cam, regardless of where he stood.

'The Cold finds us,' Shilah said. 'And not Nobles.'

I unstrapped my goggles and lowered my boilweed mask. Cam was frowning deeply, his bottom lip twitching in puzzlement. 'Cam, I don't know—'

Cam swallowed hard. 'It's okay. But maybe we could try some bigger Cold?'

We wheeled over the largest Cold Bellows that Leroi had made, inking up a few Drafts to test them out. The clouds were gigantic this time, massive plumes of inky air that made our teeth chatter and our skin tingle, but still the Cold ignored Cam completely, whilst it stained our Jadan skin so black that I wondered if the ink would ever wash off.

We even tried it with Cam turning the Bellows himself, but it was always the same, the light mist that eventually found him not even darkening the colour of his golden hair.

Cam lowered his goggles, his face more miserable than I'd ever seen it. 'I've been so trying,' he said in a sad voice. 'I don't want to be one of them.'

'Cam,' I said gently, even though my heart was racing. 'What are you talking about?'

'We're not chosen,' Cam said, backing away from the table. 'He hates my family for what we've done. He hates what we've been hiding. It's obvious. We're infected. Like firepox, but worse.'

'Who hates what?' I took a step towards him. 'Cam, just relax for a second—'

Cam held up a hand, turning it over to see how clean it was. 'I'm sorry, Spout. I can't be here.'

And with that, he ran out of the tinkershop, slamming the door behind him.

I grabbed one of the remaining pieces of clean boilweed, dipped it in the water trough, and went over to Shilah. 'Hold still,' I said, dabbing the stuff onto her face, trying to clean away some of the black from her cheeks and hair.

She stood straight and proud, a smile creeping onto her blackened lips. 'Micah. Do you get what this means?'

I nodded, wiping her forehead next. I was transported back to the first conversation I'd had with Leroi, about the first Khat being *less* than Jadan. 'I think I do.'

'I told you we're worthy. That the Drought was all lies. Cold is meant for us. Micah, this changes everything!'

I moved the boilweed down her arm, wiping the ink away from her Opened Eye tattoo. She didn't shy away, allowing me to mop her up.

'Let's get Leroi,' I said, trying to take my mind off my pounding heart. 'Maybe he can shed some light on all this.'

We went over to the study door, our knocks turning to pounds, our pleas turning to hushed shouts. He didn't answer, regardless of how much we threw ourselves at the door. Eventually, anxious that we might find a corpse on the other side, I found some tools and picked the lock. The door swung open to reveal a single anklet on the desk, next to an empty decanter. A strong stench of alcohol filled the room.

All of his tinkering materials had been piled in the corner, and there was no other trace of the Inventor himself.

We were on our own.

Chapter Thirty

I put some muscle into it, scrubbing hard, even though it wasn't necessary. The Cold had left the ink powdery and dry, so the residue from the clouds was coming off the floors and walls of the tinkershop with ease. I barely had to rub the boilweed over the black dust, but still I dug in, polishing the walls to a shine.

Abb told me sometimes the mind gets so overwhelmed that the only way to process things is through the body. I was sweating all over, my arms burning with fatigue, trying to step far enough away from the jumble of questions in my mind that I might stumble upon some answers.

'Micah,' Shilah said from my side, removing corked beakers from a shelf and dusting them with the boilweed.

I grunted in response, knelt down as I removed the black dust from a particularly deep nook in the wall.

'I think it might be enough,' she said.

'I want to keep working,' I said, trying not to let myself become overwhelmed. 'Leroi deserves to come back to a clean tinkershop.'

Shilah put a beaker back, coming over to me and putting a hand on my shoulder. 'Not the cleaning. I mean this discovery. It might be enough.'

Even though her touch sent a shiver through my body, I kept furiously cleaning. 'For?'

'Think about it,' she said, digging her fingers into my arm. 'If we can show everyone that the Cold is attracted to Jadans and not Nobles, they have to admit everything is a lie. We're the worthy ones.'

I stood up, her hand coming with me, but I didn't feel ready to face her. I kept scrubbing the wall. 'What if it's just a fluke? What if the cloud just found *us* for some reason, and not all Jadans? We don't know enough yet.'

She gave my arm another squeeze. 'Look at me.'

My hands didn't stop. The powdery ink on the walls was now an offence to me, each particle mocking my efforts. I couldn't bring myself to meet her eyes.

'Look at me,' she said again, in a softer tone.

I sighed, wiping the sweat off my forehead, and spun around to look at her.

Her face was glowing.

And not from some stray beam of light from a Sinai. She was resolute in her happiness, pure and free. Her smile struck me like Cold water, and her brazenly upright posture made her look as majestic as one of the Khat's own family. Her skin seemed smoother than usual, and her eyes gleamed with hope. I wanted to run my hands over her face and feel every angle of her joy.

'You know what I mean,' Shilah said. 'This is enough to make people fight back. The Crier wants *Jadans* to have Cold. We can prove the Drought was a lie.'

'Shilah, this isn't enough. You should know that too. If this gets out, the Khat isn't going to free us. Nobles will do everything they can to hide the truth. They'll kill us, and say you and I were just spreading the Sun's trickery, and then probably have the Priests and Vicaress do another Cleansing just for good measure. We need more. We need something bigger. Even if Cold comes to our kind in the air, it still only falls into the Nobles' hands.'

Shilah let her hand fall. 'I know.'

'I'm going to find Leroi's secret passage and use it to see my father. I need to tell him about all of this,' I said. I needed him more than ever now. 'Maybe he'll know what to do next.'

Shilah nodded. 'Fine. But I'm coming with you. And we should probably raid this place for weapons, in case—'

Three raps on the main door. Two fast, a pause, and then another.

Shilah's expression immediately became suspicious, but all I felt was relief. It wasn't pleasant to see how this discovery affected Cam. If seeing Cold prefer Jadans took such a toll on a kind, sympathetic Noble, I could only imagine the rage and denial it would inspire in all the others.

I raced across the tinkershop, tossing aside my boilweed as I dived up the stairs. Swinging open the door, I expected to find my friend, but there was no one on the other side. I chanced peeking out into the hallway, but there was no sign of life.

On the ground, however, sat a wooden chest with a note on top.

'You deserve this more than we do. I hope it will free me.'

I pulled the chest inside, noticing the odd temperature of the wood against my hands as I closed the door and slid the chain. I immediately felt very strange, my mind buckling under an odd sensation, as if I'd just walked into a barracks I'd never seen before, but somehow recognized the faces of the Jadans there.

'Where's Cam?' Shilah asked from below.

'Not here,' I said absently, staring at the box. I set it on the landing and sat cross-legged beside it, my hands running over the smooth woodgrain. The chest was colder to the touch than anything I'd felt before, and I wondered what Cam had delivered that needed to be kept in such Cold.

But when I opened the lid, I nearly fainted.

I'd never seen one before, but even after a single glance I understood what was sitting in front of me.

'Shilah,' I choked out, my fingers shaking at the sides of the chest. 'Shilah!'

Footsteps padded up the stairs. 'What? Are you okay?'

I started breathing heavily, entranced by the lovely sheen, wonder taking over my brain. It was the single most beautiful thing I'd ever seen. It wasn't dull like its kin but lustrous gold, more vibrant than any flower, smoother than any glass. And the centre had a gentle design, which seemed to rise to the surface in the shape of two thick lines with a third lying across the top. Seeing it up close, I knew instantly that these were the things shining in the night sky: that if I could fly, this is what I might bump into.

If there was ever proof of the Crier's divine touch on this world, it was this.

Shilah got to the top step, but when she caught sight of the Frost, she nearly collapsed, her legs buckling at its beauty, and only just caught herself on the railing. I would have risen to help her, if not for my complete and utter shock at what had just been thrust into my life.

'It's a— Is that—' Shilah sucked in a huge breath. 'Frost.'

I had to remember to breathe too. Only the Khat was supposed to have Frosts. What was it doing in the Tavor Manor?

I swallowed hard, shutting the lid of the chest so I could think for a moment. I felt I was back on the banks of the Kiln holding Abb's empty bucket, Sister Gale racing across the river to caress my face. The Frost had awoken some-thing in me. Suddenly my hands itched to tinker more than they'd ever done before. I felt frantic, as if I'd woken up from a long sleep and was supposed to be somewhere an hour ago.

Shilah crept closer to the crate, putting her hand on the wood. She flinched away at first, not expecting the freezing cold temperature of it either, but she breathed in, and set her hand down again.

'Maybe you did talk to the Crier,' Shilah said, her voice an awed whisper.

I took another deep breath, Shilah and I exchanging a look and then lifting the lid back off together.

The Frost was almost too much to look at. This Cold was truly holy.

I thought about all the Jadans and all the barracks that this could keep alive, and I knew it had come to me for a reason. That those nights sweating on the rooftops and sifting through rubbish had been worth the risk. That every lash I'd endured meant something, and that every piece of pain I'd suffered was valuable. That every little thing I'd created in the past had been in preparation for this very moment.

All so a Frost might end up in the hands of a Jadan Inventor.

I'd have my answers.

Half a night later and the wave of excitement I'd been riding had faded to nothing. I hovered over my tinkering table, materials and tools spread across the entire surface. My knuckles creaked as I rested my weight on the wood, my eyelids heavy and my frustration rampant.

Shilah was curled up in a chair beside me, fast asleep, her hair unbraided and blanketing the top half of her face. I stopped myself from reaching over to tuck it behind her ear.

The fatigue was winning, however. As the night progressed, my experiments shifted from thoughtful to downright weird. I'd been scared to touch it at first, but now the Frost lay suspended in a makeshift hammock I'd strung across an upside-down stool, and my current test involved sprinkling Rose of Gilead petals over the Cold to see if there was a reaction. There was none. I'd discovered early in the night that the Frost was impenetrable, unlike other types of Cold. Not crushable, not breakable, not anything. I thought maybe I could extract a small chunk to add to Leroi's solution in the marked clay pot, but found my efforts rebuffed. Scraping a blade across its surface was useless, and if anything, the sheen seemed to grow stronger under the drag of the knife, lighting up, as if the Frost was laughing at my feeble attempts. I tried wetting a boilweed swab and rubbing it gently on the surface, as a droplet of water would melt away a tiny section of any other Cold, but the Frost refused to yield.

I'd even done some nonsense experiments that I was glad Shilah was too asleep to witness. I burned some incense. I took the Bellows and blew long ineffective puffs across its surface. I tickled its belly with a silk handkerchief. Held magnets on either side. Quietly sang the Jadan's Anthem to it. Traced the Opened Eye symbol on it with melted candlewax. Dusted it with prayer sand from Marlea. In a final desperate sleep-deprived attempt, I'd even offered it a fig.

Perhaps unsurprisingly, I was getting nowhere.

Whatever I tried, nothing happened, but I couldn't shake the feeling that I was missing something.

But for now, my neck was aching, my arms were weak, and I was starting to see things moving in the shadows.

I decided a little rest wouldn't hurt, so I sat down and closed my eyes.

'Nice work putting the "ink" in tinkering, Little Builder,' Abb said with a laugh, standing on top of the Khat's Pyramid, waving his arms to keep balance.

I looked down, seeing only stone and sand and darkness

stretching as far as the eye could see. 'Looks like you've put the father in . . . the dad in the—'

'Stick with what you're good at,' Abb replied with a wink. 'Anyway, I'm going to need to go back to the barracks soon, there's only so many excuses Gramble will believe these days. How about one last story?'

I felt my chest squeeze. 'Only one?'

'You want more?' He stepped closer with a wink. 'I never thought the son of a Healer would be so greedy.'

I laughed, shaking my head. 'One is fine.'

Abb put a hand on my shoulder, and pointed over to the thousands of pieces of Cold falling to the Patches in the distance. Thick streaks fell occasionally, and I knew instinctively they were Frosts. We began walking towards the distant stars. I had missed his smell, his presence, and I leaned into him as we moved.

'Have I told you the story of Alex the Painter before?'

'I don't think so.'

He put an arm around me and hugged me tightly against his chest. 'Well, I'm glad I saved it for last then.'

He slowed our pace, ambling towards the falling stars in the distance. I thought I saw words traced in their wake, reminding me of the prayer he'd sung to me on my birthday.

Abb paused, taking a deep breath. 'Once there was a young painter named Alex who lived in the small town of Yelish. Alex had a natural gift, but he decided he didn't want to settle for being good, he wanted to be great. So he travelled the entire World Cried, discovering all the colours and textures and sights he could find. While he was on the road, if a family gave him food and shelter for the night, Alex would paint their walls with beautiful designs in thanks. If he found a sad traveller on the road, he would take out his tools and brush colour on their clothes in exchange for directions. He learned and he grew, and half a lifetime later he did indeed become great. And when Alex returned home to Yelish he painted masterpieces, on canvas and walls and streets, and for years the Jadans there rejoiced. One day Sun decided he was tired of all the beauty that Alex had at his fingertips, so he fell to the land and disguised himself as the Jadan king, showing up at Alex's door with a deal.

'"You have offended me by not coming to my Manor and offering to paint my likeness. Normally I would have a painter killed for this slight, but I'll make you a deal," the king said. "If you can paint something so beautiful that it makes everyone in Yelish weep, then I will let you live. I'll be back in one year."

'Alex bowed, accepting the challenge. As someone who knew how to use his eyes properly, he was able to see right through Sun's disguise, and knew there was no way around the deal. So he locked himself away, and for a year, he poured everything he had into his work. Every stroke was a memory; every smear was a piece of his heart. He grew thin and frail as he lost himself on the canvas, not leaving his room, only concentrating on making something utterly beautiful. One year later Sun returned disguised as the king, gathering everyone in Yelish into the town square, setting them to face the wall of the Cry Temple where Alex was to display his masterpiece.

'"Jadans of Yelish," the Sun King bellowed, "I give you, your renowned Painter."

'Alex came around the Temple on wobbly legs, his canvas in hand. He looked thirty years older and fifty pounds skinnier. When he got to the wall, his bony arms flipped the painting to set it on the easel, but just as he was putting it in place Sun took away the light that the Painting needed if it was to be seen. When the Jadans of Yelish looked, all they could see was shadow, dark and ugly. Any angle they moved to revealed the same thing.

'Nothing.

'The Sun King laughed his wicked laugh, sharpening his blade for Alex's throat, but then he realized something.

'Every Jadan in Yelish was weeping, the ground stained with hundreds of tears.

'"Why are you weeping?" the Sun King asked, both astonished and angry. "There's no painting. There's nothing to cry over."

'The town elder came up to the Sun King, tears at the corners of his eyes. "We have all known his work. The whole town has been shaped by his touch. It doesn't matter if there's a masterpiece or not. Look at the deathly state of him. We weep not for any painting. We weep for Alex."'

There was a moment of silence as Abb and I wandered through the sky.

'I'll have to tell this story to Shilah one day,' I said.

Abb bent over and kissed the top of my head, rubbing his knuckles across my hair. 'I love you, son. You have made me so proud. And I know you're about to change everything. I must be on my way now. I'll say hello to Matty for you.'

And then my father was stolen from me, falling with the rest of the Cold, his body plummeting towards the sands.

I awoke with a start, my hands shooting out in front of me, finding only empty air. I blinked a few times, remembering where I was, and then the dread filtered in.

Leroi's self-spinning hourglasses on the wall told me I'd been asleep for hours. I knew it was only a dream – how could it be otherwise? – but the feeling of happiness I'd felt at seeing Abb, and the following shock and pain at watching him fall had been real, and my heart was tightly knotted up. I felt an immeasurable sense of loss. Abb's words still rang in my ears. I couldn't fight the voice in my mind that kept whispering to me that this was the last time I'd see my father.

But it was only a dream.

I wiped a hand across my face, ridding myself of the tears that had gathered on my cheeks, and trying to keep my sniffing quiet so as not to wake Shilah. I felt as if my heart had fallen out of my chest.

'I think that's enough,' I said quietly to the giant Cold. 'As you were.'

But when I reached out to take the Frost off the hammock, wrapping my hands around the beautiful sphere, my whole world shook. An intense sensation swept through my finger-tips. I tasted Cold, and my mind was washed blank. It all happened too suddenly for me to fully comprehend, but a river of energy jolted me awake and a wave of Cold air rushed across my back, sweeping my robes inwards. And all around the workshop the buckets of Cold on the shelves crashed to the ground, the clangs of metal so loud that Shilah awoke and fell out of her chair into a defensive crouch, her hands scrambling for a weapon. The Frost lit with the same golden hue I remembered from my vision with the Crier, the three-line symbol on its belly bursting with light.

I ripped my hands away from the Frost, holding them in front of my face to try to make sense of what was happening. My fingertips were still sizzling with energy, and for a moment my skin had borrowed the golden colour of the Frost, although it faded quickly. I looked around me. Hundreds of pieces of Cold were now eerily rolling along the floor towards me.

'What's happening?' Shilah frantically looked around. She stepped up onto her chair to get a better look at the tinker-shop, the panic making her posture straighter than ever. 'Taskmasters? The Vicaress?'

'I—' I looked from my hands to the Cold, coming to a standstill on the ground, then back to the Frost. 'No. I don't know. I touched the Frost and—'

And then it all clicked, the World Cried suddenly making sense.

'Tears,' I said, gasping from the revelation. '*Jadan* tears.'

Shilah wrapped a gentle hand around my wrist, scrutinizing the tips of my fingers. 'What do you mean, tears?'

It was hard to get my mouth to work, as my bottom jaw felt so slack I worried it might just drop off. 'Crier. Tears. *Jadan* Tears.'

Shilah gestured to the mess of Cold scattered about the floor. 'You're saying *you* did that?'

'Watch,' I said, flabbergasted, the golden hue of the Frost having faded back to normal. 'Do it with me.'

Shilah's hand was still around my wrist, and I guided our arms towards the Frost, the tips of my fingers still wet. As soon as I connected with the Cold, the phenomenon started up again. Sizzling energy coursed through my entire body, making me somehow stiff and relaxed at the same time, and I could feel the golden glow in my bones, and in my hair. Shilah's grip was like a vice around my wrist, and I looked into her face while Cold continued to crash all around us, violently rolling our way, and I watched the budding golden light reflected in her hazel irises. Her mouth was agape as well, and her back went the straightest I'd ever seen it go, and somehow I could feel the energy swapping between our bodies, exploring our tips and centres and perhaps even deeper.

I wrenched my fingers off the Frost before the commotion around us got so bad that we woke the whole Tavor Manor, holding my trembling hand in front of her face. The Cold all around us had stopped rolling, some of it having tucked between our feet and nestled against our legs.

'Tears,' I said again.

Shilah released her grip and swung a hand around the back of my neck, swinging our heads together. Our lips collided a little too hard and our teeth struck, but unlike me she knew was she was doing, and gently pulled back her lips so we could properly fit before grabbing me tighter. My mouth was dry from shock but Shilah didn't seem to care, pressing her soft lips against me with the kind of passion I'd never known, firm yet gentle, tasting of fruit and sweat and a hundred different things that sent exploding powders firing across my mind, brushing out any thoughts except the exact sensations of the moment.

She let go too soon and fitted a hand over each of my cheeks, looking me deep in the eyes. 'Spout.'

'Yes,' I said, trying not to pant.

She laughed a crisp laugh, her gentle fingers moving up and caressing the corners of my eyes. 'No. *Spout.*'

I felt like my chest was so full it was going to burst. A new Idea dropped into my mind like Cold falling from the heavens. 'I think I know what we need to make.'

Chapter Thirty-one

The Coldmaker was an accident.

I'd never thought it was even a remote possibility. My logic was that if a Frost touched by Jadan tears attracted Cold, then maybe I might be able to tinker something that could *find* Cold. Shilah had agreed that this was the best next step, and together we'd experimented for the rest of the night, figuring out the strength and duration of the phenomenon, and if anything could amplify the pull. We also hoped that such a machine might help us clear up the Desert theory, perhaps finding its opposite buried somewhere in the Northern sands, where the Opened Eye was sitting on Shilah's map.

I often found myself preoccupied with vivid memories of Shilah's lips, but I tried to focus as best as I could.

The hope – as unlikely as it may have been – was that if I somehow figured out the secret of flight, I could take the *Coldfinder* into the air; which would allow me to collect greater amounts from the sky each night, dragging the Cold towards me, instead of having to fly to each individual piece.

At least that was the intention as Shilah helped me prod and tinker and brainstorm. We'd taken the Frost into the most soundproof room of the tinkershop to experiment further. We brought in the clay pots of Cold Charge to see if they might affect the Frost's pull, and if there was any materials that perhaps negated the power. A successful raid of the Manor kitchens brought back ten onions, which I cut up in order to extract a full vial of my tears, at one point slipping and slicing into my knuckle.

I never expected to stumble on what we did.

So, when shuffling sounds came from Leroi's study the next morning, Shilah and I burst in with our accidental invention, unable to keep the smiles off our faces. We found Leroi hunched over his desk looking at his decanter, which now held a branch with fuzzy red buds at the end.

'Leroi, you're back!' I exclaimed.

The tinkerer looked up at me, his face full of sorrow. 'I had to go away.'

'Alder,' Shilah said with a coy grin, pointing at the branch.

Leroi's face grew unreadable. 'Yes,' he said hesitantly.

'I'm glad you're back! We have something to show you.' I was practically dancing on my toes, so eager was I to reveal what we'd made.

Leroi looked at the machine I was carrying, his eyes narrowing at the Opened Eye I'd etched into the metal casing.

Despite the little sleep I'd had, and the anxiety I felt thinking about Abb, I couldn't help but beam. The invention in my hands was by far grander than anything I'd ever dreamed of creating.

'Shilah, would you mind grabbing the glass and water?' I asked, trying to keep calm.

Shilah nodded, rushing out of the study and into the tinkershop.

I set the Coldmaker gently down on Leroi's desk, my heartbeat racing in anticipation. The machine was compact enough to carry in my arms, but came with decent heft. I'd

used brass for the walls of the container itself, golden and
gleaming; and I'd welded strong iron for the catch-point so
it wouldn't bend out of place. The lid acted like a Belisk
Puzzle-Box, only opening with the right combination of secret
sliding levers; which meant only the worthy could look inside
and discover its secrets.

The anklet still stood on the desk as well. It was odd to
see my creation sitting next to it, but it struck me as fitting.

'Where did you go?' I asked.

Leroi's eyes were back on the Alder plant, his face gaunt
and his scalp crisped up once again. 'To visit an old friend.'

It was hard to see him so visibly upset, but I knew his
mood was about to change.

Shilah returned, setting a glass on the desk and filling it
up. She backed away, her smile possibly even larger than
mine, shooting me an excited look. We'd already witnessed
this miracle a few times, but each time it caused me a thrill
I felt could never wane.

'Leroi,' I said, feeling more alive than I'd ever felt before.
'Thank you. For allowing us to create this.'

Biting my lip, I flipped the machine on, the gears inside
turning and the droplets being extracted from each of the
different vials. The machine hummed and the air around us
took on the static we'd come to expect, the catch-point
lighting up with the golden glow. After a few moments, the
colour had coalesced into a solid bead, vibrant and holy.

I turned the invention off and picked up the little bead
which I'd decided to call an Abb.

'May we present to you,' I said, my voice slightly shaking,
'the Coldmaker.'

Leroi had kept still as we spoke, but we held his attention,
his eyes fixed on the invention. 'Excuse me?' He broke out
of his reverie. 'Did you say a Coldmaker?'

I smiled brightly, taking out a blade and slicing off a sliver of the Abb into the cup, backing away as it landed on the surface of the water.

Almost instantly the glass shattered, the two sides falling apart, and leaving behind a gleaming miracle. The block was solid, and clear, and the crystal sides beaded with gentle moisture, shining in the dim candlelight. I knew from the Gospels that this miracle substance hadn't been seen this side of the Great Drought.

Leroi's legs buckled, his hands finding the desk so he wouldn't collapse.

'Is that,' his words sounded slurred, but this time not from drink, 'Ice?'

I nodded, a lump of emotion forming in my throat. 'Yes.'

Leroi leaned forward to touch my machine. 'A Coldmaker?' he repeated.

I nodded, sliding my palm over the smooth metal. 'The Coldmaker.'

Leroi collapsed in his chair, trying to process what he'd just seen. It had taken Shilah and me some time to get over the initial shock ourselves, so I didn't blame him. 'Is this from the Crier? Did you speak to Him again?'

'No,' Shilah said, jumping in. 'We made it ourselves.'

'Is this a trick?' Leroi said, looking up at the ceiling. 'Am I awake?'

'It's real,' I said.

Leroi still looked dumbstruck. His eyes returned to the block of Ice, his mouth half-opened as though he wanted to speak but didn't have the words. Reaching out, he placed his fingers gently around the Ice and brought it to his lips, his hands shaking. 'How? This is the greatest invention of our time. This is going to change the entire world. You two found a way to . . .' his mouth seemed to have trouble admitting it '. . . create Cold.'

'Do you know about Desert?' Shilah asked, her grin still

taking up most of her face. She looked incredibly beautiful in that moment, and I thought back to the second, even more passonate kiss that she'd planted on my lips after we'd made the Ice discovery. I was desperately hoping there would be more in my near future.

Leroi looked shocked. He paused. 'Yes. I didn't want to scare you with such an idea yet. How did you—'

'We wanted to find the opposite in the North,' Shilah said proudly. 'So when Cam gave us the Frost—'

Leroi gasped at the word. 'Did you say Frost?'

'Yes,' I said. 'Cam left it on the—'

Leroi's finger shot to the Coldmaker. 'Is there a Frost in there? One of Lord Tavor's Frosts?'

I felt a wave of unease. I hadn't expected such a reaction. 'Yes, but—'

Leroi stiffened with alarm. 'Crier's light, no. Not again.'

'What?' I said. 'It's not like we stole it. Cam—'

'That damn boy is going to get you killed!' Leroi cried out. 'What was he *thinking*? Where is he?'

'Well, after we experimented with the ink, Cam got really upset,' Shilah said, the happiness finally dropping from her face. 'He hasn't come back yet.'

'What ink?' Leroi asked frantically. 'Wait. You can tell me everything on the road. We don't have time. Start grabbing everything. Cold, food, water, medicine. Any supplies we could use. We need to leave. Now.'

I held up my hands, trying to calm him down. 'Hold on, Leroi. I don't understand. Go where?'

Leroi was already snatching vials and contraptions from the room. 'Lord Tavor is going to come here looking. Here. Like the last time a Frost was taken. And you two don't have anklets on. We can't let him find you.' Leroi snapped his fingers, no longer looking at the Coldmaker. 'Go. Start packing.'

'For what?' Shilah asked, her voice strong enough to still the Tinkerer for a second.

'There's only one place a machine like that will be safe,' Leroi said, pointing a trembling finger at the machine. 'We're going to Langria.'

It was my turn to falter. 'Langria *is* real?'

Shilah's face lit up.

Leroi looked guilty for a moment. 'Yes. But it's not what you think. Hurry, we need to g—'

A thunderous knock boomed through the tinkershop.

All three of our heads turned, another crash resonating not long after.

'Hide,' Leroi gasped, grabbing the anklet off the desk. 'Now!'

I grabbed the Coldmaker and started running towards our hideaway. Shilah pushed the table off, opened the grate, and allowed me and the machine to go into the space first. She tucked herself in, making her body small. The booming on the main door grew louder with each passing moment. Leroi made sure we were completely hidden before racing towards the stairs. He undid the chain, and a swarm of bodies marched in.

Dread filled my stomach as Lord Tavor's voice filled the room. 'Leroi. You know why I am here. You have gone too far this time.'

Without so much as a greeting, Lord Tavor swept past Leroi and marched down the stairs.

'Wait, cousin!' Leroi shouted, following behind. 'I have your anklet right here. Where are you going?'

Footsteps strode across the tinkershop, using no cane this time. They went towards the study first and then to the nooks and shelves of the main workshop. Lord Tavor crossed the room with the fury and speed of a sandstorm.

I held my breath as I watched the others come down the stairs and move into view. I could make out two pairs of taskmaster feet, and what looked like a large battering ram. In the middle were Cam's buckled slippers. But worst of all, in front was a pair of black sandals, hot oil dripping at the heels.

She was here.

She'd found us.

I clutched the Coldmaker even more tightly, praying silently. If Leroi couldn't protect us then I hoped he could at the very least protect the machine. It was too valuable to be destroyed now, and I felt around the crawl-space to see if there was perhaps enough boilweed to make a cover, so at least they might not notice it when they opened the grate and wrung our throats.

'Stop!' Leroi shouted. 'I have the anklet for you.'

'If I find that it's here . . .' Lord Tavor hissed in reply.

'It *is* here.'

'Not the anklet, you blathering fool! You know what I mean. Your little slave assistant—'

'—Is dead.' Leroi interrupted. 'When you had her head cut off.'

Horror swept through me at his words.

'That's what you get when you're a dirty Jadan thief.' Lord Tavor's voice was filled with grim humour. 'And now another one of them is missing, again. My son claims he knows nothing. None of my slaves seem to know anything. And after everything our esteemed Vicaress put them through, I believe them.'

I felt my stomach clench at the thought of all the Jadans in the Manor being tortured by the Vicaress over the missing Frost. I would have my revenge for them. I needed to survive this, so I might one day watch the Vicaress scream.

'I don't know what to tell you,' Leroi responded. 'Look all you want. It's not here.'

Lord Tavor stepped over to the table above our grate, stopping so close that his sandals were inches from my eyes. My heart began to beat so wildly, I wondered if it could be heard resonating in the room. 'This is where you make them? The anklets?'

'Yes,' Leroi said, with an audible gulp.

I heard Lord Tavor pick something up from the table, but eventually his feet moved away. 'Leroi, you know the Khat's illustrious niece.'

I knew he meant the Vicaress.

'I told her about your anklets, and she's impressed with your design,' Lord Tavor said. 'And she wants to commission you. This will bring the Tavor family great prestige.'

'Is that right?' Leroi said, keeping his tone even.

'Yes. There have been problems in the slave barracks lately,' the Vicaress said in a smooth voice. 'And your invention is genius. Anklets that must be turned with a key every twelve hours or the vial breaks inside and acid melts their skin off. It's inspired. And it's the kind of threat the Crier needs to put the Jadans back in line.'

'How many do you need?' asked Leroi.

'I'm glad to see you comply, Leroi. I've come to expect more resistance from you.' Lord Tavor's voice was coldly appraising.

Leroi took a deep breath. 'For the good of the Khatdom. Praise be to his name.'

'Praise be to the Khat,' the Vicaress said with passion.

'I'll get started right away,' Leroi said. 'Now, please, if you'll leave me to my work.'

'But you haven't even heard how many?' Lord Tavor remarked derisively.

'No, you're quite right. How many?'

The Vicaress was the one to reply. 'Considering the workload this represents, we will start with head Jadans. I will need one for each barracks' head Jadan. The population has been getting uppity ever since the Cleansing. And we can't be too careful after finding that cave garden.'

Leroi clenched his teeth. 'You want a *hundred* anklets?'

'Ninety-nine,' the Vicaress corrected him calmly. 'I've already taken care of the Healer in barracks forty-five last night. Can you believe a Jadan had the gall to gather a group and openly talk about rebellion? And as chance will have it, his son was my missing Jadan as well. He wouldn't tell me where the child was, but I found illegal items in his quarters. It seemed very much to me that he had undertaken illicit tinkering activity. So I killed him in front of the whole barracks. I think they now know better than to defy the Khat's orders.'

I didn't remember much after that.

Chapter Thirty-two

The smelling salts pulled me out of my stupor.

But I desperately clung to where I was. I didn't want to be back in reality.

I wanted to be numb.

I wanted to be back in the black river.

I wanted to be back with my father in the sky.

Leroi practically shoved the salts up my nostril until I finally gave them a sign that I was awake, jerking away from the pungent odour.

Shilah came up to me first, bending over so I could smell her hair. I was sitting in Leroi's chair, the Coldmaker on the desk in front of me.

'Abb,' I said, the word stinging my tongue.

'Spout,' Shilah put a hand gently on my cheek. It was strange to see such a consoling look on her face. 'You can grieve all you want later. I'll grieve with you. But right now you have to get up. We *need* to go.'

I looked from side to side, noticing all the supplies and inventions around the study. Three sets of Rope Shoes. Bags of Cold. Waterskins. A whole sack of figs. Clothes. A portable Sinai.

Cam was there too, standing, his head bowed as though it was too heavy for his body.

'Cam,' I said. 'You came back.'

Cam swallowed hard. 'I'm sorry. I only wanted to punish my father. I thought that giving the Frost away . . .'

Leroi flicked him on the neck. 'And look where it got us. Why, why didn't you *think*, Camlish?'

Cam's hand flew to the Coldmaker. 'But, Leroi, look. I was right. That Frost got us a miracle.'

'A miracle that will have us all killed. Then what good will the machine be when they toss it to the bottom of the Singe?' Leroi stuffed the salt block in his pocket. 'Spout. We need you up and moving. We have to go.'

I looked to the study door. 'Lord Tavor . . .'

'Will be back,' Leroi said in a solemn voice. 'I know my cousin. He doesn't trust me. He'll be back with all the task-masters he can and search the tinkershop top to bottom. He knows that we have the Frost. We need to go.'

'To Langria,' Shilah said, her voice soft. 'Can you believe it? We're actually going, Spout. Freedom.'

Leroi gave a barely audible snort and scooped up a small black velvety bag which rattled with objects as he slinged it over his shoulder. 'Some inventions, just in case,' Leroi said, answering the question that played on my face. He looked to the side of his study where the door had been painted the same colour as the walls. It stood open and ready, and through the threshold I noticed a set of stairs leading down into the pitch blackness.

I tried to get up from the chair, but my legs were too weak. I thought I'd felt grief after my dream where Abb had died, but now that it was real, that my father, the best Jadan I'd ever known had been killed because of me, those feelings seemed laughable in comparison.

Leroi pulled a flask out of his desk drawer and offered it

to me, but I waved it away. He gave a satisfied nod, tossing it into a corner of the study.

'Then I won't either,' Leroi said, looking to Shilah and Cam with a different nod.

Both of them came to my sides, lifting me out of the chair, moving my arms around each of their shoulders so my weight was suspended.

'You can do this,' Cam said. 'You're a natural.'

I thought about where I had ended up. Where Abb had pushed me to be. Because of him, my friends and I had been led to the most important finding since the Great Drought began. Perhaps ever.

My father would want me to be strong.

'The Cold doesn't matter,' I whispered to Cam. 'You're one of us. Family.'

'Thanks, Spout.' Cam gave my side a squeeze where his hand was, keeping me up. 'I'm glad you think that.'

'I need you all to be quick,' Leroi said. 'We don't stop until we're far, far out of Paphos. Then we can break for water, not before. There are Tavors up in the Glasslands. They don't particularly care for this side of the family, so I think we'll be safe to stop there and resupply.'

'I can do this,' I said. I stepped away from my friends' support and took the bag which sat beside the Coldmaker on the desk, nestling the machine inside it. Someone had thought to put in some boilweed for cushioning, and I buttoned it closed, slinging it over my shoulder. 'I want to carry this.'

Leroi nodded understandingly. 'Course you do. We wouldn't have it any other way.'

Everyone loaded themselves with as much as they could hold, our bodies practically caravans, and we followed our gaunt leader into the secret tunnel. The passage was narrow and the stairs steep, but miniature Sinais had been set on each of the landings, and there was enough light to travel by.

We moved silently, anxiously. It felt awful to be leaving my new home so soon, but now that I had the Coldmaker I knew the Crier needed me out in His world.

I'd make more Coldmakers with my blood and tears and Frosts.

I'd figure out how to reach into the sky itself.

Perhaps I'd even discover how to rid the world of Desert.

My legs found strength, and for just a moment I thought I could feel Abb's touch on my arm, his telltale chuckle over my shoulder.

Soon enough a door appeared at the end of the tunnel.

Leroi stopped just before the exit, turning to us with an odd look on his face. 'I just want you all to know—'

'What are you doing?' Cam asked. 'I thought we have to keep moving.'

Leroi set down his Rope Shoes so he could hold up a hand. 'Just give me a moment. I want to thank you all. I never thought I'd know hope again. It's good to know that it's been there all along, even though I couldn't feel it.'

Then he turned and kicked open the door, the Sunlight striking us as we all spilled out into a garden.

Everything afterwards happened in a flash.

Before us stood the Vicaress, with an army of taskmasters at her back. 'Get the slaves!' she yelled. Lord Tavor was standing by her side, a huge smile plastered on his face. 'The Crier says they have the Frost!'

I stumbled back in shock, but Leroi was prepared for this. Moving fast, he reached into his purse and pulled out a round device, whose glass centre was filled with something dark and menacing.

'Run!' Leroi said, hurling the little device. 'To the gate! Go!'

The sphere landed in front of the taskmasters, and the ground exploded, sending grass, plants and fruit flying in every direction. Vicious fire burst from the heart of the explosion, and began to spread. The taskmasters were tossed backwards by a violent wind, nearly colliding with the Vicaress.

The Vicaress snarled. 'Forward!'

A dozen more taskmasters hopped through the wreckage, but Leroi was ready. He hurled another explosive, which landed closer to the oncomers this time. Bodies flew into the air, the Vicaress and Lord Tavor both stumbled backwards.

Leroi turned and pushed me in the direction of the gate. 'Go! I'll keep them off. Leave! Now!'

Numb with shock, I did as Leroi commanded. Cam and Shilah ran by my sides, our bags colliding in messy thuds, slowing us down. Panicked, I dropped everything except the Coldmaker, which I pressed tightly against my chest.

There were more bangs, a flurry of shouting but I couldn't bear to look back. The thump of bodies hitting the dirt seemed to be coming from every direction, and I could feel each explosion in my chest.

The Vicaress's screams pierced the air.

Cam looked petrified, but only fierce determination shone in Shilah's eyes as she led us through the garden. She pushed open the gate, and we raced behind her.

I looked back with horror. Leroi was the only barrier keeping all the taskmasters at bay. He hurled sphere after sphere, the land itself opening under his wrath. Fire was now consuming the garden, moving through the green as easily as wind moving across the dunes, and the flames were growing higher and higher. The big tree in the centre of the garden had fallen, the Vicaress and Lord Tavor nowhere to be seen, but more taskmasters were spilling out from other parts of the Manor every second, charging through the garden towards Leroi.

'Shivers and Frosts, Spout! Come on,' Cam yelled over the blasts. 'We need to go.'

'Spout,' Shilah said, a hand finding my shoulder. 'There's too many of them. We have to run. We need to keep the Coldmaker safe!'

She was right. There was only one way to free the Jadan people, and that meant staying alive.

I squeezed the bars of the gate, taking one last look at the brave Inventor.

I silently thanked him.

Then the three of us ran into the sands.

Acknowledgements

There are far too many people to deeply and sincerely thank, and even if your name does not appear below, know that I am forever grateful.

First and foremost, thanks to my agent, Danielle Zigner: the Dream-maker.

Thanks to my mother, for being the only one who believed this book possible from the very beginning.

To Jardin Telling, for being the most loving and supportive girlfriend a struggling young writer could ever ask for. I could not have gotten through this grueling process without you.

Thanks to Natasha Bardon, Lily Cooper, Jack Renninson, and the rest of my HarperVoyager family. My family family (I finally mentioned you in text itself, Ray Ray!). My Waking Fable family. Fierce Kelly family. Spencer Hill Press family (Kate Kaynak and Rich Storrs is particular). Firehouse and House Wine family. Brad Payton and the Payton family. Thanks to William Goldman, Patrick Rothfuss, Ted Chiang, and Brandon Sanderson (not that I know them personally, buy they deserve all the thanks in the World Cried for showing me the way). And finally, thanks to Sara Hahn for the many mountains of inspiration.